TWICE THE SHOOTIN', TWICE THE LOVIN' FOR ONE LOW PRICE!

SAN FRANCISCO STRUMPET

The buggy kept on coming. When it was opposite the point where McCoy had entered the woods, it stopped. He heard a voice.

"Spur McCoy, you stupid bastard, you better start thinking about dying, 'cause that's what you're going to be doing before this day is over. Christ, but I've waited a long time for this."

As soon as the man stopped talking, a shotgun boomed and Spur jerked his head back behind the big oak, as half-a-dozen big slugs hit the tree and the brush around him. Double-ought buck! He knew how well it killed, but he had never been on the receiving end before.

BOISE BELLE

Spur plowed his fist into the man's chin, sending him reeling across the coach to the opposite seat. Coughing, choking on the dust that spun in through the opened window, Silas renewed his attack. McCoy's foot connected with his stomach and sent him back.

"Damn!" Silas said, rubbing his gut. "You're asking for it."

Spur drew before the gunman had even grasped the Dragoon's holster. "This ain't no place for shooting," he said in an even voice.

SPUR

SAN FRANCISCO STRUMPET
BOISE BELLE
DIRK FLETCHER

LEISURE BOOKS **L** **NEW YORK CITY**

A LEISURE BOOK®

April 1994

Published by

Dorchester Publishing Co., Inc.
276 Fifth Avenue
New York, NY 10001

SAN FRANCISCO STRUMPET Copyright © MCMLXXXIV by Chet Cunningham/BookCrafters, Inc.

BOISE BELLE Copyright © MCMLXXXIX by Chet Cunningham/BookCrafters, Inc.

Printed in the United States of America.

SPUR

SAN FRANCISCO STRUMPET

CHAPTER ONE

(Oleomargarine, the common man's butter, was patented by H.W. Bradley in Binghamton, N.Y. in the year 1871. Ulysses S. Grant was President of the United States. The National Rifle Association was organized in New York City. The first of many Chinese Tongs in San Francisco, Kwong Dock Tong, was organized a year earlier and was growing in strength. Cement was patented by D. O. Saylor in Allentown, New York. Wild West outlaw Ben Thompson surfaced in Abilene, Kansas, the first cow town, and began a lifelong feud with Abilene Town Marshall Wild Bill Hickok. In October 1871 the great Chicago fire destroyed Chicago with an estimated loss of more than one hundred and ninety-six million dollars.)

Spur McCoy adjusted the white tie he wore with his formal evening coat and relaxed. It had been a month of holidays since he had been in a formal suit — not since he had worked in Washington, D.C. He sipped a cup of slightly spiked punch and watched the ladies in their beautiful long gowns and the men in white tie wearing a version of what San Francisco's social set considered formal wear.

And it was society. This was the official celebration of the opening of the San Francisco Opera Society's 1871 season. It was a gala evening. The performance of *Don Giovanni* was fair, Spur decided, but the lady who just danced past him was remarkable.

He watched her over his punch cup. Maybe five feet five, taller than most women, and the proud, determined way she held herself when dancing piqued his interest. She was a brunette, with hair to her waist in a silky black waterfall, and he thought she had brown eyes in the moments he saw her face. A round, pretty countenance, with wide set eyes, and a small nose over a pouting mouth.

The soft pink gown cinched delightfully at her waist, and the top showed a generous amount of soft white breasts and a dark line of cleavage.

Yes, he would have to dance with this one.

Spur was in San Francisco on business. He was a Secret Service agent of the United States Government, with St. Louis as his base, and he had the entire western half of the nation as his territory. Which meant he was seldom in St. Louis. The Secret Service was still the only federal policing agency that could cross state lines, and as such it was called upon to handle a wide range of problems.

His current assignment was simple: find and stop a major counterfeiting ring in San Francisco that specialized in minting double gold eagles, the gold twenty dollar piece that was still the only solid medium of exchange considered as actual hard money by many cantankerous Westerners.

The pair danced back toward him in the large Pacific Ballroom, and Spur moved quickly through the dancers and tapped the young man on the shoulder. He turned.

"May I cut in?" Spur asked.

He saw a glint of surprise and pleasure dart across the woman's face. Twenty-five, he judged.

"Oh, damn, not another one. Katherine, you are simply much, much too popular tonight."

The man stopped talking, shrugged, bowed gently and walked away.

"May I?" Spur asked again.

She put one hand on his shoulder and held her other out to him.

"Of course. And a man with manners in San Francisco! Really, I am going to have something to tell everyone!"

He accepted her hand and danced her around the room.

"I know we haven't been introduced, but when I saw you I couldn't stop myself from cutting in. If I may say so, Katherine, you are the most beautiful lady I have seen in a century and a half."

She laughed, a small tinkling sound that sounded

exactly right for her. She leaned back in his arms to get a clearer look at him, and smiled, one dimple showing, her eyes crinkling slightly as she nodded.

"Yes, I like you. Now, so we can be formally introduced, I am Katherine Sanford, of *the* Sanfords. He's my father although sometimes he is loath to admit it."

"Delighted to meet you, Miss Sanford. I am Spur McCoy, but I am not a cowboy. I come from New York City by way of Washington, D.C. and St. Louis."

"A New Yorker! I knew you had to be someone special. And you dance beautifully. Could you hold me just a bit closer so I can follow you better? Yes, that is ever so nice. I love it."

They circled the ballroom, and Spur was getting used to the heady scent of her hair and the interesting perfume she was wearing when someone tapped him on the shoulder. He stopped and stepped back. Spur saw the girl shaking her head at the man behind him, but Spur already was thanking her for the short but provocative dance, then the young man whisked her away into the rest of the dancers.

Spur went back to the punch bowl, then to the person in the room he knew best, J. Anderson Dumbarton II, one of the biggest bankers in San Francisco, a man who had a knowledge of his city and his thumb on its pulse as well as anyone.

Dumbarton was a tall man who could look eye to eye with McCoy at six feet-two inches. He had considerably more girth as well as financial reserves and resources. He waved a welcome to Spur as he walked up.

"McCoy! Glad you could come. How did you enjoy our opera? We'll all proud of the organization we have here. Our Opera Society seems to fall apart every few years, but we've got it in high gear now. And I see you picked the prettiest girl in the place to dance with already. You always did have a good eye for the ladies."

"Jay, good to see you. I found your note and the tickets on my dresser when I checked in this morning. Thanks, I enjoyed the music. How is the banking business going?"

The financier frowned. "Fine, except for that little problem I wired you about. It isn't out of hand yet, but I'd hate to think what would happen if the story gets out. We weather bad publicity about the paper certificates every year or two, but the double eagle is the standard."

"That's why I'm here, Jay. I'll be past your firm in the morning to check over those items you have to show me. You have caught twenty of them so far?"

"Twenty-two now."

"That's bad. But to more pleasant topics. What can you tell me about Katherine Sanford?"

"As much as you want to know. Daughter of Amos Sanford, the Sanford Emporium, the biggest and best mercantile in town. You can buy anything from a diamond necklace to a steam engine at Sanford's. He's a whiz at sales and promotion, probably the best man on advertising goods we have in town. Daughter is just like him, bright, quick, even graduated from college. She and her father don't get on the best, both a hell of a lot alike, on the stubborn side."

"And she's not married?"

"Nope, she must be twenty-five or twenty-six now and that's one of the problems. Old man wants her married off and out of his hair."

"Thanks. And I'll be in about nine tomorrow."

"Fine, fine, now don't stand here, go out there and cut in on her again."

Spur did. She smiled.

"What took you so long?"

"Checking up on you. You are a Sanford."

"Yes, now hold me close before I scream."

He did. Halfway around the floor there was a set of french windows leading to a patio. He headed for them, and she smiled as he opened one and motioned for her to go through. Outside he closed it, saw no one else there and took her in his arms and kissed her lips tenderly.

"Yes," she said when their lips parted. "That was nice. Mr. McCoy, do you believe in impulses?"

"Usually, do you?"

"Always. I have a tremendously strong impulse right now to kiss you back." She stretched up on tiptoe and held his face and kissed his lips hard. When her lips came from his her eyes opened and she nodded. "Oh, good lord yes!" she said softly, took his hand and led him across the patio to another set of french windows which opened inside to a hallway, and down it on the right, she opened a door and went through it quickly.

A lamp burned low on a dresser. It was a waiting room, with several chairs, a couch and two mirrors.

She reached up and kissed him again, then turned to the door and threw a small bolt.

"Spur McCoy, would you think it terribly bold of me if I asked you to kiss me again?"

He shook his head, took her in his arms and kissed her. As he did he felt her push against him, from her ankles right up to her hips and then her breasts pressed hard on his body. His mouth softened to hers and his tongue flicked out, brushed her lips and suddenly they were open.

McCoy gave a little moan of pleasure and thrust his tongue deep inside her mouth, finding her tongue and dueling with it, chasing it, struggling to capture it again. Then he withdrew and waited and slowly her tongue darted in and out of his mouth, then came in firmly in command, probing, pushing, exploring.

When at last their lips parted, she sighed.

"Now, that, Mr. McCoy, was a real kiss." She looked up at him a moment, smiled, then took his hand and put it over the bareness of her upper breasts.

"I'm hoping that you have some impulses right now that you would like to follow, Mr. McCoy."

She reached her hand down and rubbed it over the growing bulge at his crotch. Katherine smiled, and with one deft movement pulled her dress off one shoulder, and then the other, letting the fabric slip

13

slowly down until it revealed her breasts.

Spur's hands caught them, his fingers massaging them as if they were rare gems, exploring her heavy nipples, brushing them until they heated and rose and filled with hot blood to stand even taller. He could feel her breasts throbbing.

Her hand had opened the buttons on his fly and wormed inside, grasping his erection.

"Darling! Darling!" she breathed softly.

Spur bent and kissed her pulsating breast and she whimpered. He kissed the other one.

"Yes, yes, sweetheart!" she crooned.

Spur bent lower and nuzzled her big orbs, kissing around and around, then winding up at her nipple. He kissed it firmly and bit the brown bud until she yelped in joy. His mouth continued to work until he was sucking on her nipple, pulling half the big tit into his mouth as Katherine gasped and moaned and leaned back against the door.

Her hands were busy as they worked his stiff pole from his fly. She cried out in success when he came out and she sank to her knees in front of him, staring at his penis.

"So wonderful, marvelous, so beautiful!" She kissed the stem and saw him jump. She kissed him again, and then worked toward the purple headed tip.

It was Spur's turn to moan in delight as her soft lips closed around him and she licked and sucked his rod. It had been a week for Spur and he wasn't sure how long he could take this kind of specialized treatment. He looked at the couch, then lifted her up.

He kissed her lips, looked deep into her eyes and found her nodding.

"Yes, yes, and quickly, I am ready, darling, I am so ready I am almost undone."

He started for the couch, but she pulled him back, leaning against the door and lifted her skirts. She wore no other garments. She pulled her skirts to her breasts, spread her legs and leaned against the door.

"Darling, kiss me," she said. Spur dropped to his knees and parted the fragrant, dark hair to see her pink nether lips and he kissed them, then again as she crooned above him. He found the magic node and he twanged it again and again with his tongue until she shrieked in ecstasy, her hips driving against his face as she trembled and shook and cried out. The tremors boiled through her slender body and her hips pumped a dozen times against him.

Somewhere in the process she lost her hold on her skirts and they billowed around Spur, but he held one cheek with each hand and kept massaging her clit and driving his curved tongue deep into her wet and eager pussy.

That set off another series of climaxes and she held his head through the cloth fast to her crotch while she vibrated through another long shattering series of climaxes. At last they trailed off and she sighed, then giggled and lifted her skirts and petti-coats, and used them to wipe off his mouth and his face. Holding her skirts she pushed her legs wider apart.

"Your turn, darling."

Spur bent his knees, moved toward her and she directed him until a moment later he plunged into her wet heartland and drove upward until his pubic bones ground against hers. Katherine let out a long wail of delight. She screeched with delight as he began to surge upward into her, retreating and then claiming her vagina as he own, again and again.

"Darling that is so beautiful!" She said. "Darling you make me feel like a real woman. That is fantastic! You are so fine, so fine!"

He felt the pressure growing, slowed and stopped, then he bent low until he could pull her breast into his mouth and suck it. As he did she climaxed again and it set him off on another pounding driving set of thrusts upward into her.

Somewhere deep in his system the small valve opened and the trigger pulled, the hammer dropped, and he could feel the primer charge go off, igniting the main powder supply and ramming his load upward through the tubes, along the highway of no return, until he cried out in joy and rapture. He jetted his load into her grasping and throbbing vagina.

As he finished he wanted to slump to the floor. But she held him tightly against her body, keeping him upright, nailing his body inside of hers.

It was five minutes before she sighed, and let go of his back.

"Just beautiful, darling Spur. I've never fucked anybody against a wall this way. It was tremendous."

Spur grinned at her vocabulary, sucked in air trying to get his breath and his strength back. It was true what they said about Samson, only it wasn't cutting his hair that made him weak.

She hurried to the dresser, found a towel and turned to minister to herself. Then she lowered her skirts, and walked toward him with her breasts bare.

"One more kiss?" she asked. "It will be the last time you ever see them or ever touch them. I won't even dance with you again so don't try. I like it this way. Always something different, someone new."

He bent and kissed each breast, licked her nipples and felt them rising again. She turned away.

"No!"

"Katherine, I will see you again. I will make love to you again, only the next time on my terms, in my bed, and with lots of time." He bit each nipple until she shuddered and then moved up and kissed her mouth. When he broke away from her he saw her self-confidence decaying. He kissed her once again and made sure that his clothes were arranged properly. He slid the bolt open and left the room as she worked at getting her breasts covered and her dress properly adjusted over her shoulders.

Spur left the gala, and headed for his room at the San Franciscan Hotel. It was just about two A.M. He wanted a good night's sleep before his work day tomorrow.

Spur McCoy was a big man, standing six feet two

inches and hitting the scales at two hundred pounds. He had sandy red hair, a full red moustache and sandy mutton chop sideburns. He was an excellent horseman, a crack shot with derringer, six-gun or rifle and was in fine physical condition. He could fight with a gun, knife, his fists or a four foot staff.

Not many people knew that Spur McCoy was a United States Secret Service Agent. The service was established by an act of Congress in 1865 with William P. Wood as its first director.

Spur came to the service by a round-about way. He was born and educated in New York City, went to Harvard and graduated in the class of 1858 at twenty-four years of age. His father was a well known merchant and trader in New York, and after two years with his father's import business, Spur joined the war time army with a commission as a second lieutenant and advanced to a captain's rank before Lee surrendered. After two years in the army, Spur went to Washington as an aide to Senator Arthur B. Walton, a long-time family friend from New York. In 1865, soon after the act was passed, Charles Spur McCoy won an appointment as one of the first U.S. Secret Service Agents.

Since the Secret Service was the only federal law enforcement agency at the time, it handled a wide range of problems. Many were far removed from the group's original task of preventing currency counter-feiting.

Spur had spent six months in Washington's Secret Service office, then was transferred to head the base in St. Louis where he handled all problems west of the Mississippi river. He was chosen from ten men because he was the only one who could ride a horse well and because he had won the service marksmanship contest. Wood figured the man in the west would need both skills.

CHAPTER TWO

Spur McCoy had walked only half a block from the Pacific Ballroom when he sensed that someone was following him. He had turned toward the San Franciscan Hotel, which took him down a side street with fewer lights in the buildings. He had no weapon with him, with the exception of a hideout derringer strapped to his ankle. As soon as he turned the corner, he ran hard for fifty feet to an alley mouth and stepped into the darkness.

McCoy pulled the derringer out, checked the loads by feel, then held it ready for his trackers.

Two of them came around the corner quickly, looked down the street and stopped. McCoy stepped into the street sure that they could not see him in the gloom, but they could hear his boots against the bricked-in sidewalk. He strode confidently away from them, listening behind him. Two sets of foot-falls continued to follow.

Spur slowed, reversed his direction and walked toward the pair. It was some time before they realized what had happened, and when Spur was almost upon them, he ran forward attacking. McCoy slammed into the smaller man spinning him sideways into the street where he fell. The second man caught an angry left lead fist into the gut which doubled him over. The small man got to his feet and ran.

Spur patted the man down, found no weapon and spun him around and slammed him against a store front. He took too long to recover and when he started to lift his head he came up with flying knuckles in front of him. Spur slammed his fist down on the back of the attacker's neck, dropping him to the sidewalk on his face.

Spur followed him down, planted his knee in the middle of the man's back and put all his weight on it. He grabbed the ambusher's head and turned it where Spur could see it.

"Talk, you son of a bitch before you die. Why the hell were you trying to follow me?"

"Wasn't, wasn't following nobody."

"Hell you wasn't. You want me to find a police-man and have you thrown in jail?"

"No, no!"

"Then talk, fast."

"Don't know who he was. This gent gave us a dollar each to find out where you was staying."

"Who was he?"

22

"Didn't know him. Some swell in a fancy suit like yours."

"How were you to tell him my residence?"

"Write it down and take it to this address."

McCoy took the slip of paper and read the numbers in the faint light. It was a downtown address, probably some business. McCoy slid the paper in his pocket and took out a small, thin one dollar gold piece. He gave it to the man.

"Thanks, friend. There is your dollar. Now you don't need to take care of the delivery, I'll handle it myself. I expect a much bigger payoff when I find out who this gentleman was."

The next morning Spur was up and dressed promptly at 6:30, went downstairs to the dining room where he ordered a breakfast of steak with scrambled eggs, a stack of hot cakes and hot syrup. He finished with coffee and read the *Examiner*. There seemed to be no burning problems in the world, and, most important, there was no story about counterfeit gold double eagles being circulated in San Francisco.

He had been in San Francisco many times during the past few years, and never ceased to be surprised by the vitality, the cosmopolitan atmosphere of the former village now all grown up. Ships from dozens of nations were anchored in the harbor. Many different races were represented in the people walking the streets.

Spur walked a few blocks to the Dumbarton-

Pacific Bank and went inside. It was the most impressive bank building in town and fairly shouted that it was four-square and solid, firm and safe for your money.

On the second floor, behind two secretaries, Spur was ushered into the private office of J. Anderson Dumbarton, founder and majority stockholder of the bank. He looked a little worse for his late night out.

"Just a touch of the scurvy this morning, McCoy. Sit down. I have those items we discussed."

Spur looked at them critically. There was little counterfeiting done on gold coins since it was technically so difficult. It involved a foundry, usually plating and always a big stamping press to strike off the coins themselves. When they did find counterfeited coins, many of them were of excellent quality and workmanship.

Some of these were good, some not. One had been sawed in half. The gold on the outside was real, but it was paper thin and had been put on the blanks by simple gold plating. There were places on the finished coins where the sharp edges would lose their gold plating and in other spots it had chipped off. These were the obvious forgeries and easy to spot. Others were harder.

"An even dozen in there. Some are real, some ringers. Can you pick them out?"

Spur found two of the real double eagles, but was not sure about two more.

"Two out of three isn't bad, McCoy. Actually the two you are suspicious of are genuine, just well used.

The other bad coin is so good we weren't sure until we nicked it and turned up the copper, zinc and lead base metal."

"Any more clues who might be passing them since your wire?"

"None, not of any value. We did trace back one of the coins we took in deposit, but it could have been picked up anywhere."

"Is the person reliable?"

"Totally, but she can't remember where that particular coin might have been given to her. She wrote a draft for cash at another bank, but surely they wouldn't have passed it, unless it was a new teller who hadn't proper training. You know the lady, by the way, she is Katherine Sanford."

"Curious," Spur said. "Seemingly little motive for her to be involved in something like this. Must have been duped somewhere. What about the San Francisco police?"

"I haven't alerted them. It would be in the papers at once. This seemed the best way. We don't need a run on the banks for anything as ridiculous as this."

"Right. Could I borrow one of these for comparison?"

"Take any of the bad ones you like. I'd suggest the perfect one for a tough look."

Spur took the paper from his pocket with an address on it. "Oh, I have an errand and I can't remember this street, Olivera, do you know where it is?"

"Olivera, yes, it's down in the edge of Mexican Village. It's a tough neighborhood. Makes the

Barbary Coast look like a church picnic. Be careful."

"My Spanish is passable."

"Is this some kind of a lead?"

"That's what I'm going to find out."

They parted and Spur caught a hack in front of the bank and asked how far it was to Olivera Street.

The driver flicked his reins on the bay's back and scowled.

"You don't want to go there."

"Why not?"

"You're not Mexican. They eat you alive."

"Why?"

"You're a *gringo*. That's Juan Pico's street. It's only one block long. He owns every building on it, and every cutthroat on the sidewalks."

"Let's just drive through."

"No, anywhere else."

"Let's drive past the end of the street."

The one-horse-rig driver thought about it. "For a dollar, and we go fast."

It looked like any of the other streets in the area. A lot of wide Mexican straw hats, women in colorful clothes, shops, markets, stores. So why would someone from Olivera Street try to follow him last night?

He pondered it as the hack drove him back to his hotel. It gave him a moment to think over his leads in this case. The only hard facts he had were the twelve counterfeit coins. From Washington he had received the names and last known addresses of two convicted coin counterfeiters in San Francisco. He had little hope for either. Counterfeiting paper bills was so much simpler these days with the good printing presses available, that the talented men had moved from coins to paper long ago.

At the hotel there were three messages. One was from a Mrs. Mildred Engleton. She said she was membership chairman of the San Francisco Opera Society and wanted to talk to him about becoming a sustaining member. He remembered her from the dance, a large, pretty woman draped in diamonds who was quick to tell him she was a widow. She was about forty.

The second note was unsigned. It said: "I know you are with the Secret Service, others do also. Be on your guard."

The third note was from Juan Pico. "My Dear Mr. McCoy. I must see you as soon as possible. Come to Olivera street and give this note in Spanish to anyone. You will receive every courtesy and be brought to my office at once." McCoy read the Spanish words at the bottom of the paper. He didn't understand all of them but in essence it said that the bearer was a friend and was to be taken to Juan Pico's office at once.

Ten minutes later Spur was back at the entrance to Olivera Street. The cab driver let him off and hurried away. Spur had walked only ten feet down the street before a large Mexican with a scar on his cheek stepped into his path and muttered in Spanish. Spur held out the paper and the man scanned the bottom of it quickly, returned it to Spur and motioned with his hand to follow.

They entered a new three-story brick building

near the center of the block. Spur noted that it was the same address as the note he'd taken from the pair who tried to follow him. The building was well made and decorated with Mexican murals and framed paintings. The lobby was spacious with two desks and luxurious furniture. Up an open staircase he could see offices with glass walls. They went up the steps and then on to the third floor where the scarred Mexican knocked on a wide beautifully hand-carved oak door. It opened a moment later and a well dressed woman glanced at him, then smiled.

"Yes, you would be Mr. McCoy. Won't you come in. Mr. Pico has been hoping that you would come. Right this way."

She led him through an outer office furnished and decorated with an understated elegance that surprised Spur. It looked like a senator's outer office in Washington. The small dark girl knocked once, then opened the door and walked inside. Holding the door for Spur she motioned him inside.

The office was luxurious with thick carpet, original oil paintings on the paneled walls. Two large windows looked down on Olivera Street. The whole office was professionally decorated with a decided macho theme.

Spur took this all in with a glance, then turned to the man sitting behind a massive cherrywood desk. He stood and held out his hand. Juan Pico was tall with soft brown Mexican skin, dark eyes and a lot of black hair which he combed straight back. He wore spectacles which he now held in one hand.

"Mr. McCoy. I have been trying to get in touch with you. It is good that you came so quickly."

Spur took the hand and met the firmness with equal force.

"Thank you, Mr. Pico. I have heard a lot about you in a short time."

"Do not believe all that you hear, Mr. McCoy. I am here only to help my people, to see that they are treated fairly, and that they can live a good life." He waved Spur to a softly upholstered chair at the side of the desk. Now to business."

Spur had not heard the door close behind him, but assumed it had. Now he sat and looked at Juan Pico. Before he could say anything he felt cold steel pressed against his neck and the ominous sound of a six-gun cocking. Spur did not move, he only looked up at Pico.

"Yes, Mr. McCoy, a gun at your head ready to kill you. I promised you every courtesy in my note, I said nothing about killing you. Tell me, Mr. McCoy, Secret Service Agent for the United States Government, how does it feel, knowing that you are about to die?"

CHAPTER THREE

Spur felt the cold gunmetal at his neck and chuckled deep in his throat. "No, no, Señor Pico. I simply can't believe what you say and what the pistol suggests. It is not reasonable, it is not rational, it would not be good for your people, and mostly because you obviously are a cultured man, a person of taste, breeding and education. But the main reason why you did not invite me here to kill me is because it would be of no value whatsoever to your people. And that, Señor Pico, is your purpose in life, your reason for being, your goal, your mission."

The slight sneer on Juan Pico's face faded and was replaced by a grudging smile. As his smile broadened the pressure of the gun muzzle eased and then stopped as the weapon was removed.

"Si, Señor McCoy. They told me you were no ordinary man, no run of the mill civil servant. I had to be sure what kind of a man I was dealing with. Now I know from my own experience." He stood and reached out his hand again. "Now I take your hand as a friend. Come, I want to show you something."

He moved to a case along a wall with a glass top. Inside there were gold double eagles. He opened the case and motioned for Spur to examine them.

"Yes, counterfeit, all of them I would imagine, or they would not be here."

"True. So far we have found a hundred and twelve. That represents two thousand, two hundred and forty dollars. Which would have been a tremendous loss to my people. The average shop owner in the street below makes a net profit of between eight to ten dollars a month, with his whole family working ten to twelve hours a day. He cannot afford a twenty dollar loss, even once a month. The bank has *retained* ten of these coins which had been deposited by some of the larger businesses. I have made good on these others to my people."

Juan Pico paused and watched Spur closely. "I understand that the prime responsibility of the United States Secret Service is to control and stop all counterfeiting."

"That used to be our only task. Now our duties have far outreached that and we handle any interstate felony problems."

"But counterfeiting is still a major work?"

"Yes, Señor Pico. That is why I am here, to stop this particular counterfeiting." He took the perfect counterfeit from his pocket and tossed it to Pico.

"The work is excellent. Only the thinness of the gold plating gives it away."

Pico examined it, found the gouge where the base metal showed through and frowned. "It is good work. I don't think I would have caught this one." His black eyes snapped. "So what can we do about it?"

"Have your people seen anyone passing them? Could it be a Mexican? Not many *gringos* shop on your street."

"That is the bad part. We have seen no *gringos* passing the coins. Most are new like this one, and only through use do they grow tired and we catch them."

They went back to the desk and sat down. Spur rubbed his hand over his face for a moment in thought. "Señor, would you do me a favor?"

"Of course, that is why I invited you here."

"Ask each of your people to nick every twenty dollar gold piece they take in with a knife, gouging it to see if the gold is plating or real. Then they should get a description of any person trying to pass the bad coin. A caution. There may be many of these counterfeits out there passing as real. Innocents must be using the coins without knowing it. But we may be able to establish some pattern of passing and perhaps spot one or two persons."

"That will be done within the hour."

"Don Pico, have you lived in San Francisco for many years?"

"Since my birth, Mr. McCoy."

"Good, you and your people must know this city

as few others could. It is a complicated process this counterfeiting of gold coins. Certain unusual equipment must be available. Could you discover for me where in the area such coins could be produced? There would need to be some basic foundry and metal working and plating equipment, as well as a heavy metal forming press or stamping press, the kind needed to strike the coins from the plated base metal."

"Yes, good. We can have that information within twenty-four hours. There will be no *siesta* or *mañana* here. We will find all the places where such work can be done. They should be both in the same plant?"

"Yes, that seems logical."

The same small woman who had let him into the office appeared with a tray holding coffee and some confection. They were a foot long and dusted with powdered sugar.

"Coffee?" Pico asked. Spur nodded. "You must try this sweet we have. We call it *churro*, something like a long donut."

Spur sipped the coffee, then took a bite of the *churro*. It was like a light, delicious donut, tasteful and sweetened with powdered sugar. Before he realized it he had eaten a whole one.

Pico nodded. "Yes, there are few who do not love our *churros.*" He became more serious. "Mr. McCoy, we need your help. We do not often ask for outside assistance. Our Mexican community likes to think it is self-sufficient. We are not, of course. We do not even have our own bank. But we are growing.

34

Olivera Street has a bad name among the Americans. You will hear that it is filled with cutthroats and thieves. That is not true. We are hard working men and women protecting ourselves, and trying to make a living."

He motioned to the door and two men came in. They were well dressed in white shirts and neckties and dark trousers. They were young and well groomed. They listened attentively to Juan Pico and the instructions he gave them in Spanish. A moment later they were gone.

"Come, let me show you Olivera Street, introduce you to my people, and you will see how gregarious, outgoing and loving they are. Anytime you wish to walk Olivera Street and buy a *churro* or other goods, you may do so with total freedom and absolute safety. Already I am spreading the word that the tall *gringo* in the soft gray cowboy hat is our friend. Come."

They toured the street, which turned out to be an area seven blocks long and three blocks wide. It was filled with shops and businesses of all types, and everywhere Don Pico went he was treated with utmost respect, and McCoy sensed a deep love and appreciation of what he was doing for them. Spur bought a sack of *churros* and a softly delicate lace *mantilla*.

Don Pico chuckled when they left the shop. "My friend McCoy, you are a true *gringo*, you do not bargain. You paid the first price you were asked. The *mantilla* could have been purchased for half what you paid."

It was Spur's turn to smile. "Don Pico, I have haggled with the best that Tijuana, Mexicali, Nogales and Ciudad Juarez have to offer. But here, with the people of Don Pico, I gladly pay what is asked as one small way of helping."

Don Pico blinked tears from his eyes and grasped Spur by his shoulders and kissed both his cheeks in a familiar manly embrace of the greatest respect.

"Señor McCoy, you are one of us, you are *amigo.* We thank you."

Spur had the *mantilla* wrapped at a shop and addressed it to Katherine Sanford, and asked Don Pico if he could hire a messenger to deliver it. A boy of twelve hurried up at Pico's call and Spur gave him a quarter to deliver the package. The boy's eyes grew large and he asked if it all was for him. Spur nodded and the youth smiled broadly as he ran down the street.

An hour later Spur finished his tour of the *barrio,* and caught a hack back to his hotel. He munched *churros* on the way and gave one to the driver who said he had seen them but never tasted them. He was happily surprised.

At his hotel Spur wrote two short letters, one to Jay Anderson Dumbarton at his bank telling of the one hundred and twelve counterfeit coins Don Pico had found, suggesting that the situation was much worse than they first assumed. "There could be hundreds more coins out there circulating undetected. This could cause a serious economic problem, even business failure for some small businesses. Suggest holding all coins for eventual reimbursement by some means."

His note to Katherine Sanford was short. "Miss Sanford: The lace was so beautiful that I thought of you, and could not leave the shop until I had it sent to you. Hope to see you again soon." He signed it McCoy.

At the desk downstairs he got envelopes, addressed the notes and had the desk clerk find someone to deliver them for a quarter each.

Back in his room, Spur thought for a moment about Katherine Sanford. She was the most vigorous and responsive woman he had ever known. Every little touch and caress seemed to explode her sexuality. He would see her again, he was positive. He wondered what she would be like over a bottle of wine and some cheese and a big hotel bed with a lock on the door and all night to make love. It was only a dream, but a delightful one.

CHAPTER FOUR

For the first time that day, Spur McCoy thought about his cover. He had come to San Francisco as a representative of his own art wholesale house in New York on a buying trip. He would have to spend a respectable amount of time looking at art. He sized up the list of four galleries and individual artists whom he was supposed to contact in the city. He picked out one with the most impressive name: San Francisco Artists.

The address was only a short distance away, so he changed jackets. He wore a soft blue with his dark blue trousers and a flashy vest of blues and greens over his white shirt and tie. He decided that he looked artistic enough.

San Francisco Artists was off the main streets on the ground floor with a dozen good oil paintings exhibited in the window. He went inside, heard the bell ring and a small man with a large belly, rimless spectacles and a smudged white painter's smock came through a connecting door.

"Yes, may I help you?"

"McCoy is the name, McCoy Galleries in New York City."

His pleasant expression sweetened to delight.

"Mr. McCoy! Pardon my appearance. A commission I'm rushing for a dear lady on the hill. Look around a moment while I change and I'll show you everything we have. Just a minute."

Spur knew enough about art to bluff his way through. He favored naturalism, without a lot of shifting around of the subjects. And in portraits, the mole better show or he was not pleased. He noticed several paintings that were good. At the end of the display room one painting was positioned where it caught the morning light and was highlighted with reflecting mirrors from two angles. It was a seascape, a rocky area and a cliff with a glittering sunset. Close in the foreground there were two seagulls. It was an outstanding painting. He guessed it would bring over a thousand dollars at a New York auction.

The little man came back, his hair slicked down and wearing a suit coat to match his pants. His eyes shone with anticipation.

"Well, Mr. McCoy. The art colony here must be thrilled with your visit. We have some outstanding artists in town and we all pull together. Here at my gallery we have over twenty professional artists represented. All local, and all excellent."

"I'm sure they are, Mr. . . ."

"Excuse me, the name is Locklaw, Ira Locklaw."

"Mr. Locklaw, I'm looking for specifics. One type painting I need is marine oils. Do you have any good ocean scenes, beaches, rocks, cliffs, the mighty Pacific in a storm, that sort of thing?"

They spent an hour sorting through paintings, and Spur quickly selected half a dozen he was interested in. The painting on the wall had been discussed first. The artist wanted five hundred dollars for it but Locklaw said he would take less from a New York gallery just to get his work shown and owned there.

"Would you like a drink, Mr. McCoy? I could go with a spot of Irish whiskey about now with just a brace of branch water."

Spur nodded, studying the painting of the ocean on the wall again. It was an excellent job and easily worth the thousand dollars he'd originally estimated.

The whiskey came cut with only a splash of water and Spur worked on it slowly.

"I do have one other item to show you, Mr. McCoy. It's called *Triplets*. Three interesting female figures. It's in the back studio. Would you care to see it?"

Spur waved his drink and followed the pauchy little man. It was in the back studio which had excellent northern exposure and a skylight. The canvas was a large horizontal, three by five feet. There were three woman on it, all nude and in various provocative poses. The background had been completed and the figures half filled-in.

The little man was wringing his hands.

"Of course it's only started. I have all the detail work to do, but what do you think of the concept? I'm calling it three wood nymphs . . . as in nymph-omaniacs."

"Your basic composition doesn't excite me, Mr. Locklaw. Not that it's wrong or bad, but it just doesn't move me. This is obviously for a select audience. Whoever buys it will want it to be sexually explicit, to arouse him, to excite, to stimulate. Have you considered mixing a man in with the three women?"

Locklaw stood for a moment frozen in thought then he smiled. "Yes, yes! I think the patron who's interested would be enthusiastic about such an addition. Yes! Would you like to see the models themselves? They are still here since they were sitting for me." He didn't wait for Spur's response, but waved his hand and there was motion behind a screen Spur had seen to the right.

Three young women came out wearing white cover-up robes. One was a striking Chinese girl with long black hair. She had a pouting face that could not be called pretty, but the gown was wrapped around what Spur had seen on the canvas, a voluptuous body. The second girl was a blond with her hair cut short. She was small, slender with a quizzical smile. On canvas she appeared to be fuller bodied than in real life.

The third girl was a huge Spanish girl. She was

older than the other two, perhaps twenty-two. Her jet black hair was cut short, and the robe had slipped open in front. She was about five feet two and must have weighed more than two hundred and fifty pounds.

"Ladies, ladies! This is no time for modesty. You are models, your bodies are your fortunes." Spur saw that Locklaw was rubbing a bulge behind his fly. "Come, come, ladies, let's get to work. Pose on the mattresses, now!"

They went to three single blue mattress pads on the floor and each took off her robe characteristically, Spur decided. The tall Chinese shrugged it off her shoulders letting her large, heavily nippled breasts surge out, then flipped the white robe away as if it were a trifle. She lay in her position on the mattress with her slender legs spread, one straight, one knee bent, and leaning up on one elbow, her other arm draped across her knee, her breasts bouncing slightly with her movements.

The small blonde turned half around as she slid the robe off, then in a teasing move walked to the pad and turned so that Spur could see her front as she assumed her pose. She stood with her legs spread, her blonde crotch hair glistening, her legs bent and her hands lifting her breasts which were small and delicate with light pink nipples and aeolas.

The heavy Mexican girl knelt on the pad, her huge breasts sagging almost to the floor as she presented her chubby ass to the artist. She looked over her shoulder with what Spur decided was her version of a coy expression.

Locklaw was openly rubbing his erection now through his pants.

"Mr. McCoy, that is what I call arousing. God, doesn't it get your pecker up?"

The artist dropped to his knees on the floor, pulled open his fly and jerked out his hard penis. "Oh, God, you kids are just beautiful, so sexy, so damn sexy!"

It was a signal. The girls dropped their poses. Two of them simply sat down and waited. The small blonde moved toward Spur. She rubbed against him and then began unbuttoning his vest.

"Damn, but I'd like to see you naked as I am."

"You are a pretty girl."

"And sexy? Do you want to fuck me?"

"Of course."

"Then get your pants off."

"They watch?" Spur asked amused.

"The girls won't be able to stand it for long. It was my turn first. Old Ira there will play with himself for a half hour then want to work again and put us in those asshole poses."

She had his vest unbuttoned and half his shirt. She pushed her hands inside touching his warm skin.

"Oh, nice! I like a man with chest hair. I go wild playing with it." She pulled his hand up to her breast.

"You like tits? Start out with these and work up to the Chink and the greaser. They got cow tits."

Spur laughed and fondled her breasts. "Can you feel that? Do you respond at all?"

"Shit, not to that little feel. I'll get going about the third time. I ain't no fucking virgin, you know." She had his pants unbuttoned and his underwear down and pulled out his still limp prick.

"Hey, fuckers, look! A man with some staying power. Tits don't get him hard!"

The three girls cheered. The others came over and helped pull off Spur's pants. Then they carried him to the biggest mattress and flopped down beside his prostrate form.

"Come on, Tiny Tits, you was first," the Mexican girl said.

The blonde yelped and rolled on top of Spur, then knelt over him and worked on his hardening staff. She gave a little cry of success and positioned herself over his hips and holding his penis upright, she stabbed it into her vagina.

"Oh, lordy, I ain't lost the fucking touch!" she shouted. "I still got the way in the hay, I smooch in the kooch, I'm a hell in the bell, and I fuck like a duck."

Spur hardly moved. She lifted herself off him and plunged back down and soon achieved a familiar rhythm. Forgetting that he was on the bottom, Spur responded as he always did with a jolting, hip-thrusting climax that pitched the blonde three feet in the air and brought squeals of admiration from the naked girls.

As soon as the blonde was impaled, the other girls lay down beside Spur. The fat girl held his hand to her huge breasts, urging him to play with them. The Chinese girl leaned close to him, tongued his ear and

45

assured him that she was *not* cut sideways as the myth warned. She plunged his hand between her legs and squeezed it, then let him find his own way into her heartland.

Spur looked at Locklaw. He was on his knees, his right hand pumping his surprisingly long penis in the traditional male masturbating pose. Sweat beaded his forehead but still he pumped and pumped, his eyes fastened securely on the four naked bodies on the mattresses, anticipation showing on his face.

Over him the blonde was screaming, wailing, pumping at Spur harder than ever as she climaxed again and again.

Suddenly she was gone. The big Mexican girl had shoved her to one side, breaking their connection.

A large brown face loomed over Spur.

"Honey-fuck, now you gonna see something, a real Mexican ten dollar piece of ass. You know how *good* that is? Shit, you don' know." She bent and put a piece of elastic three times around the base of his penis and laughed.

"Yeah, now we got that big prick captured. He ain't gonna droop on Carlotta, tell you that for sure." She got up on her hands and knees and pushed her big bottom toward him. "Hey, man, you got it up, get it in. You the big toro and I'm the little heifer in the pasture. Plant it in me, Big Cock. Sock it right in my old pussy!"

Spur was getting into the swing of it. He got on his knees and powered forward, heard a shriek as he entered and then a long squeal and a moan.

"That's too high, you're in my fucking asshole."

"Enjoy it while you can," Spur said, reached around her and grabbed a big tit with each hand and pumped into her, slapping with each stroke against her fat buttocks.

Carlotta bellowed and moaned, screeching so loud it caught Locklaw's attention. He climaxed, jolting his load into his hand, but kept right on pumping for seconds.

Carlotta kept up a steady stream of moans and chatter.

"You sexy prick, you can't get me pregnant in there. What the fuck I have to show you how to do everything? Bet you don't even piss straight. Damn like to have you for a month. I'd get your ass straightened out. Get some good chilli beans and peppers into your gut and clean out your asshole. Yeah, and you could ream mine out every night. Oh, shit-fuck but that is wild. You a mean fucker, man, a mean fucker."

Spur worked it up a long time, then knew the rubber band was stopping him. He pulled out of her, slid off the elastic band and jolted back into her upper slot and climaxed almost at once, slamming her forward onto her fat belly on the mattress, bringing a wail of torment and ecstasy from Carlotta who gave one last shuddering climax and went to sleep without moving.

He pulled out of her and turned to find the Chinese girl with her large, shapely breasts kneeling in front of him. She had a wash basin, warm water and soap and she washed off Spur's genitals tenderly, yet thoroughly. She smiled.

"Mr. McCoy. We save best for last. I born in Hong Kong. Do not know American ways. Only Chinese way, all right?"

Spur nodded. He wasn't doing much to find the counterfeiters, but hell, he had to maintain his cover. Too many people in town already knew that he was Secret Service. That could get him killed. A good cover was worth its weight in gold.

"Little darling," Spur said. "I don't think there's anything you could do that wouldn't be all right with me."

She smiled. "Name, LoLing." She bowed.

"Shit, here we go again," Carlotta said.

LoLing ignored the jibe and began a soft little chanting song in Chinese. It fascinated Spur who had no idea what she was saying, nor did he understand the strange musical sound, but still he was caught up.

She finished the song and bowed again, then took his hands and placed them gently on her breasts. "Play." she said.

Spur felt himself suddenly shoved to one side. Locklaw knelt there glaring at Spur.

"Not this one. LoLing is mine. All mine. You fuck around with them other two sluts, but nobody touches LoLing but me!"

Spur watched him for a moment, looked at the inviting, lush young body of the Chinese girl, her heavily nippled, large breasts and her slender waist and perfect legs.

"Yes, Locklaw. Yes, I can understand that. I

48

understand." He stood and found his clothes and let the small blonde girl help him put them on. She buttoned every button and pulled on his half boots. Then she kissed his fly.

"When you coming back? You wanna come to my place? Not much but it's got a quiet bed." She laughed. "Sure, you think I'm a slut just because I like to fuck. Hell, men like to fuck, why can't a woman like to pump it up the way men do? No goddamn reason. Men just afraid of us. You wanna come over to my place right now, stay a week or so? Fuck this job. He can do the rest of it from memory, he's been in me enough in the last two months so he won't never forget me. How about it?"

It took Spur a half hour to get untangled from the girl with the short blonde hair and back to the street. Locklaw was still entwined with the gorgeous LoLing, and Spur didn't blame him a bit.

McCoy checked his watch as he stood outside the gallery. He would have time enough to get to the U.S. Mint and find out more about how they made gold coins as well as some of the major problems that counterfeiters confront. He found a hack and was soon talking with the professionals in the field of minting coins. He would learn as much as he could, as quickly as he could and then see what Juan Pico had turned up. There was a good chance that Juan's men could find out what he needed to know and do it much faster than Spur. He needed all the help he could muster.

CHAPTER FIVE

Katherine Sanford sat in her room in the Sanford Mansion high on the hill and studied her reflection in the mirror. Yes, she was pretty, and her figure was good enough to trap almost any man she wanted whether he was married or not.

She studied the eyes, brown, with tiny flecks of emerald green. Yes, but were they excited? Were the eyes ready for something new? Someone new? A new thrill? Damn right they were!

And it would happen today. Katherine had awakened that morning cheerful and happy, realizing that she had enjoyed a new experience the previous night. Good Lord, she had been fucked standing up against the door twenty yards from the Opera Society's gala dance! Now that was worthwhile! And the man, this Spur McCoy, had certainly put his

51

spurs into her. Usually she forgot the man an hour later, but there was something about this one, this cowboy who was sleek and slick and intelligent and surprise of surprises, had manners. That held her interest.

Yes, she was ready.

She went out the side door, walked three blocks down the hill to a cross street where a row of small houses stood. They were quaint and poor and she always wore a cover-up bonnet when she came. Now she slipped in the side door of one of them, relocked it after her and went to the back bedroom. There she tore off her clothes, the skirts and petticoats, the wrapper, the fluffy drawers. She wore only a cut-off pair of drawers and a thick, tight chemise that bound her breasts close to her chest.

Quickly she put on a shirt too big for her that bagged at the chest covering her breasts, hiding them. She stuffed the shirt tail into a pair of breeches that were also cut slightly large for her figure, concealing her womanly hips. Her hair had been braided and pinned securely on top of her head before she came. Now she pinned on a hat with a dozen pins so it couldn't fall off, and put on knee-high boots.

She looked at the effect in the mirror. A pair of thick rimmed spectacles with plain glass completed the disguise. Her own mother wouldn't know her from three feet away. She smeared dirt smudges on her cheeks, and wiped off the rouge she had put on last night. With a mask added to her disguise there would be no way anyone could identify her.

Kate went out the rear door into the alley, saw that no one was there and walked quickly down the street to a livery and rented a gentle nag she had used before. So far she hadn't said a word. Her voice could be a problem.

She rode for an hour and left the fringes of houses at the south of San Francisco behind. Less than a mile ahead and only a quarter mile off the main trail down the coast in the direction of a growing community known as Los Angeles, sat a small farm house. She rode to the rear where four more horses stood.

Kate tied her horse to the rail and went in the back door. As she opened it she heard someone say:

"Easy, it's her for sure."

Kate walked into the farm house kitchen slapping a riding crop against a gloved hand. She looked around at the familiar room and at the four men waiting for her.

"Gentlemen. You are all here. Good. Any changes in our plans?"

Foster Burke, who went by the tag of Foss, hunched his shoulders and stood.

"Kate, we got to thinking. Can't see much profit in this one. Twice we hit them before and sure as hell they going to have more guns out this time. Seems like one hell of a big risk when we got a sure thing going tomorrow night."

Burke was the best gun in the group and the tallest at five feet ten. He also had an annoying habit of exaggerating things. It offended Kate but she tried not to let it show. He had been much easier to handle since she had taken him to bed and promised him more later. He had a shock of red hair they always had to keep covered and one missing tooth that showed when he smiled. She guessed he was about forty years old.

"I've told you each time that this is a volunteer operation. Anyone not wishing to go is excused. Of course, you also know it's a little like fishing. You never know who or what you might catch in the stage from Los Angeles North. And as is always the case, I take no share in anything that you find.

"There might be twenty dollars in silver and two pocket watches, or there might be a bank strong box on board with fifty thousand dollars worth of gold in it. The choice is yours."

Kate looked at Tim Hackett, a man five feet tall who was the best metal worker and die man she could find in San Francisco. He was even tempered, about thirty-five and married. He was also an excellent locksmith. Now he pawed one hand back over straggly brown hair to cover the growing bald spot on top and shrugged.

"I like to fish, it's a gamble. Hell, I'm in the game if we get enough players."

The third member of the team was a Klamath half breed raised in Oregon and who had learned English at his white father's knee. He was the best tracker in half of California, and good with horses, with a natural instinct to calm them.

He nodded. "Yes, I'll go."

She looked back at Foss. He shrugged. "Christ the three of you would bungle the whole thing and get somebody killed. I better go along and keep you out of trouble."

Kate smiled. "Then it's unanimous, since Hop Choy always votes with me."

When he heard his name, a huge Chinese looked up from where he sat on the floor. He was six feet eight inches tall and weighed three hundred pounds. But he was all muscle, no flab. He had been neutered as a boy in Canton by a regional War Lord to be a guard for the Lord's women. But the War Lord was defeated and the victor freed all the slaves. Eventually he was captured near the coast and sent to the new world to work on the railroad. Afterward he drifted to San Francisco where Kate saw him, befriended him so she could seduce him, and only after two tries did she realize that he was mute as well as castrated. The War Lord had cut out his tongue. She set him up in her house and supported him, using him in various ways when she could.

Kate smiled. "Well, then, we still have a few minutes. Our original time schedule called for us to leave here at 10:30. It is now fifteen minutes from that hour. We will have ten minutes of dry shooting practice. Burke will direct."

They went in back and Burke again gave them directions in the best way to fire a six-gun, and the best way to hit a target. Burke was a natural teacher, and an excellent shot with any weapon.

Promptly at 10:30 they mounted up and rode out. Each wore a blue handkerchief around the throat ready to be pulled up as a mask. They rode ten miles along the coach road south to a spot where it entered a thick patch of live oak and brush.

Burke positioned them where the roadway made a turn and the rigs would slow. He was the only one with a rifle, a heavy Sharps with a .50 caliber slug and enough stopping power to drop a horse in its tracks.

Hackett, with a shotgun would be front insurance, Burke was at the bend in the road and would stop the rig. Hop Choy was at the back and would let the rig pass him. Kate was on the up trail end near Hackett, and the Breed would be sandwiched between.

Burke had worked out the strategy on the first stage they took two years ago in Nevada, and he had not varied his plan. They all were in position a half hour before the stage was due. Knowing the schedules the coaches maintained, they realized it could be from one to three hours late.

Today they were lucky. A half hour after its due time, they heard the rig coming up the trail. Burke cocked the big Sharps and rested it over a fallen oak tree that hid him and offered him excellent protection in case of a fire fight.

All his people had protection.

Five minutes after they heard the rig they could see it. It swung around the bend and Burke was standing following the lead horse. He head shot it and the animal died in mid-stride going down in the traces. The other five horses tried to bolt ahead but twelve strong reins in the driver's hands pulled them down after dragging the dead animal for less than forty feet.

Burke had positioned himself perfectly. The rig was opposite him. As the harness stopped jangling he called out.

"Guard! Pitch your shotgun and pistols into the trail, then stand up and hold your hands on top of your heads. You too, driver, only tie them reins tight first. If them horses move, you die!"

The orders were carried out.

"Now listen carefully and no one will get hurt. There are ten men around you, you are surrounded." As he finished Burke fired a pistol shot under the coach. The four others fired at the same time.

When the noise died down Burke called out again.

"Everyone inside, get out and sit in the road. Do it now, facing the trees."

Slowly the door opened and two men and two women got out. Then out came a small boy and an elderly woman.

Burke called to the youth. "Boy, use that black hat and gather up everyone's wallet, watches, jewelry. I can see all of you, so no holding back. If you think that hiding a twenty dollar gold piece is worth your life, you are betting your life on it. Do it, son, right now."

It took nearly five minutes for the boy to gather up the money and jewelry the passengers were carrying.

According to the plan Breed had crossed the road below the bend and come back on the off side, worked to the coach and checked the interior. He jabbed with his knife and a cowering man in a black suit erupted from the coach.

"Well, well, a coward, a holdout. Walk straight toward my voice, sir, we'll see what you are trying to hide." The man looked behind him, saw Breed's war-painted face and the ugly knife thrust at him. He walked.

In her position to the rear, Kate saw the man and giggled. She knew him, a pompous ass, one Reginald Compton. She was glad Breed had flushed him and wondered what Burke would do. He had strict instructions that no person was to be harmed in any way.

As Compton vanished into the woods toward Burke, he called out again.

"Now, the strong box up there in the boot. We know where it is, driver. Take your hands down now and toss it to the ground. Then unhitch your lead horse and see if you can move this lopsided buggy around the animal."

Three minutes later the dead horse had been cut free and the coach maneuvered around it.

"Thank you, son, for your help. Now, put the gentleman's hat with the loot in it on top of the strong box, then everyone place beside it any personal weapons you might have and reboard the coach. Your journey will continue shortly."

There was a scream from the woods, and Reginald Compton came running from the trees. He was stark naked, and ran behind the coach. He refused to move until one of the men gave him a coat to cover himself.

"Driver, move it out!" Burke called and fired the rifle again over the heads of the men riding on top. "Get it out of here!"

As the coach rolled along the trail, the men who had been ahead of it fired a shot behind it to keep it moving. Soon it was a dot two miles down the road.

"Let's take a look," Kate called and they all ran into the roadway. Burke looked over the wallets and jewelry.

"Maybe two hundred dollars worth," Burke said.

Hop Choy lifted the strong box and slammed it down on the top of a buried boulder at the side of the roadway. The wooden box split apart and the top flopped open. It contained no big gold shipment.

Kate looked in the envelopes. She smiled.

"Not such a bad day. Two bank envelopes each with five hundred dollars in it!"

Everyone cheered.

"Now, let's get out of here. Everyone take a different route back." Kate was directing. "Burke and I will bring the loot. Remember, all jewelry to be sold must be taken to Los Angeles or Sacramento, someplace well away from San Francisco. Let's get moving."

Burke and Kate rode knee to knee for a mile straight toward the coast after the group split up. She watched him and nodded.

"Burke, I think you deserve a bonus after today's performance. You were excellent. If nobody can see a stage coach bandit, nobody can identify him or his horse. Beautiful!"

She kicked her horse. "I feel like a swim in the surf. Race you to the water!"

They came out at the beach in a deserted stretch of gently sloping sand and crashing Pacific waves. They dismounted and tied their horses to some brush. She stood close to him. "You haven't said yet if you want your bonus."

He reached down to kiss her, but instead she put both her hands on his crotch and rubbed. A few seconds later she smiled.

"Yes, I think he's saying he wants his bonus." She stepped away from him and began pulling off her clothes. There was no one within sight a mile in each direction. She was naked in thirty seconds and Burke stood watching her with mounting excitement.

When she ran for the water he undressed and followed her.

They jumped waves and swam in the cool Pacific as long as they could stand it, then raced to a grassy place and lay in the sun until they were dry. They made love three times before they dressed and rode back to the farmhouse. The men would be happy, they had earned three hundred dollars each. That was as much as a cowboy earned working all year on a ranch!

Kate watched her gang, her team, she called them. She reminded them that they would work the next night. Two of them were assigned to stop at the small house to pick up the gear they needed before gathering at the usual place.

"Three or four more sessions with the press and we should be set for life," Kate said.

"Good," Burke said. "I'm getting the feeling that it's about time for me to be moving again. Hate to overstay my welcome anywhere."

Kate watched them, they were a good crew. She signaled to Breed. He would ride with her back to town. One of these days she would give *him* a bonus. He was the only one she had not favored, but he didn't seem to mind. On the way to the small house she told him he would get a bonus the next night. He stared at her a long time, then nodded, and rode back to the ranch house.

CHAPTER SIX

There was a note in McCoy's key box at the San Francisco Hotel when he returned from his research at the U.S. Mint. It was a message inviting Spur to dinner with Don Pico at a restaurant in the Mexican Village at seven. It also indicated in a guarded way that Pico had some useful information. The note had been sealed, opened and sealed again.

Spur wondered if someone was watching him or if it had been a desk clerk's idle curiosity. To be sure he didn't make himself an easy target, Spur slipped out of the hotel by the side door. He had changed into a lightweight, white summer jacket.

Don Pico was waiting for him at *La Valencia* restaurant, and was working on a frosty, salt-rimmed *margarita*. Spur ordered the same and Don Pico came at once to the point.

"We have found twelve small and large foundries in the area, and four of them contain the large stamping presses you mentioned that were essential to counterfeiting. As you suggested we did this quietly."

"Good. I'll go on a midnight patrol and check them out. Do you have the addresses?"

Don Pico handed Spur a paper with the names and locations neatly printed, including small maps of each to pinpoint the location.

"Thank you, highly efficient."

Don Pico smiled. "Efficient help produces excellent work. I only have highly qualified people around me."

They had not ordered but dinner came. First *tortilla* chips with a spicy dip that set Spur's mouth on fire. He used up two glasses of water. Don Pico smiled and signalled for a milder *salsa*. The appetizer was finished and a series of courses came, each could have been a full meal. Spur ate until he was stuffed, and held up his hands.

"I surrender, Don Pico, everything was delicious. I'll learn to eat that hot *salsa* yet."

The Mexican leader smiled. "Perhaps, Señor McCoy. Now, back to business. May I offer you some assistance? I have two young men who could work closely with you if you wish in any capacity. They both speak excellent English, can use weapons, know the city thoroughly, and have had training in unarmed attack and defense."

Spur shook his head. "Thanks, Don Pico, but I wouldn't know what to do with bodyguards. So far it doesn't look like anything that I can't handle. I'll keep them in mind if I need some quick help and I really appreciate your offer."

"They will be available at any time, day or night. Just send word to me at my office, and say where they should meet you. They will come armed." Don Pico paused. "This is the top task on my schedule, Mr. McCoy. It is vital that we put a quick stop to this dastardly drain on my people. We are struggling, and twenty dollars sometimes looks like a fortune to a small pottery maker. I believe that you understand."

An hour later Spur was back in his room in the hotel. He decided on a good night's sleep before investigating the foundries. He would go to them tomorrow, posing as a small manufacturer of decorative fences and gratings. That way he could inspect the facilities with the help of the owners. It was not only legal, it would be easier.

There were no messages in his key box, so he went up to his third floor room. He walked to the fourth floor, waited a moment and stepped part way into the open stairway going down and waited. No one seemed to have followed him. Good. He went back to room 310 and locked it securely behind him. As an added precaution, he put the key in the lock and turned it half way so it could not be pushed out. Then he wedged a straight backed chair under the door knob. Now he felt safer. It was a five storey building so no one would be climbing up to his window.

He blew out the lamp and lay on the bed. The

weather was still warm, even at night. For a moment he wondered what Katherine Sanford was doing. He laughed remembering the quick, sexy time they had together last night. It had been a total serendipity for him. He was thinking about her luscious body as he drifted off to sleep.

It should not have wakened him. Spur wondered what time it was. He rolled toward the outside of the bed and slid softly to the floor. The bedcovers humped up in the middle of the bed and a bright moon outside beamed a ray of light inside. He saw a shadow at the window and found his six-gun on the chair by the bed and cocked it just as the window shattered and gunshots boomed from outside. Three slugs tore into the covers of the bed where he had been. Before the last shot sounded Spur had snapped off two rounds of his own toward the figure at the window.

Spur heard a cry and then nothing more. He rushed to the broken window and saw a sturdy rope hanging down. He looked through the shattered pane and spotted a figure sliding down the line to the ground thirty feet below. Spur took a quick shot, missed and the figure hit the dirt running and darted behind a buggy in the alley and was gone.

Who in the hell was that? Spur wondered. He must have come down the rope from the roof to the third floor room window. Spur pulled on his pants, then his boots and shirt and went down to the desk where he registered under three different names in three different rooms. He left the registration in 310 under his real name.

Spur pushed his six-gun muzzle under the clerk's chin.

"Son, if *anybody* knows about this, and I mean one other person besides you and me, I'm going to carve your heart out and eat it for lunch! Am I making an impression on your small mind?"

"Yes, sir, Mr. . . . ah, Mr. Green."

"Good. Now remember that. I know you will."

Spur went up the steps to room 310, left his suitcase and took some essentials and slept the rest of the night in room 322. No one bothered him. His new worry was now who out there was trying to turn him into dead?

The next morning, Spur got up at 6:30, dressed in a new lightweight cotton suit and had breakfast. He turned in his 310 room key but kept the other three in his pocket. He found a livery and hired a horse and a rig for a week and made arrangements to bring it back when not in use and at night.

He found the first foundry on the list. It was not large and specialized in small decorative iron pieces and even some jewelry metal work. The big stamping press was seldom used now, and the owner even tried to sell it to Spur. He could see the rig had not been worked for months.

The second foundry was at the far north end of San Francisco, and Spur enjoyed the drive. He was near the ocean for a while, then the street curved back inland and he saw the smokestacks of the foundry. This was a large one, with a great volume of heavy steel work. There were a variety of heavy stamping presses and plenty of capacity for the plating needed for counterfeiting. Spur did not use his prospective customer story here, saw what he could and left. It did not look like a likely prospect for the counterfeiters' use.

The last two spots he checked were closer to the downtown section, along the bay and smaller in size. There was no night work done there the guard on the gate had said. Spur's tour of the second place told him that the equipment would work well.

All that would be needed to operate clandestinely was to bribe a guard or two and use the equipment late at night or early in the morning. He decided that he had better watch both these foundries.

By the time he got back to the hotel it was past lunch time. He wandered to the wharf and ate crab fresh off a boat. A little stand sold a cupful of a tasty seafood sauce along with a dozen crackers for ten cents. He had two of the crab cocktails and a bottle of cold beer. Spur had always wanted to be a fisherman, going to sea every morning, working the poles and nets and coming back at night with the catch. The open sea and the struggle and battle with the elements appealed to him.

When this assignment was over Spur told himself he was going to go fishing on one of the boats. He should be able to find a small boat owner who would take him into the bay fishing, maybe even out to the kelp beds along the coast. Yes! That would be a small pleasure he could look forward to.

Back at his hotel he found a message in his 310

box. He took it up to his room, found that the hotel had reglazed his window with a new pane of glass, and then sat on the bed and read the note.

It was on scented lavender stationery and Spur hoped it came from Katherine. It did not. The paper inside was also lavender. It had been written in a flowing, neat hand. He looked at the second page and saw the signature, Mildred Engleton. He thought back to the gala, yes, Mildred, the membership chairman, a large, pretty woman about forty who quickly told him she was a widow. He read it:

My dear Mr. McCoy. I do hope you don't think me a nuisance, but I would love to talk to you about New York. It has been some time since I lived there, but it would be interesting.

Of course, I will try to talk you into supporting our San Francisco Opera Society as a sustaining member. I have a dozen reasons why you should join.

Would you do me the honor of coming to a small dinner party this evening at seven? I know this is short notice, but it came up quickly and I wanted to be sure to invite you. I will be devastated if you can't come. No reason to reply, just be at the address below at seven and I will be in heaven!

Remember, part of the civic duty of those who have been blessed with more than average wealth is to realize their responsibility to use their money to promote the cultural activities of our city.

I just know that you will come, so I am counting on it. Until seven this evening. . . .

Spur felt trapped. She was playing on his cover story, and the assumption that he was rich, and that he *owed* something to the community. Perhaps he could make an appearance, say he would support the Opera Society, and then beg off pleading an appointment. That sounded reasonable. He did have to maintain his cover for a while yet.

That decided, Spur drove, where he had wanted to go all day, up the hill to the elaborate entrance. A uniformed butler answered the bell. When McCoy said he would like to speak with Katherine, the butler brightened and hurried away.

It was almost ten minutes before Katherine came down the curving marble stairway from the second floor. She wore a soft pink dress that looked so thin it wasn't there, but multiple layers defeated his straining eyes.

Her long black hair was braided, forming twin ropes down her back. She smiled and ran up and kissed his lips quickly, then caught his hand, and led him into a garden greenhouse, off the living room.

"That was so sweet of you to send me the *mantilla*. It is just beautiful. You are an intelligent, cultured, manered, and sexy man. I think I'll marry you for a week." She giggled and led him behind a big fern and kissed him hard, pressing her hips against his until his hot blood began to flow.

"Thanks, but I'm busy this week, so I can't marry

you. However, I would like to take you to the theater tonight. Shakespeare's *A Comedy of Errors* is being played by a traveling troupe. . . ."

She kissed his lips into silence and pushed her breasts hard into his chest. When she leaned back she shook her head.

"Sweetheart, I would love to go tonight, but I can't. Some damn social thing. But why not tomorrow night? Will they still be playing?"

"Yes."

"Then why don't we go then?"

"Fine, I'll be here about 7:30."

She put her arms around him. "Hold me close, sweetheart. I missed you so much. I wanted you in my bed last night so we could make love all night long. Maybe tomorrow?"

He nodded. Her hand worked down to his crotch, and Spur pushed his hand through the folds of the bodice until he could hold her bare, throbbing breast in his hand. She sighed, kissed him one more time and pushed him away.

"Another minute of this and I'll be flat on my back in the orchids spreading my legs," she whispered.

He stepped back. "Yes, Miss Sanford. Then until tomorrow night for the Bard." He turned, walked into the living room where he found the butler ready to open the door to the hallway. There was a twinkle in the man's eye, and Spur figured he had seen the fondling in the greenhouse.

Spur was walking to his rig at the curb when the sound of a pistol shot jolted him back to reality. He dropped to the ground and looked around. He saw a man aiming another shot from around a tree. Spur jumped and ran behind his horse. He worked back and pulled out a six-gun he had hidden in the buggy seat and returned fire hitting the tree. The man's weapon evidently jammed.

Spur ran hard for the tree, firing once more into it. He saw the man look out before he turned and charged down an alley, over a fence and into another yard before vanishing. Spur stopped. The man had been terrified at being shot at. He was running on adrenalin and fear and no one could catch him. McCoy got back in his rig and drove away. No one in the posh neighborhood came out to investigate the gunshots. Either it was common enough or they simply did not feel involved.

Something bothered Spur that he couldn't tie down. The man's face. That was it. He had seemed familiar. McCoy knew he had seen that man before and had dealt with him. The more he thought about it the more convinced he became it had been on an official basis. Where had he arrested the man?

By the time Spur got his rig back to the alley behind the hotel and checked his message box, it was mid-afternoon. He decided to have a bath, and ordered hot water for the third floor bathroom. He enjoyed a sudsy tub until the water cooled. He checked the counterfeit coins in his possession and was ready to leave for his dinner engagement at 6:45. Spur decided to look over the two small foundries for any unusual activity that night. He would leave the dinner party as soon as he could get away. A little support of his cover was all right, but he didn't want to let it monopolize his time.

CHAPTER SEVEN

McCoy parked his rig on a street in the Nob Hill section of San Francisco near the Engleton Mansion. It was two minutes after seven and Spur wondered where all the other buggies were? Perhaps people had been dropped off by drivers and the carriages were parked somewhere else.

He went to the door hoping he wasn't overdressed. Spur was wearing the same basic formal outfit he had worn for the Gala, plus flashier studs and cuff links.

Before he rang the bell, the door opened. Mrs. Engleton greeted him in a floor length gown of sequined gold and wearing a large diamond necklace around her throat which fell into a thrust up cleavage. Her smile was one of delight.

"Mr. McCoy! I am simply overwhelmed that you

have come. It was one of my greatest desires, and here you are. The stars are indeed kind to me tonight. Do you believe in astrology? Well, my dear, you should, it is simply fascinating." She took his arm possessively, her large breast pushing comfortably against him.

"Come in, come in, I want to show you my house. Would you mind? I'm still fascinated with everything that my late husband had built into it for our pleasure. This is the entrance hall, and that funny bathtub is an Egyptian sepulcher, which dates back to the early pre-Christian era. My husband loved Egypt."

The house was a mansion and Mrs. Engleton spent an hour showing him every room, including her bedroom, done in pink satin. She lingered there for quite some time.

Spur kept wondering where the other guests were. They had not yet seen the dining room.

"Mrs. Engleton, this is all remarkable, but where are the other guests?"

She smiled and led him to double walnut doors that opened into a dining room with a table that would seat forty. At the far end next to a large bay window stood a table set for two.

"Dear Boy, I thought I explained that. I said it would be a small dinner party. It's for the two of us, of course. I hope you didn't misunderstand."

McCoy recovered in a second. He smiled. "Then I have you all to myself," he said.

She beamed. "Dear Boy, you do say the sweetest things. Now, let's have a cocktail before dinner."

They sat on a shaded terrace and looked out over the lights of the city. They could trace the bend of the bay and see faint traces of the Pacific ocean far to the west. They sat close together on a couch and her thigh pressed against his through the cloth. She didn't move away. Dinner came a few minutes later.

They went inside and sat at the small table. Their knees touched under it, and she smiled.

"I do so like the small, intimate dinner like this. Then you can really get to know a guest." She sighed. "Spur McCoy, it has been a lonesome ten years for me living here without Wally. He was the most romantic man I have ever known. The patio was his favorite spot. He would take me out there and put down a blanket and seduce me. He didn't have to, but he told me to fight him off a little, he said it made it all the more sweet." She turned. "I hope I'm not embarrassing you. But a relationship is special. Have you been married, Mr. McCoy?"

"No."

"Pity, what a waste! But I bet you have entertained a young lady or two in your bedroom." She laughed. "Yes, I would say a goodly number." She moved and her knee pressed higher on his leg.

Dinner came, a seafood delight. Fresh lobster with melted butter, a dozen clams on the half shell, broiled salmon and the largest, crusty fried shrimp Spur had ever seen.

A small black girl in a maid's uniform complete with little cap served the meal. Her skirt was so short Spur could not avoid seeing the starkly white panties she wore under it.

When she brought the second course she had removed her jacket and the low cut blouse showed more than half of each of her small breasts.

Mrs. Engleton looked at her pointedly. "Celeste, my dear, you do look too warm this evening. Why don't you get cooler?"

"Yes, Ma'am. Right away." Celeste set the tray of desserts on the edge of the table, unbuttoned the blouse and let it drop to the floor, Her chocolate brown breasts had dark, nearly black areolas, and her small nipples were jet black. She wasn't the least concerned with her top nakedness. She served Mrs. Engleton a strawberry tart, and then offered the tray to Spur.

"Take whatever appeals to you, Mr. McCoy," Mrs. Engleton said.

Celeste leaned in toward him, her breasts the closest dessert to Spur. He smiled at her, took a French cheese cake and put it on his plate. As Celeste moved her breast brushed Spur's cheek as she walked away.

"A dear girl, Celeste, but sometimes a little too proud of her dainty figure. I didn't think you would mind my helping satisfy her small fantasy."

Spur grunted a response. He had been pleasantly surprised when the girl was asked to strip, evidently for his amusement. Now he saw the pattern and he had to suppress a chuckle. This society *grand dame* was trying to seduce him, teasing him on with the black breasts and saucy bottom. He wouldn't be surprised if little Celeste came out the next time bareassed naked.

But there was no reprise. Mrs. Engleton put down her fork and stood.

"Mr. McCoy, I hope you don't mind if I call you that, I've never been a first name person. Please come this way. Oh, I am interested in your participation in our Opera Society, but I understand you will be here only a short time. Pity. I hoped we could count on you for support."

"I really do have a great number of charities . . ."

"Yes, that is what I expected. Don't worry about that. What I have ready for you is much more important. I want you to see my art collection."

They went to the third floor and in a door that opened to a hallway. On each side of the hall were pedestals with African tribal statues and fertility rite objects. Some were obvious, a twelve inch phallus and huge testicles. Others were breasts and variations on a woman's pubic area.

On the last pedestal stood a lifelike woman figure with her naked legs spread and her hands opening her nether lips. The statue came alive. It was Celeste who ran ahead and opened a pair of double doors into a large, high ceilinged room.

"This is my treasure, Mr. McCoy."

Spur looked around in amazement. It was an art gallery. The walls were covered with expensive oil paintings, the floor spotted with statuary, and every art object was pornographic. They were sexually explicit, men and women having intercourse in every imaginable position; homosexual lovers, trios of lovers and one depicted six naked bodies connected in a chain.

"This is my hobby, my love," she said softly.

Spur turned and looked at her. She slowly let down the front of her dress revealing big, firm breasts with the largest nipple he had ever seen. She brushed them with her hands, the diamond necklace extending between them.

"Tonight is for us, Spur McCoy." She took his hand and led him past a painting of a swan and a naked woman having sex, to a round bed in the center of the sixty foot long room. She sat down and patted the spot beside her.

"We move the art pieces around for variety, but I have my favorites here near the passion center," she said.

Directly in front of them was a rough sculpture of a man's torso, his erect phallus in the face of a woman who had taken half of the rod into her mouth. Another marble statue standing beside it showed the buttocks of a fat woman with a penis about to penetrate her.

"Mr. McCoy, you haven't said a word. You do make love, don't you? You do like women and tits and cunts and sucking mouths?"

"Yes. It's such a surprise. It must have taken you years to gather all this."

"I have friends who help, who come here once a week. Six of us now, for group sex parties. I wanted to invite you but I thought slow and steady would be more appropriate at the beginning."

Celeste walked in, still darkly naked. She went on her knees behind Mrs. Engleton and began undressing her. It took only a few moments before the two women were naked.

Celeste moved to Spur, edged a breast toward his mouth. He kissed it. Both women cheered, then they undressed him.

They sat side by side on the bed, Spur still amazed at the variety of sexually explicit art around him.

"What is the sexiest thing you can think of, Mr. McCoy?" Mrs. Engleton asked.

Spur looked at them, stroked the breasts of each, surprised at the differences in the black and white, large and small. He thought about it a few seconds.

"At the moment the sexiest thing I can think of is watching you two make love to each other. But don't worry, I'll be a participant before too long."

Mrs. Engleton looked at her maid, who smiled. "Celeste, I don't think I have told you often enough how much I love you, how I enjoy having you here, how I am delighted with your compact, sexy body, and how I adore having your hands touch me." She lay down on the bed, closed her eyes, and Celeste bent over her, the girl's long, slender fingers barely touching the larger, white flattened breasts. Flying over the flesh, teasing, touching, moving away, leaving a wanting for more.

Mildred Engleton moaned softly. "Yes, yes!"

The touching continued, more and more contact was made until the black hands were fully engaged, stroking softly the large half orbs, then working harder around the big nipples, until they began to rise, harden and enlarge.

"Yes, darling Celeste. Oh, yes!" The larger woman rolled over and lifted to her hands and knees, letting her breasts hang downward swaying like two pendulums.

Celeste turned on her back, worked under the hanging mounds and began licking them gently. Her mouth worked around each breast, then lower and lower until the pulsating, hot nipple was drawn into her mouth and she chewed gently on it. As she sucked on the nipples, Mrs. Engleton jolted into a surging, shrieking climax. The walls bounced back her cries of satisfaction, and Spur wondered if they could not be heard outside.

As the climax wound down, Celeste pushed from under the white woman and sat on her back as a jockey would and with her left hand spanked Mrs. Engleton's fat round buttocks.

The wailing now had a note of pain in it as the woman reacted to the rougher sexual treatment, but this too brought on a climax that set her bucking and bouncing until the rider was thrown off, and both collapsed on the bed.

Now Celeste was facing the older woman's feet. She slowly pressed the white legs apart and with one hand smoothed the pubic hair over the nether lips. Slowly the caresses increased in tempo and force until at last Celeste's fingers parted the silky crotch hair and exposed her love nest.

With soft, gentle fingers, Celeste feather brushed the pubic area and around her crotch and then back as she came nearer and nearer to the sensitive, pink lips. When at last she touched them tenderly, Mrs. Engleton erupted in a long awaited climax and surged a dozen times with her hips as her whole body shook and vibrated and rattled as if it would never stop.

It was another two minutes before Mrs. Engleton quieted sufficiently for Celeste to find the tiny node, the joy trigger, the clit that she stroked back and forth.

At once Mrs. Engleton shivered and wailed in a different kind of a climax, one that started her crying with short potent sobs of joy-pain-relief-satisfaction all at once.

Suddenly Celeste pushed her face into the very center of Mrs. Engleton's nether lips, her tongue jamming in as deep as it would go. The white woman bellowed out in surprise and total joy. Celeste turned around, fell on the older woman and began humping her hips at the other's hips. Each picked up the rhythm and slammed against each other for two or three minutes before they whimpered again and again. Then the pumping slowed and stopped and they relaxed in each other's arms. For a moment they slept.

They woke up three minutes later, and Celeste jumped up and ran from the room.

Mrs. Engleton sat up and smiled at him. "Isn't she good? She is so delicious I'm afraid someone else will hire her away from me." Mrs. Engleton smiled. "Did you think that was sexy?"

"I've never seen anything so tender, so gentle, and so violently sexy all at the same time. I thought you were going to have a heart seizure."

"I almost did." She smiled. "Now it's my turn to please you. Whatever you want, however you want me, anything, just anything at all."

"I do like tits," Spur said. "Hang those two for me again and I'll pretend they are vanila cones of dessert!"

They made love twice, gently and with feeling, then Celeste brought in cheese, grapes and melons all cut into small squares and a variety of salted nuts. She put down the food and two bottles of wine and left quickly, by direction, Spur was sure. She was still naked.

After the snack they experimented trying to duplicate some of the poses they found in the art works, but they usually ended in a tangle of arms, legs and torsos.

It was just after three A.M. when Spur finished dressing and kissed Mrs. Engleton goodbye. As he did she pressed something into his hand.

"Don't look at it until you get back to your hotel," she said. "It's just a small gift so you'll remember me and this night. And when you're back in town again, you might send me a note asking about my art collection."

Spur nodded, kissed her again, and went out the big front door to his buggy in the street. He was glad it had been a dinner party for one, after all. Before he drove away he opened the small box she had given him and looked inside. He found a man's ring, a wide gold band set with black onyx surrounding a large diamond. He frowned as he looked at it. It must be at least a two carat diamond, and worth half a year's salary.

Was it a bribe or a gift? He frowned a moment, then grinned. It was simply a gift to a friend from a rich and oversexed lady.

CHAPTER EIGHT

Katherine Sanford had stopped telling her parents where she was going five years ago when she began going out nights. Tonight they were sleeping when she slipped out of the mansion, walked to her own small gray house three blocks away and changed quickly into her Kate uniform, baggy shirt and pants, hair on top of her head and the pinned on hat to turn her into a young man.

Tonight she drove a buggy she had left in back of the house earlier, and met her four gang members a block from the foundry and metal works owned by a Mr. Nelson. He was an elderly man, not much interested in his firm anymore, and there was no activity at all there after five o'clock. His night watchman was a poor man and for a twenty dollar gold piece he would help them come in and use the equipment, just as long as they didn't steal anything or break it.

Seven times they had been here, coming over a back fence, lugging in the various types of metal they had used for the stamping blanks and the gold to use in plating. Tonight things went according to plan.

Hop Choy was lookout near the street. If anyone came or if the police were about to disrupt the stamping, he would fire one shot in the air.

Tim Hackett was boss tonight. He was the expert die man who had created the dies and knew how to use them in a stamp press. He also handled the gold plating of the base metal stock. Tonight they had strips of copper two and a half inches wide and five feet long.

Tim had tried to explain the stamping process to Kate one night, but she couldn't wade through the details. He could do it, so she told him to do it.

He explained that they would use a method over two thousand years old, although the pressure may have been delivered in those days through the use of a crude sledgehammer. The upper and lower dies were embossed and engraved with the design of the double gold eagle. The metal blank was then fed to the lower die which was positioned securely on a solid base and with a knurled ring around it so the metal was confined and could not spread as the upper die was powered down on it with a great force.

It usually took Hackett about an hour to set up the stamping press with his dies and to get everything right. First the metal strips were fed into the press and the cutting die stamped out the individual coins. They had to be cut out first so the gold plating would coat the sides of the metal as well. Tim cut them with a die that was perfectly round and exactly the size of the double eagle and would even leave the required serration on the edges of the coins. After the blanks were plated they would be *struck off* with another hit of the stamping press to finish them. It was a two strike process.

When the press was set up correctly, Hackett got ready to plate the blanks. Tonight they had enough stock to strike up two hundred coins — if everything went right.

Breed prowled the outside of the buildings, watching, listening, looking for any trouble. Twice he rushed in and told everyone to remain silent as someone passed close by.

Foster Burke was along to carry stock and to help with his gun if there was any trouble which gave him time to talk to Kate.

Foss edged up beside Kate as she watched the plating process and put his hand on her shoulder.

"That was a terrific swim we had yesterday," he said.

She brushed his hand away, her eyes cold. "I don't remember anything about a swim, and you better not either. Today we have new work, new problems. We take care of today today."

"Yeah, sure, only I thought maybe tonight, after we're done here. . . ."

"No."

Foss cocked his head in surprise. "Just a flat no? Not even a maybe or a later, or something?"

"Just a no. I run this outfit, Foss, don't forget. I put it together, I paid the bills when you were knocking over stage coaches and going broke. It's my gang to do whatever I damn well please with. Without me you'd be back hustling whores on the Barbary Coast. Now, let's get these blanks moved over where we can get them into production."

"Yes, Ma'am!" Foss said with an exaggerated amount of snap and subservience.

Kate watched him go, wondering if her romp with him yesterday had been a good idea after all. He could think he was getting too important for his own good. She dismissed it and watched Jim Hackett cutting out the round blanks that would soon become double eagles. The coin blanks came from a strip of copper the correct thickness, two and a half inches wide and five feet long. They could cut out thirty coins from the strip.

When all two hundred and fifteen blanks had been cut out, Tim took them to the hot plating area and gold plated them, let them dry and then brought them back in racks.

Back at the press, Tim changed the dies, putting in those with the gold eagle engravings and began to *strike off* the actual coins.

They were done by four A.M. and Kate gave each of the men three coins and warned them.

"We must be careful where we spend these. I got one mixed up the other day and deposited it at a bank. They caught it and asked me where I got it. I

90

told them at a store somewhere. We must spend these only at large stores that take in hundreds a day, then the clerks will not be able to remember who passes them. A small shop owner will remember."

They spent the next half hour taking the dies off the press and putting all the equipment back the way they had found it. By 4:30 they were across the fence and heading for their various houses. Hop Choy stayed at the little gray house in the city, Burke and the Breed were out at the ranch house and Tim Hackett had a wife and a small house in the north side of town.

Hop Choy drove the rig for her on the home trip. He also carried the 200 coins to the buggy. They had struck 215, so she had 203 to put in her hoard. Kate had made a fair profit for the night's work, four thousand dollars! She had an arrangement with Tim that every other time they struck off coins, he would get 25. It was payment for his work on the dies and his expertise. The others were satisfied with their sixty dollars. That was two months' wages for most factory workers and laborers.

Before Breed rode away, she told him to stop by at the little house. He nodded and left.

She wondered about Breed, his Indian blood, his savage redskin mother. Would he be different? She shivered. It would be exciting finding out.

A half hour later she removed a section of the floor boards in the back bedroom and lowered the heavy sack into the hidden vault-like safe she had created there. The house could burn down and not harm the gold. She looked in her small notebook and made an entry. Now she had a few over two thousand of the coins! They had spent another three hundred perhaps. Her goal was fifty thousand dollars. She could have that in three more strikings!

She would start her deposits of four hundred dollars in various small banks around town, then transfer the credits after a month or so to one bank, and the counterfeit coins would be washed clean and pure. No one could trace them, and her credits in her main bank would be secure!

She was thrilled at the thought. Fifty thousand dollars all her own, that she had made herself. She didn't care if her father was rich, if he was worth five million dollars. This was money she had earned herself!

Hop Choy went to the back door and let in Breed. She covered up the safe and put the rug back, then sat on the bed and called to Breed to come back. He stepped inside the room, his dark eyes darting a quick look at her shirt. He was a man all right.

She closed the door and began talking. It would relax him, make him more sure of himself.

"Breed, I know you said once your name was Tom, may I call you that? It will be so much better." She closed the door and began unbuttoning her shirt. "Tom, could you help me with these buttons?" He nodded and unfastened them, then pushed the shirt off her shoulders and frowned at the tight wrapper she had put around her breasts to flatten them for her disguise.

Kate laughed. "Yes, Tom, I do have breasts, I

had to hide them. Here, unwrap this for me." He did and her breasts lifted and she shook them and Tom's eyes glowed.

"Tom, I don't think we're going to have any trouble at all. I do hope it hasn't been a long time for you. Remember you must be soft and gentle."

Breed bent and sucked half of one of her big breasts into his mouth and began chewing on it.

"No, Tom, I don't think we're going to have any problems at all this first time."

Outside the small gray house, Foss Burke settled down beside a box in the alley. He rolled a smoke and watched the horse that Breed rode. The back bedroom light had stayed on in the little house, and he could imagine Breed kneeling over that glorious white meat and lunging forward, taking her and making her like it just the way Burke had done three times yesterday.

Foss grinned. Yes sir, a man could take orders from a woman for just so long, then there came a time to settle up. He knew all about the floor safe and how to get into it. He figured she must have sixty, maybe seventy thousand dollars worth of counterfeit double eagles in there by now. Hell, with money like that a man could hole up in some little town and live as top dog for the rest of his natural life. Just take some careful *investing* in small banks and then getting letters of credit when he moved on.

The only problem was the timing. Things were going so damn smooth right now. She put another two thousand dollars worth away tonight.

Shit! He should do it tonight!

He could rent a rig, give Hop Choy the choice of going with them, or taking a .44 slug in the gut. Then him and Breed could light out with the gold in the buggy and live high on the hog!

Foss snorted. Damned if he almost talked himself into it. But not quite. He wanted like crazy to have another go round with that sweet little pussy. Breed was getting his tonight. Foss should come due in another week. She was always hot to get punched. It gave her some wild thrill to play at being a damned outlaw. He'd seen other women react that way. One night a woman *knew* that he had robbed a stage outside of town that afternoon and it got him the best piece of ass he'd ever had. The woman had gone crazy because he was laying her.

Foss knew who Kate was, a Sanford for Christ's sakes. She could buy and sell half the merchants in town. Her father was good for maybe ten million dollars!

No chance to marry into that kind of money, but he was going to get one more good fuck into it before he took off with her little stash of coins!

Fuck away, Katherine Sanford, you have met your match in Foster Burke, he thought. She just didn't know it yet.

CHAPTER NINE

Spur woke up the next morning at 6:30 as usual, put on his light blue suit and flat heeled boots. He felt like a wet dishrag that had been drawn and quartered. He rinsed his mouth out with a swallow from the china pitcher on the wash stand slicked back his hair and went down the back stairs for a walk down to the waterfront and back.

That got his blood circulating and his mind in gear. Without thinking about it he suddenly remembered the name and problems of the gunman who had tried to put holes in his hide yesterday.

Rich Turneau was a small time counterfeiter from St. Louis. Spur had sent him to prison four years ago. He was a one man operation then, dealing in five dollar bills. He had used poor plates and he was not a good counterfeiter or passer.

Could Rich have developed into a big timer? Doubtful, Spur decided, but possible. At least it was a solid lead. But how to find Rich? Why not let Rich find him . . . again? At the same time if he let Rich find him, there had to be a plan not to get suddenly dead.

Spur went into the San Franciscan by the side door, charged to the dining room and ordered a breakfast of six eggs and bacon, three slices of toast and two cups of coffee.

Upstairs he went to room 310 and dug out his gunbelt and cleaned and oiled his .44. Today should prove interesting.

Just after 9 A.M. Spur brought his rig around to the front of the hotel, had a boy carry a big empty box out to the buggy and made a fuss about getting it in the rig just right, then sent the boy away laughing with a dollar bill in his hand.

The scene was designed to make sure that Rich Turneau saw Spur and knew that he was leaving. Nobody could have slept through that performance.

Spur drove south, the quickest way out of the built up area and toward the low brown hills. He made sure that he did not obviously look to the rear, but twice he caught glimpses of a rig a hundred yards behind him. Both times it was the same one. Spur made a detour down a side road and then back to the main track south, and his black topped Democrat buggy was still with him.

Soon they had passed the houses, and Spur noticed an occasional small ranch and small farm. The road leveled out, then turned toward the coast, and just as Spur made the turn he heard a rifle shot. His horse stumbled and went down. The buggy crashed into the animal, almost tipped over and then settled on its wheels. One final scream of fear bellowed from the mare before she lifted her head and died in the traces.

Rich was getting serious. Spur jumped out of the buggy away from the other rig and sprinted in a zig zag course into a small clump of live oak trees and brush. He couldn't see anyone in the buggy behind him, but it had stopped in the road.

Spur edged around a tree and watched the black rig. It moved as if a person were getting in or out. It began rolling forward, but no driver, no one was visible. It was a moving blind, a protective cover for the ambusher.

Now Spur wished that he had his seven shot Spencer rifle along. He would make short work of this attacker, but as it was the other man had the advantage. He had a long gun, he was on the offensive, and he had murder in mind.

The Democrat buggy kept coming. When it was opposite the point where McCoy had entered the woods, it stopped. He heard a voice.

"Spur McCoy, you stupid bastard, you better start thinking about dying, 'cause that's what you're going to be doing before this day is over. Christ, but I've waited a long time for this."

As soon as he stopped talking a shotgun boomed and Spur jerked his head back behind the big oak, as half a dozen big slugs hit the tree and the brush around him. Double-ought buck!

He knew how well it killed, but he had never been on the receiving end before. Nine to thirteen .33 caliber sized slugs packed into a three-inch shotgun shell. Two rounds was like having ten men each firing two shots at you with a .32 caliber revolver.

So Rich had a rifle, a shotgun and probably a pistol. Spur was tempted to put a round through the soft canvas top of the buggy, but decided he had better save his ammunition. He had only the five in his weapon and eighteen in the belt loops.

"You get out of prison legal, or you bust out, Turneau?"

"Parole, and I learned plenty inside. The first thing I learned was to wipe out the sonofabitch who jailed me, and that's you, Spur, and you're as good as dead. I've got plenty of ammunition, how much do you have?"

Spur aimed carefully with the .44 and slammed a round through the canvas low and he hoped just over the seat. Before the sound of the round had echoed away, he was up and moving through the woods, deeper into it, running hard before Rich realized he had left. Principal number one here was to get the enemy away from his rolling fortress and ammunition supply. If he had to carry a shotgun and a rifle and a pistol, he would have less room for additional ammunition.

As Spur ran he heard Rich say something behind him but he didn't stop to listen. He ran as silently as possible, without smashing branches or snapping brush. He took a route that went gradually down a slope and merged into a small brush filled creek.

Knowing that Rich would come after him, he needed a protected ambush spot, where he could lure Rich to within twenty yards without Rich realizing it was a trap.

It was the only way Spur could take on the shotgun and rifle and have any hope of living more than a few more hours. He heard the shotgun roar again near the road, then the crack of a heavy long gun, maybe a Sharps.

He needed rocks for protection, but there were no boulders on these smooth, sparsely wooded San Francisco rolling hills. The high ground? He looked around and saw a stretch of timber that climbed to the left up to the highest point around. He ran again, working through the heavier brush and trees toward the top of the small hill. The live oak were thick here, and many of them were old when Columbus discovered the New World.

Spur lay behind one at the brow of the slope and looked around its three foot diameter at the land below.

After ten minutes he saw a figure moving carefully through the woods. The day had turned hot, the humidity was low, and the sun burning down.

He watched the hunter below. He was good, not taking any chances, moving from cover to cover. For a moment Spur thought he might be able to circle behind him, get to the road and take the Democrat buggy and drive for town. But then Rich moved laterally a hundred yards and swung back. He too had thought of that and would cut off any try.

Spur settled down to wait. Rich could not track

him, he wasn't even watching the ground. He was guessing, and so far his logic had been as good as Spur's. Now if he chose the high ground and started up. . . .

Spur looked to his left and could see the ocean. Close by long dry grass covered many areas. It would provide no protection. The dry wind came again and Spur was surprised at its heat. It was one of those hot winds that come off the California deserts and blow toward the sea, a Santa Ana, the natives called them.

When Spur saw Rich come through a small stand of live oak and brush he could tell that the man was tracking him. Spur had made no attempt not to leave a trail or to conceal it. Rich had more talent at tracking than making counterfeit ten dollar bills.

Rich was still a hundred yards away. Much too far for Spur's .44, but easy range for a rifle. He looked around at his alternatives. His forehead sweated as he considered them. He could turn and run down the hill toward the beach a half mile over, but what good would that do? He still needed that ambush chance, but now the possibility seemed to be growing less all the time.

Circle back to the Democrat buggy? That was one good chance. A run for it? What else? A do or die ambush behind a big oak tree, allowing Rich to walk right up to him in good pistol range.

It wasn't just a case of run or fight. Spur would have to go across two open places to get back to the buggy. Rich would have a clear shot at him, probably six or seven shots. He should not miss with those odds.

So it was stand and fight. He ran down the hill fifty yards and found the tree he needed. It was live oak, with shiny green leaves that stayed on the trees all year round. New leaves grew all year replacing those that dropped off. This one was four feet across, ancient, scraggly, partly dead, but with plenty of bulk to hide him and offer a good shooting fort. To one side there was a hole all the way through the trunk, probably carved out in some long forgotten grass fire.

The growth up hill from the big tree was young, nothing big enough to hide behind. Rich would have to stand and fight.

It was several minutes before Rich came over the crest of the hill. He stood up from behind a small bush where he had been watching the downslope. He was good. Spur had been under cover all the time. There was no chance Rich could know where Spur was, or whether he was hiding or running. Rich would watch the big tree with caution, probably walk well to one side of it as he passed.

Spur would be edging around it until he could get his shot. He had to be on target with the first one. Now Spur noticed that Rich did not carry the shotgun. That was one less weapon to deal with. He had two six-guns on his hips, however.

McCoy waited. The odds in this match were not in his favor. He had to do everything right, do it lightning fast and be dead on target.

Rich came forward twenty yards and stopped. He stood near a downed oak that would give him good cover, if he needed it. Ahead there was no cover. Spur watched him from the base of the tree through some two foot high squawbush.

Rich loosened the six-gun on his right, and made sure there was a round in the long gun, then he moved ahead, slowly, angling away to his right around the big oak. He glanced at it each step, then swept the land in front of him on the downgrade to the thick growth of cottonwoods and scrub oak. Behind the oak, Spur had the six-gun up and leveled, braced with both hands and ready to lean out, refine his arm and fire.

Rich was still thirty yards away, too far. A lucky shot might save him, but Spur could not rely on that. To Spur's surprise, Rich lowered the rifle, held it with his left hand and pulled his six-shooter from the right holster and thumbed back the hammer.

Why? A ruse to get Spur out in the open, then use the long gun? Probably. Rich had already shot at him twice from ambush, he wouldn't hesitate to use any dirty trick he could think of. Spur stayed where he was.

Twenty-five yards away.

Not yet. Spur wiped sweat from his forehead, peered through the brush again.

Suddenly Rich was running, not toward the tree, but at an angle around and past it. He had been twenty yards toward it, now he was twenty-five. Spur lifted up, stepped out, pulled down in a dead aim at the running man and fired three times. He saw the first two rounds miss. He saw Rich turn, surprised, and whip off two shots.

Spur's third shot had hit Rich in the right leg above the knee and he tumbled into the dirt and rolled. But Rich had fired his third shot and Spur felt the hammer blow to his left shoulder and saw himself thrown backward, behind the protection of the big oak.

He almost dropped the gun. His left shoulder was on fire. The bullet had gone in high, near the bone. It throbbed like the time he spilled bacon fat on his hand, only this was ten times worse. Spur watched the blood soak his jacket sleeve and then drip off his left hand. He had to stop it. First he lifted himself up and looked past the tree to the spot where Rich had been. He lay in a small depression. Spur could see only part of his back.

With a great deal of effort, Spur moved and stood up. He had a better angle on the counterfeiter. Spur aimed by resting the six-gun against the oak. He fired, but dug up dirt in front of the blue shirt. Rich moved so he could see none of him.

Sweating and swearing softly, Spur used his right hand and pulled the four fired rounds from his gun and pushed in four cartridges from his belt loops.

Then he took off his blue coat so he could look at his wound. His knife sliced through the hole in the shirt fabric, and he saw the black hole where the bullet had entered just below his collar bone almost under his arm. He didn't think that the lead slug came out. It bled more as he watched. How could he get a bandage on it? He cut off the sleeve of his shirt and folded part of it into a compress. Then he cut strips from the rest and clumsily tied them together.

Every half minute he leaned out and looked through the brush at the spot where Rich had dropped. Nothing.

He pushed the compress in place with his hand, then held it there with his chin as he looped the strips of cloth over his shoulder and under his arm and tied them with loose double overhand knots. Good enough, it would stay in place for a while. He discarded his coat and stood, lifting himself as high as he could. He could make out the edge of some brown cloth.

Was Rich still there? Had he faked the wound and circled around to zero in on Spur with the rifle? Spur stepped on part of the burned, hollowed section of the oak and boosted himself up another three feet. Now he looked through a crotch in the ancient tree. Rich Turneau lay exactly where Spur thought he had.

"Turneau, you might as well give it up. You'll never get away from here with a shot up leg. Throw out your weapons, all four of them, including the hide-out, and I'll help you back to the buggy. You'll still have to face an assault with a deadly weapons charge."

His answer came in a rifle shot that slammed less than two inches over Spur's partly revealed head. He dropped down. Strategy. Spur was mobile; he wasn't sure how active Rich could be.

Should he get away or end it here, Spur wondered? He could angle away from Rich, up the hill where Rich couldn't see him or shoot at him. But then Rich would still be trying later to kill Spur. He had to end it now, one way or the other.

But how? Spur wished he had some of those half-stick dynamite bombs he had made from time to time. They would be perfect. He could make a small bomb with all the black powder from his remaining pistol rounds, but that would leave him out of ammunition.

Burn him out? Yes, the wind was right, but it also would burn all the way to the coast and could easily sweep north into San Francisco. Not a good idea.

Circle.

Spur looked where Rich was down, then looked away up the hill in a direct line with the tree and Rich. The rifleman could not see him for forty yards, then he would have ten yards to cross before Rich saw him or got a shot off. The odds were the best he had all day. He pressed the bandage on his shoulder again, gripped his shirt front with his left hand, turned and ran hard on the one line of retreat that was safe.

Spur looked back as he passed the small tree he figured was the end of his cover. He could not see Rich. Digging in his boots he bolted the last ten yards and got over the top of the ridge.

Automatically he swung left, to go downhill and circle so he could come out in the heavier woods below and have a good view of the low place where Rich should still be hiding.

No one lay on the hillside.

Rich had done exactly the same thing Spur had. Only he must have moved much slower away from his spot, using the tree as his cover, hoping Spur wouldn't look out just then.

Spur lined up the two positions and moved silently

through the trees toward the spot Rich could have entered the thicker growth. He found the spot, something dragging, perhaps a broken leg, then he spotted dark red stains of blood on a leaf. Where ahead could Rich be?

He would try for the buggy. That was the key now. Spur angled away from the shortest route back to the road and the transportation. He circled slightly to the left through heavy woods and came out on the road two hundred yards toward San Francisco from the rig. No one was there.

Spur crawled through the grass working silently and he hoped unseen toward the buggy. Five minutes later he was within thirty yards of the rig. He raised himself to search the route from woods to buggy but saw no one. Spur eased back down and waited.

Twenty minutes later he heard a soft groan of agony from ahead. He lifted himself up but saw no one. Then he realized that Rich was crawling through the grass too, not to stay unobserved, but because he probably couldn't walk.

The sounds came closer.

Spur waited.

The sounds changed, Rich turned. He was almost to the buggy.

The shotgun! Spur should have found the shotgun and had it as his second weapon. Too late.

Rich eased out of the grass and reached for the buggy wheel to help himself stand up.

Spur put a slug into the side of the buggy over Rich's head.

"That's far enough, Rich. Hold it right there."

Two pistol shots blasted toward Spur but they had no target, finding only grass and dirt.

"That won't help you, Rich. You have no target. I have a big one. Shall I try for you this time?"

"I won't go back to prison. I'll die first."

"Talking that way you will. Throw down the pistols and the rifle."

"I don't have the rifle, dropped it back there, before I started crawling."

"Drop them."

Rich shrugged. "What the hell, prison is better than dead. You win, McCoy." He leaned against the buggy wheel with his back, let the six-gun fall into the dirt. "You win."

Spur stood, leveled the gun at Rich and walked forward. He stumbled in the grass, almost fell but caught himself, bringing a scream of pain as he jerked his arm around suddenly.

When he looked back at Rich he saw a six-gun firing. Spur fired four times, and saw three of the heavy slugs pound into the counterfeiter's chest, smearing it with blood and slamming him against the wheel, then to the ground under the rig. He was dead before he hit the ground.

Spur moved up cautiously. The counterfeiter's eyes were glazed, there was no pulse. The gun remained frozen in Rich Turneau's hand in a death grip.

It took Spur ten minutes to get the body lifted into the buggy. His shoulder burned now, every small movement dug daggers into the wound. Lifting the dead body was excruciating.

He turned the buggy around and drove back to town, to the police station, showed them his thin Secret Service identification card taped between two photos of his parents, and at last the police understood. The livery sent someone out the south road to cut the horse loose and to bring back the buggy. Spur had to pay forty dollars for the dead horse and another five dollars for bringing back the buggy.

"It figures," Spur said. "Now they'll probably have both spinach and eggplant on the menu at the hotel dining room." He was wrong. They only had spinach.

CHAPTER TEN

Police Captain Vuylsteke had looked at Spur's shoulder and recommended a doctor who was good with bullets. The sawbones had given Spur a long smell of chloroform, and he entered an amazing world where everything was strange and funny. He was almost unconscious and couldn't feel a thing.

For an hour after it was over he kept asking the doctor when he was going to start taking out the bullet. Then Spur came fully conscious and saw his arm in a sling, his shoulder bandaged and a feeling that his main assignment was all shot to hell.

"You'll be as good as new in two weeks," the doctor said. "Go home, and stay in bed for a week. Then come see me again."

Spur nodded gravely and got outside as soon as he could. Captain Vuylsteke said he would send two men to Turneau's address which they had found in his wallet. Spur had insisted on going along before he went to the doctor. In the rooming house they found plates for five and ten dollar bills, and some new ones that Turneau was working on for twenties. In his belongings they found over ten thousand dollars in counterfeit bills and about five hundred in double eagles. He evidently had been passing the bills and converting them into gold.

Back in his hotel room, Spur had stripped and washed as best he could in the china bowl, then put on a clean suit and took a cab to the Sanford residence. The butler seemed surprised to see him. When he asked to talk to Katherine, the man frowned and asked Spur to wait in the library.

It was a half hour before Katherine came in. She looked at his injured arm.

"What in the world have you done? Injured yourself seriously it looks like. Whatever am I to do with you men. Always showing off and hurting yourselves. Well, we'll just have to take your mind off your hurt. It's a glorious day, much too nice to stay in town, let's go sailing on the bay."

"I know nothing of boats, Miss Sanford."

"Silly, you don't have to, neither do I. It's father's boat and he has a crew to sail it. All we have to do is enjoy the wind and the water. It will be delightful. Cook will send ahead a nice lunch for us. You simply can't say no."

"I'm not supposed to get this wet," he said showing her his arm.

She touched it and smiled. "We won't get wet at all. How did you hurt it?"

"I could tell you I got drunk and fell down. I could say one of the wild San Francisco fancy ladies bit me. Actually I got shot."

"If you don't want to tell me, fine. Today I want to enjoy life and have fun. I'll have some things from my room and see you right back here in two minutes. My carriage is in back."

Her driver took them to Bay Street where several docks held small sailing boats. Small compared to ocean going clipper ships, but much larger than Spur had ever seen privately owned. The Sanford boat was forty-five feet long, had twin masts, and more lines and ropes and cables than he had seen before.

"This is it, the *Francisco Belle*. She's not new, but she sails well."

Two men in sailor blues and wearing white hats met her at the rail and helped her on board. She shook hands and talked to them a minute.

"Just around the bay, and no fishing. We have an important meeting to take care of so please don't disturb us. I'll let you know when we want to dock again."

She took Spur's right hand and gave him the guided tour. Below there were two cabins forward, a galley and dining area amidships, and a large captain's cabin aft. The big cabin had a full sized bed, dressers built into the walls, a gas lamp and all the comforts of a luxurious living room and bedroom.

Spur felt the ship tremble as it edged away from the dock. Then it quivered as the sails went up and caught the wind.

"Let's go up and watch us moving out," Katherine

said. "This is the exciting part of sailing."

The men scurried around the deck, hoisting sail, working out through incoming ships. They lifted another sail that billowed out in the afternoon breeze. At the helm a seaman turned the rudder and they angled half into the wind toward the inland side of the bay. Katherine took a deep breath. "The salt spray is so invigorating! I just love to sail." She turned and went below to the big cabin and Spur followed.

As soon as the door closed, Spur caught her with his right arm and pulled her gently to him. When he bent to kiss her she was ready. His lips clung to hers as he rubbed her back, then he let go of her and his right hand wormed between their bodies until he found her breasts. She moaned softly.

"Yes, beautiful man! Oh, yes! Sailing just sets me on fire! I don't know what it is, but as soon as we start sailing I want to tear off my clothes and attack anything with a pecker." She giggled and helped him as he unbuttoned the top of her dress.

She kissed him again, her tongue barging inside his mouth, fighting him, licking his teeth, searching for his tongue. Her arms wrapped around him so tightly that it made his arm throb, but Spur didn't mind. His blood was boiling and he pushed his hips hard against her pubic center to show her. She murmured deep in her throat and stepped back so that his hand could find her nearly bare breasts.

"You like my tits, don't you, Spur?"

"Yes, they are perfect and so big I want to try to eat them up."

The boat turned and slanted and they both fell on the bed giggling.

She rolled on top of him, pushed her dress down so her breasts hung out. She moved upward and one dangled deliciously over his face.

"Now, beautiful man, now you can try to chew me flat busted."

Spur's mouth closed around the heavy nipple and sucked in more of it and she yelped when he bit her.

"Easy, dammit! I was just kidding about chewing me off. Nibble but don't bite!"

Spur laughed and moved his right arm, then went back to his feast of hanging tits.

As she let him suck and chew, she found his fly and opened the buttons, working inside until she caught his erection.

"Now there is something worth getting fucked with," she said and laughed. "I don't know why it makes me feel wicked to say fucked. It's just another word. Fuck, fuck, fuck. As in I'm going to fuck you!" She tittered. "It still makes me feel naughty."

"I may recuperate here all day and all night," Spur said between bites. "This is good therapy for my arm."

"And it will be a shrinking therapy for your long, hot cock," she said.

They both laughed.

She gently rubbed his erection and watched him eating her breasts.

"I don't understand most women. They try to act so aloof and pure, like the only reason they *ever* let their husbands have their way with them is to produce children. Dammit, women *like to fuck* as much as men do. Some women have to get warmed up to the idea, but they love it. They say they don't, but I heard my women relatives talking one night, three of them, women in their thirties, all married, all with four or five kids each. They began talking about fucking, which they called *doing it*. I have never heard a sexier, explicit talk about making love.

"The way I look at it, all women are whores. Most of them don't get in bed with a man until they get him to marry them, that's supposed to be the big prize, their wet little pussy. But then they fuck away, give it away, but in return they work at it, doing his clothes, raising his kids, taking his money. How are they any different from the girls down in the red light district who give you men your two dollars worth and push you out the door? The married woman just gets her security and her keep in a different form of payoff."

She rolled over beside him, lifted his erection from his pants and sighed.

"A cock is the most beautiful thing in the world, did you know that, McCoy? It is. Look at him. Straight and tall, and pink and purple and throbbing with life, wanting to spread life." She pushed her hand lower and gently picked up his scrotum. "Of course your balls are fucking important too."

She sat up and waited for him to sit. The boat rocked and she nodded. "When the boat rolls when we're fucking you won't believe the new, wild sensation." She stopped and stared at him. "The other night you said the next time would be long and slow.

Good! This is it. I want you to undress me, slow and easy, kissing every part of my clothes off, just kissing me all over!" She shivered. "Then, beautiful man, when I'm all naked, I'll kiss off your clothes and we'll see how long we can hold off before we have to fuck each other or explode!"

Spur pushed her down on her back, kissed her lips to softly she hardly felt him. He worked down her cheek and chin and her neck to her breasts, where he anointed each one and moved to her shoulder where he pushed off the fabric kissing it down as he went.

"Oh, yes, Spur! That is heaven, so soft and gentle, so easy and relaxing. Yes. Did I tell you my one big dream, Sweet Man Spur? What I really want to do more than anything else is to take this boat and the crew of two and sail her to Hawaii. Then I want to stay there. Just sit in the sand and play, and fuck the big Hawaiians when they want to, and swim naked in the warm waters and walk around without any top on all the time. I have heard that they are extremely casual about sex and that children often belong to everyone because they are not really sure who the father is."

Spur pushed the dress fabric lower off her arms and lifted her up and pulled it off her back bunching it around her waist.

He kissed down across her breasts again to her soft stomach and worked down to her waist.

"Now this is getting more interesting," she said. "I wonder if he has guts enough to kiss down any further."

Spur pulled the fabric down more. He was sure

the dress was supposed to slip over her head, but he was too far down to change directions. He pulled the fabric over her hips, caught the top of her under drawers and worked them down over her soft belly until he saw fringes of pubic hair.

He stopped and kissed rings and squares and designs on her flat tummy and moved down, ever down to the soft dark hair. She began trembling as he pushed the cloth lower, kissing as he went. He circled around the pinkness showing through the silky black crotch hair.

Katherine was moaning now, her legs twitching, her hips grinding against the mattress. Spur shoved the clothing down to her knees and pushed his face into her pubic hair, kissing down farther, circling her glory spot and then reaching down and parting the forest of dark hair to expose the wet, pulsing pinkness of her nether lips.

"Now, Spur, fuck me now!"

He ignored her, saw her hips rotating, then pumping up gently and retreating, then coming high again. He worked in closer, kissed her wet, steaming nether lips and she exploded with a scream and a sharp series of tremors that shook her body. Her cries came again and again, and her hips went wild with gyrations. She moaned and bounced and swore and cried and at last shuddered to a stop. Only then did her eyes come open. She brushed joy-tears away and stared at him.

"God, nobody ever did that for me before, actually kissed my pussy! I think I am in heaven. Do that twice more and I'll kill my parents, inherit all the money and marry you!'"

116

She panted and he smiled, watching her.

"That was wonderful, marvelous. It's the best one I've ever had. I thought I was going to break in half and die right here on the bed. God, what a fucking good feeling, and your prick wasn't even inside me! It's going to be a half hour before I'm anywhere near back to normal. If I dressed and said hello to somebody, anybody, they would grin and know that I had just had the fuck of my life!"

"We can't let you get back to normal, then, can we?" Spur said. He pulled the tangled clothes off her feet and threw them on the floor. He lifted her to the center of the big bed and kissed her breasts, then dropped to her pubic hair and kissed around her heartland. When she started to gasp in anticipation, he kissed her nether lips again, tasting the soft fluid that came out, and kissed her again, then flicked out his tongue to strike her clit and Katherine exploded. She lifted upward, humping him high, then she bellowed a scream that Spur was sure would bring the crew running, but no one banged on the locked door.

When her screaming faded she mumbled over and over.

"Omigod, Omigod, Omigod. I'm dying. I'm dying!" The spasms shot through her, shattering her whole body with trembling and jolting and shaking until she seemed one moving mass of flesh.

It was almost five minutes before she tapered off, and the spasms stopped.

He kissed her lips and she smiled. Spur realized that she was almost asleep.

"Don't touch me, I'm dead and I'm in heaven

right now." She smiled again, curled up into a fetal ball and went to sleep. She was awake almost at once.

"My God! You did it again. When are we going to get married? I want that every night for the rest of my life. I'll keep you in luxury, you can have six mistresses if you want just so you eat me every night!"

Spur chuckled. "I've heard it just gets better and better."

She looked at him and saw that he was slipping out of his clothes.

"You haven't even been in me yet and I feel like I've had the best fuck of my life."

"You're young yet, Katherine, so very young."

She lay on her back, spread her legs and lifted her knees and held out her arms to him. Spur was more than ready. He went to her with a sudden need, with a moment of knowing that he should have a wife and settle down, that he should stop all this cuntmongering, but also knowing that he wasn't likely to for a long time. With that in mind he bent and thrust into her with one sharp move that brought a cry of pain and desire and satisfaction from Katherine.

His own surging climax was an anticlimax to the tremendous exhibition Katherine had shown him. They lay there panting for a few minutes and she held him tightly.

"Let's have a little nap," she said. "It feels so safe, so warm and protected with you on top of me this way. Just a short little nap."

She was sleeping almost before he agreed, drifting off to a pleasant and he imagined dream filled few minutes.

Five minutes later Spur moved and she woke up.

"Wake up time, everyone," she said. "I'm hungry. I had some food sent on board before we got here." She stood and moved with the same erect, proud carriage he had seen on the dance floor. Most of Spur's women had been self-conscious when naked and could not move gracefully when unclothed. But Katherine's self-esteem enabled her to move just as beautifully naked as dressed.

Katherine went to a small cupboard and brought out three kinds of cheeses, four small melons, all different varieties, and a bottle of white wine.

"You thought of everything," he said.

"I try. Do you know that you're the first man I've ever made love with on two different days?"

"Curious. You like variety?"

"Yes, and I don't want to be tied down. Men get so possessive. If I fucked one three or four times, in three or four weeks he would assume we were going to be married."

"So for you it's simply recreation, a sport, a kind of intimate game to play, to strike back at convention, at the mores of our society, at the idea that women can't enjoy sex before marriage."

"Exactly. You sound like my college professors."

"Did you take any of them to bed?"

She laughed. "My philosophy professor stole my virginity, and it cost him an 'A' grade in his course. He kept trying but I wouldn't get near him again. I was too busy after that with college boys to bother with older men. The boys were so much more active."

Spur cut the melons. They ate melon and salted

nuts, drank the wine.

"Where did you get all these cheeses? I love good cheese."

"It's made locally up the coast somewhere." She stretched, one arm high, the other low, her breasts straining forward, thrust out to their maximum. Spur grinned.

"Now that is a beautiful picture. I wish I were an artist, I'd paint you in that pose."

She did it again, and he reached out and kissed the forward thrusting breasts.

"You are amazing, Katherine Sanford. A marvelous body, great tits, lovely shoulders, a flat little tummy and no waist at all, gently rounded hips and legs so slender and perfect that they take my breath away."

"I like you, let's fuck again."

They laughed.

"And all this long black hair. I love to get tangled up in it when I undress you."

"You should undress me more. Want me to come to your hotel room late tonight?"

"No, I couldn't satisfy your insatiable appetites. I'm not sixteen anymore with unlimited climaxes available."

She laughed. "I bet you caught your first little girl before you were sixteen."

"Somewhere around there, but she was nothing like you." He kissed her breasts again. They finished the wine and half the cheese. Then she stood to put away the things. Her reticule spilled from the side of the bed and a dozen gold double eagles rolled onto the floor. Spur dropped to the deck which had a soft

120

carpet over it, and began picking them up. One caught his eye and then another. He thought he noticed the small peculiarity he had seen on the counterfeit coins. He palmed one of them as he put them back in her purse. When he picked up their clothes, he slid the coin into his pants pocket. He would check it later.

"Hey, let's go on deck and watch the water."

"Like this?"

"No, silly. We'll get dressed."

"Can I watch you dress? It's a very special spectacle watching a lady dress."

She shrugged. "If you like. I don't take long. Race you!"

They dressed and went on deck. The afternoon sun was still high and the boat had worked well down the southern half of the thirty-mile long San Francisco bay. The water was blue, the sky the same shade and the wind brisk as the boat sliced through the bay waters. A large clipper ship came into the bay to the north of them, and they saw how big it looked. It swung into a berth at the San Francisco harbor.

The bay was dotted with fishing craft and a few pleasure boats. Few people could afford boats to play with, and those who could usually didn't have time to sail just for the enjoyment. Katherine was an exception.

They moved in close across the bay and almost touched at a green park-like area on the mainland side, then swung around.

Spur wished he could stop beside some of the fishing boats and get on board for a few hours, but he knew that now wasn't the time. Perhaps later.

Katherine signalled the crew that it was time to head back to their berth, and the sailing craft turned into the wind and they began tacking back toward the San Francisco docks.

Spur had found that he could move his arm more freely now. He took it out of the sling and realized that the movement from his elbow down did not hurt the wound at all. There was no reason to continue using the sling.

An hour later they docked and left the boat. Katherine thanked the crew and gave each a double eagle. Spur wondered if they were real or counterfeit.

Spur turned down an invitation to dinner, explaining that he had to see two artists' work. She argued with him and at last gave up.

"But I do want to see you again tomorrow. Perhaps we could drive out into the country on a picnic, up along the coast somewhere. I'll bring a blanket and some lunch."

"I hate to say no, but I'm not sure. I'll send a note over in the morning one way or the other."

She dropped him off in front of his hotel with a formal handshake and was gone.

Spur stood watching the buggy roll away. He took the double eagle from his pocket and pricked the back with his pocket knife. The gold flaked away showing base metal underneath. It was counterfeit. He stared after the buggy. To have so many of them, she must somehow be involved. Exactly how she was tied into the ring would be his next assignment.

CHAPTER ELEVEN

The coffee was still hot a half hour after the waitress at the hotel restaurant had fixed Spur's dinner to take out. He had ordered two ham and cheese sandwiches, an apple and a quart mason jar full of coffee. She had wrapped the jar with a hotel towel to help it stay warm.

He sipped the coffee and looked for the millionth time at the two doors. He had parked his buggy in a position where he could see both the front and the side doors to the Sanford mansion. As far as he could tell there was no regularly used door leading into the alley. The house sat on a corner and the side door opened to a walk leading to a sparsely traveled side street.

McCoy had nothing more than a hunch. Katherine was stubborn, she was strong willed, she had not

123

been welcomed into the management level at the store her father owned, and she was a real sexual rebel. Why not a counterfeiter too? She had been caught depositing a counterfeit coin. Granted that could happen to anyone if there were hundreds of them in circulation. But the dozen or so coins that Spur spotted in Katherine's purse were probably counterfeits. This led him to new and tougher conclusions.

Now all he had to do was try to prove if she was working some scheme, it most surely would be done either in some disguise or during the night. Perhaps both. The front door opened and a couple he assumed were Mr. and Mrs. Sanford came out. They went to the curb where their driver waited with a fancy carriage.

Lights came on in the house at dusk. Spur moved his rig a half block closer. The side door was not lighted by any windows. If she left, he guessed it would be by the side door.

By nine that night Spur's coffee was gone, both the sandwiches had vanished and he had eaten one of the apples. This might be a fool's errand after all. The poor sex crazed girl was probably no more than a nymphomaniac. He knew for certain that she qualified for that title.

Another hour and Spur found himself nodding. It was by a stroke of luck that he didn't miss her. His horse grew tired of the stationary position and jolted the rig ahead six feet, bringing Spur out of a doze. He shook his head and checked the side door just as a shaft of weak yellow light stabbed out as the door came open, then disappeared quickly. A shadow in a black coat and large hat left the house, walked quickly to the street and down the hill toward the lower priced houses of San Francisco. Spur had no way of telling who it was, but the steps were short, the stature about five-five, and the carriage . . . Yes! it was Katherine. There was no hiding that proud walk, chin high, shoulders back, chest out stance that had first caught his attention on the dance floor.

Katherine Sanford was going for a walk at 10 P.M. when *nice* girls were home in bed with the door and windows locked.

Spur let her come past him on the far side of the street. She turned and went down the steep hill that led to Charter Street. The horse and rig would make too much noise. He slid off the buggy seat and followed her, keeping her in sight, but not venturing too close.

She went straight down for three blocks, then over one block. As he paused behind a tree, he saw her go into the second of a row of five nearly identical gray houses. Lights were already on inside. He moved up as close as he could and noticed a new light glowing in the back room. There were two windows on his side of the house but both were carefully curtained, and the blinds had been drawn.

He gambled she would be in the house for some time. He checked in back and at the side. In the alley he found a rig that looked surprisingly like the one she had driven to the sailing ship that afternoon. She might be stopping here and moving on.

Spur turned and ran quietly back up the hill, panting at the exertion. He got in his rig and brought it to a stop at the end of the alley where her rig would emerge if it didn't turn around. Again he waited.

An hour later, just at 11:15, a horse and rider came out of the alley. It was a tall, sturdy horse, and the man who rode it was equally as tall. Spur figured the man was over six feet eight inches and maybe two hundred and eighty pounds. A lot of man, a lot of horse. He wore a hat that came down over his features.

Fifteen minutes later, he heard harness jangling, and the buggy in the alley came out. Spur crouched down in his rig so as not to be seen. The other buggy turned to the left in the same direction that Spur was headed. He followed a block behind, and after three blocks thought he was onto something. He could not see who was in the rig, but chances were that it was Katherine Sanford. Where the hell was she going?

Ahead Spur saw the big man on the horse pass the buggy and ride his way. The man turned around and followed the rig almost a block behind.

Spur scowled. Was this big man following her? Or was he protection? He found out a block later when the big man wheeled his horse and charged straight at Spur's buggy. Only by turning aside quickly could Spur avoid a collision. Twice more the large rider and his huge black horse charged Spur's carriage and twice more Spur had to pull sharply to the side to miss him.

As quickly as he attacked, the man was gone.

Spur looked ahead but could find no evidence of the other buggy.

He raced down one street after another looking, but he could not find the rig anywhere. He had been challenged and detained and thrown off the scent.

Spur took the next logical step. He continued in the direction he had been going and half a mile later he jogged over one block to the first prime suspect foundry. This one had all the needed equipment, and it was small enough. He found a watchman near the front gate and stopped.

"Good evening, sir. Are you the watchman here?"

" 'Pears as how, young feller."

"Been with the company long?"

"Ten year if it's been a day."

"Good. Notice anything unusual tonight?"

"How unusual?" the watchman said and sent a squirt of tobacco juice into the dust a foot from Spur's boots.

"Any people trying to break in, trying to use any of the machinery."

"Hail, why would they want to do that? They got to work here all day. You want them to come back at night, too?"

"No, not the regular workers, strangers."

"Hail, no. Nobody wants to get in there. I just walk around and scoot the kids away now and again."

"You sure, nothing unusual has been happening around here tonight?"

"Damn sure. Now I got to make my rounds. Promised Mr. Nelson I'd do that every hour on the hour, and sure looks like it's coming up on just after midnight."

"Right, yes, you do that." Spur waved at the watchman as he went back through the main gate and locked it. McCoy looked around. A stamping press striking off the coins would make considerable noise. This was a business and light industry area, no houses, no small shops with owners living over them. Might not be a soul within a mile.

That, along with the press being in a sturdy building which would muffle sound, were two big reasons this could be one of the Foundries used by the counterfeiters. He would check the other. If it was as dark and dead as this one, he might slip back here for an unannounced look around.

Spur stepped into his buggy and drove away.

On the other side of the board fence, Hop Choy watched through a crack between the boards as Spur talked to the guard. Hop had his pistol out and hammer back. He decided he would shoot the stranger and not simply warn the others. This was the same man in the buggy he had seen before.

The big man knew he should warn Miss Sanford, but he did not know how. He had never learned to read or write. His tongue had been gone for twenty years. He watched in satisfaction as the stranger drove away. It was safe after all. There was no reason to tell Miss Sanford that he had seen the man following her from the small gray house. Everything would be all right. Miss Sanford told him that she would take care of him. She promised he would be safe and would not have to go back to China. He liked it here. He had a house of his very own! Yes he shared it with Miss Sanford sometimes, but she told him it was his for as long as he wanted it.

Hop Choy smiled as he let the hammer down gently on the round in the chamber and put the six-gun in his holster. He would walk his rounds again. He had to protect Miss Sanford.

Spur McCoy drove to the second foundry. It was smaller, and he soon found out it had no night watchman. He jumped over the fence from the step of his buggy and toured the plant. There was no lights on anywhere, no one hiding in the shadows, and no one was trying to counterfeit coins. The foundry was uninvolved, at least for now. So where had Katherine Sanford gone? And why had the big man on the large horse made sure that Spur could not follow her?

He drove back to the small gray house and watched it for an hour. There was no movement in or out. He waited another half hour by his pocket watch, then drove away.

McCoy had tried to reason it out. Katherine was up to something. Fact: she had in her possession counterfeit coins. One had surfaced at the bank and the second time there were at least a dozen of them. Fact: she had gone in disguise somewhere. Fact: she had an accomplice who shielded her, and prevented Spur from following her.

Speculation: right now Katherine and some helpers could be striking off counterfeit gold double eagles.

Fact: he had not walked around the Nelson foundry and metal plant. He had taken the watchman's word for it. Why couldn't the watchman have been one of them, sharing in the proceeds? It might not have been the real watchman at all.

Spur turned his rig toward the Nelson foundry. He would come up quietly from the back. He would listen and watch. They would need lights, and he imagined that there would be considerable sound.

He parked the rig a block away from the back of the large yard and moved up silently.

Lights! He could see lights in on one of the buildings near the center of the complex. The board fence in back had been put up as a boundary marker more than a barrier. He went over it easily and crouched in the darkness. He heard a hiss of steam and a metalic clang somewhere ahead. Was that how it sounded like when a coin was struck? He wasn't sure.

Spur moved forward, misjudged a step and kicked a square of sheet metal, tipping it over and slamming a loud foreign sound through the back yard.

He bent low and waited, but neither saw nor heard anything unusual. Hoping that no one heard the noise, Spur moved forward again toward the lights and the sound. He came to a large building that was dark and edged around it. The next one was his target. But the building where he had seen lights was silent and dark. It must have been the following one. He hurried around the side of the dark structure and checked the next two buildings. Both were also dark.

Spur stood and rubbed his jaw. He had seen lights. He knew that. Had someone heard him coming and blown out the lamps? He could get the guard and demand to investigate the whole area. But that could be difficult, since he had no real authority here, no warrant to search.

Only suspicion.

He waited and watched.

After five minutes he had heard nothing. The only light he could see was a small lantern in the shack beside the main gate where the watchman sat. He could have been mistaken about the lights. The sound was better evidence. He would come back tomorrow and talk to the owner again, perhaps inspect the area.

Spur made his way to the back of the lot, climbed over the fence and drove away. A half mile down the street, he turned and came back past the plant. It was quiet and dark, just the way he had left it before. Perhaps tonight wasn't the night. But he became more convinced that this was the place where the counterfeiting was being done.

All he had to do was catch them at it.

He drove back to the hotel, parked his rig in back and went up to one of his four rooms he hadn't used, 319. Spur pulled his boots off and his jacket and pants, then fell on the bed and tried to relax. But his mind kept churning. Tomorrow he would go see Juan Pico. The Mexican had offered help and now he would take it. He wanted a dusk to daylight watch kept on that foundry. He wanted to get the description of anyone passing a counterfeit double eagle. And he was going to find out who owned that small gray house. The county clerk would be able to tell him. Then Spur slept.

CHAPTER TWELVE

It was 10 A.M. before Spur awoke the next morning. He seldom slept in that late. He shaved carefully, put on his conservative brown suit and sent his other two out to be cleaned. Then he had a quick breakfast and took a cab to the San Francisco county building and found the county clerk. It took them ten minutes to find the legal description of the property from the address. The ledger provided the tax paying owner.

"Legal owner of that plot is Katherine L. Sanford, and one Hop Choy, Chinese, I would imagine. They are listed as co-owners." As the clerk with a green eyeshade said it he shook his head. "Now why would a rich lady like her want a dumpy little place like that?"

"Maybe she has two or three thousand little

houses like that one," Spur said. He thanked the clerk and left knowing that things were looking worse for sweet little Katherine. Her troubles were not only sexual, that was growing plainer all the time.

He drove to a point where he could see the front door of the small gray house and waited. It was his major connection to the counterfeiters. He was sure now that they used the house as a headquarters, or at least Katherine did. She must have more men than the giant. But he had seen no others at the house. Surely she couldn't do it all by herself.

Spur had a quick lunch at a nearby café and watched the front door again. Within a half hour the big man came out and Spur now saw that he was Chinese. He had to be Hop Choy. In the daylight Spur increased his estimate of the man's size: He would go six feet eight and three hundred pounds. Not a man to tangle with. Hop Choy turned at the sidewalk and started off downtown. Spur tied the reins on his rig and followed.

Ten minutes later they were still walking. Spur had brought his gun and gunbelt along and had put half a box of loose shells in his jacket pocket just in case.

They passed through the busy shops and stores going toward a section that residents had long since dubbed *China Town* because of its high percentage of Chinese residents. Hop Choy worked his way through a crowd, avoided a small prancing dragon made of paper and animated by half a dozen children. He vanished into a store that seemed to cater to non-Chinese customers.

Spur walked in and stayed to one side as the man bought several items, paid for them with a double gold eagle, and then left with his change. Spur wanted to run up and test the coin, but there wasn't time. Already the mountain of a man had left.

Spur hurried out and spotted Hop Choy's head and shoulders over the shorter Chinese as he went down the street passing the time window shopping. He bought nothing else, but looked at various Chinese items offered for sale.

For a moment the man turned back and Spur was worried about getting too close. Then he realized Hop Choy would not know him. He had never seen Spur's face close enough to recognize him.

But he did. Hop Choy looked directly at Spur a moment later and he growled and pushed aside two small Chinese women and rushed toward Spur. The Secret Agent saw him coming. His back was at a plate glass window of a store, and a dozen children and woman surrounded him. There was no place to run.

He pulled the .44 and shouted.

"Hop Choy! Stay there. Stop!" He kept coming. Spur lifted the .44 and blasted a shot into the air. Hop Choy looked up and snorted, charging the last ten feet toward Spur. It was a beautiful and dramatic way to get a tracker off your trail, Spur thought in the few seconds before the Chinese mountain landed in his face.

Hop Choy didn't hesitate. He dove straight for Spur, his big hands out. Spur waited until the last critical split second, then he pivoted away as Spanish bullfighters did and brought the side of the .44

135

pistol down hard on the back of his attacker's neck. Hop Choy pawed at the empty air where McCoy had been, then felt the blow on his neck and dropped to his knees. He turned growling, making angry non-words in his throat as he started to get up. Spur powered another stroke with the .44 along Hop Choy's head and the huge man grunted, his arms dropped and he sank slowly in the street, his head a foot from a string of Chinese firecrackers.

Excited words in Chinese came from every side. Spur realized he was a stranger in a foreign land. He held the pistol up and waved his free hand for people to get out of his way. By then the street was full. Curious Chinese hurried up to see the fight.

The people were parting for him. Some seemed to be just off the boat in their coolie hats and Chinese robes. Others were smartly dressed Americanized businessmen. Many wore old clothes, and he saw more than one with the bleary eyes of the opium pipe.

Another half block and he would be out of the mess and free to turn down a street that led out of China Town. But Spur did not make it to that corner.

Three large men over six feet tall, thickly built and each carrying a two foot long Chinese sword, suddenly blocked his path. Two had angry scars on their cheeks. The third had a half healed slash across one arm and another on his bare torso.

All three were bare to the waist. They wore red bands around their heads and he heard someone behind him whisper to someone. The words were "Kwong Dock Tong."

Spur steadied himself. Tong. The strong, vicious, ruling gang that had usurped regular policing in China Town, and had taken it over much the way Juan Pico controlled his sector. Only here there were competing tongs. Spur knew that the Kwong Dock group was the first of the Mainland China societies to be transferred to America. It was the strongest, and it looked like these three enforcers were unhappy with him.

One of the trio edged around Spur and ran to Hop Choy who still lay in the street. The other two advanced slowly, moved six feet apart and came toward him.

Spur waited for them. He calmly thumbed a round into his six-gun to replace the fired bullets, and put a sixth in the empty chamber where usually the hammer rested. He would need six shots to get out of this he was certain.

McCoy called up his best parade ground voice and bellowed at the two Tong enforcers in front of him, shouting with such derision that they didn't have to understand the language to get the idea.

"You sorry looking women's helpers! You couldn't whip a house full of little boys and old women! Your sisters could knock you down with one backhanded slap!"

The first tong man roared in anger and charged forward swinging the sharp blade like a scythe. Spur fired twice, both rounds jolted into the Chinese's right leg, one .44 round broke the smaller leg bone and the enforcer crashed to the street and rolled over twice before he dropped his sticker and screamed as he grabbed his broken leg.

The second Chinese pulled two four-inch throwing knives from his belt and showed one to Spur. He laughed and came forward.

Police whistles down the street slowed, then stopped the big Chinese. He turned and stared toward the whistles. As he did Spur sprinted into the first shop behind him, ran through it to the back where he found another building filled with Chinese women working at some kind of craft. He hurried on through into the alley.

A dozen children looked up, screeched in terror at seeing a white man in their play yard. They watched silently as he ran down the street. The man who had gone to see Hop Choy appeared in the alley in front of Spur, cutting off his escape.

Spur turned to a door, kicked it open and rushed inside. He saw only a dimly lit room and a surprised Chinese woman who stared at him as he ran past.

The corridor narrowed, then went down, and he knew he should turn back, but there was no chance with the tong man following up behind him. The passage became smaller, and then the floor turned to dirt and the walls became raw wood. The roof was held up with mining type square set timbers. The only lights were torches placed at ten feet intervals. The smoke was heavy. He ran on. Ahead he saw a light, and soon the dirt floor gave way to planks, and the walls were covered. The route slanted upward slightly. Spur came to another corridor that opened into a long, low ceilinged room filled with pallets. On each small bed lay a man. Here and there lay a woman. All were smoking the long tubed pipe, and the sweet smell of opium smoke filled the chamber.

Glazed eyes turned to watch him. No one moved more than eyes as he ran to the far side where he entered a higher priced den, with bunks and tables. There was also a slender, naked Chinese girl giving comfort to the customers and always there was the long stemmed pipe and the tubes and the water jars.

Someone shouted at him in Chinese and he ran ahead. Now the hallway had doors on both sides. An occasional scream stabbed through the dimly lit rooms as Spur kept moving. The level dropped again and he descended a steep slope into a sunlit room where three naked men sat on cushions watching six nude Chinese girls dancing.

Two men shouted at Spur who hurried on into a closed room where a small Chinese woman nodded at him and waved to him to follow her. He noticed various pictures on the walls, all Oriental pornographic art. Each depicted a different method of intercourse.

The small woman led him into a room to one side and turned. She was holding a small caliber pistol in her hand. She smiled and took the revolver from his holster. There was no chance to knock away her weapon or beat her to the draw. She was crafty and wise in the way of guns. When she had his weapon, she lifted her gun and smiled.

"Now, crazy American, how do you want to die?"

Spur watched her closely. She was serious. He held his wounded arm as it throbbed again.

"American. No white man has ever been in this room before. None would dare to come here. Some

•

of my small friends must have been chasing you."

"They are not small."

She laughed. As she did one of the tong enforcers burst into the room. He lifted his sword, but a curt command in Chinese stopped him. The two spoke softly for a moment, he angry and arguing, she with the tone and manner of authority. She looked at him. Then nodded and laughed. She said something to the man with the sticker and walked away.

The point of the sword touched Spur's side.

"Go," the Chinese commanded. Spur moved in the direction indicated. They went through another corridor, down some steps, up another flight and finally to a building where Spur thought he could hear people in the street.

They stopped at a door, and Spur found no chance to break away or to attack the big guard. Then his hands were tied behind his back and he was blindfolded while the big man held the sword at Spur's throat.

He was marched outside and helped into a buggy. After a short ride, Spur was taken out of the rig. He could smell the salt air. They were at the waterfront. A moment later a net dropped over him and he was pushed off his feet. He tried to yell as he was hoisted into the air upside down and swung to one side. He hit something, bounced off it and then was lowered with a bump as he fought the heavy net.

It came away quickly and hands caught him, carried him and then untied his hands. When they removed the blindfold Spur found himself below deck on an ocean going sailing ship. A big sailor with a patch over one eye waved a foot long knife at Spur and shouted at him in a foreign language. He pointed to a black hole.

Spur was shoved and pushed and jammed down the three foot square hole and dropped six feet to the hold below.

Shanghaied!

The tong had sold his body for three dollars, and unless he did something quickly, he would be on a year-long cruise to the South Pacific and perhaps Europe.

"Anyone else here?" Spur asked.

Someone laughed from the far corner. It was so dark Spur couldn't see his hands. Another voice came, half drunk, half frightened.

"Hell yes, six of us so far. Welcome aboard."

"Hear we're heading for the Philippines," another voice said.

"Not me," Spur said. "I'm heading back to the docks. Anything down here to use for a club? Feel around, anybody sitting on a board or a stick, part of a crate, anything?"

"Not me, mate. Clean as a baby's bottom."

"Nothing here."

Spur looked around. The hatch cover fit loosely and let in a little light. Now his eyes had adjusted and he could see the twenty foot square hold, and five other men sitting or lying on the deck. A ladder led up to the hatch cover. He crawled up and tried to lift it, but it was locked down.

He took stock. He still had the four inch knife in his boot they had not taken, and the .44 rounds in his belt and in his pocket.

"Anybody have a hide-out gun they missed?" Spur asked.

Again negative answers.

"What about a pair of pliers? Hell, that's too much to ask for." Spur checked the hatch cover again. There was a spot near the top where he could put in a charge and the force would be directed upward. Great. He dropped back to the bottom of the hold and sat down, took a small note pad from his pocket and ripped six pages from it.

"Anyone ever taken .44 rounds apart to get the black powder out?"

"Yeah, I did during the war," an older voice said.

"Come over here and help me," Spur said. "And just maybe all of us can get out of here. When are we supposed to sail?"

"With the midnight tide," the older voice said.

Spur took from his pocket twenty .44 rounds. He got his knife from his boot and began loosening up the lead slugs in the copper casings. The older man was a dark shadow, but he took one of the loosened rounds and twisted the lead out with his teeth.

"Yes!" Spur said. "That's the way. Now empty the powder on these sheets of paper. They'll have to do for containers."

They worked for almost ten minutes. Eventually Spur and the older man had emptied the twenty rounds from his pocket and the eighteen from his belt. They made a stack of six of the pages filled with powder.

"Any sailors here?" Spur asked.

"Yeah, I been over the line a few times," a voice from the far corner said.

"What's the procedure on deck? When will the least men be up there?"

"Most of the hands will be on shore leave today. Just a few to load, and then the rest will come back two hours before sailing."

"How many up there right now?" Spur asked.

"Five, maybe six."

Spur took off his three inch wide leather belt with the heavy silver buckle. He pivoted a four inch blade from the buckle and locked it in place so it extended three inches beyond the end of the buckle. He had shaved with it from time to time. By wrapping the end of the belt around his hand he was able to make a sharp and dangerous swinging type weapon.

"Now would be as good a time as any?" Spur asked.

"Yep, if you want to get your head bashed in. Nobody knows you're here. They got nothing to lose."

"I have plenty to lose by sailing," Spur said. "Any of you with me?"

Four were. Spur explained what they would do. He went up the ladder and placed the packages of black powder in the corner of the hatch cover and trailed a quarter inch wide line of powder a foot along the two-by-four from the small bomb as a fuse.

"Ready?" Spur asked below. They were. He took a sulphur stinker match from his pocket and lit it. When it blazed up fully he touched it to the powder

143

trail and swung out and dropped to the bottom of the hold. He rolled to the far corner with the others as the black powder bomb went off.

It made twice the explosion Spur thought it would. As soon as it crashed, he was up and running for the ladder. The charge had splintered the hatch cover, blown half of it off and broken the wooden latch that held it down. Spur jammed the rest of it upward and jumped on deck just as a seaman came out of a forward cabin, a knife in one hand, a half eaten apple in the other. He yelled and charged, but Spur stood his ground. At the last moment, Spur swung the belt once around his head, then leaped forward and aimed the blade at the seaman's legs. It missed one but slashed a three inch wound in the other leg. Blood poured out and the seaman screamed as he fell to the deck. The other men had streamed out of the hold. Two ran and jumped into the water on the bay side, another charged a second sailor who had answered his friend's alarm. The man took a slash to the shoulder, but kicked the seaman in the groin and rushed for the gangplank.

Spur ran in the same direction. A large man lumbered into their path. Spur swung the belt, missed, swung it again and the blade slashed across the sailor's chest before he knew what he was fighting. He yelled and fell to one side. Spur and an older man from below ran down the gangplank, bowled over a small seaman who tried to stop them. They were free and ran along the dock and up the nearest street.

When they were two blocks away, Spur and the other man stepped into an alley and rested.

Spur held out his hand. "Spur McCoy," he said.

"Lenord Bruce, and I thank you. I had about given up. I'd been down there two days, and I don't think I could have survived a voyage on that windjammer."

"Where did they capture you?"

"A bar. I was drunk and broke. They sold me for four dollars."

"I was worth only three." Spur reached in his pocket, and found two gold double eagles, real ones. He gave them to the man and wished him luck, then hurried up the street where he could find a hack and get back to his hotel. A throbbing pain forced him to think about his shoulder. It was bleeding again. He'd have to go back to the doctor for a new bandage. He also wanted to see Juan Pico and talk about having that twelve-hour dusk to dawn watch on the three foundries. He was convinced that the gang was using one of them, probably Nelson's. All he had to do was catch them in the act. He would have the evidence any court would require for a quick conviction.

CHAPTER THIRTEEN

It was nearly four in the afternoon before Spur made it to Olivera Street to talk to Juan Pico. The Mexican leader received him at once.

"A watch on the foundries? Yes, I agree. A good plan. And if we see or hear any activity, my men will report it directly to you. Where? Your hotel room at the San Franciscan?"

"A message in my key box room 310 will do it. Could they start tonight?"

"It is now being arranged for a team of two men to be on guard at all three of the firms. That way one can report to you while the other observes."

"Thanks, Don Pico. I appreciate your help. The United States government appreciates your assistance as well. If this turns out the way it looks now, there should be enough money recovered so all of the counterfeits can be redeemed at face value by a local banker. They will have to be picked up, of course, but I don't think any of your people will lose a peso because of these bad coins."

"Good! *Bueno!* I am glad." He frowned. "I know it is not polite to ask but you seem a bit worse for the wear. Have you had any problems with my people?"

Spur touched a torn place on his jacket sleeve, a bruise on his cheek and the newly bandaged shoulder.

"Not at all, Don Pico. I enjoy coming to Olivera Street. It was China Town where I had my problems. I got involved in an underground maze and never did find my way out."

"You were in the *Palace of Pleasure?*"

"I'm not sure, but there were a lot of pleasures offered the paying customers."

"You are a lucky man to come out of there alive. Even most of the Chinese living here don't know where it is."

"It was not a memorable experience. I better get moving. Thanks again for your help."

Twenty minutes later Spur sat in the afternoon sunshine. He decided that another stretch of watching the small gray house might be productive. This time he chose the far end of the alley where he could see the house and the buggy that was usually tied up behind it. It appeared to be the same one Katherine had used before.

A little more than an hour after Spur took up his watch, a man rode in on a sorrel with a white mane and tail. He tied his mount to a fence and sat down in the shade and waited. He kept looking up the alley, away from Spur.

For a second Spur wondered if this man was watching the gray house as well. No other law enforcement people in town knew about the counterfeiting. Who could he be? Spur waited a half hour more and the sun was beginning to go down. A young boy came out of the back of the gray house and put something in the buggy. As he moved, Spur recognized the stride, the proud carriage. It was Katherine dressed as a boy again.

The watcher ahead of Spur turned away and became busy with some boxes in the alley. Obviously he didn't want to be recognized by Katherine. Spur watched the man in the late afternoon light. He was maybe five feet ten, red hair showed under a high crown range hat. He wore a six-gun tied low on his right leg.

If he were with the San Francisco police, they should compare notes. Spur left the buggy and walked down the alley toward the man, making just enough noise to make him aware that someone was coming. Spur's gunbelt was back in place, with a replacement .44 and belt rounds repositioned.

The man with the sorrel looked up quickly, stared at Spur for a moment, then mounted up fast.

"Hold it!" Spur shouted. But the redhead pulled the sorrel around and rode out past the gray house toward the street. Spur leaped in his buggy and slapped the reins on the horse's back as he tried to follow the man. He didn't have a chance of staying with the horseback rider, but he could get a general direction where he was headed.

Spur came around the mouth of the alley. The rider was half a block ahead. He turned left and headed for the bay side of the peninsula. Spur stayed with him. Soon the redhead had a full block lead, but he didn't try to lose Spur. Was he simply leading Spur on, working him into some kind of a trap?

Spur kept driving, saw the sorrel turn again toward the bay and ride down a street fronting the harbor where the fishing fleet tied up. There were a hundred fishing boats, none over thirty feet long. Most were identical, with one mast and no cabin. They were piled with nets. Some had outriggers for lines to be let down.

The man left his horse at the embarcadero and rushed to a pier and stepped on board a fishing boat. As Spur watched from the pier the man hurried from one boat tied along side another until he was half way across to the next pier. Spur couldn't figure out what he was trying to do.

Maybe he was working over to the second pier in order to get away. Spur left his rig and made his way to the next wooden structure jutting into the bay. As unobtrusively as possible he went past the fish sellers to the midpoint and watched the redhead's progress. He ducked into one fishing boat after another, coming out on the other side and stepped into the next boat tied alongside.

It had to be a tangled problem when all those boats started out for a day's fishing first thing in the morning, Spur decided. For a moment he lost the redhead. Then he spotted the man moving across the last three boats to the pier. Spur was between the man and the shore.

Someone behind Spur shouted. He looked back and saw two men rolling a fish box on wheels toward him. It was filled with silver, flopping fish. Spur leaped to one side but was too late. The fish box hit him, tipped over and a hundred pounds of wet, sticky fish flooded down on top of him on the pier. He saw the redhead run past. By the time Spur got to his feet, the man was almost to the street.

McCoy threw a fish at the fisherman who had dumped them on him and rushed after his quarry.

McCoy lost the redhead twice, picked up his trail in the sparsely peopled dock area, and at last caught him just before he slipped into a small seafood restaurant. He did not even try to draw his gun.

Spur grabbed his shirt front and pushed the man against the side of the building.

"I told you to stop back in the alley. Why did you run?" Spur asked.

"Thought you were trying to rob me."

"That won't work, try another reason."

"Look, I wasn't supposed to be in the alley. I figured you were working for her."

"Who?"

"The woman who lives in the gray house."

"Why were you spying on her?"

"She owes me money. I thought she was leaving town."

"Who is the lady who lives there?"

"Dorothy Jones."

"Never heard of her. Who is she?"

"Nobody you would know." He turned. "Why were you in the alley?"

"I'm the one asking the questions, and you've been lying to me. Now why were you watching the place?"

"She had been meeting someone there, and I had to know who it was. It was a lover."

"And you're her husband."

"Yes, of course."

"Wrong again. I know who owns that house. It isn't anybody named Dorothy Jones. When are you going to start telling me the truth?"

"I don't have to tell you a damned thing!" Then his shoulders slumped, his face turned sad almost to the point of tears, and he shook his head. "No, no. Maybe I should tell someone." He rubbed one hand across his face and Spur followed the motion.

Too late McCoy realized he had been fooled. The redhead's other hand flashed down, drew his pistol and waved it in Spur's face before he could draw.

"Now, back off you sonofabitch, or I'm gonna cut you down to size with a few lead slugs. You savvy? Lay down on the sidewalk, face to the boards. Right now!"

Spur could do nothing else. He went down, stretched out on the wooden sidewalk.

"You stay there for five minutes or I'll blast a hole a foot wide through your belly! You try following me and you're going to discover yourself dead and gone to hell!" The redhead glared at Spur, then ran down the block and around the corner.

Spur stood and let the man go. He wasn't San

Francisco police, and if he were one of the men working with Katherine, why would he be spying on her? Another piece to the puzzle. He had to get all of them put together, and the quicker the better.

It was a little after six when Spur returned to the San Franciscan Hotel, ordered up bath water and washed the last of the fish scales out of his hair. He would smell like fish for a week.

There had been two messages in his 310 box. One was from Juan Pico. It read:

The situation with the counterfeit double eagles is reaching critical proportions. My people took in twenty more of them during the past two days. These have come through my unofficial banking fuction for the smaller merchants. Something must be done at once.

If the situation is not cleared up in two days, I will put a ban on the use of the double eagle in my area. This could have startling effects on the rest of the business firms in San Francisco, and could lead to a collapse in public support for the gold standard in the city.

This is by no means a threat. Only to urge you on to greater efforts for everyone's benefit. My men are on post watching the three foundries. Any activity report will come directly to you.

Spur read the note again. He could watch the small gray house tonight or he could go see Katherine. His shoulder ached again and he changed his mind.

He read the second note. It was from Mrs. Engleton, the society matron with the sexy little black maid. She suggested they have a late dinner at her place. He smiled but shook his head. He wasn't strong enough for that kind of a workout yet.

Spur decided it was time for a real rest. He would have a good dinner downstairs and get to bed early for a long sleep.

That was when he remembered his appointment for tonight. He had to see one more artist to help keep his cover intact. He wasn't even sure who it was. Then he remembered. The artist who signed himself Radiji. Sounded like an East Indian. Spur would much rather have caught up on his sleep, but he had that 8 P.M. appointment. He would go. This would be his last artist contact. His cover wasn't going to be that important after the next two days.

Tomorrow he would see Katherine and try to trip her up about the gold eagles. It was either that or make a raid on the gray house. He had to know where they were doing the counterfeiting, and catch them in the act.

Spur left the hotel by the side door at ten minutes to eight and took a hack to the address. It was not the best section of town and in a two storey building. Artists always wanted a skylight.

He went up the steps to the second floor and knocked on the only door there. Nobody answered. He knocked again and at last someone came. When the door opened a short chunky woman stared at him, then she smiled.

"Oh, you're the buyer from New York, the important big man coming to bless us with his presence. Come on in. I know you won't buy nothing. You big shot fuckers never do, but come in anyway. Hell, what I got to lose?"

"I was looking for Radiji. Is this the right address?"

"Yeah, right, it is. I'm feeling bitchy tonight. Come on in. What do you want to drink?"

"Nothing, thanks. I wanted to see some of the work of this person called Radiji. Is he here?"

"Damn! You did it too. I am Radiji. Radiji ain't no goddamn man, she's me, I am Radiji!"

"Well, good. What a pleasant surprise. If you would sign your work Helen or Ruth, the whole world would know that you're a woman. Why hide behind one name?"

"I ain't hiding. Tried it the other way. Sold maybe five or six paintings a year, all to women. Started using Radiji and I sell enough to live on. Not well, as you can see, but I get the rent paid." She stared up at him. "You really want to look at my work, or you just here because you said you would come?"

"I want to look, otherwise I wouldn't be here. You may not believe it, but you're not the only one with problems."

"Yeah, all right, sorry. I guess I did get shouting there before I knew your feelings. Back this way."

She led him down a hall to a big studio with a skylight. The room was thirty feet long, and he saw that a wall had been torn out. Along one side there were canvases hung on the wall. All were of nude women.

"You knew I only did tit paintings. Tits and ass, that's what you men like on the wall and in the bed. So that's what I paint. Not dirty pictures, artistic ones. Beautiful women with a few or no clothes on. Men buy them. Some women hate them. I make a living. How many do you want me to send to New York on the train?"

Spur moved a lamp and checked one two by three foot horizontal picture. It was beautiful. A woman lay on a velvet couch. She was well rounded, like a Rubens, big breasted and painted in an artistic pose that could be thought of as sexy. Her crotch was delicately covered with a trailing hand, but her breasts thrust up and out invitingly.

"You do good work."

"Hell, I know that, not great, but good. That's why I'll sell wholesale, no consignment. Sell outright a dozen, twenty, two dozen. And I'll give you a fifty percent cut in my retail price. Means you can double your money fast."

It was true. Spur had seen paintings of less quality in some New York galleries at three times the price she asked. He suddenly wished he were a real art buyer.

They moved the lamps so he could see the rest of her work. Every piece was good. The faces were as marvelously done as the nude bodies.

He asked her prices.

"You want a dozen, they are eighty dollars each. You want twice that you can have them for sixty-five dollars. Any of these tit paintings will sell in New York for a hundred and fifty. I used to work there, I know."

"You're right. I just don't have that kind of money left in my budget. I wish I had stopped here earlier on my trip."

The woman nodded. "Shit! That's happened to me the last two times. I don't sell on the street. I'd be busted."

"How much do you get for one painting?"

"That bitch there with the pink tits is sixty-five on the street. I haggle down to about forty You want her she's wrapped up for you for twenty bucks. You can do me some good back east."

Spur pulled out a good double eagle from his pocket and handed it to her. "Sold."

"Hot damn!" She grinned. "You want the bonus that goes along with the picture?"

"What's that?"

"Surprise. You come over here while I wrap up the picture. Can't let you carry Polly there around the street all naked."

She led Spur into an adjoining room. It was small and had a couch, chair and a mirror.

"This is a model's dressing room. I'll be right back. You wait here."

She left and a minute later the opposite door opened and a young girl no more than thirteen came in. She wore only a chemise that barely covered her crotch. Her young, small breasts made only dimples in the chemise.

Spur frowned. "Sorry, I must be in the wrong place."

"No, this is the right place." She turned around slowly. "Do you like me? My name is Willa."

Spur was slowly beginning to understand. She

pulled the chemise off and stood nude before him. Her breasts were just beginning to swell. Only a soft brown hint of crotch hair showed.

"You like Willa better this way?"

"No, Willa, put the chemise on." Spur turned to the door. Radiji came in carrying the wrapped picture in front of her. When she put it down she was naked as well.

"Well, you've met Willa. She and me, we're the bonus. You can bang away on either one of us, or both. That's the fucking bonus you get for buying a picture."

Spur grinned at Radiji. She was pleasingly and frankly fat. Her large breasts sagged halfway to her belly, which bulged over her crotch so no pubic hair showed. Her arms and legs were chunky as well.

Spur waved at the girl. "Get her out of here."

Radiji nodded and the girl went out the door. Her expression hadn't changed the whole time she was in the room.

"You'll get in trouble offering that young girl," Spur said.

"Haven't yet. She's my daughter."

"That's worse yet."

"Ease up, McCoy. Ease up and relax and enjoy a good fuck. You got a pecker in them pants of yours or not?"

Spur watched the fat woman moving in front of him, doing a little bump and grind, waggling her huge, sagging breasts.

"Hey, I give a nice, soft, easy cushion of a ride." She knelt in front of Spur and pulled open his fly, dug inside until she found his hardness and yelped in success.

"Damn, he's small, but I found him. He grow any bigger?"

Spur laughed and let down his pants and drawers and followed her to the couch.

She flopped down on her back and spread her legs.

"Want me to pee a little to give you a target?" she said and wailed in laughter.

While she was laughing Spur dropped between her legs and jolted inside her ending the laugh with a gasp of pleasure. Then she looked up and frowned.

"Someday women is gonna be appreciated, you know that? We'll get the vote and be equal in the law. Now men think of us as tits and cunt, that's it. They ball us and expect us to raise the kids and feed everybody and spread our legs and open our cunts to them whenever they bellow. Hell, that's partly why I left my old man. He kept demanding. I told him to stuff it up his own ass for a change. Came out here. So I fuck when I want to, why not? Men sure as hell do. Why can't I? I want to let a man have a go at me, that's my own fucking business." She laughed at her own pun.

"Christ, you got a cock like a big oak tree, you know that? I ain't been touched in deep that way in years. Oh, god! That is pure wild. Usually I don't come at all, no fucking climax. Sometimes I pretend, but this time for damn sure I feel it building up. Oh, yeah!"

Spur concentrated on jolting into her so he scraped past her tender clit, and each time she worked her own passion higher and higher.

Before Spur reached his climax, the chunky woman screeched in pain and delight. She rattled and shook like a cattle car on the railroad. She roared and bellowed her delight and soon she was panting and wailing as if she had never been here before.

Her performance jolted Spur into action and his climax kept hers alive. She worked through the whole gambit of her joy ride again, screaming at the end, then nearly fainting.

Spur slid away from her and watched her recuperate. Her breath came in ragged gasping surges. Sweat beaded her forehead and ran in a little stream down between her breasts. She moaned softly and reached for him.

"Don't go. Once more. Give Willa a ride like that. Show her how good it can be."

Spur hadn't even taken off his pants. Now he pulled up his clothes and shook his head at the chunky woman sprawled on the couch.

"I told you. I don't touch anybody that young. Forget it."

She sat up and he grinned at the way her breasts swung around.

"You got too damn many principles."

"Probably, but that's just the way I am. You got your bonus, I got my bonus. We'll leave Willa out of it." Spur paused. "I'm going to try to rustle up some demand for your work. I'll be in St. Louis soon, and

I should be able to get an order for you there. Keep watching your mail." Spur left her on the couch and went into the front room.

Willa sat there, still in the chemise. She was looking at a magazine. She smiled at him.

"Thanks. I really don't like to do it."

"That's natural. You shouldn't yet. Tell your mother. Maybe she'll listen."

"Doubt it, but I'll try." She blushed. "Mr. McCoy, could I ask you something?"

He stopped. "Sure."

"Could I kiss you on the cheek? I'd really like that."

"So would I, Willa."

She jumped up and kissed him and stepped back. She smiled and ran toward the inside door. "I better get some clothes on, somebody might come in."

Spur McCoy picked up the painting which he planned to ship to St. Louis. It would hang over his bed. Fleurette would either love it or slash it to pieces. It would be interesting to see which one.

He went down to the street and walked back to the hotel. Now he could work on that good night's sleep.

CHAPTER FOURTEEN

As Spur was catching up on his sleep, Katherine Sanford held a special meeting of her gang. She loved to call them a gang, and made it clear to them that she was the leader, and that Burke was second in command.

They met in a small back room of a bar and gaming house near the outskirts of town, well away from any place that Spur McCoy might be seen. She waited until the bar wench had delivered warm beer to everyone, and a glass of white wine for her, then she grabbed their attention.

"We may have to kill someone," she said. She watched the reaction of each man. Tim Hackett, the die and metal expert, turned slightly pale and had a long pull on his beer. Burke Foster grinned and drew his six-gun and slid it back in leather three times. Hop Choy touched the bandage at the side of his face and nodded solemnly, anger, hatred in his usually calm eyes. Breed's face showed no change whatsoever, his black eyes flicked up to her face to see if she were serious, then he looked back at the table and nursed his beer.

"Anyone we know?" Burke asked.

"That's what I want to find out. Hop Choy has indicated that a tall white man hit him with a pistol. He does not know when the white man started following him, but, if I am right in interpreting what he tells me with sign language, he was the same fellow who was nosing around Nelson's the other night. The same man who talked to the night watchman."

"Christ, that is big trouble," Burke said. "Does he know about the gray house?"

"I don't know," Katherine said. "Have any of you seen him around there watching the place? Have you seen a tall man with sandy hair and a moustache in the alley or down the block, just sitting around, waiting, maybe watching?"

"Christ, that would be bad," Burke said. "If this guy knows about the gray house! Maybe we shouldn't use it for a while. Didn't you say we were about coming to the end of our string on this one, anyway? Maybe we should close it down now and take what we have and split it up the way we talked."

"No, it isn't that drastic. I know this man. His name is Spur McCoy. He says he's an art buyer from New York, but I don't believe him. I saw him one

164

night with my banker, the banker who asked me about the counterfeit I let slip into a deposit I made."

"Maybe he's government," Hackett said. "They have one bunch of guys that worry about counterfeiting. Yeah, I think it's time we split the coins the way you said and go different directions."

"Stop it!" Katherine said. She hadn't changed clothes, and wore a dress that she realized now was too tightly revealing. Burke was drooling. "Just relax, everyone. When it's time to quit, I'll tell you all and everyone will be free and safe. This money is going to be no good if we're all in prison. So let me handle that end of it. All I want to know is if any of you have seen this Spur McCoy."

She looked at each of them again.

"Hell, we might have," Burke said. "I don't imagine you got a tintype of him so we could be sure."

She shook her head.

Burke shrugged. "Hell, I'll keep my eyeballs peeled." But inside Burke was worried. Her description fit the *hombre* in the alley who chased him down to the docks. He said he knew who lived in the gray house. If he knew and he suspected, then this McCoy could close in anytime. Burke had to get into motion. He had to get the coins out of the gray house. No big job, simply shoot the Chink and take the goods about two A.M. Easy. He would bring Breed along for protection, then give him a lead sandwich out the trail a ways. It had to be tonight. Things were closing in too damn fast. There was no chance that he was going to admit to Kate that he had seen McCoy and that McCoy knew about the gray house. If he did that, then he would have to explain to the damn black widow lady just what he was doing spying on the little gray house. He could not risk it if he wanted a shot at that treasure chest under the floor in the back bedroom. Best to dummy up and wait.

"I was hoping that some of you men had seen him hanging around. Even without that, it is now decision time. Tomorrow I'll be going on a little picnic with Mr. McCoy. I want Breed to follow us out of town and take care of him. Breed, I don't care how you do it, but don't get me all messed up. Understand? I don't want him falling on me or anything."

"Do a head shot, Breed," Burke suggested.

"I don't want to know the details. You better not follow us out. We'll go to Moon Rocks Bay, just south of town. You be there and take care of it. Then we won't have to worry about anything and we can finish five more strikings."

"Five?" Burke asked. "Thought you said two more the last time we were at Nelson's."

"Yes, but we can strike off four thousand dollars a night. I think we all could use just a little bit more cash when we split it."

Around the room heads nodded.

"Using that as a vote, we'll take care of Mr. McCoy and then have five more strikings. Now, that's all we need to settle. It's nice talking to you rich men, but I have to get back to a damn meeting about the opera."

Katherine went to the meeting, then to bed so she could get up early. She sent a note to Spur's hotel room inviting him to a picnic lunch, expounding on the beauty and seclusion of this place just out of town south. She told him to be at her door by eleven the next morning.

The following morning, Katherine was pleased to hear Spur arriving ten minutes early. She looked in the mirror one last time, pulled on her dress to show more cleavage, then went downstairs to give Spur a loving kiss and a promise of more to come.

"Mr. McCoy! It's so good to see you. I'm glad you can come on the picnic. The basket is all packed, and we have plenty of wine this time so we don't run out. It's in the carriage and I'll even let you drive."

She held her cheek out to be kissed and Spur brushed his lips against it. Then he turned her face and kissed her lips.

"Now that is better," Spur said. "I was hoping I could see you today. It's almost time for me to move on to Los Angeles. They are developing some very fine young artists down there, and some of the Mexicans are producing again."

"Oh, so soon? Then we shall make this a special time, an extra special, personal time for just the two of us. Darling, I almost can't wait!"

"Then let's get moving and see this idyllic glen you have found on the coast."

It took them an hour to drive there, and they reached it after going through a gate on a private road, then turning off and working up the coast a half mile. It was beautiful; one of those miniature coves less than fifty feet wide, with a sandy beach and rocks all the way around it and the surf crashing on the rocks and then sliding into the cove that was blue-water deep and calm.

Behind the beach lay a dense stand of young live oak and cotton woods. They walked the last two hundred yards where they spread the blanket out in the grass at the edge of the sand in the shade.

"Let's swim first," she said, and they raced each other to take off clothes. He stopped and watched her pull off her garments, throwing them on the grass. When her breasts burst into view he clapped and cheered. But she was off, running for the clear, cool waters.

Spur raced right after her. They both came up gasping for air and his arms went around her and they kissed and sank below the water laughing as they surfaced.

They stood in waist deep water and she kissed him hard, her tongue boring into his mouth, her hands playing with his growing erection. When the kiss ended, she yelped in delight.

"You did it! You're hard underwater. Oh, do it now, put it inside me when we're both underwater. I don't know if it can be done or not."

She wouldn't let him go and pulled at him. Spur shrugged, lifted her and positioned himself. With one stabbing thrust he penetrated her shrunken nether lips and she screeched in real pain. Then she burst out laughing.

"My god! It can be done. Just don't lay me down

on my back out here or we'll both drown."

She began moving back and forth, then forward and back as she built his passion and too soon he exploded inside her and sagged under water, rolling away as he came out of her. He swam twenty yards underwater to shore until he hit the sand, then he was up and running for the picnic basket.

"I'm starved, let's eat," he called. Spur used the few moments for a quick security check. He had not seen anyone when they drove in. There was a small farm or camp to the south, but they had turned north and there didn't seem to be anyone within two miles. Still he had a strange feeling, a hunch. Why was she so set on coming out here for a picnic? Spur was thinking of her more as a suspect than a casual friend and lover.

She came running up, her magnificent breasts swaying and bouncing and still dripping salt water. She sat on his lap and demanded that he kiss her all over. He started but never got past her breasts.

"You are so good!" she said. "We will make love ten times today, and you will be great. I have ways to help you. Now, the lunch."

They sat on the blanket, one on each side of the basket, and began the picnic. There was fried chicken, potato salad, fresh fruit, a half a dead-ripe watermelon, bottles of beer and wine, and cheese and a dozen different kinds of crackers.

She showed him some thin sandwiches made of crushed small shrimp and mixed with a little thick cream and chopped onions. It was delicious. He ate four. Once he saw her looking into the woods, and he wondered why. She might have heard someone.

"Are you nervous? Do we need to dress?" He asked her.

She shook her head. "Cover up that beautiful body? I won't let you. No, there is not a soul around for five miles. That's why I like it out here. We can go bare all day if we don't get sunburned. It is a marvelous fling."

She opened the wine and poured him a glass, then took a drink from the bottle before pouring her glass. "I get ahead that way." She stood and rubbed her breasts into his face and he caught one and chewed and she crooned.

Fifty yards away in the deep woods, Breed lay in his protective covering, not making a sound. A .50 caliber Sharps rifle lay beside him and his hand pumped up and down over his crotch.

"Damn, oh, damn! Oh, damn!" he whispered as he ejaculated into the hundred year old mulch of decomposed leaf mold under the trees. He wiped sweat off his forehead and picked up the Sharps.

She was so beautiful! Twice he had been ready to shoot, and then she moved or waved her bare ass in his direction or her big tits, and he put down the rifle and grabbed his stiff penis for one more masturbation.

Now he had to do it. They had been there an hour. He wanted to kill McCoy and then run up and throw her onto the blanket and demand sexual compensation. She would give it to him. She had loved his work a few nights ago.

Breed picked up the Sharps, made sure that it was

170

loaded and ready, then sighted in on the broad back of Spur McCoy. He would put a round through his spinal column, a much better target than a head. Sweat misted his eyes and he slashed it away.

Katherine stood and rubbed her breasts over the naked man, then lowered one breast into his mouth.

"Oh, damn, no!" Breed croaked. He pushed the Sharps to one side and a stick caught in the trigger. He pushed it again as he reached for his phallus. The pressure of the stick was more than the trigger could withstand; the trigger pushed, the hammer fell and the Sharps round exploded and screamed six feet over Spur's head.

McCoy dove away from the naked woman toward his clothes. He dragged his gunbelt off the top of his clothes and sprinted fifteen yards toward a sturdy live oak that would shield him.

Breed swore, jammed a new round into the Sharps and looked for his target. Katherine remained on the blanket. He checked the rest of the beach and the grass, then looked at the trees. For a moment the thrill of a fight settled over him. He realized that in the thick trees and brush a man with a six-gun would have the advantage. It was not a long range duel.

Spur checked his loads in the .44, then peered out from low on the oak, searching for the source of the rifle shot. He did not think it had been a warning. The elements were too perfect: it was a bushwhack killing. Only something had gone wrong. The report had been from a heavy rifle, a Spencer or a Sharps. If the gunman had been over thirty to forty yards away he had been a fool. How could he miss at that range?

Spur had thought it through. He called to Katherine.

"Take your clothes and get back to the buggy. Drive for town if you can. I'll hold this hardcase off whoever he is. Just go. Leave my clothes, but take yours. Now move before he fires again."

As soon as Spur shouted the commands, he dropped to his knees and crawled from his tree to another one to his left. The sound of the shot had come from that direction. It was the sort of sound placement he had learned to recognize and remember. It helped a person to stay alive.

Now he stood behind another big live oak and listened.

Nothing.

He detected movement ahead and to the left. Only a whisper. He knew Indians who couldn't move through dry woodlands that quietly. More soft sounds to the left. Retreating. The bushwhacker was moving out. Spur watched through the trees, but could see no sign of anyone. He ran lightly from tree to tree, working quickly out of the acre sized woods. As he remembered there was grasslands all around the spot of trees. Once to the edge of the oaks the ambusher would have no cover. The grass was waist high, but not heavy enough for a man to crawl through undetected.

Five minutes later Spur was at the edge of the woods. He stayed behind a big oak and scanned the area ahead. For a moment he saw movement a hundred feet ahead, then it blended back into the shadows.

The man was down there, worried about his next step. A horse? There should be a horse nearby. Spur sniffed the off shore breeze but could not detect any horse smells. Too much to hope for.

He waited.

Spur remembered a time in Arizona when he had outwaited an Indian lying half covered with sand in the desert. After two hours the Indian had moved an arm, and Spur shot him. He hoped this would not entail that much patience.

To the right he heard harness jangle and the sound of the horse moving the buggy. At least Katherine was away with no harm done. Now it was his turn to even the score with this bushwhacker.

Spur dodged around his tree and bolted fifteen yards to the next big oak to his left. It provided cover for him after ten steps and then he was behind it, panting, trying to hold his breath to listen.

No sounds.

Spur waited for five minutes.

A startled pheasant flew up from the grass twenty yards from the trees. Spur watched the spot with interest. Pheasants will let you walk within a foot of them and not move, blending in with the grass and shrubs. If one moved. . . .

Spur watched the flushing spot with intensity, and saw a wand of grass jiggle, then bend to the left, away from the woods.

His bushwhacker was moving through the grass. He was out of sight, which also meant he couldn't see out. Spur crouched and watched the gently swaying grass where he figured the killer had to be. He ran softly through the grass paralleling the bushwhacker. Soon he was ahead of him with an off shore wind blowing in his face. The waist high grass was tinder dry from the Santa Ana dry winds. Spur ran another twenty yards ahead of the crawler and cut at right angles to his former path until he estimated he was directly in front of the bushwhacker.

Spur brought a small packet of stinker matches from his pocket, broke off one and bent low, striking it on the bottom of the pack and touching off the dry grass. Flames leaped at the grass and Spur knelt there upwind, watching the breeze fan the flames.

It crackled, then the wind raced the flames through the grass as fast as a man could walk. Spur watched ahead, his .44 up and held with both hands. He heard a startled cry, then a figure leaped upright twenty feet in front of him and only a half dozen feet from the flames. Black smoke billowed toward him and he stared at it a moment.

That was when Spur fired. His round caught Breed in the left shoulder and knocked him down. He screamed as the fire raced toward him. Frantically he jumped up, holding his left shoulder, the rifle forgotten. He ran to the left to go around the end of the fire. Spur fired twice, aiming low into the grass hoping to hit his legs.

The first round missed, but the second sent Breed tumbling into the grass. He screamed in terror and hopped on one leg as he frantically worked around the far end of the fire.

Spur figured the grass would burn itself out when it came to the live oaks where it would have little grass to continue. He would worry about that later. He ran hard now around the end of the blackened grass until he found Breed lying on his back, breathing heavily of the sweet non-smoky air.

Breed looked up at Spur and spat at him. Spur lowered the muzzle of the .44.

"Indian, aren't you? Who paid you to kill me?"

The man didn't reply.

Spur shot him in the other leg. Blood gushed out as the Indian screamed.

"Who paid you to kill me?"

"I won't tell you."

"You don't understand. I don't like people to shoot at me. It makes me unhappy with whoever does it and whoever hires him to do it. I plan on seeing justice done on both counts."

Spur shot Breed in the right arm. More blood surged.

Breed screamed again.

"I understand this is remote and isolated. No one ever comes here, so you won't get any help. Who paid you to kill me?"

"They will kill me if I tell you."

"That way you live a few days longer, because if you don't tell me, I'll kill you where you lie with pleasure."

"Help me."

"Just the way you helped me, bushwhacker."

Spur knew it was an obscene situation. He stood wearing nothing but a gunbelt, holding a .44 on an Indian lying in tall grass with four bullet holes in

175

him already.

A gust of wind whipped a heavy pall of smoke over them and Spur ducked to avoid it. As he did Breed used his left hand, jerked a hideout from his ankle and pulled it up to fire at Spur.

The motion registered in Spur's side vision. He dove to the ground and fired the last round from his six-gun at the figure on the ground. There was no time to place his shot. The slug caught the Indian under the chin, smashed up through his mouth, through his brain and exited with a four inch square of scalp, hair and brain tissue.

Spur sat where he had stopped moving. Automatically he re-loaded his .44 from the rounds in the belt. There was no sense in checking on the Indian. He was as dead as any man ever gets.

Spur scowled as he went back for his clothes. He dressed quickly, put the picnic things in the big wicker basket and folded the blanket. He guessed that the horse and buggy might be a short way down the road.

He took one last look at the fire. It was all but out. It had died at the edge of the woods. He went to one spot and tramped out the last of the flames, then began his walk back to town.

He was wrong about the buggy. When he reached the main road, he ate a piece of chicken, finished the bottle of wine, and threw the blanket and the basket in the ditch.

Now he was sure. Katherine had set him up for a killing. She had picked the spot. She could have sent one of her men out in advance and had him all ready to blast Spur into a quick coffin. Katherine Sanford was also the counterfeiter. All he had to do was prove it.

CHAPTER FIFTEEN

Spur McCoy caught a ride with a farmer taking eggs and chickens into market. He got back to his hotel just after two o'clock. He moved to a new room again, resupplied his gun belt with rounds and carried some in his pocket. From now on he would move cautiously. If Katherine tried to have him killed in the country, she would undoubtedly continue the contract in town. He would use the back door and a low hat and change his habit patterns.

His prime job was to follow Katherine and hope that she led him to the next counterfeiting party. Nothing would happen there until dark. He changed jackets and slipped out the back door of the hotel through the kitchen, and went to see the banker, J. Anderson Dumbarton.

"We've found another twenty-five of the coins,"

Dumbarton said. "So far we are simply holding them, waiting the outcome of your investigation. How is it going?"

Spur told him he had a good idea. "Something may happen tonight, I'm not sure. If it turns out right, there should be enough funds to cover all of your counterfeit coins. That way you can simply replace the coins and we won't cause a panic in the public confidence of the double eagle."

"Good, this is one problem I'll be glad to have cleaned up."

"Have you ever thought about opening a branch of your bank in the Mexican Village?"

Dumbarton laughed. "No I haven't. I couldn't get in there in the first place."

"You might. With a partner. There are a lot of small merchants up there. They need a bank. You know who is doing the banking function now?"

"Juan Pico, and he's probably charging them twenty percent."

Spur smiled. "Mr. Dumbarton, I can see you've never met Juan Pico. He is tough, but he is also fair, honest and as far as I can tell, absolutely devoted to the betterment of his people. Do you know that right now he is holding more than three hundred double eagle counterfeit coins? Somebody flooded his merchants with them. If he wasn't holding them, it would wipe out every fifth store in the Village."

"He's holding over six thousand dollars worth? Amazing. We don't have a tenth of that amount." He rubbed his chin. "This Juan Pico, I've heard of him for years. Could you arrange a meeting with him?"

"Of course. I'm sure he would want to hand pick the people who worked in your branch. It would have to be bilingual all the way, and serve both anglos and Mexicans."

Dumbarton nodded. "Yes, we could work that out. And Pico, what would be his share?"

"You'll have to talk with him about that. But I would guess knowing his people had the services of a reliable bank would probably be reward enough for him."

"Maybe I've had this Pico all wrong."

"It's hard to know a man until you have met and talked with him for a while. Are you free now? Let's go and see Juan, and start discussions about this."

"Fine, but I'll leave my rings and watch and wallet here."

"Suit yourself, but you'll be safer in the Village than you are on any other San Francisco street."

The two men talked that afternoon and laid a foundation. The following day Juan Pico would visit Dumbarton in his office and they would make more plans.

Spur ordered a steak dinner sent to his room along with a pot of coffee and he ate every scrap of food. After that he had a short nap. Just before eleven o'clock he was up, dressed in black pants and a black shirt, ready for business. He had a feeling this was the night.

He planned to leave the hotel at midnight and drive straight to the Nelson Foundry. His plans changed when someone knocked on his door at

11:45. It was one of the men he had seen in Don Pico's office.

"Nelson's," the man said, still panting from running up the stairs. "We saw lights and heard voices and loud metal sounds. It began about twenty minutes ago."

Spur slipped on his gunbelt and buckled it, then put on a low crowned black hat.

"Thanks. This may be the time we catch them."

"Can we help you? Don Pico said we are at your command."

Backup. They could come in handy. The young Mexican touched a .44 on his hip. Spur nodded.

"Come on, we'll work it out as we ride."

Spur had changed his rented buggy for a rented saddle horse tied behind the hotel. They went out, again through the kitchen, and rode for the foundry. By then his plans were made. He left the two young Mexicans at the fence and told them that if he fired three shots in a row, they should come in, he would need help.

Like a dark shadow, Spur skimmed over the back fence, moved through the yard without a sound, then settled down behind some heavy sheet metal and watched. He saw the big Chinese man making a guard round of the fence. So they were here. When the way was clear, Spur moved toward the building where he could see a faint light. The heavy metal sounds had stopped about five minutes before, the Mexican lookout reported.

The Secret Service agent wasn't exactly sure what process they used, but he knew it couldn't be over

182

yet. He moved up again, slid through a partially open dark door and was inside the building with the lights on. Three lanterns glowed at the far end. He worked his way slowly forward, making sure of each step.

After five minutes he could see two men moving around, then he spotted Katherine dressed again as a man. It looked as though they were in the plating process. Evidently they plated the round blank coins before they were struck off with the counterfeit dies. He moved closer. He could identify the man he had chased out from behind the gray house. He was helping a smaller man with the plating, dipping the coin blanks into a small vat that held the liquid gold. Spur had no idea how hot gold had to be to melt, but assumed that it had to be extremely hot.

He moved up again. The small man used a long handled, heavy metal dipper to move more molten gold from a furnace area to the vat where the blanks were immersed, shaken, and immersed again.

Spur had seen enough. With the dies in their possession this was plenty to convict.

He jumped out from his hiding spot and covered them with his six-gun.

"Hold it, right there!" he barked. "Nobody moves. You are all under arrest for counterfeiting." They froze from surprise more than fear. Spur walked forward. He had the three of them well covered. He could not see any guns but he was sure there were some around.

"Oh, shit!" Burke said.

The small man holding the cup sized dipper of

molten gold looked as if he was about to faint. He teetered on his feet, and the dipper wavered.

"Hold it steady!" Spur shouted. He was within six feet of them now. The youth he assumed to be Kate was furious but silent.

"Now, all of you lie down on the floor. Quickly! The small man with the molten gold looked at his treasure and shivered. He stumbled forward, tripped and the cup of pure gold jolted forward and splashed out of the container. Drops of it hit Spur's leg, bigger spots burned through his pants and into his ankle. Most of it splashed on the toe of his boot, the gold paltering the heavy leather in an instant.

As the gold burned into Spur he bit his lip and groaned at the searing pain. He concentrated on getting the gold off him and didn't notice Katherine slipping behind him swinging a half inch iron rod downward, striking his gun and slamming it out of his hand.

Burke pounced on Spur driving him to the floor and nailing his hands behind him.

"Now, big man, we get a good look at you," Burke said. "For as long as you live, that is. Good work, boss, you put him down just right."

"The gold! I spilled a whole ladle full of gold!" Tim Hackett cried.

"And a good thing you did," Katherine said. She had grabbed the six-gun and now held it on Spur. "Tim, get on with it, finish plating the blanks. We must hurry now. Even though I think Spur McCoy is working alone."

Spur lay on the floor. He could see two quarter

inch holes in his pants over his thigh where he had been burned. More serious was his ankle. The whole thing seemed still to be burning.

"So at last you know," Katherine said, looking down at Spur.

"I've known for several days, I just couldn't prove it. Now I can."

"You'll have a hard time proving it from the bottom of the bay. Because very soon you will be feeding the fishes."

"Want me to blow his brains out right now, Kate?" Burke asked. He had drawn his .44 and glared at Spur.

"Not here, we can't make any more noise than necessary. Maybe in time with one of the press strikes, that would cover up the sound nicely."

The plating was done and they walked Spur over to the lanterns lighting the huge press. Tim arranged the dies again, checked his set-up and then put one of the gold plated blanks in the die and tripped it. The powerful die press came slamming down on the blank, compressing the metal and leaving ridges and lines to form a near-perfect likeness of the double eagle. Tim examined the first one and smiled.

"Wonder how the great Spur McCoy would feel if his hand happened to get under that press?" Burke asked with a snarl. "Use his hand instead of a gold blank?"

Tim shivered, shaking his head. "Mess up the die, have to clean it off."

"What the hell, be worth it!" Burke yelped. "Hell,

I'll clean it up. Come on, this sonofabitch has it coming!"

Katherine smiled. "Why not, pain for pain I always say. Move over there, McCoy. Let's see how you stand pain." She sent Tim out to find Hop Choy and bring him in to help hold Spur. The big Chinese roared with anger when he saw Spur. When Tim told him what they were going to do he grinned. He put his hand over the die and gurgled what could have been a laugh.

Spur was hoisted up, his ankle still a roaring, almost debilitating agony. Burke pushed him beside the big press and Katherine and Hop Choy held him there. The big press was up. Hop Choy grabbed Spur's hand and pulled it over the lower die until it centered on McCoy's palm.

Spur shook his head. He knew what was happening, but the shock and the pain of the burn had him woozy. He shook his head again, saw his hand over the die where the gold blank should be. Slowly he realized what they were going to do. No, it wasn't right! No! He forced his mind to concentrate. He had to do something. The damn wires seemed to be down to his arm. He screeched at them in his mind. Move! Move!

Tim Hackett gritted his teeth as he reached with both hands, touching the safety handle with one, then tripping the press trigger with the other hand. Spur saw the press start to descend. It moved slowly, hundreds of pounds of pressure smashing downward.

He roared and the sound came out this time. It

186

wasn't only in his head. He saw Hop Choy jolt with surprise. At the same time Spur lunged backwards, dragging his hand out from under the die. Hop Choy didn't let go. He held fast to Spur's fingers. Hop Choy's hand and wrist moved over the die. Just as his wrist was over the lower die, the upper one powered down with tremendous force.

Hop Choy screamed, but it came out only as a terrified gurgle as the tongueless Chinese tried to jerk his hand away. He moved it only a fraction of an inch before the top die powered into his soft flesh and bone. In a second it was all over. Hop Choy's wrist was vomiting blood. His hand dangled by threads left where the die had cut out a round hold through his skin, tissue, and bones.

Hop Choy bellowed his shock and horror. He swung his hand at Spur but Spur and Burke had tumbled to the floor when Hop Choy released him. The nearly severed hand broke free and sailed onto the floor in front of Katherine. She stared down at it.

The huge Chinese bellowed in terror and agony, his voice in full volume. His bloody stump grazed Burke's shoulder, then came back and hit Burke in the face, slamming him sideways to the floor. He came up with his six-gun.

"Stop it, you wild, crazy Chink!" Burke screamed. He waved the gun at the marauding giant, who batted it aside and swung his good fist at Hackett, battering him away from the press, knocking him six feet down the shop to the floor.

Hop Choy kept on screaming, swinging at anything that moved. Spur edged into the shadows. He saw Burke moving away too. Then Burke stood, lifted the six-gun and fired.

The round went wide of Hop Choy, but he turned toward the sound.

Spur crouched in the shadows, working silently, deeper into the blackness. His ankle burned with a thousand demons but he tried to ignore it. He had to move or die, it was that simple. When Burke killed the crazed Chinese, he would come after Spur. McCoy made it to the door and rushed outside, putting all his weight on his left ankle for the first time. It gave way and he sprawled in the dirt.

In the shop behind Spur, Burke screamed at Hop Choy.

"Stop it, Choy! You're hurt damn bad. Let us help you. We can stop the goddamned bleeding and you'll live. You keep charging around this way and you won't, because you'll bleed to death in five minutes."

The huge Chinese neither heard nor understood. He could only see those who had pained him. He ran for the cowering Tim Hackett. Burke shot Hop Choy in the leg. He fell sideways, got up, but by then Hackett had vanished out of the pool of light coming from the three coal oil lamps.

The Chinese roared his anger and turned on Katherine still staring at the severed hand lying at her feet. Hop Choy walked toward her, his good right hand balled in a fist the size of a chopping block. He swung it back watching Katherine. She didn't move. Her eyes were glazed with fear.

Just as Hop Choy began to swing his big fist, Burke shot him in the forehead. The heavy slug penetrated his brain but still the mountain of a man came forward. Burke shot him again, this time the slug entered his right eye, slanted upward and cut off the brain's nerve centers to Hop Choy's legs. His knees buckled and he sat down, still staring at Katherine, then his eyes closed and he fell backwards.

Outside Spur had raised himself at the shots. He surged toward the back fence, hopping on his right foot.

The two Mexican lookouts saw him and one jumped over the fence to help. They lifted Spur over and were just turning when Burke ran up screaming at Spur. One of the lookouts fired a shot that grazed Burke's arm and drove him to cover. The three men beyond the fence scurried into deeper shadows, mounted up and rode for town.

It was nearly three in the morning when the Mexican doctor in the Village finished working over Spur. Don Pico stood by and asked only one question.

"Did you get the evidence you need?"

Spur shook his head. The doctor had used gas on him making everything fuzzy.

"I have enough on the two I guess are still alive. But the girl is a problem. I didn't see her there often enough to positively identify her out of her disguise. It could have been any woman about her size dressed that way. I have to be positive. I will tell Nelson about the problem and have him fire his night watchman and put on two new men until this is settled."

"Gold!" the doctor said holding up a tray with the splatters of gold he had removed from Spur's flesh and off the pants where it cooled before it burned through.

"It's yours," Spur said. "Gold is still worth $20.67 an ounce." He sat up wobbled a little and one of the men held him.

He looked at the bandage around his ankle. With a pair of pants on no one would notice. Now if he could walk. He pushed off the table to his feet and fell to the floor.

They helped him up and using a heavy cane he tried walking to the door. He walked back, then to the door and back again. After making the trip ten times, he dropped the cane and walked out to Olivera Street.

Spur thanked Don Pico for helping him.

"It is nothing, Mr. McCoy. Because of your help we are going to have a real bank here in the Village for the first time. It will make my people feel more like Americans, less like foreigners."

Spur nodded. "Good. I hope it works out. And I hope you insist that everyone learns to speak English. For your people to get out of poverty, they must know the language."

Don Pico sighed into the night air. "*Si*, that is true, but it is also harder. But I will soon start a school for adults. I will make it known that every adult must know English. Yes?"

Spur was taken in a carriage to his hotel and

helped up to his room. He rolled onto the bed and slept. He woke up at five in the morning, stood and walked around his room, then walked the length of the corridor three times. Good, his ankle was responding. The burns were not as deep as he had feared. He slept again, woke up at noon and walked again. After a quick lunch, he returned to the alley behind the gray house. He wore a large Mexican straw *sombrero* and a red and white *serape*, over his shoulders. The sun was not as hot today. He had brought his saddle horse, tied a few yards behind him.

The next move was up to Katherine.

CHAPTER SIXTEEN

Inside the gray house Spur McCoy watched from the alley, there was a heated discussion in progress. Three people had been talking for almost an hour.

"I say we go ahead and do the job like we planned," Burke said. "So we had some problems last night. We got the Chink dumped in the bay and got the place cleaned up so they won't notice anything. Way I figure it we're done with our coin making anyway. We might as well try for a big pay day."

Katherine Sanford had mixed feelings about it. She listened as Tim Hackett shook his head.

"Hey, we were lucky last night. That damn Chinaman could have killed us all. I say it's an omen, we do our money division right here, right now, and I can get out of here and vanish for a few years. We know practically for sure that this McCoy is a federal man. Who else would spend so much time on a counterfeit case? I say we call it quits right now, divide and disappear. McCoy will be down on us like a ton of horseshoes if we make another try at anything."

Katherine stood and walked the length of the room.

"The trouble is that both of you are right. We should stop and we should cap it with one big haul. There is supposed to be fifty thousand in gold coins in that bank. And it sits out there like a lonesome chicken surrounded by foxes. Then there is McCoy. He knows damn sure what's going on now. But why would he watch a bank?"

She studied the two men. Only two left out of the four. It would work better with five guns.

"You both agree that majority rules? Whichever way it goes the other one will dig in and help get the work done." The men nodded. "Then I say we take the bank this afternoon, right now, as soon as we can get out there. We have the saddle horses from the livery. Check your weapons and let's get out there."

Burke grinned. "I knew you would figure it out right. We go separately and meet at the bank."

"Yes, and don't be late. When we all get there we go right in. The safe will be open. No guards. Like taking candy from a baby."

Tim shrugged. "Hell, I figured I was done with all of this. I don't like guns."

"Well, bucko, you'll hold one today, and you'll use it if you have to," Burke said. "Hey, Tim, relax. I'm just trying to make you into a rich man."

Burke and Tim had left their horses in front of the house. They went outside and rode off. Spur missed them but he did see Katherine as she left the back door. He heard the screen slam and he faded behind a box in the alley, peeked out and watched her mount up and ride out at the far end of the alley. She was on a bay saddle horse. He would have no trouble following her.

She never looked behind. It was either a mark of confidence or stupidity, Spur wasn't sure which. She moved north, to the far edge of town and stopped half a block from a small cluster of neighborhood stores. Shortly two riders came up and joined her and the three talked for a minute, then rode separately down the street and tied up their mounts near the door to the small bank. Spur recognized Burke and the little metal expert from the foundry.

Bank robbery? Spur wondered. They were not depositing anything. That was certain. Spur rode forward and tied his horse to the rail, then edged up and looked inside the bank. All three had masks over their faces and their guns out. It *was* a robbery.

Spur checked the protective cover in the street. A horse trough sat directly across from the bank, forty feet to the front door. He ran there and lay behind it, waiting.

A woman moving down the boardwalk in front of the stores, stared at him in surprise, then hurried on.

Four minutes later the three in the bank came out. Spur put a round into the bank door over their heads.

"Drop your weapons, you're covered by ten guns. You don't have a chance."

Katherine pushed Tim toward the sound of the voice and sprinted for her horse. Spur fired once. Tim screamed and fell off the boardwalk into the dust of the street.

Burke and Katherine mounted up and rode hard. Spur couldn't shoot because a dozen people crowded around. He ran for his own horse, mounted and told someone to sit on the shot man and go for the police. Then he rode after them.

Following the pair was no problem. They rode fast and went nearly a mile before they split up. He followed Burke, the cowboy with the fast gun.

Spur had barely noticed the weather, but now he realized the sun was not shining, and the air smelled heavy and damp. The clouds boiled above them and before Spur had a chance to catch up to Burke, lightning split the skies apart, thunder rolled in and crashed, and rain came down like it was the forty day flood. It was a thunder shower trying to become a cloudburst. Spur wheeled his mount under a thick tree and waited out the rain.

When it tapered off to a fine mist, Spur went on a muddy street that angled back toward the downtown area. They were still out where great open spaces lay exposed. No buildings or even streets had been installed. Yet nowhere did he see the figure of Burke on his sorrel. The white mane and tail made it stand out like a flagpole.

Spur turned and galloped back to the bank. San Francisco police were there. They had hauled the small man back inside the bank where he had been identified and questioned. He grinned at them, steadfastly maintaining that he had done the whole thing himself.

When Spur arrived Tim changed his tune and demanded to be taken to jail at once. The bank had lost nearly three thousand dollars in gold coins. None was recovered from Tim Hackett's saddlebags.

Spur knew he should step forward, identify himself and take the city police into his confidence about the counterfeiting. He decided to tell them later, fearing that they would blunder and ruin his case against Katherine. He had seen it happen before, not here by the bay, but in other towns.

By the time he rode back to his hotel in the gentle mist, he was completely wet through and his ankle was burning as though it was inside a blast furnace. He put his horse behind the hotel at the rack and stumbled when he got off. He had to test his ankle three times and work at it before he could walk up the steps and into the side door. Then he hobbled to his second floor room and sprawled on the bed.

He knew that it was time to send word to the police, but he didn't. His ankle would be better soon and he would move in and close up Katherine and her little coin factory.

His forehead felt warm and he realized he had a fever. No! He could not get sick, he had a damn case to finish.

Katherine was furious when she returned to the

small gray house. She tied up her horse, carried the bank sack with the double eagles inside and pulled the six-gun from her holster. If she could only have had a shot at him! It was McCoy again. How could he possibly have known that they were there or that they were going to rob the bank? He must have seen them on the street and followed them. Clearly he knew about her disguise.

She paced the floor, then took the coins and opened the floor vault. From it she scooped a hundred of the counterfeits and placed ten genuine eagles on top of the pile in the heavy leather sack. It was time she began depositing some of the coins in banks around town.

At once she changed her mind. Too risky. Surely the San Francisco banks had been alerted to the counterfeits. She had to get away, south to Los Angeles! Yes, it was a long trip, but they would not be suspicious there. She had enough real coins to front the others.

Katherine took all the coins out of the impromptu floor safe and distributed them among several large leather bags. She could load them one at a time in her buggy. Quickly she changed into her afternoon dress, hid the sacks of coins in the closet and hurried home. She took only a few things in a carpetbag, some spare clothes, a letter of introduction from a banker, and then slipped out of the house without seeing her parents. She drove her best buggy to the alley and quickly loaded the leather pouches into it. She put some on the floor, others under the seat cushions. She was not dressed for the trip.

Back inside the house she changed into her boy's costume, put her hair up and packed her other clothes in her carpetbag.

She took one quick look around and ran out to the buggy. She had done it! She was a rich woman by her own hand. And she would go to Los Angeles, deposit the money, spend a few days and then return. She would write for letters of credit to the Los Angeles banks and have the money transferred to her bank up here. It would take a month, perhaps, but well worth it. The only stumbling blocks she could see were Spur McCoy and Foster Burke. She had expected Burke back before now. Hopefully McCoy had caught him before the rain hit and solved one of her problems.

Spur still felt light-headed as he turned his saddle mount into the far end of the alley behind the gray house where Katherine had changed her clothes. He blinked when he saw a fuzzy buggy and horse in back of the place. He shook his head to clear it and saw Katherine run out of the house carrying a carpet bag. She was in her young man disguise. Spur sat quietly as she stepped into the rig and drove out the other end of the alley.

McCoy had no idea where she was heading. But he knew he had to follow her. She could be on the way to her house on the hill. No, his fuzzy brain was not thinking straight. She never went up there in her disguise. Running away?

Possibly. What about Burke? She was probably running out on him too, taking his share of the gold. That sounded like Katherine Sanford. Spur kicked the mount into motion. He had to follow her, had to stay with her. His ankle churned with pain. His shoulder wound had started bleeding again, and his fever was a notch higher. He was in great shape!

After a half hour, Spur realized that they were heading out of town. It was the same road they had taken when they went to the picnic. This time there would be no picnic. The sky had cleared. It was not yet three in the afternoon.

He was as prepared as he was capable of under the circumstances. He had the six-gun and two boxes of rounds. He also wished he had his repeating Spencer. He didn't think he would need it in the civilized environs of San Francisco.

They passed the last businesses, and as they did Spur saw a sorrel with white mane and tail being ridden toward the buggy. It was Burke. It had to be. He rode alongside Katherine's rig and Spur wished he could hear the conversation:

He could imagine it: *Of course I'm not running out on you. I knew we had to get the gold away from the house. McCoy must have known where it was. It was get it away or lose it. You still get your half, Burke.*

How the talk actually went, evidently Kate won. She stopped the rig, and Burke tied his mount on behind and stepped into the buggy. Good, Spur had them both together. He felt sure the gold was on board too. Where was she heading? There were few little towns between San Francisco and Los Angeles, nearly four hundred miles to the south. Santa Barbara? There would be a bank there. Perhaps.

Spur shook his head and grabbed the saddle horn. He had almost toppled off his horse. He pushed his eyes open wide and stopped at the side of the street, which was quickly turning into a muddy country road. He would have to stay farther back now or they would notice he was following. He couldn't permit that. He had to wait until the proper time, when he would have an advantage, when he couldn't lose and they had no chance of winning. Spur shook his head to clear it. He prayed that the perfect time came soon. He wasn't sure how much longer he could sit in the saddle.

CHAPTER SEVENTEEN

Spur McCoy discovered that the route from San Francisco to Los Angeles in 1871 was not a grand highway. It was a poor imitation of a road and in places it came down to a track of a trail running across ranches and around bluffs and through the low mountain passes of the coast range. Never was it simple and easy.

Spur also found out that there were few inns along the way catering to the traveler, simply because there were few travelers. The stage did run, but it made its normal stops.

Spur figured he was about two hours behind the pair in the buggy when he came to the first stage coach overnight stop. These were usually spotted at twenty mile intervals. If a ranch was not available with its buildings and water supply, the coach company built a small station, crude, minimal and practical. Spur came to one of these down the coast about eighteen miles from San Francisco.

He looked it over carefully from the protection of some trees and made certain that Katherine and Burke had not stopped there. He wondered why they hadn't since it was after seven P.M. and the sun was almost drowning in the Pacific Ocean.

For the last mile Spur had been holding tightly to the saddle horn, not sure if he could sit the saddle or not. Once he had almost fallen off and the horse had stopped until he pulled himself upright. His head was pounding, his arm was bleeding again and his ankle felt like the liquid gold had just been splashed onto it.

When he rode up to the rail outside the coach stop, a wrangler saw him coming and hurried out and led the horse. He helped Spur down and walked him inside. Spur sat down at a long bench with a table in front of it and promptly lowered his head on his folded arms.

Someone brought him a steaming mug of coffee. The manager poured a slug of whiskey into the coffee and helped Spur drink it. Right then Spur could think of nothing better than a bottle of whiskey and a cot where he could sleep. They fed him first, then gave him a glass of whiskey and helped him to a bed. A woman came, put a new bandage on his shoulder. She chattered away about having done the same thing during the big war, but Spur barely heard her. She placed his foot in a pail of cold water and it stopped hurting for the first time since he was burned. Later she put some salve on the ankle and wrapped it. Spur McCoy knew nothing else until morning.

Five miles down the road, Burke and Katherine moved off the trail into a small bluff overlooking the ocean and camped.

She had brought along a few essentials when she left the house, including some blankets and two cooking pots. She knew she couldn't stay at the inns and coach stops with Spur looking for her. She also carried some food, and before they passed the last bit of San Francisco, Burke had stopped at a store and bought some bread, beans and bacon, the three B's of any travel cook, he told her.

Burke was an efficient camper. Within an hour after they stopped he had a cooking fire going, a spot cleared for their blankets, and a small lean-to built over the blankets. He made the lean-to of branches and some boughs from a pine tree.

"All the comforts of home," Katherine said after they had eaten and cleaned up the cooking things.

"Almost all the comforts," Burke said. He leaned in and kissed her lips. She didn't respond but neither did she pull away. She was thinking. All along she knew that she had not fooled Burke about not running out on him. She had been watching for a good moment to eliminate him, and she had the chilling idea that he would kill her at the first opportunity. Yes, the idea built. She could get him worn out with sex play and when he slept afterward she would shoot him. The idea was horrifying but there was no other way.

She returned his kiss, surprising him.

"There's no reason we can't be friends, Foss," she said softly, working a hand inside his shirt, rubbing his thick mat of chest hair, working down toward his crotch.

"I've always said we make a good team, Kate. I've got the know-how, and you have the contacts. We can take that town back there for plenty, then move on." He kissed her again, then put one hand over her right breast and rubbed softly.

"Foss, that feels so good! You know how to get me excited so quickly. Foss, why don't we seal our partnership right here by making love five or six times!"

"Yeah! Great idea. We will make a good team. You fuck so fine and you *like* it. A lot of women don't. Yeah, you and me, Kate, just you and me!"

She opened her shirt and pulled both his hands to her breasts. She knew she had him. He believed her about the partnership. So he wouldn't be trying to kill her. She could take her time, enjoy him once more for most of the night and it would be the last night Foss Burke ever knew.

She moaned in appreciation as he fondled her breasts.

"Damn, but you've got big tits, Kate, so big and beautiful, God! What a perfect set of tits!" He went down on them, kissing them and sucking them. She responded quickly and she didn't have to pretend. Any man could get her motor running, but she remembered the times with Spur and she knew he had touched her, and excited her more than any man ever had.

She pretended she was with Spur as Burke chewed on her breasts until she yelped with pleasure/pain. She pushed him away and stripped off the shirt. She wiggled out of the trousers and her cut-off drawers and sat on the blanket naked and passionate wanting to make love.

She helped him pull off his clothes, then turned on her back and put her legs high in the air.

"Right now, Foss darling, fuck me right now!"

Foss moved over her, not quite believing his good luck. All that gold and a good fucking woman like Kate! He kissed her flattened breasts and then probed and jammed and pushed into her with one hard stroke that brought a scream and then tears of joy from her as she yelled and shouted telling him he was the best man she'd ever had.

Foss had caught up with Katherine as she was riding out of town. He had gone to the gray house, saw that the gold was gone and wondered what she would do. He figured the banks wouldn't accept any counterfeits now, and the only thing she could do with them was to travel. For Kate that meant going south. He had gone down one street and missed her, doubled back and found her on the third main street out of town.

Now he was a little unsure. At first when he saw that she had gone he swore he would kill her. At the first chance he would fuck her and then kill her. But now with her new attitude, it might be different. He would go slow. He might give her a few days down the road. If he could get taken care of this well every night, goddamn, yes, he would give her a few more days.

Vaguely he realized that Katherine couldn't change her leopard's spots so quickly. Maybe she just wanted him to help her along the flight to Los Angeles.

Burke rammed her again and again, watching her smile and scream as she found her own climax four times before he was even ready. She was young. Hell she was rich too and she fucked. What more could a man want?

She locked her legs over his back and lifted her hips off the ground to meet his thrusts and within fifteen seconds he was blasting his load into her, grunting and yelping at the intensity of his climax.

Later they lay side by side on the blanket. The moon was out now and the clouds had all blown away.

"That was marvelous, Foss. Just wonderful. You're the best fuck I've ever had. The very best!"

"Kate, you're the most passionate woman I've fucked. You get so damned excited, you climax so quickly and you just keep going. I think this partnership is going to work in and out of bed."

"You bet it is, Foss. You bet! And we'll work at keeping it good. It won't go stale. Way I figure it is the way I told you. We take all the coins to Los Angeles and I'll use the letter of introduction from my banker, and we'll open an account in several banks. We'll put a bag of coins with some of our real ones on top. Let them check the top and they will be solid. We get it all deposited, then we go back to San Francisco, and we get the balances transferred up there. But the counterfeits stay in Los Angeles and they won't know where they came from."

"Fine, good thinking. We won't have to worry about robbing the stage coach anymore." He caught her breasts and rubbed them. She rolled over on top of him.

"Once more with me on top. I kind of like it up here. I can ride you like a pony, bucking and jumping and fucking away like crazy."

Foss laughed. "You are wild, a crazy, wild, best fucking woman in the world. Ride away, I'm ready." The idea of having to shoot the woman slid further and further from his mind as Foss reveled in the moment.

Katherine half lay and half sat on top of him, riding him like a pony, giving him satisfaction as well as enjoying it herself. A fleeting thought that she might need him down the road flashed through her mind, but she could find a guide at one of the coach stops if necessary. She could always put the gold in her big carpet bag and take the next stage south. This far from town it would be perfectly safe. Yes, it was sounding better all the time.

About two more fucks and Foss Burke would be so worn out he would sleep like a dead mule. *Planning, you have to plan all the time,* she told herself.

Later, she guessed it was a little after midnight, Katherine was still wide awake. Burke slept with one hand cupping her right breast. He snored softly, his naked form beside her on the blanket in the soft September night. She moved his hand. He mumbled but didn't awaken. His other hand cupped his genitals.

Kate eased away from him and crawled to the bottom of the blanket where they had left their clothes and their six-guns. She made sure his was there, took it and lay it in the buggy seat, then came back and checked the loads in her .32 caliber six-gun. All were there. She wondered how many she would need.

She had never killed anyone before. A sudden shiver of anticipation drilled through her. It was surprisingly like a climax! Her hand went to her crotch and she stroked her clit twice and felt the sensations building. Yes, why not? A first! She kept stroking her clit and knelt across the blanket from him. He had been a good fuck, and now he would give her the ultimate sexual thrill—a death climax!

Her body responded faster. She pushed the magic node again and again. It came, that surging rapture, that ecstasy of boiling sexual triumph.

She aimed and pulled the trigger. The round missed Burke's heart, tore through a lung and severed several large arteries.

Her climax surged and she screamed in delight as Foss tried to sit up.

"Bastard!" he shouted. "Fucking, murderous bastard!"

Her climax built higher and she shot him again, then again and again. Each of the five times she shot Foster Burke her climax seemed to escalate into wild peaks of rapture. When the gun clicked on the empty round, she fell on the blanket so exhausted she couldn't move. For a half hour she lay there trying to recover.

Then she reloaded the little gun and worked herself up and did it all again, shooting him, climaxing, driving her passion into peaks of pleasure.

When the gun emptied and the last crashing climax left her, she lay down beside Burke's body and went to sleep.

Katherine was up early the next morning, flipped the blanket over Burke to avoid seeing him and put her gear in the buggy. She intended to drive to the next coach stop down the road, sell the buggy and horse and take the first coach south to Los Angeles.

So far her scheme was on schedule and progressing nicely. She presumed that she had eluded Spur McCoy or he would be on her trail by now. She smiled grimly. If he did find her, she would give him the same treatment that she had given Burke.

She shook her head in amazement. She still couldn't believe the fantastic heights to which she had risen when she worked her special magic on Burke.

Would it happen again? Could she make the same thrill occur with just any man? What about pulling the trigger when the man was inside her, fucking her?

Yes, there were new worlds to conquer. She would

make the experiment just as soon as she could. Perhaps at the coach stop if she had to wait over a night. She could even lure a stranger into the woods, experiment and be gone the next morning before anyone knew the man was missing.

And Spur McCoy. Yes! She almost hoped that he would find her. She would take triple pleasure in testing her new passion on him when his big cock was deep inside her!

CHAPTER EIGHTEEN

When Spur woke up the next morning, it was after eight. The morning stage had come in and driven on through to San Francisco. He sat up in his bed in the common room and saw that none of the other bunks was occupied. His head spun and whirled. He had to reach down to steady himself.

Better? Yes. He touched his forehead. The slight fever was gone. Even his ankle felt better this morning, but he wasn't going to enter any foot races.

His shoulder was stiff but at least it was not leaking blood. He was not sure about last night. He remembered that he ate some food and had some whiskey and the woman had fixed his shoulder. She made his ankle feel fetter.

Spur swung his feet to the floor and overcame the whirl of dizziness. Standing up was difficult, but once up he walked back and forth in the room until he was sure of himself. He adjusted his clothes, the old brown suit, and checked his six-gun. It was there and loaded.

The proprietor was surprised when Spur walked out to the main depot room a few minutes later.

"Thought you was out for a couple of days there, friend," the big man said as he eyed Spur.

"I'm feeling much better. What do I owe you for the night's lodging and nursing care?"

"Quarter should do it." He stopped. Curious. "You going to be moving on south? It's twenty miles on to the Gonzales Ranch."

"Heading that way. Did you see a buggy go past here yesterday? Pretty, long-haired woman and a man in it, trailing a sorrel with white mane?"

"Yep. Rode right on past. Figured they might stop for the night, but evident they were going to camp out."

"Thanks. I best get moving."

"Not before breakfast. Been saving some flapjacks and a pound of sausages for you. And coffee. Hate to see you leave in your condition. You a lawman?"

Spur didn't reply, just dug into the food when it appeared in front of him. The woman who brought it was short, round and happy. She smiled at him and he remembered her face from the night before. He still had the bandages around his ankle she put there.

"Before you try to sneak out of here, you let me look at that shot-up shoulder and your burned ankle. I'd be right down angry if you didn't let me play nurse one more time."

He nodded and she went back to the kitchen.

"Figured you had to be a lawman, otherwise any sensible man would be in bed getting himself well. But that ain't my row of corn to hoe. Just enjoy the victuals."

Spur ate until he could hold no more. There were four eggs on the side and a pitcher of maple syrup and a big cup of coffee the woman kept filling.

"Like to see a man eat," she said.

Spur thanked her. She checked his bandages and told him to get to a doctor for the shoulder as soon as he could.

"Course, I know you're heading away from the doctoring, but I got to tell you anyways."

The stable man had to help Spur mount his horse. He noticed that it had been brushed down, watered and given some oats to eat.

He gave the stable hand a silver dollar, paid the proprietor, and rode south down the trail.

There had been little traffic since the rainstorm. He saw the stage tracks and to one side the thin wheels of a buggy and one horse. Several times he lost them, the stage tracks were over them, which meant that the stage had traveled the road after the buggy had driven through.

Three more miles down the road, he saw the opposite was true. The buggy tracks were over the wide stage coach wheel marks. Which meant the buggy had been off the road for some time, probably all night, then moved out again in the morning. Spur was not far behind them.

The food and the kindly ministrations were all helping Spur to feel better. He brought the horse to a canter for a quarter of a mile, then eased her back. The jolting made him hurt all over. At least his head was clear.

He had to catch Katherine and bring her back for trial. He was sure she had the bank robbery gold and the counterfeit coins, otherwise Burke would not have gone with her. He could look forward to a double job as soon as he caught them.

Every half hour he put the horse in a trot and kept at it for as long as he could stand the jolting. He hoped he was gaining on them.

Just before noon the trail wound around a hill and came out near the coast where it crossed a small stream. A flash flood had washed out the temporary bridge made of logs and laid end ways in the stream. The water was not more than a foot deep now. Ahead he could see that a buggy had tried to cross it. The stage coach probably crossed as well, but the fording was not as kind to the narrow wheels of the buggy. The rear wheels were sunk in the mud up to the axle.

Spur turned into the trees and watched the rig. For ten minutes nothing moved. Then he saw a small figure get out of the buggy and step gingerly into the water. There was no mistaking the carriage or the stance. It was Katherine. Where was Burke? Spur noticed that the sorrel was no longer tied to the back of the carriage. Had Burke gone ahead for help?

No, help was closer to the rear. The second horse

would have been enough to pull the buggy out of the mud. Spur had a chilling thought. Burke was not helping get the buggy out because he was no longer with Katherine. Spur guessed the fast gun had met a faster gun and was probably at the overnight camp the couple must have made.

He rode through the woods, circling around so he could come up to the buggy in the cover and not be seen. Brush and live oak came to within twenty yards of the stalled rig.

Spur McCoy left his horse tied to a tree and went the last twenty yards on foot. When he looked around the oak tree closest to the buggy, he saw Katherine Sanford facing the buggy and screaming at the horse. She tugged at the bridle urging the horse forward, but the horse could not pull it out. She raged and swore at the horse. Finally she took out her pistol and aimed at the animal's head and fired. At the last moment she had lifted her aim over the head to miss. The horse shied away as far as the traces would let it and lunged forward, but still the rig was mired.

She shoved the gun back in the holster and began to unhitch the animal from the buggy. It was immediately obvious that she did not know what she was doing.

Spur stopped her with a pistol shot over her head.

"Morning, Katherine Sanford. Don't move, that first shot was a warning. The next will cut your pretty little legs right out from under you."

She glared his way.

"Don't just stand there, stupid. Come help me get

this rig out of the mud."

"First, some talk. One: You are now under arrest for counterfeiting U.S. gold coins. Two: You are under arrest for bank robbery. Three: You are under arrest for the murder of an accomplice in said bank robbery, one Foster Burke. Four: You are now to take the six-gun from your holster and drop it in the stream, then lace your hands on top of your head. Do you understand all these directions?"

She drew the gun slowly, then fired the last four shots in the direction of his voice. She didn't move. When the gun was dry she tossed it in the creek, and put her hands on her head.

"It's safe to come out now, Spur McCoy, you big bad United States Government agent."

Spur walked out, his gun back in the holster.

"I should have shot you when I had the chance," she said.

"The same way you shot Foster Burke?"

"No, not that way, something different, more interesting."

Spur came up and stood in front of her.

"I'm going to check to see if you have any other weapons. Don't move or I'll knock you down." Spur patted her down along shapely legs, around her waist, up to her breasts. She had no other weapons.

"Now what?" she asked.

"Now we get you unstuck and we drive back to the San Francisco police who take you into custody on three charges."

"Nobody will believe it."

"All we need are twelve good and true men to

believe it, and you'll be in prison for the rest of your life."

"It's a long way back to San Francisco."

"Will you stay here while I go get my horse, or do I have to tie you up?"

She glared at him, then noticed his limp.

"That foot Tim splashed with molten gold hurt you a little? And I see your shoulder is still bleeding. Too bad. I'll stay. It's a lot of miles to San Francisco."

Spur brought up his horse, tied it to the frame of the buggy, and with one surge the two horses pulled the rig up to dry land.

Spur got on his horse and they towed the buggy back across the ford with no trouble. He made Katherine walk across in her boots and pants, then told her to sit down on the grass while he inspected the buggy.

He found the gold, and a .44 six-gun.

"Burke's?" Spur asked.

"It was. He gave it to me."

Spur found nothing else dangerous on board, so let her get in and tied his mount to the rear. Spur took the reins.

A half hour later she spoke for the first time.

"You better stop, I have to go to the bathroom."

Spur looked at her with suspicion, shrugged and stopped the rig. He went with her to the side of the road where she let down her pants and squatted.

"You could hold my hand and squeeze," she said.

"You won't get any hand holding in prison."

He heard his horse snort and looked at the rig,

and when he glanced back she stood up, kicked off the pants and was unbuttoning her shirt.

"That won't work, Katherine. I'll take you right through to San Francisco naked as a new born if you want it that way."

She threw the shirt down and ran to him, pushing her body against his and talking fast.

"Spur, once more! Think how long it's going to be until I have a man again. Come on, Spur, fuck me just once more here in the open while I'm still free. Just one more good one!"

Spur pushed her down and she fell on the grass at his feet.

"Is that how you caught Burke off guard, with his pants off, maybe even inside you?"

"Burke was going to kill me, I just beat him to it."

"It won't work here, forget it. Do you want to dress again, or ride on into town that way?"

Before she could answer a rifle spoke nearby and the lead whistled past so close to Spur's nose that he could smell the heat. He dropped down, but had nothing to hide behind.

The voice that came from the brush was southern-mean. Spur reached for his six-gun.

"Your hand touches that iron, you get a .50 caliber slug right in your belly. You want that, friend?"

Spur moved his hand away from his gun.

"Now that's good. You, pretty baby, stand up and turn around slow, want to get me a good look at all them tits and cunt."

"Well, sure. This guy was attacking me. You

220

came just in time. I can be nice to you, would you like that? Right here, right now!"

She turned around twice, then stood watching the woods.

A man emerged with his rifle covering them. Spur frowned, rawhiders, and there would be more than one. Probably renegades left over from the war, living off the land, robbing and killing anyone they ran across, living in the hills and woods, moving all the time. To them human life was no more important than that of a rabbit, a dog or a mosquito.

The man was thin and tall, clad in dirty jeans and a ragged shirt too large for him. His beard was greasy, his hair matted under a filthy black hat. Small dark eyes showed from a smoke and dirt stained face. His fingernails were dirty and ragged, his teeth half black stumps.

He turned Katherine around again, then rubbed her breasts.

"Damn good tits, little whore." He turned and called toward the buggy.

"Come on in, Sacks, I got'm by the tits." He laughed and kicked Spur in the leg. "You got any cash money, boy?"

"Yes."

"Get it out, slow. And lay that six-gun over there on the grass."

Spur did, putting his wallet beside it. He looked up to see a small woman dressed in the same kind of ragged clothes, just as filthy as the man.

"Leave her tits alone, you bastard!" the woman

shrilled.

"Lilly Mae, ain't them something. Look at all them tits! Christ, she got twenty times the knockers you got."

"Shut up, stupid. She'd sooner shoot you as fuck you. Now you gonna do it, or should I?" Spur saw that she carried a sawed-off shotgun. The barrel was not over eight inches long.

"Now wait a minute," the man argued. "She offered, Lilly Mae, before I said a dang thing. She offered!"

"That's right," Katherine said. "I'll go down on you right now, you open your jeans. And I'll fuck you twice a day. You'll have these good tits all to yourself. Shoot the old hag there and take me with you. Shoot both of them!"

The rawhider grinned at his woman. "Damn, Lilly Mae, she's like us. God, what I'd give to fuck her just once. Lilly Mae, you put down the shotgun and look through the buggy. You come back and it'll all be over, then we finish our business and move on. Remember that redhead last week? He was your turn. This one is my turn, then it'll be even again."

"Shit, what a bastard you are," Lilly Mae said. She shrugged and lay down the shotgun. "Hell, make it fast, I don't like being this close to no highway." She walked back toward the trail.

At once the man opened his pants and his hard penis shot out. Katherine hesitated only a fraction of a second, then she opened her mouth and knelt in front of him and went down. The man moaned in delight, the rifle lowering. Spur eyed his six-gun forgotten three feet from him. The shotgun was ten feet away. But his own pistol was a chance.

Spur lay where he was, watching the rawhider. He was getting excited. Suddenly the rawhider pushed her away.

"Get on your hands and knees," he said. He leered at Spur, and laughed. "Damn, dog fashion fuck!"

Katherine went to her hands and knees quickly. She was sideways to Spur now. The man still held the rifle in his right hand near Spur as he knelt behind Katherine trying to make the right connection. When he was inside he yelped with delight and howled like a dog, his head high, his eyes closed.

Spur dove toward the gun, rolled in the grass on his shot-up shoulder, caught up the weapon and fired three times. The first round missed, the second took a half inch off the rawhider's nose, and the third went in just behind his ear, roared through his brain and came out over his eyes. The force of the slug knocked him to the left away from Katherine who dropped to the grass on her stomach.

A scream of fury sounded near the buggy, then Lilly Mae came running toward them firing a six-gun.

"No, no, not me!" Katherine shouted. "I want to go with you. He killed your man, Spur shot him!" Katherine sat up as she said it. Lilly Mae was twenty yards away, and Spur had held his fire. He still had two rounds and couldn't waste them. He looked at the shotgun, still six feet away. It was double barreled.

Lilly Mae screamed again and ran toward them,

firing again. Now Spur saw she had two six-guns. Spur fired a warning shot, then she fired twice more.

One of the rounds caught Katherine in the chest, staggering her. She slumped to the left. Now she was waving her hands, pointing to Spur. Lilly Mae shot twice more and both rounds caught Katherine Sanford in the face, one tearing upward into her brain, destroying vital nerve centers and slamming her backward into the long sleep of death.

Spur fired his last round at Lilly Mae, missed and rolled toward the shotgun. He came up with it as the woman was frantically reloading one of the six-guns.

"Put it down, Lilly Mae," Spur said. "Drop it now."

"Fucking shotgun ain't loaded," she screamed.

Spur snapped in the last round and brought up the gun.

Spur fired. The buckshot caught her in the stomach and almost tore her in half. She jolted backwards and screamed a last threat but gurgles of blood were all that came out.

Spur ran back to Katherine. She was dead the moment the bullet struck. The other two were gone as well. He had no shovel. He picked up Katherine and took her back to the buggy. There he dressed her in her pants and shirt and sat her in the seat. Then he collected the shotgun and two handguns and the rifle, and drove slowly back to the stage coach inn where he had spent the previous night.

They would be surprised to see him. He would hire one of the men to come back and bury the two. Katherine he would take on into town. He should be able to get there well before midnight. There would be a lot of explaining to do, and he would have to identify himself again. He looked at Katherine and shook his head. For a girl with all the advantages, she had taken the wrong road. She had been willing to go with the rawhiders, to kill the other woman and become the man's new woman, to become a rawhider herself, just so she could stay out of jail.

Spur urged the horse on faster. He had a corpse, and what he guessed was about sixty thousand dollars in counterfeit gold double eagles.

He had to deliver them tonight.

CHAPTER NINETEEN

Spur tied up the horse in front of the San Francisco police station just before 10 P.M. and called a passing officer to bring out the captain in charge.

"I've got a dead body here I want to talk to him about," Spur said and the man ran inside quickly.

Spur wasn't sure how long he could stand on his ankle. It was throbbing again. The watch captain came out quickly, his name was Streib. Three officers stood behind him.

"Is this a joke, sir. You have a corpse out here?"

Spur motioned at the figure in the buggy and the captain investigated quickly.

"Call the undertaker or the mortician or whoever handles that sort of thing. Then notify her father. The lady is Katherine Sanford, daughter of Amos Sanford."

"You're joking," Captain Streib said.

"I'm not joking. My name is Spur McCoy and I am a United States Service agent. I'll show you my credentials later. Right now there is forty or fifty thousand dollars worth of gold double eagles on this buggy. I want some lock boxes I can transfer it to until I can go over it and separate the real ones from the counterfeit."

"You must be drunk!"

"Captain Streib, am I going to have to call your police chief from his home? Just do what I ask you. Katherine Sanford is the counterfeiter. She also robbed the Thirtieth Street bank yesterday. Now bring out those lock boxes and send someone to take the body."

It was a half hour before the undertaker came. Amos Sanford stormed up at about the same time. He was a short man, slender and wiry. He carried a silver headed walking cane he liked to wave around. He stood in front of Spur as the undertaker's buggy rolled away. Tears showed in his eyes.

"Sir! I demand some explanation! How did my daughter die? Did you shoot her? Why did it happen?"

Spur quietly told him the story, what she had been doing, and how the rawhiders killed her.

"I don't believe any of it!" Amos Sanford said through clenched teeth. "I'll have you charged with murder before daylight. I have some powers in this town. The chief of police is a good friend of mine."

Spur's kind attitude changed. "Good, because

when it comes out in the papers what Katherine did, the people she killed and had killed, the counterfeiting and the bank robbery, you are going to need all the friends you have. Besides, the Secret Service functions directly for the President of the United States, and *he* happens to be a good friend of mine."

Spur walked over to the buggy and supervised the loading of the gold coins in the two lock boxes. He searched the rig three times, and when he was certain all the coins were in them, he snapped the padlocks on the hasps and took the keys.

It was almost midnight.

Spur went inside the station, saw that two locked boxes were placed in the police safe and the door shut, then he turned to Captain Streib. He took the thin card from between two others in his wallet and showed it to the policeman.

"If you need further proof, send a wire to William Wood, Director, the Secret Service, Washington, D.C. He will confirm my authority and description."

Captain Streib read the card and handed it back.

"No, Mr. McCoy, that won't be required. You just gave me a start hauling a corpse right up to my door, and a buggy with fifty thousand dollars in it."

"Sorry, it just turned out that way. Do you have a doctor on call? I have a bad ankle that needs attention."

A half hour later Spur sat in a small medical office two blocks from the police station. A bear of a man worked over the ankle, shaking his head.

"Infection. I just hope we can stop it in time so you don't lose the foot. Looks bad." He applied some medication and told Spur to stay off the foot for a week at least.

"The shoulder is healing. Would do better if you stop breaking it open. May bleed a little more, but it's coming along well. You tend to get yourself hurt a lot, don't you, Mr. McCoy."

"Seems as how, Doc."

Spur found a police rig waiting for him outside the doctor's office to take him to his hotel. He fell into bed and slept at once.

At 8 A.M. the next morning a knock on his door awakened Spur. There were two reporters from the newspapers. He told them to come back in two hours.

His ankle was swelled half again its size. He sent notes to J. Anderson Dumbarton and Juan Pico, explaining his injury and asking if they could meet him in his room at eleven o'clock. Then he went back to sleep.

Spur was up and wearing a clean shirt and his foot rested on a pillow when the two men arrived.

"We heard the news," Dumbarton said, a big grin on his face. "Amazing. It was that pretty little Katherine Sanford behind the whole thing. Remarkable."

Juan Pico smiled. "And this should stop the flood of counterfeit coins, right?"

Spur told them what had happened. "We should have most of the counterfeits. In cases like this there are always a few floating around that haven't been found yet. What I suggest is that Mr. Dumbarton wait a reasonable time and then talk to Amos Sanford. Tally up all the losses on the counterfeits by everyone, you, Don Pico, other banks, and build in a contingency for those not found. Show Sanford the figure. He may simply write a check for the amount. If not you might suggest that the cash come from Miss Sanford's property. She owns that gray house we mentioned. If this doesn't work, you may have to threaten a civil suit to recover damages, but I don't think Mr. Sanford would let it go that far."

Don Pico, nodded. "This all seems fair and proper, Mr. McCoy. My people thank you. More than two dozen small shop owners thank you for saving their stores. To show our appreciation we are holding a *fiesta* tonight in Olivera Street. Everyone is invited. There will be music and dancing and more food than anyone can eat.

"Mr. Dumbarton has promised to come. We are making good progress on talks about the new Olivera Street Bank."

Dumbarton agreed. He looked around the room. "I've made some other arrangements. There will be a nurse coming in at noon with your lunch. She will be on duty here twenty-four hours a day until you can get around. The doctor said to stay off the foot, right? She'll be in the room next door, but we'll have a hole cut in the wall and a string put through so you can ring a bell whenever you want her."

"There's no need for that . . ." Spur began. Both men looked at him sternly. "All right, thank you," he said meekly.

"There will be a buggy at the door for you and your nurse at six tonight, so you can come to the fiesta," Don Pico said.

The men started for the door. Dumbarton turned.

"McCoy, just relax, rest and get well. We might need you again out here. We want you to think well of San Francisco."

As they went out a bell boy came in with two telegrams. One was from General Halleck, his immediate superior in Washington. It read:

"Good work re counterfeiting stop Hurry and get well stop have two more assignments waiting stop Halleck."

"Figures," Spur mumbled, moving his foot on the cushion. And knowing Halleck his next job probably would be somewhere in the Texas desert or the wilds of Montana.

The second wire was from Fleurette Leon, his assistant in the St. Louis office, and cute as a fluffy kitten. He read the message:

"Hear you've done it again stop Go easy on that hurt ankle stop Please don't get shot anymore stop We need you stop Hurry home stop All my love stop Fluerette."

Spur put down the wires and smiled. It was nice to be appreciated by someone, even if she was a slip of a girl half a continent away.

The knock on the door came softly. He called for the person to come in.

Spur McCoy stared. She was tall and slender, with wheat straw colored hair billowing around her face and shoulders. Soft blue eyes twinkled at him over a pug nose and dimples dented her cheeks. She was so pretty, and her smile so radiant that he kept staring.

She laughed softly, and the animation in her face was delightful.

"Mr. McCoy?"

"Ah . . . yes. Yes."

"Oh, good, at first I thought I had the wrong room. I have your lunch. I'm your nurse."

Spur shook his head. "Tell me I'm not asleep and dreaming. This must be a dream. You are absolutely gorgeous! You're the most beautiful woman I've ever seen."

She smiled and he knew she had heard compliments before.

"Well, aren't you nice! But remember, the doctor said you were not to get excited or walk around. Our job is to get you well."

"I may stay sick for six months," Spur said and she laughed softly.

"They said you were a perfect gentleman. Are you really from New York, and Washington, D.C.? Have you really met President Grant?" Her soft blue eyes were wide with wonder.

"Yes, to all three. I just remembered. I didn't have any breakfast. Did you really bring me lunch?"

"Oh, gracious! I almost forgot." She went into the hall and rolled in a small cart with a covered tray on it. She closed the door, then looked at him quickly.

"Is it all right to close it?"

"Fine with me. After all, you're the nurse."

"I wanted to ask." She uncovered the tray, showing him two kinds of sandwiches, a bowl of ranch stew, two desserts, a glass of milk and a pot of coffee.

"We want to be sure you eat to keep up your strength."

"I'll try. You have to eat with me."

"Oh!" She shrugged. "All right."

He ate and she nibbled on a sandwich. He caught the scent of her long blonde hair as it came close to him. She wore a blue dress that swept the floor and buttoned to her neck. It was molded to her body and showed good breasts and a small waist.

When the lunch was over, she cleared the tray and rolled it outside the door, then came back. She adjusted the pillows around his head and his foot and checked the bandages.

"Your foot is fine. The doctor will come tomorrow to check it. You are a most important man in town. Mr. Dumbarton says we have to take care of you in every way. Now, let's look at your shoulder. Off with the shirt." She unbuttoned it for him, and helped him out of it.

When her fingers touched his shoulder to check the bandages he felt a tingle. The cloth showed no bloodstains.

"There, that is fine, too." She stood and smiled. "Now I think you should have a nap."

"I should get at least one kiss good night," Spur said.

She sat on the bed beside him.

"That's not usual nursing procedure."

"But you are not the usual nurse. You are a beautiful, wonderful, marvelous, highly desirable nurse."

"Oh, thank you! And you are as nice as they said. Maybe just one small goodnight kiss."

She leaned down and kissed his cheek, but lingered. He took her face in his hands and brought her lips to his. She didn't protest. Spur kissed her tenderly, then with more force, and brushed her lips with his tongue.

She leaned away and he gave up her lips. She didn't move far.

"Now, that was nice, Mr. McCoy. But, gracious, you aren't asleep yet. Do you need one more?" He nodded. She bent down to him gently, then touched his hair with her hand and this time her tongue brushed his lips. He opened them, then his tongue darted through into her mouth. The game began of search and find, touch and retreat and her tongue played along.

She pulled away gently. "I don't think you're going to sleep."

"I could sleep much better if the door were locked and the key turned half around in the lock," Spur said.

She grinned, kissed him gently and stood. "Mr. McCoy that was not in any of the nursing training I took. However, I think it might be good therapy."

"I don't know your name," Spur said.

She locked the door as he asked, then came back. "I'm Millicent, Millicent Young. Call me Milli." She sat on the bed beside him.

"Now for that therapy," Spur said. She bent down and kissed his nose, then his cheeks, and then his mouth. Her lips came to his softly and parted. She moaned in delight as his tongue penetrated her mouth. She stretched down until she was lying beside him, half on top of his good side. She purred.

When the long kiss ended she sat up and unbuttoned three of the fasteners down the front of her dress.

"It's warm in here," she said.

Spur agreed and motioned for her to bend lower. He finished undoing the buttons to her waist. She bent down and he worked his hand under the chemise and captured one of her hanging breasts.

"Oh, dear!" she said, gasping slightly. "That is so, so delightful!"

Spur sat up beside her, pushed the dress off her shoulders and spread kisses across her chest above the white chemise. Then he pushed the chemise straps down and moved it lower until one pink-tipped breast showed.

"You really shouldn't," she said softly.

"I know," Spur said and bent and kissed the breast. Milli sighed softly. He licked the throbbing breast and watched her nipple enlarge and stiffen. A moment later he worked on her other breast. He found her hand and moved it down to his crotch and helped her unfasten the buttons on his fly.

"Milli, I think this is going to be a slow but fantastically successful recuperation. I'm going to need a week at least to get well enough to travel, maybe two weeks."

236

"Spur McCoy, I'll certainly do everything possible to make your recovery just as pleasant and memorable as I can."

"I was hoping you would," Spur said and kissed her pulsating breast again.

BOISE BELLE

CHAPTER ONE

Silas Mander wouldn't take no for an answer.

"Come on! Show me your piece! Bet it won't stand up to this little baby!" The mustachioed gunman twirled his gold-plated Dragoon revolver as the stagecoach creaked along a rutted track. Dust laden sunlight shone on its walnut handle.

Sitting across from him, Spur McCoy sighed. "Don't you believe in getting the latest? The relic must date back to 1848."

"It do," the balding man said, nodding. "I just keep what's worked for me. Now you gonna show me your pea shooter or am I gonna have to—"

"Have to what?" Spur sighed. "Here." He unholstered his weapon and handed it to the man.

Silas took it and guffawed. "Hell, an old Navy revolver? This thing couldn't hit a—a—holy shit!" He stared down at it. "I'll be damned!"

"What's wrong now?" Spur tried to make more room for himself on the seat. The two men on both sides of him seemed to be taking up more than their fair share.

"What's wrong? What's wrong?" Silas thundered. "I'll tell you what's wrong! That's mine! That's my old piece! Lost it to a sonofabitch thief on the trail outside Phoenix last year. And you're him!" His nostrils flared.

"No." Spur clamped his hands on the man's.

"Nothin' doin'! That's my revolver! I oughta kill you right here and now, you thieving bastard!"

McCoy pried his revolver from the man's grip. "You're wrong, Mander. I've had this for four years. Picked it up in St. Louis. Griswold's Firearms, if I remember the name right. Have a bill of sale in my bags."

"Like hell!"

"Rein it in, Silas," the man to his right said. "You're keeping me awake!"

His face beet red, Mander made a fist. McCoy rocked left when Silas drove it into the stagecoach wall. As the wood splintered and the big man howled, Spur calmly holstered his revolver.

"You've got some kind of nerve, Silas. One revolver looks like any other," Spur said.

"Not that one!" Mander massaged his hand and sat back on the seat. "It had a snaky picture in the grain on the handle. I swear that's mine!"

"You heard him," the passenger beside Mander said.

"No!" Mander grabbed his Dragoon. "Now we'll see whose it is!" He levelled it at Spur's chest.

"Jesus! You could shoot someone with that thing!"

"Yeah, Reinhart. Him! I'll plug that thievin' bastard!"

Spur shook his head. "Use it or holster it!" he shouted.

Silas stared at Spur, sweating, his upper lip curling under his black mustache. He hesitated.

"Go ahead! Just kill me and take it!" McCoy's voice was harsh. "But remember this day when you feel the rope tighten around your scrawny neck and squeeze the breath outta you! Remember how your stupidity cost you your worthless life!"

Mander eased off on his aim. "Well, well," he stammered.

"Gentlemen," Reinhart said, brushing off his black suit. "Can we keep this civilized?"

"Well, I don't wanna hang if I'm wrong." He holstered his revolver and lunged at Spur. "We'll just see if I am!"

Spur grabbed Mander's hands and threw them off his gunbelt. "Jesus!" he cursed.

Undaunted, the big man threw his weight against Spur, falling on him, legs and arms flailing. The men on both sides of McCoy groaned as the two grappled.

"It's mine!" Mander screamed.

"No!"

They fought it out. Spur plowed his fist into the man's chin, sending him reeling across the coach to the opposite seat. Coughing, choking on the dust that spun in through the opened windows, Silas renewed his attack. McCoy's foot connected with his stomach and sent him back.

"Goddamn!" Mander said, rubbing his gut. "You're asking for it."

Spur drew before the gunman had even grasped the Dragoon's holster. "This arn't no place for shooting," he said in an even voice.

"Damn right."

"Shut up, Reinhart!"

Three explosions broke through the relentless clatter of the stagecoach and the horses' pounding hooves.

"Jesus, what was that?" Silas asked.

Spur looked out the window. "We got company, men."

"Indians?" Mander looked at him.

"No. White men." He ducked back inside. "Three of them. Kerchiefs around their faces. And they're shooting." He stared at Silas Mander. "Friends of yours?"

"They're still pretty far back," Reinhart said, peering through the window. "Out of range."

The men drew their weapons.

"Now's a good time to show me what you can do with that thing, Mander!" Spur shouted, and peeled off a warning shot toward the advancing gunmen. It was quickly returned.

"Hell!"

"What's the matter, Silas? Ain't up to a little gunplay?"

"No, it's not that, it's just . . . ."

"Save it for later!"

The driver rode the horses as hard as he could, forcing them to a gallop as they tugged the heavy load. The stagecoach bounced and bucked like a wild steer. Spur tried to steady his legs as he took another shot.

"Funny that they ain't gettin' any closer," Feingold said.

"Yeah. This stage isn't moving that fast." Spur craned his neck. The three mounted gunmen seemed to be riding just out of range.

"What in hell's going on, Geoffrey?" Silas said to the thin man seated beside him.

"Damned if I know!"

"Maybe they're driving us into a trap." Spur glanced out again. "But there doesn't seem to be a good place for an ambush up ahead."

Mander fired two shots.

"You're wasting lead, Silas!" Geoffrey said.

"I know, but I gotta do something!"

Spur thought hard. "There's nothing we can do, men. Nothing except wait this out and see what happens." He settled back on the seat. "This happen much around these parts?" McCoy asked the fellow on his right.

"Nope. It don't happen nowhere. Something mighty strange going on here."

"Yeah. Are they still hanging back, Reinhart?" Spur asked.

"Yup. No way we can hit 'em from here."

"And I don't suppose the driver'll slow down none to let us shoot 'em."

"I don't understand!" Silas said.

Three more shots boomed out behind the rollicking stagecoach.

"Boise's gonna be the most glorious sight a man could see," Reinhart said.

"Yeah."

The gunmen took a few more shots. Then silence.

"Well, that's it, men," Spur said as he looked out the window. Yellow dust boiled up in the air around the retreating horses. "They're heading back."

Silas Mander smiled smugly. "We scared 'em off."

Reinhart shook his head. "Hell, Mander. You got crazy ideas. We didn't scare them off."

McCoy grinned. "Obviously not. It's almost as if they didn't want to hit us. Didn't even want to stop the stage."

"Maybe they decided we didn't have anything worthwhile." Reinhart scratched his chin and took one last look out the window. "Maybe they had second thoughts."

"No, that's not it at all. I know exactly what those men were doing—what they were hired to do."

Spur turned to the thin man seated beside him. "How?"

He smiled. "I'm Geoffrey Evans. My father's the governor of Idaho Territory."

"So? That make you an expert on thieves?" Silas said.

Geoffrey ignored him. "My father sent me a letter telling me the trouble he's been having. It's almost election time and someone's trying to scare him off. They stole one of his horses, knocked down the front door of the governor's mansion, sent him threatening letters—and now this. Seems likely they knew I was on the stage and decided

I was as good as my father to harass."

Spur nodded. "I've heard about your father, and what's been happening in Boise."

Geoffrey smoothed out his corduroy pants legs on his thighs. "Just another indirect attack on the Territorial governor, as far as I can tell."

"I see," McCoy said.

He knew all about Martin Evans. In fact, the Secret Service was sending him to Boise to look into the man's complaints that someone, or a group of men, were out to kill him.

"Is your father really fearful of his life? Does he believe someone'll kill him?"

"Maybe. That's why I'm going home for the day. I'll be heading back in the morning." Geoffrey Evans smiled. "My father wants some free legal advice."

"Well, lawyer," Spur said. "What do you think of Silas there?" He glanced at the man. "Should I charge him with attempted murder?"

"Now hold on, stranger!" Mander sighed and straightened his shoulders. "Push yer piece out here. I won't touch it, I'll only look at the handle."

Grinning, Spur held it between the seats. Silas peered at the walnut grain and finally sat back.

He coughed. "Guess I was mistaken. Ain't no snake on that handle."

"Only snake around here's you, Mander!" Reinhart said.

"Well hell! You can't blame a man for looking out for himself," Mander said.

"Sure, when he's got his eyes closed." Spur pushed the revolver into his holster. Boise wasn't far now. Boise and Governor Evans.

"It only makes sense. Those men were attacking my father through me." Geoffrey shook his head. "Sometimes I wish he'd never gone into politicking."

"He might think the same thing." Spur kept an eye out for the gunman until they'd safely pulled into Boise, Idaho.

CHAPTER TWO

"So what do you think about my father's town?" Geoffrey Evans asked him as the stagecoach rattled into the bustling heart of Idaho Territory.

"I won't know until I see it." Spur looked out the window as the driver reined in the horses. "Looks like a fine enough town. But looks don't tell a man everything."

"I know what you mean."

As his boots dug into the inch-thick dust of Goldrush Street, Spur wiped trail grit from his face and thought about his assignment. His superior's telegram had been concise. General Halleck wanted Spur to halt the terror that had been stalking Governor Martin Evans for the past few weeks as election day grew nearer.

McCoy slipped his hat off his forehead and ran a bony hand through his hair, waiting for his

carpetbags to be thrown down from atop the stage.
If it stayed as hot as this, he thought, he wouldn't
even want to touch a woman even if he did find
one—and she was willing.

Though it probably got cooler after dark.

"What's the holdup?" Spur finally yelled to the
driver, who stood on the seat and rummaged
through the bags.

The grizzled man winced. "My shoulder's what
it is! Darn thing's acting up again." The driver
stepped aside. "Git 'em yourself!"

"Alright, alright." McCoy sprang up and
reached for his bags. "Hard to get good help these
days," he muttered.

"And that brown leather one!" someone said
below him.

"Yeah and the green bags!"

Spur dropped the dirty luggage into the street,
finally found his at the back and hauled them
down.

"Mighty nice of you, McCoy," Geoffrey Evans
said, gripping his oversized, heavy leather bag.

"No problem," he huffed. "Is your father
expecting you? Think he'll be home in an hour or
so?"

The lean man smiled. "Possibly. My father isn't
one to keep schedules. Poor mother, before her
untimely death, had to put up with him working
all night. Burned more midnight oil than
counterfeiters—if you know what I mean."

Spur nodded. "I'll track him down. Where's the
governor's place?"

"You'll find the mansion, as my father likes to
term it, at the end of Thistledown Avenue. It's a

big brick thing. Take one look at it and you'd swear you were back east." Geoffrey laughed.

"Fine. Thanks." McCoy trotted across the street to the Goldrush Hotel and got a room.

A half hour later, wearing clean pants and a slightly wrinkled blue shirt, Spur found the street. Two blocks of Thistledown extended from either side of Goldrush. Governor Evans' place was the showpiece of Boise. The two story brick monstrosity, surrounded by a six-foot iron fence, dominated one end of the short street. Smoke rose from one of the spiralled chimneys.

He moved toward it, tipping his hat and greeting a few residents. Boise was a fairly large town. He certainly hoped the governor had some leads.

McCoy found the gate open and looked up at the brass eagle that surmounted it. His boots clicked on the brick walkway that led to the front porch. Manicured gardens extended down both sides of the big house—he hadn't seen roses for years. Their scent hung in the air, reminiscent of a certain blonde-haired woman lost in his memories of St. Louis.

The doorknocker banged twice on the solid oak door. Spur waited until it whipped open.

"Yes?"

He instantly took off his hat. "Ma'am, I'm looking for Governor Evans."

The petite girl smirked. "So am I." She shook her head. Soft, curled blonde hair spread out like a halo around her. "My father's been gone all day long, and Geoffrey's waiting to see him. Honestly, you'd think he'd have time to talk to my brother." The thin-nosed girl smiled sweetly. "I'm terribly sorry, he isn't here. Who may I say called?"

"McCoy. Spur McCoy."

She glanced down at his boots. "You, ah, aren't wearing any, Spur. I mean—Mr. McCoy." Her gaze slowly trailed back up to his face.

"Just when I need them, ma'am. Tell your father I'm staying at the Goldrush Hotel. I'll stop by to see him again in the morning."

"Okay. If you have to go . . . ."

He grinned, planted his low-brimmed Stetson on his head and turned.

"Do come back in the morning," the girl called out. "I'm sure he'll be here!"

"Fine. I'll do that."

She couldn't hide the urgency in her voice, McCoy thought as he walked out through the gates and onto Thistledown. How old was she? Sixteen? Seventeen?

Probably too young. He stifled a yawn as he returned to the Goldrush Hotel. Maybe he should rest up for a night. A good stretch of shut-eye would feel good.

A yellow half-moon nearly touched the western horizon, scattering scant light on the countryside.

The five men gathered a half mile out of town. Mounted, kerchiefs covering their faces from the eyes down and hats pulled low over their heads, they waited. The horses whinneyed and jostled on their legs. They were eager to be off, and so were the men.

Finally, a sixth rider quietly approached from the east. The assembled men watched, straightening their backs, clearing their throats.

"You all made it. Good. We know what we have to do," the gruff-voiced rider said.

They nodded.

"Then let's go!" he shouted. "Let's do it for the town, for the people of Boise. Things have gotten out of hand. No one's in control of him. Are we gonna let that man get away with it? Are we gonna let him live?"

"Hell, no!" one called out.

"That's the spirit. Let's ride back to town and wipe that scum off the streets!"

The men fell in behind their leader at a slow trot, saving their horses.

At nine they slipped into town and, without talk, headed toward the Lucky Dollar Saloon. As they rode down Goldrush Street, other riders and men walking along its broad avenue moved aside. Eyes turned to watch them go, but no one challenged the men who wore the kerchiefs.

"Good, no trouble," their leader whispered as they gathered across the street from the green batwing doors that led into the bright saloon. Raucous laughter and the slap of the boots on the floorboards echoed from inside.

Weapons drawn, the six men waited for the right man to step outside.

The doors spread open. In the three seconds of light that followed, the man's face was clearly illuminated. The six rode forward.

"Thomas Fairchild!"

The paunchy man stopped and stared across the street. "That's me. Who're you—SHIT!"

"Citizens' Vigilante Council!"

Fairchild raced down the boardwalk, nearly

tripping over a stray dog that lay sleeping beside a water trough. The six mounted men took off after him.

"Help!" he called out.

Riding alongside the boardwalk, the leader of the vigilantes overtook the fleeing man and halted his horse directly in front of him where the rickety porch dropped down to bare earth. The others quickly closed in. He was trapped.

"What in hell are you guys doing?" Fairchild asked.

"Thomas Fairchild, you're a worthless gambler who doesn't deserve to walk the streets of this town!"

"No!"

"As county treasurer, you've stolen over $10,000 in public funds and wasted it all on women, whiskey and cards. You've squandered the monies of the fine citizens of Boise." The leader motioned with his free hand to his men. "Get him!"

Ten people assembled 50 yards away, watching silently as the vigilantes grabbed Fairchild and dragged him to the square where Goldrush met Whitten Avenue.

"No! God no! I haven't done anything wrong!" Fairchild frantically searched the men's eyes.

"Like hell!" the leader spat.

"You have no right!"

He broke free and ran ten feet before two vigilantes sent him sprawling to the ground.

"The rope!"

It was produced. The leader sat on his mount, arms crossed on his chest, watching as the noose was lowered around Tom Fairchild's neck and thrown over the highest branch of the ancient oak tree in the middle of the square.

"For God's sake, people, help me!" he screamed at the men and women watching from a distance.

"Save your breath, thief!" the head vigilante said. "Your stealin' days are over!"

The five men hauled him onto a horse. Bullets quenched the four kerosene lamps surrounding the square. The darkness that swallowed up the scene was soon broken by snorts and a long, agonized scream.

"Let's get the hell out! Now, men!"

The five raced to their horses. They rode out of town, joking, whooping and sending hot lead into the skies above them.

The assembled citizens turned their backs and walked away, muttering to themselves, shaking their heads.

In the public square of Boise, Idaho Territory, the county treasurer kicked and screamed, feeling the coarse hemp rope squeeze the breath from his body until he felt nothing but a long, endless drop into eternity.

Spur's brain exploded with the sound. Gunfire. He buckled on his gunbelt and looked out the window.

Nothing. Absolutely nothing but the distant sound of hooves biting into the earth. The few people he saw on the street didn't seem concerned. Maybe he'd imagined hearing the shots. Maybe he'd dreamed it.

Maybe he really did need some sleep.

Spur yawned, scratched his stubbly chin and

pushed the brownish-red hair from his eyes as he continued staring out the cracked window. If anything had happened, surely men would be reacting. But the few citizens of Boise walking the streets at that hour seemed calm, strolling along as if nothing unusual had occurred.

It must have been his imagination, Spur McCoy decided. He'd heard so many weapons discharged, had been in so many fights and had seen so much trouble in his years with the Secret Service, that it was catching up with him.

Nothing had happened out there.

The Secret Service officer groaned and felt the weariness wash over him. It had been a long ride and he was exhausted. Sleep, he told himself and stretched out on the pigeon-feather bed.

He'd have to ask the sheriff what all that was about in the morning.

CHAPTER THREE

"Missy told me what happened last night," Lacey Evans said, staring at her father as they sipped coffee in the mansion's dining room.

"Yeah." He was absorbed in the latest edition of *The Idaho Statesman.*

Around her, silver and crystal glistened. The table was set with the finest Irish linen. The plates, strewn with the remnants of their breakfast meal, were rimmed with gold.

"Yeah." Governor Evans rustled the paper.

"On his way to the stage, Geoffrey heard about it and he told Missy."

Martin Evans grunted and stared harder at an article about his opponent in the upcoming election. "So what? You shouldn't worry about things like that, darling."

"Why not? I live here, don't I?" The 18-year-

old girl dabbed a lace handkerchief at the spot of
strawberry jam on her chin. "Those vigilantes
went and hung poor Tom Fairchild by his neck
in the square. And no one tried to stop them!"

"I know, I know." Governor Evans sighed and
looked at his daughter over the paper. "How could
anyone? You know what they're like. If anyone
tried to stand up to them they sure wouldn't be
able to do it again."

The petite girl fluffed her hair and pushed back
her plate. "Father, I'm worried. You keep getting
all these threats against you, and those vigilantes
are riding around killing whomever they please."
Lacey grabbed his arm. "What happens if I wake
up in the morning and you're—you're—"

Evans put the paper down and smiled at her.
"They won't touch me. Besides, it isn't them I'm
worried about. It has to be one of my opponents
who wants to take over this territory." A smile
creased the governor's face. "Someone's just trying
to scare me, is all, Lacey."

She blinked her blue eyes. "I hope so. Maybe
the man who's coming to see you can help, like
you said."

"Maybe. That's why I sent for him. Oh, that
reminds me. Missy!" he yelled toward the kitchen.
"Get rid of these breakfast things and make this
house presentable. We've got company coming—
important company!"

The gaunt faced man stared up at Spur McCoy.
"So you're some kind of government agent?"

"That's right, Sheriff MacElravie. Governor
Evans called me here to secure his safety until after

the election. I'm sure you know all about the threats against his life?"

"Sure, sure. I've seen some of the letters that were mysteriously delivered to Evans. No way a man could tell who sent them." MacElravie glanced over his glasses. "Who's paying for all this? Your visit, I mean?"

McCoy smiled. "Courtesy of the U.S. of A."

The sheriff sighed. "Good. Nothing irregular about the money, then. That's just what Governor Evans would need, something else for Judd Feingold to talk about."

"This Feingold's running against the governor, I take it. Saw some posters about him. Actually, I saw a lot of posters." Spur crossed his arms.

"Yep. 'Course, Feingold's the type to take a direct attack with words. It doesn't seem likely that he'd stoop to something like that."

"I'll look into it." Spur started for the door.

"Don't you worry none about that hanging last night," the sheriff said.

McCoy stopped and turned back to him. "Hanging?" His voice was weak.

"Sure. Didn't you hear about it? Maybe not. The vigilantes were busy again. Strung up Thomas Fairchild in the public square. Lots of folks watched him, too."

Damn, Spur thought. "I thought I heard some unusual activity last night, but everything seemed so normal in the streets."

"Yeah, it's happening with regularity. Fairchild's just the latest one that someone's crossed off his list of men to kill."

"What'd he do to attract attention?"

''Fairchild was the county treasurer. He made a small salary but was out gambling every night. He'd lose $100 in 24 hours. That made some men suspicious.''

Sheriff MacElravie shook his head and tasted the coffee that had been cooling on his desk. ''Too weak.'' He took a small bottle from his desk and poured some amber colored liquid into the brew. ''I heard from a reliable source that Fairchild had been stealing money from the public funds for over a year. And he lost it, every cent of it.''

''How much?''

''Hard to figure. Probably around $10,000.''

Spur nodded. ''And you didn't take him into custody?''

MacElravie glared at him. ''Don't try to tell me how to do my job! I just heard about it this morning. What am I gonna do, have a corpse sit up before Judge Mostad?''

''Of course not.''

''As I figure it, the vigilantes saved me the trouble of hauling him in.''

McCoy changed the subject. ''With these death threats and bodies piling up, you must have your hands full.''

MacElravie sipped the spiked coffee and shrugged. ''Nothing I can do about the vigilantes, they're becoming the law around here.''

''Can't you track them down? Round them up and press charges against them? Hell, sheriff, how many innocent men have they murdered?''

MacElravie winced. ''Look, McCoy. If I did, or said, or even thunk anything against them, I'd be kicking the wind by morning.'' He shook his head.

"Like I said, they run this town, whether we like it or not. I value my life too much to run up against that bunch. Besides, most of their victims have been guilty of something or another."

Spur let it sink in. "I see."

The sheriff didn't seem to want to stop them.

"That isn't exactly by the book, MacElravie."

"No, siree. But it works. I do what I have to to survive." He swallowed down half of the bitter, burning liquid. "And as for Martin Evans, he don't need my help. The governor can take care of himself." MacElravie smacked his lips. "Mighty fine coffee!"

"He have friends in this town?"

"Friends? Business acquaintances, more like." He took another sip and pushed back his glasses on his nose. "You'll meet him. Judge for yourself. The governor's a powerful man, and that scares off a lot of folks. And it keeps the fellas away from that dangerous daughter of his." He raised his eyebrows and sipped. "Ah, nothing like coffee in the morning!"

"Thanks for your time, sheriff. I'll be checking in with you."

"Fine, fine. And give my regards to Evans!"

As Spur walked down Goldrush to the mansion, something bugged him. Sheriff MacElravie might be at the mercy of these vigilantes, the whole town might be afraid of them, but that didn't seem like a good enough reason to sit back and let them do whatever the hell they wanted.

Maybe the sheriff wasn't telling him everything. Maybe he liked sitting behind his desk and not taking charge. Maybe he'd grown used to having a band of wild men doing his job.

Vigilantes were bad news. Wherever they popped up they had absolute power over the local people until they were stopped. If Governor Evans hadn't hired him, Spur thought, he just might spend some time finding out who they were.

He arrived at the end of Thistledown and knocked.

"Yes?"

A pleasant-faced older woman wrapped in layers of blue and white checkered cloth stared at him.

"I'm Spur McCoy. Here to see Governor Evans?"

"And I'm Missy—answerin' the door." Her eyes were hard, lips tight. "What you here to see him about?"

As she leaned closer to him, Spur caught the fragrance of onions hanging on her clothes. "Well, ah, just who are you?"

"I already done told you!"

"Missy, Missy, really!"

A vision of white silk appeared beside the woman. "You don't have to be so careful. Do you think someone who was here to murder my father would knock on the door?" The girl turned to face him. "We meet again! I'm Lacey Evans. My father's expecting you. If you'll come this way?"

Spur took off his hat, stepped past Missy and followed Lacey. The swing of her hips nearly mesmerized him. He didn't know how old this girl was, but she was old enough.

Lacey glanced back at him. Spur realized he'd been caught and quickly raised his gaze. She

laughed. "Right in there. The governor'll be with
you in a minute."

"Thank you kindly, ma'am."

"Oooh, aren't you one for manners! You could
teach a lot to the menfolk who come around here!'
She tossed her head and disappeared through the
parlor.

If she was any indication of her father, Martin
Evans would indeed be able to take care of
himself. Spur walked into the oak paneled room
and studied the books lining the walls. Law.
Astronomy. Agriculture. Mathematics. The man
wasn't stupid.

A chair turned toward him, revealing a paunchy
man in shirtsleeves. "You must be Mr. McCoy!"

He walked to him. "I am indeed. Good to meet
you, Governor Evans."

They shook hands. Spur nearly winced at the
strength of the pudgy, tall man's grip.

"I sure am glad you're here. Election day's not
far away. For some reason I wanna be sure I'm
still alive to see it." The robust man laughed and
waddled to the bar. Wild red hair stuck straight
out from his scalp as if he hadn't brushed it for
weeks. "Care for a brandy, Mr. McCoy?"

"No thanks. Too early in the morning."

"I remember when it was for me, too. Before
all this started." Evans smoothed out his black vest
and poured an inch of brandy into a well-dusted
snifter. "Maybe I shouldn't have run again."

"From what I hear, you've been doing well, and
the territory's in pretty good shape. Why shouldn't
you run?"

The governor sighed and swirled the alcohol in the glass. "I'm gonna level with you, McCoy, seeing as how you're here to protect me. Politicking ain't all picnics and kissing babies. Sometimes you gotta step on toes." He sniffed the brandy. "You try to give the majority what they want but the minority doesn't like it. That makes a man lots of enemies."

"What about your opponents? Could one of them be who's behind these threats?"

"Hell, I don't know. Maybe. Only one man's a real danger. That's Judd Feingold. Just moved in here last year and he's trying to take over my territory."

"Would he stoop to something like this?"

"I don't know him well enough. Maybe." He took a drink. "Hell, McCoy. I ain't exactly the most impartial man to ask. Feingold's out to ruin my life. You mark my words—Idaho will be a state soon enough, and I wanna make sure I'm still here to see it through the transition."

Spur nodded and looked around the room. "You build this place yourself?"

Martin Evans smiled. "Sure did. All my own money too, so even if that damned Feingold wins I'll stay right here. I've got some business interests in Boise and Idaho Falls." The governor drained his glass. "But I don't wanna lose at the end of a rope or with a pound of lead in my chest." He burped.

"That's understandable."

He poured another glass. "I can hire my own protection, but I need someone to oversee the whole operation. Someone who'll keep an extra eye out for my safety. That's you." Evans glanced at the Seth Thomas that ticked on the mantle. "Hell, I got a meeting with the Ladies' Church Auxiliary. Think over what I've said and see if you can come up with any clever ways to keep the undertaker from getting his grubby hands on my carcass. Got that?"

McCoy grinned. "Sure. Sure, Mr. Evans." The man was treating him like a slave.

"Good."

The young girl waltzed into the room. "Father, I—oh, I'm sorry, I didn't know you still had company."

"Lacey! You're worse than ever."

"Hello, Mr. McCoy. Good seeing you again "

"Good morning, Miss Evans." Spur kissed the hand that she extended to him.

Evans stood back, watching, "You've ah, met my daughter before?"

"Yesterday afternoon, when I came to see you, governor."

Martin Evans smiled. "Heck, Lacey, let the poor man get on with his business. He's got too much to think about without your foolishness clouding up his brain." He lifted his glass once again.

"What's so foolish about love?"

Evans spit his brandy. "Get up to your room, girl! I know you're growing up fast but I won't stand for such boldness in my house!"

The blonde haired girl pouted. "Okay. Be seeing you again, Mr. McCoy?"

"Almost assuredly."

Lacey grinned. "Well then, I'll be off. I should get out of this old dress and take a bath."

"Git, girl!"

She flounced out of the room.

"She's quite a young lady," McCoy said.

Evans looked hard at him. "Yeah. Between her and my campaign . . . ."

"What about the vigilantes?" Spur said as he followed Evans out of the study. "I realize they're a problem, but you think there's any connection between them and those letters?"

"No. I don't think so. They may be too untamed for some tastes, but all in all they're doing a good job of cleaning up this town. Besides, they wouldn't send me any letters. They'd just string me up."

"That makes sense."

"You just concentrate on keeping me in one piece. I'll see you later, McCoy!"

CHAPTER FOUR

Spur ducked as the small explosion cracked the air inside the saloon. As he rubbed his ears the bullet slammed into the far wall, plowing into a portrait of Governor Martin Evans and knocking it from its tack.

"You take that back, George!" a gravelly voice shouted.

"Hell no!" a man shouted back. "Thomas Fairchild deserved to hang! He was cheating all of us, the whole town! The whole territory! You know it as well as anyone."

"Don't tell me what I know!"

Spur peered over the table. Two men faced each other at the bar, weapons drawn. The well dressed man's Colt sent a column of blue smoke up toward the overhead kerosene lamps.

His opponent snarled. "Come on, Jackson!

You're just pissed old Fairchild won't be lining your pockets at the table ev'ry night! You never liked him, even if you did let him squire your daughter around town! You just liked his money!"

"I never saw you throw it back in his face," he said. "You took it same as every other man's silver and gold. And don't you go bad-mouthin' my little girl! She took a shine to Thomas Fairchild, she did!"

"He was just using her to get to you, to get to that bank of yours, to get to your money!" George said.

"Yeah!"

"Who called for your two bits?" the banker asked, staring hard at the drunk beside him at the bar.

McCoy watched with interest as the pair delivered their outbursts. The recently hanged man certainly wasn't too popular, at least in that saloon.

"Come on, Jackson, forget it. Sorry I even brought the whole damn thing up. Let's just play some cards."

A brassy-haired saloon girl put her hands on her hips and yelled at them from the stairs. "Boys, boys, don't end things like this! A little fightin's good for business. Makes everyone drink!"

"Stay outa this, Kelly!" George said.

"Okay. Just don't be askin' me for any more discounts!" She lifted her hem and sauntered up the stairs. Before she'd made it halfway, a love-starved rancher had stormed after her, grabbed her waist and squeezed.

The cowboy watched the happy couple disappear, then turned back to Jackson. "You just messed that up for me real good!"

The banker laughed. "Hell, let me buy you a drink. Okay?"

"Well . . . ."

Spur returned to his seat as the apron slapped two glasses onto the oak bar. If nothing else, Thomas Fairchild had been a controversial figure. If his dirty dealings were common knowledge, anyone could have decided to clean up the problem. McCoy wasn't surprised a vigilante group had sprung up in Boise with men like him walking the streets.

"Looks like Jackson's a mite upset."

Spur shrugged at the man across the table from him. "Was this Fairchild all that bad?"

The craggy-faced man stared into his whiskey. "That's a fact. Bad from the inside out. Some say he's been stealing since he was appointed two years ago. He sure never had no trouble making ante. That made some men wonder."

McCoy nodded. "If he wasn't well-off, it would at that. So some boys around here decided to take the law into their own hands."

His drinking companion glared up at him and slightly nodded. He leaned closer to Spur. "Yep," he whispered. "Fairchild's the last bad seed in town, as far as I know. We shouldn't be hearing any more about them."

The man was afraid of the vigilantes, Spur thought. "No one's ever stood up to them? What if they made a mistake, hung the wrong man?"

"They did once. Yeah. Feller named, ah, Gilroy. Michael Gilroy. Damn fine dentist he was too, before they strung him up." The wizened man glanced both ways. "They got him a while back and killed him. Then everybody found out he hadn't done nothing, he hadn't hurt a flea. A couple teeth, maybe, but that's all."

Spur lowered his voice as well. "Then that should have been the end of them. The public should have driven them out of town, put a stop to the killing before they did it again."

"I know, I know, but folks around here—" He sighed. "Look, it ain't right talkin' about this here, in the open and all that. What's done is done. Them boys are in power in this town now and, because no one knows who they are, they're gonna stay right where they are." He narrowed his brows. "Not even the newspaper, *The Idaho Statesman,* has printed a word about the vigilantes or the mysterious killin's."

"I see." Maybe Governor Evans hadn't told him the truth. Maybe these vigilantes were getting power-happy, testing the limits of the town's tolerance, riding on the sensations of omnipotence.

" 'Course, they may not be done at that. Fairchild might not be the end."

"Why?"

The man drained his glass, swallowed, then smacked his lips. He carefully set it back on the table and looked at Spur. "Mormons," he said. "They're coming up here from Salt Lake. Lots of folks in town aren't happy to see 'em, if you know what I mean. Some of them have been forced to leave. Houses burned. Horses killed!"

"Vigilantes?"

He stared at the empty glass, mute, motionless.

Spur was certain from the man's reaction that the vigilanties were connected with the threats against Evans' life. Maybe he'd better look into them, even if the governor didn't think it was necessary.

"Look," his drinking companion suddenly said. "I don't know why in hell you'd be interested, but there's someone who may know something about these men. A woman."

Spur nodded in encouragement.

"She was the wife of that dentist I told you about. Name of Vanessa Gilroy. Lives on Maplewood, the two-story with weeds in the yard."

"Right. Thanks." Spur started to rise but the man violently grabbed his wrist.

"Get them!" he whispered.

McCoy walked out of the bar rubbing the red bruises that creased his arm, his mind fixed on his mission.

Vanessa Gilroy opened the door. The statuesque women was draped in black, from her satin bonnet to the wisps of petticoats that dragged across the floor as she let Spur into her home. With the veil covering her face and black gloves on her hands, Vanessa looked like a woman in mourning.

"I don't know why you want to talk about my husband," she said as she took a chair in her parlor. "Please."

Spur sat on the couch she motioned to and held his hat in his hands. "Just trying to gather up some facts, Mrs. Gilroy. I'm looking into the matter."

The women arched her back, lifted the veil and laughed. A fair, gloriously beautiful face glowed beneath the black lace. Flashing green eyes drilled into his; her lips, though devoid of paint, were red and full.

"Looking into the matter? I'm sorry, Mr. McCoy, but those are strange words around here. I'm not used to hearing them." She calmed herself and peeled off her left glove.

"That's quite all right. You've been through a terrible loss, and everyone in town's afraid to help you. Is that the way it is?"

She threw one glove onto the table beside her. "Close enough!" Long, beautiful fingers extricated the second sheath from her right hand. That finished, Vanessa turned to Spur. "So why on earth are you here? Why are you talking to me? I'm sorry, Mr. McCoy; I can't figure this out."

"I'm not here from the governor, and Sheriff MacElravie didn't send me."

Vanessa rubbed her fingernails together and frowned at the name.

"Let's just say I'm an interested party, interested in righting the wrong that's been done to you."

The thirty year-old woman separated her hands, unpinned the bonnet and let it fall, trailing the veil after it. Vanessa shook out the hair that she'd gathered under the hat and let it cascade to her shoulders in red ringlets that glowed in the morning sun.

"Does that bother you?" Spur asked. Something didn't seem right.

"No, no, help me all you can! I'm glad for that.
But I can tell you're from out of town. Every man
within fifteen miles of Boise's afraid to do anything
now that the citizen's committee's watching what
goes on here." Vanessa moved her chin from side
to side. "I just don't think there's anything you
can do."

Her eyes were bright, her lips pressed firmly
together. This wasn't a woman drowning in
despair, Spur thought. Had she loved her husband?
Or had she accepted what had happened and the
fact that nothing could be done about it?

"Leave that to me," McCoy said. "How did it
happen?"

Vanessa sighed and crossed her ankles. "Six men
rode up one afternoon when Michael and I were
reading our Bible. He used to like to do that.
Anyway, they barged in here, grabbed him and
hauled him outside, yelling and carrying on like
they'd eaten the wrong kind of mushrooms."

"And then?"

She wet her lips. "And then they accused him
of murdering Frank Glapion, the blacksmith's son.
We tried to tell them that was nonsense—Michael
was in Mountain Home the day Frank turned up
dead, but they wouldn't listen. They made me
watch as they—they—" Vanessa turned to Spur,
tears brimming in her eyes. "They did it."

"I see."

The woman angrily wiped away the drop that
rolled down her cheek. "Do what you want. But
I'm gonna find out who killed my husband, and
I'll see that they get what's coming to them!"

Spur rose. "Maybe you should leave that to me."

Vanessa laughed. "We'll see who finds them first!" She smiled and stood. "I hate to rush you out, Mr. McCoy, but I have some things to attend to. I'm sure you understand, it's only been two weeks and there's papers to go through and everything else."

He nodded. "Okay. Thanks for the talk, Mrs. Gilroy. And if you find out anything, or have any ideas regarding the identities of the vigilantes, I'm at the Goldrush Hotel."

"Fine." She walked him to the door. "Goodbye!"

Spur stuck his wide-brimmed hat low on his head and walked out into the brilliant sunshine. Vanessa Gilroy wasn't a woman to underestimate, he decided, kicking through a maze of dying plants that flourished in her overgrown garden. Under all those tears and lace she was as tough as steel.

A woman like that would get what she wanted. Spur hoped she'd share it with him.

CHAPTER FIVE

McCoy slumped on the chair in the Goldrush dining room, exhausted. He'd been on an overnight trip with Governor Evans, who gave four speeches in as many towns in two days, jubilantly painting verbal pictures of the glories that Idaho Territory would see if he remained in office.

Even as he dug into the food he'd piled on his plate, Spur could hear the man's powerful voice blasting away at him. After hearing the same speech four times, McCoy figured he almost had it memorized.

And the people seemed receptive to Evans. Many that Spur talked with were suspicious of newcomers, "Especially that danged Feingold, with his outsider's ways." Quite a few were well aware of the *Mormon problem*, as they termed it.

The candidate's views on the Mormons seemed highly important to the people of Idaho Territory.

Evans had been straightforward—he wasn't too happy that they were moving in, but there was no way of stopping them. He went on and on about "opening your hearts to these strangers, giving them a chance to fit into the framework of the community."

During each speech, this remark had been met with boos and hisses. The governor always seemed surprised for a second, then smiled broadly. "And if that doesn't work, well, maybe they'll get tired of fighting us and move back home. That'd be the best for them and the best for us. After all, men," Evans said with a wink, "they do unnatural and ungodly things. Those boys each got three or four wives. If they move in here there'll be a painful shortage of unmarried girls!"

Cheers and shouts of approval always met this statement, and Spur was impressed by Governor Evans' ability to work the crowd that came to watch him. He was a professional, playing up to their fears.

His re-election seemed certain.

Spur had guarded the governor but nothing happened, save for a minor scuffle when some Mormons spoke up after he'd asked for questions. Their comments sparked the non-converts in the audience to action, and McCoy had to break up two fistfights before calm was restored.

Maybe Evans was only in danger at home, he thought, flaking a baked potato apart with his fork.

The bad feelings about the Mormons, and that

man's comments about them the other night in the saloon, brought the vigilantes to the forefront of his mind again. Spur sighed. He had two jobs to do in Boise.

The food quickly disappeared, giving the Secret Service agent renewed energy and vitality. Spur wiped his lip and walked outside, enjoying the cool evening air.

"Why, hello again!"

He turned to see Lacey Evans walking primly across the street, keeping her skirt well above the mud and dust that lay there.

"Good evening, Miss Evans," Spur said, tipping his hat. He took her hand and helped her onto the boardwalk that fronted the Goldrush Hotel.

The young girl stared up at him, her eyes wide under the silk bonnet that glowed a dull pink from the moon and the spill of light from the hotel.

"I hope you can help me," Lacey said.

"With what?"

"I didn't realize how late it was getting. When I left my friend's house it was already dark." She lowered her chin and pouted. "I'm afraid. I mean, I don't like to walk the streets alone at night. Could you escort me home?"

"Of course, Miss Evans."

"Thanks! And call me Lacey. Everyone calls me that. Except my father."

Spur took her arm and they walked toward Thistledown Avenue.

"What's he call you?"

"Trouble."

He chuckled. Somewhere in the distance a

rooster called, stirred by some bizarre feeling that dawn was about to break.

"Why would he call you that?" he teased. "A fine, upstanding, young girl like you?"

"I'm not a girl," Lacey said, turning to him. Her face shimmered. "I'm a woman. After all, I just reached my eighteenth birthday."

Her crinoline skirt crackled as they walked. The scent of roses drifted up from her hair. Spur held her tighter and Lacey clasped his arm. Her hand was warm. She was so small and tiny, so fragile looking. And so arousing.

Down, boy, Spur told himself. She might be of age, and she was certainly the kind of woman any man would be happy to have in his bed, but this was Lacey Evans, for God's sake. The governor's daughter!

"I love the night!" she said, looking up at the stars. "It's so cool. I just feel different after the sun goes down. Don't you?"

"Mmmm."

"I feel different tonight, like I could do anything—just anything." She swung her head farther back. "Maybe it has something to do with that moon up there."

"That moon?" Spur glanced at the pale yellow orb. "That's the same moon that's always up there. Nothing different about it."

She sighed. "Then perhaps it's the company."

Spur looked at the young girl, who squeezed his arm and laughed as they turned onto Thistledown Avenue.

"The place looks deserted," Spur said.

The bulk of the mansion loomed against the sky, dark save for a few lit windows.

"Yes. Everyone's away. Missy at her mother's— that's where she stays. My father's out doing something or other. It's amazing how he works. Why, sometimes he's out till one or two AM."

"I see."

They cleared the gate.

Lacey stopped and turned to him. "Come see the garden!" she urged him.

Spur laughed. "It's dark, Lacey."

"I know. I have a night garden!" She tugged at his arm like a child after a cookie. "Please?"

This could be dangerous. But he was used to danger—even from eighteen-year-old girls.

"Okay."

Lacey squealed with delight and took off, pulling him along with her as they raced between the manicured cherry trees and huge lilac bushes that hugged the brick walls.

"Slow down!" Spur said, feeling the old lethargy creep up his legs.

"We're almost there!"

They passed by nameless plants until the narrow path beside the mansion opened up into a vast garden. An owl that had been resting on the central sundial hooted and flew off toward the sky, its wings rasping the air.

"Alright." Lacey stopped beside a stone bench. "Close your eyes," she said, "and tell me what you smell."

"Lacey, this is crazy."

"I know, I know! Just do it. Please?"

Spur nodded and shut his eyes. The girl's hand took his. They moved forward ten feet. She pressed on his back, so McCoy stooped down.

"What is it?"

He sniffed. The scent was intoxicating, drenched with femininity and the sweetness of honey. Spur smelled it until his head grew faint.

He sighed. "I don't know, but it's frying my brain." He moved upright.

"Don't open your eyes yet! That's jasmine. Now what's this? I'll hold it up to your nose."

Lacey giggled. A bush rattled. A few seconds later Spur smelled full-blown roses.

"If I didn't know better, I say that was your hair."

He grabbed her arm and opened his eyes.

The young girl lowered the lock from his nose and glanced up at him. She smiled invitingly. "You were right. Look, Spur, we're all alone. There's no one around, and no one can see in here."

"So?"

Lacey moved closer to him until their bodies were touching. "And so? What do you think?" She gazed up at his face, lips parted, and pressed firmly against him.

Her warmth, the erotic feeling of her breasts crushing against his chest and the delightful scent of jasmine curling up around them overpowered Spur.

Old feelings began to stir inside him. "Lacey, you're beautiful. Don't misunderstand me. But you're—"

"I'm old enough!" She ground her groin against

his thighs. "I told you I'm eighteen. Since the 27th of last month."

"You're also Governor Evans' daughter."

Spur felt the primal excitement grow within him. Her body nourished it, built it up to an almost undeniable level.

"Don't think about him!" Her voice was breathy. "That old man isn't around. What he doesn't know can't hurt him."

Lacey pushed her hand under Spur's hat and scraped her fingernails across his neck. It filled him with chills.

"I can feel that thing growing down there," she said, her voice dripping with invitation. "Are you going to refuse my offer?"

Something snapped inside him. Spur moaned and took her head in his hands, gripping it, tilting it upward. "Hell, no!" he grumbled, and kissed her.

Tongues clashed. Bodies clung to each other. The earth beneath his feet seemed to shake as Spur explored her mouth. His erection strained against the corduroy pants, against the insistent pressure from her young body.

He lifted his lips from hers. Lacey threw back her head and gasped. "Oh, yes!"

"Let's go inside," he said, pulling her closer to him.

"No. Let's do it right here!"

Spur looked around. "Here?"

"Yes!"

Lacey pushed away from him. She tugged at her bonnet. The ties unravelled and she threw it onto a mignionette bush. The girl took Spur's hand, curled his fingers under the bodice of her dress and pushed them downward.

Spur went to her as the cloth ripped and fell open. He tugged at it, tearing and rending the fabric. The garden echoed with Lacey's laughter as he tore off her clothes, denuding her piece by piece, until the last petticoat and her creamy chemise lay in a heap at her feet.

"Jesus, Lacey, you're some fine woman!" he said.

"And you're some fine man!"

Her moonlight-splashed body glowed with a firefly's glory. The white shoulders, full breasts, slender waist and flaring hips were perfectly proportioned. Lacey reached for his crotch, unbuttoned his trousers and hauled them down. Her hands were experienced, Spur noted with wonder.

She lowered his drawers and smiled as the obvious proof of his arousal sprang out toward her. "I like that, Spur! I like that a lot!"

He threw back the hand that she extended toward his crotch. "You touch it and it's liable to spit at you!" he said, his voice husky. Spur quickly removed his shirt and pulled his pants off over his boots.

"So soon?"

"It isn't my doing. It's all your fault, Lacey!"

She nodded, sat on the petal-strewn earth and lowered her back. Spur stared between her upraised, parted knees. The blonde patch there drew him in. He knelt before her.

''You like my garden?'' Her voice was dreamy. She circled her hips, lifting them to him.

''God, yes!''

Spur stretched out over her and fit his body between her thighs. He rubbed his erection back and forth over her opening.

''Oh!''

''Now?'' he asked.

''Can't you feel how wet I am?''

''Yeah. I guess you want it.''

He drove into her. Lacey gasped and puffed as he joined his body with hers. The long, slick slide was too exciting, too stimulating. He slowed his penetration, inching into her warmth, extending the timeless moment until his testicles pressed against her.

''Oh, Spur!'' Lacey said, shaking her head from side to side.

''Lacey! What you do to a man!''

He kissed her, ripped his mouth from hers and sucked her right breast. The tight, wet feeling enveloped him with ecstasy, demanding action.

Spur pulled out and plunged back in. Their hip bones crashed together. He lifted his head from the groaning woman and pumped into her with short, deep jabs. The pebble beneath his toes didn't bother Spur as he pleasured her. Lacey sighed and arched her back, offering herself to him, giving him access to the most precious part of her body.

''Yes. Yes. Yes!'' she chanted with each thrust.

''Lacey!''

The sound of flesh slapping against flesh broke the stillness of the garden. His groans rose with hers as they struggled together, hands clasped, mouths locked.

Staring up at him, Lacey caught her breath again and again, finally exploding into tremors and gasps, her breasts heaving up and down below him.

The increased pressure and the young woman's excitement pushed Spur over the edge. He drove blindly into her, bucking deeper, his mind whirling. The spasms, the spurts and deep release rocketed through his body. Again and again he blasted his seed into Lacey as their eyes locked and their bodies trembled.

McCoy kicked his heels as he spent himself, rustling the jasmine bush that grew above them. Fragrant white petals rained onto the panting pair as the liquor of total release dripped through their veins.

As jasmine flowers landed on Spur's head and back he kissed her again, slowing his spasmic thrusts, breathing out the paroxysms of pleasure that tore at his very being.

Lacey gathered him up in her arms, moaning against his tongue. The scent of jasmine mixed with their musk as he stopped moving and hugged her. He broke the kiss and gasped into her ear, puffing out the fine hair that lay scattered around her head.

A breeze swept through the garden, evaporating the sweat that seethed on McCoy's back. "Whew, Lacey!" he said.

"My feelings exactly, sir."

He deliberately thrust his foot into the bush,

renewing the aromatic rain and completely covering their bodies with a thick layer of gleaming jasmine flowers.

CHAPTER SIX

Vanessa Gilroy banged her thumb as she pounded the last nail into the window frame.

''Darn!'' she said, sucking it, trying to soothe away the sudden pain with her lips. She put down the hammer and glanced outside. The night seemed quiet enough, but the widow knew that at any time six cowards on horseback could ride into town and snuff out a life as easily as a cigar butt.

The memories of that awful day swept through her. Vanessa choked back a sob, straightened her back and checked her appearance in the small mirror over the coatrack. Satisfied by her somber clothing, she smoothed the veil over her face, turned down the kerosene lamps and walked outside.

Some day I'll have to do something about those

weeds, Vanessa thought as they pulled at her skirt. The sheriff's office wasn't far, but she hurried down the darkened street, her leather boots scuffing through the dust. It wasn't much after eight; he should still be there. Sheriff MacElravie rarely went home before nine at night.

Vanessa Gilroy smiled beneath the black lace as she walked. She was finally doing something, not just hiding in her house, moaning about the injustice of it all. She'd wasted enough time with those womanly things. It was time for action!

The widow quickened her pace as pictures of the coming event rolled around in her mind. She was so caught up in her planning that she was surprised to find herself standing in front of the building.

She went in.

"Widow Gilroy!"

"Sheriff MacElravie, I have to talk to you." Vanessa wrung her hands. "I can't believe what I've seen!"

"What's wrong?" the lean-cheeked man asked, respositioning his thick glasses on his nose. He pushed his chair away from the desk.

"It's hard to explain. Just come with me. Please!"

"Now?"

"Yes! Before it's over!"

"Well, well," he stammered.

"Please, sheriff, you wouldn't want to miss this! It's unspeakable!"

He sighed and rose from the chair. "Alright." They walked to her house.

"What's all this about?" Sheriff MacElravie asked as they hurried along the street.

"I was just finishing up dusting when I saw it, right out my bedroom window."

He sighed. "Saw what?"

"Saw what? A pagan wedding, that's what I saw!" Vanessa increased her pace. "There was a wedding going on in the house behind mine—you know, the old Martin place? I guess it was sold, because there was a man standing up with three women. They were getting married. *All of them!*"

"Land sakes!" MacElvravie said, huffing as he tried to keep up with the woman's strides.

"It's one thing for those Godless souls to live here, but it's another to let them do that kind of thing! We can't have unholy unions taking place in Boise, can we?"

"Absolutely not!" The sheriff touched her shoulder. "I'm mighty glad you told me about this, Vanessa."

She shrugged. "Everyone knows what you think about those Mormons. I thought you might want to see it."

"Indeed I do!"

They were both winded by the time they stood on her front porch. "Sheriff, could you take off your gunbelt and leave it out here? I don't feel comfortable with firearms inside my house."

"Sure, Widow Gilroy. I understand." He unbuckled it and let the heavy apparatus fall onto a rattan chair.

"Fine. Follow me!"

She let him in and raced up the stairs.

MacElravie trudged after her and finally walked into her bedroom. The low lamps cast a yellowish glow.

"Which window?" he asked, loosening his collar.

"That one!" Vanessa pointed to the glass beside her plain iron bed.

The sheriff went to it and peered outside. "Nothing there now. The place looks deserted."

"Really? Damn it! I guess it's over." Vanessa crossed her arms as George MacElravie turned to her. "Can you imagine something like that? Taking three wives?"

"They're un-Biblical. They bring their wicked, blasphemous ways into our own town! We can't let this thing happen!"

"Maybe they were just using the Martin house for the wedding. I couldn't see who they were from up here. I don't think it was one of the locals." She raised the veil from her face and smoothed it out over her black bonnet.

The sheriff smiled. "You did right in telling me about this, Widow Gilroy. I'll have my boys look into it. This has gone far enough!"

"Some folks say the vigilantes have gone far enough, too." Her voice was low.

He grinned at her. "What did you say?"

"You heard me, Sheriff. The vigilantes are taking over this town, killing innocent citizens!"

"Now hold on, woman! The Mormons are one thing, the vigilantes are quite another."

Vanessa laughed and turned up the flame on the wall lamp. The light that welled up in the room illuminated the sheriff's confused face.

"They're just the same. Both Godless people breaking the laws of Jesus and man alike! Wouldn't you agree with that?"

He set his jaw. "No, ma'am. No, I would not! You don't fully comprehend what you're talking about."

"Yes, I do." She sweetly smiled and lifted her left eyebrow. "And so do you. You know all about the Citizens' Vigilante Committee. More than you've told anyone."

George MacElravie stared hard at her, his left cheek twitching. "Just what are you driving at, woman? What are you trying to say?"

She closed the bedroom door and faced him again. "That you're one of them! You're one of those murdering sons of bitches!" Her fiery eyes burned into his.

He broke the stare. "Get off it, Vanessa!" MacElravie said. "That's a pile of horsedung if I've ever heard one!"

"You killed my husband! Murdered him in cold blood. Took the only man I ever loved away from me!" she screamed.

"Stop it! Act like a grown woman. Have you gone out of your mind?"

"No. You did, the minute you ganged up with them, the moment you slapped that horse and left my husband dangling by his neck from the limb." She ripped off her hat and veil. "Admit it! You're one of them!"

The sheriff planted his feet on the floorboards, his hands at his sides. "So what if I am?" he asked,

smiling. "Just what the hell are you gonna do
about it? I'm the law in Boise, Vanessa! I'm the
goddamned sheriff!" He pounded on the star
pinned to his chest.

She snickered. "The law? Or *lawless!*"

"Widow Gilroy, you shut your mouth and keep
it shut!" MacElravie reached for his right thigh.
His fingers closed around empty air.

Vanessa poked a hand into her skirt pocket. "It's
out on the front porch. Remember?"

"You bitch!" He lunged at her.

Cold steel flashed up in her hand. The sheriff
stumbled backward out of her reach.

"Hell! Where'd that thing come from?"

Vanessa grinned and stabbed the air with the
knife. "You're not going to kill another innocent
victim, George!"

"Now, now, Widow Gilroy," MacElravie said.
Glistening drops poured down his face, slipping
his glasses nearly off their perch. "Don't go and
do anything stupid with that thing. Give it here!"

"I'll give it to you, like you gave it to my
husband!"

Vanessa advanced on him, gripping the Bowie
knife with a firm hand, her arm strong, muscles
tight.

The sheriff backed toward the door. "What the
hell are you doing?"

"Justice!"

His hands scrambled at the doorknob behind
him. His face tightened as he tried to turn it.

"I thought of everything. Your revolver's
outside. Door's locked. Windows nailed shut. You

aren't going anywhere, sheriff!''

He flattened against the oak door, the muscles in his neck popping out as the deadly steel blade closed in on him.

"Jesus, no!" he whispered, frozen in disbelief.

"Yes!"

Closer.

"You wouldn't really—"

Vanessa Gilroy grunted and plunged the knife into his chest. She smiled at the satisfying crack of bones and the disgusting sound of ripping tissues as it slid into the sheriff's body.

The man's face contorted. "No! God, no!"

Before his hands touched the knife the widowed woman pulled it out and rammed it back in, digging into the murderer's heart, ripping and tearing the big pump.

The sheriff collapsed, clutching the knife buried in his chest, gurgling and staring up at her in shocked surprise. Eerily wet sounds issued from his throat.

"You killed him!" she said, and sat on the floor before him, staring at the stain that slowly spread on his checkered shirt front.

His chin slumped to his chest.

Vanessa Gilroy patiently waited, even hummed a hymn as she watched the man die. The bleeding finally halted, the spasms stopped shooting through his form. Sheriff MacElravie was finally dead.

The smell of blood rose up from his body, sickening her, but the widow's jubilation overcame the urge to vomit. She yanked out the knife and wiped it clean with a monogrammed handkerchief that her husband had given her when they were courting.

"Michael, this one's for you," she whispered to the spirit that she felt hovering around her, and unlocked the bedroom door.

Ten minutes later she'd hauled the sheriff down the stairs. Vanessa stared at the grandfather clock that ticked comfortingly near the fireplace. Four hours to wait.

She did some needlepoint, returning to the seat cushion she'd been working on lately. Once in a 'hile she glanced over her close work at the lifeless form that lay on her parlor floor and smiled. Everything was finally going her way.

At midnight, Vanessa Gilroy went behind her house and hitched her old mare to the carriage. She drove up to her front door and hauled the dead man into the conveyance, silently thanking her father for working her so hard, remembering how he'd forced his daughter to help out with the boy's chores after her brother had died in an accident on the farm.

She calmly drove three streets from her home. Dressed in black, the veil covering her face, no one could tell who she was even if they did see her. But she met no one. The houses and the streets were dark.

The woman kicked and rolled Sheriff MacElravie's body onto the dirt, thrilling to the dull sound as it hit the earth. That done, she slowly drove home, put the horse in the small shelter and wiped up the stains that covered

the parlor floor. Next, she cleaned up her bedroom.

Vanessa took the soiled cloth and the
handkerchief downstairs and threw them into the
fireplace. Her clothing soon followed it, every
stitch until she stood naked. The shivering woman
lit a taper from the wall sconce and lit the pile
of blood-smeared clothing.

As the flames lapped the stiff black material and
rose up the chimney, destroying the evidence of
what she'd done, Vanessa laughed until the vivid
memories of her beloved husband flooded through
her. Her triumph dissolved with the tears that
splattered onto the polished hardwood floor.

"Did you hear what happened last night?"
Governor Evans shouted as Spur McCoy walked
into his library. "Sheriff MacElravie is dead!
Stabbed through the heart and dumped onto the
street!"

Spur took off his hat. "No, I hadn't heard."

He'd been cautious about facing the man the
morning after, but Evans seemed oblivious to what
may have happened between McCoy and his
daughter.

"Jesus, I can't believe it!"

"The vigilantes?" Spur guessed.

Evans turned to him. "Hell, no!" He sighed and
rubbed his forehead. "I don't know. Everything's
all messed up now."

"Did anyone see anything?" Spur asked
remembering the ineffectual sheriff. "Was this
another public execution like all the others?"

"No." The governor went to his brandy. "Nothing like it. This wasn't them vigilantes. It couldn't have been. They hang men, they don't stab them. And they make sure everyone sees them ride into town. You can't miss them."

"Maybe they've changed their methods. Maybe hanging got boring after awhile. You string up three or four men and where's the excitement?"

Evans splashed some liquor into a glass and downed it in one swallow. "I don't know."

"Seems like you're not the only one in town who might not wake up in the morning. Lots of murders going on here," he pointed out.

"You think I don't know that? But I'm not gonna cancel that big speech I have scheduled for this afternoon. Nothing's gonna scare me away from meeting the voters!"

"Okay. I'll plan security for it." Spur mulled over the situation. "That's the one in the church. Right?"

Evans nodded and took another drink.

"Fine. I'll see you there at noon. Meanwhile, think I'll see what I can find out about the sheriff's murder."

"You do that, McCoy! Find the bastard who killed him!" He refilled his glass.

As he left, Spur was surprised at the governor's reaction to MacElravie's death. He'd breezed through the other recent murders without a care, but this one seemed to have gotten to him. Why?

He shook his head and wandered over to the saloon. That's usually a good place to gather information in a hurry, and the whole town should be buzzing with the news—if, indeed, the vigilantes hadn't killed the man.

What had the sheriff done?

When the man was gone, Governor Evans sucked up another glassful of brandy and sat at his desk. The burly man slammed his fist onto its slick surface, almost enjoying the pain that ripped up his arm.

This was unthinkable, he raged in his mind. Absolutely unthinkable! Who the hell had killed him?

He stood and paced back and forth, thinking. The longer he waited, the more questions he'd have. He walked out of his house and saddled up his fastest horse. He had some people to talk to!

CHAPTER SEVEN

Vanessa smiled, thinking over what she'd done last night. The incident was fresh in her mind—the glorious feeling of ultimate triumph. Victory was sweet.

She had feigned shocked surprise when she'd heard of the sheriff's murder on her way to the dry goods store earlier that morning. It seemed that was the biggest thing that had happened to Boise in recent years.

Doubt crept up inside her, boiling like a teapot kept too long on the flame. No one had apparently connected John MacElravie's death with the vigilantes. That had been her mistake. If she could find a way to make it seem like they had done the killing it would serve them right, Vanessa thought. It could have maintained her innocent appearance.

Widow Gilroy wondered what the other

vigilantes thought when they heard that one of
their own was dead. She wished she could see
their faces.

The woman stared into her own eyes in the
hallway mirror. The memories swept over her
again, twisting and turning through her mind like
a prairie storm. The widow again felt the hands
biting into her shoulders and neck as two men
forced her to watch. She remembered her
husband's tortured words to her just before it
happened. Once again, she saw him hanging like
a dead chicken from the tree.

Vanessa had watched every second. When the
horse had bolted forward, when the rope had
snapped tight, when Michael Gilroy had screamed
as he was suddenly suspended in midair, she had
sworn vengeance against those men. The vivid
recollections of that hideous day possessed her.

One down, Vanessa thought. Those words
soothed her. She smiled at her reflection and sat
in her beloved rocker. One down, and five to go.

When it was all over, maybe she'd be able to
sleep all through the night unhaunted by the eerie
sound of hemp rope creaking as it swayed back
and forth and fresh wood snapping under the
weight it bore.

Maybe.

Jake Bancroft pushed his boots into the braided
rag rug. "Come on, Candra; you know that's our
mission! That's why we're here in the first place.
I don't like Boise any more than you do, but we're
doing the work of the Lord."

The twenty-year-old woman stopped stirring and set down the wooden bowl. "Jake, I realize that. But how much can we do if they kill us?"

"Candra, really!" Maureen said as she sat near the fireplace, stroking Lois' fine blonde hair. "They aren't savages, you foolish girl. They're human beings."

"You're quite right, wife of mine. Misguided, unenlightened—but human."

"But they aren't God-fearing souls. They don't follow our ways! They don't even understand us!" Candra gasped and pushed the spoon into the cornbread dough. "All we have is the Stones across the street and our faith to sustain us. I'm just not sure that's enough."

"It is, child, it is!" Jake kissed her cheek. "The Lord will protect us!" He stepped back and frowned at her. "And I'll talk to Governor Evans again. He wasn't pleased with my words, but he will hear me!"

Candra stared across the room at her sister wives. As usual, Lois and Maureen were having a great time. The two women were inseparable. They met her gaze with laughter and smiles. She turned back to the counter, gripped the wooden spoon and stirred the stiff mixture.

Jake wiped his hands on his pants. "And besides, the election's coming up. Maybe Judd Feinhold will win. He's sympmathetic to our cause."

"Candra! You aren't losing faith, are you?" Maureen said. "I'd hate to lose you as a sister!"

"I'm not your sister," she said bitterly into the dough. "I'm Jake's wife."

"And so am I."

He walked to the fireplace. "Girls, do everything you can to bolster up Candra's faith. I have some chores to attend to."

"Yes, husband!" the two chanted in unison.

"They hate us!" Candra said. "They hate us enough to kill us!"

Jake hesitated at the door, shook his head and walked outside.

Candra saw Maureen's mocking face in the bowl and stabbed it with the spoon, slicing her perfect cheekbones with huge gashes.

Everything had been fine. She'd just converted and Jake had married her, saving the young girl from a life of lonely darkness. They had built a house and she had enjoyed caring for him.

Then it had begun. She'd heard all about polygamy, of course, but Jake had never mentioned it in relation to them. One day, he brought a young woman home with him and introduced her as his next wife.

The shock had been so severe that Candra just smiled and talked with the stern-faced woman. Jake had let her sit down to dinner with them that night. At first, Maureen had been as friendly as she could under the circumstances.

After a while Candra noticed a distinct change. The woman kept her sentences short and clipped. Her smiles were less frequent and she clutched Jake's hand under the table.

She's jealous of me, Candra had thought. Jealous of the first wife! Maybe she could drive the woman away, make her so mean and ugly that Jake would forget all about her.

It hadn't worked. They'd been married and soon the bitch was sharing her bed every night. Candra fought back tears as she remembered lying beside them, shaking back and forth with the bed, forcing her head harder into her pillow to block out the revolting sounds of their couplings.

By the time Lois, too, had moved in, Candra was beyond caring about it anymore. Everything about their religion was right except this. It wasn't natural. It was evil.

But there was nothing she could do. She waited it out and eventually grew to like Lois, the short, soft-voiced woman who was the exact opposite of Maureen. They even stitched together and talked about future babies, though none of them had any on the way.

But Maureen hadn't warmed to her. A year after their nuptials the woman was cold and harsh with Candra, exploding over the tiniest thing.

Now, here in Boise, she couldn't put up with it anymore. She'd stayed with Jake because she loved him, and had realized that sharing his love was better than being alone. But now the danger— the whispered comments on the street, the ugly rumors spreading around town about them, the real anger that showed in the people's faces— forced her to face the truth. She couldn't face a whole lifetime of Lois and Maureen. She couldn't live in a place that hated her and everything for which she stood.

''You gonna beat that dough to death?'' a voice cut into her thoughts.

Candra turned and stared at Maureen, who frowned at her.

"You know better than that. You keep that up and that cornbread'll be flatter than your chest!"

She hurled the bowl at the wall, flinging it with the hatred that surged through her body. It crashed against the bricks and slid to the floor with a dull rattle. "You bit—"

"Maureen!" Lois said. "You promised to be nice to our sister wife."

"Dear, sweet Lois!" Maureen bent down and kissed her head. "I never said such a thing. How can I be nice to a woman that hates me?"

"She's still new. She doesn't understand everything about our faith." Lois sat up and smoothed down her apron.

Maureen laughed. "She just wants Jake for herself. She thinks she's woman enough for him!"

Candra fought back the words, biting her index finger as her body racked with silent sobs.

"Oh, did I make you cry again?" Maureen asked with mock sympathy. "Get used to it, sister wife!"

"Come on. Let's play." Lois snuggled up to the woman.

Candra watched in revulsion as Maureen cupped the younger woman's breast and squeezed it.

"Don't you want to join in?" Her voice was wicked.

"No!"

Candra ran from the room and collapsed on the bed. As she cried she felt the four distinct impressions that creased the huge feather mattress, and rolled into the familiar one that hugged her body every night while Jake wrapped his arms around Lois and Maureen.

"Your speech sounded better than ever," Spur said as the governor led him up to the front door.

"Yep! Talk's one of my strong points." Evans reached for the knob. "Not another one!" He bent and retrieved the piece of paper that had been tacked to the front door. "Another note!" He shook his head and let Spur into his mansion.

In the library, Governor Evans unfolded it and laid it on his desk. Spur bent over his shoulder to read it. The block letters were written in blue ink:

WARNING! EVANS, YOU DON'T LISSEN.
LEAVE TOWN ORR WE BURIE YOU!

"I see he hasn't learned how to spell yet," McCoy said. "It seems to be close to the last one."

"Identical in intent," Evans said. He scratched his chin. "You think I should be worried about this? Nothing's happened to me. I'm as healthy as a bird!"

"I don't know. In situations like this it's best to act as if the threat was real. If it isn't, it doesn't matter. If it is, you're prepared." He eased into the leather-upoholstered chair in front of the governor's desk.

"I know all that," he said with a snarl. "That's why I sent for you! I just want your gut feeling on this." The big man stared down at the note.

Spur sighed. "I don't know. All the vigilante activity in town might have been inspirational."

"How so?"

"A few citizens righting wrongs could set a trend. Others could take actions against those they assume have acted against them. Maybe someone's toes still feel the pressure from your feet."

"Yeah, but why wait? This man hasn't tried anything directly against me. Sure, he's sent notes and broken a few windows, but that's it."

"He's nervous. Threatening to do something is a hell of a lot easier than doing it."

Evans shook his head. "Maybe I don't need you after all, McCoy." He looked at the bottle of brandy in the corner of the room. "I think this guy's talking big. It's probably one of Lacey's would-be suitors that I turned away at the door."

"That's a possibility," Spur admitted. "But I'm here. I might as well stay in town and look into things."

"Fine with me!" Evans rose.

"Governor, think you could give me some ideas?"

"Ideas?" he asked, mystified.

"Yeah. Can you think of anyone in town who's been upset with you? Someone you've tangled with in the past, bad enough to make him want to do something like this?" Spur McCoy tapped the note.

"Well, sure! There's Judd Feingold, my opponent." Evans pinched his brows. "And, of course, the Mormons never have settled well with me. There's only two families left in Boise." He thought. "Jake Bancroft and I had some words a few months back, right after he moved in with his family on Plainfield Way. He didn't seem to like me. And the feeling was mutual, I might add."

"A Mormon and a politician. Well, it's something," Spur said. "Thanks for your help."

"I doubt it'll do you any good, but you're welcome to try." He pushed out his hand.

They shook.

"If by some miracle I do get a man to confess to writing these letters I'll surely let you know, Governor Evans."

"I'd appreciate that. Well, I'm sure you know the way out."

Spur did, and walked there quickly, trying to avoid a danger that lurked in the stately halls of the mansion. But before he reached the front door soft hands grabbed his waist, yanked him back and twisted him around.

"You wouldn't leave without giving me a kiss, would you?" She pressed up against him.

"Lacey!" Spur moved back and glanced at the library. "Keep it down, okay?"

The girl pouted but spoke softly. "You didn't keep it down last night." She eyed him and twirled a curl of blonde hair around a finger.

"I know. I just don't want your father to stain his carpet with my blood!"

"Didn't you like it?" she asked, flapping her lashes over widened eyes.

"Of course I did! We can't talk here. Come on, Lacey; let's go outside."

She happily followed him, smiling and bouncing in her plain blue dress. Out in the bright sunshine

Spur grinned in spite of himself at her youthful glee.

"As much as I hate it, I don't think we should see each other when your father's around. You know why."

She nodded. "If he even suspected, he'd fix it so that you couldn't ever love me again. And that wouldn't be any fun for me at all!"

"You have a way with words, Lacey," Spur said, and kissed her cheek. "I have to be going. See you later."

She grabbed his shirt. "When?" she insisted.

"Soon. Ah, soon. When I have the time and the governor's busy with something else—somewhere else."

"Alright. I'll try to wait until then!"

Spur wrested himself from her grip and walked toward the eagle-topped iron gate.

CHAPTER EIGHT

When he got to Plainfield Avenue, Spur soon realized it wouldn't be difficult to find this Jake Bancroft. The street was much like any other in such towns—houses spaced well apart with plenty of empty land between them.

But as he walked beside them he saw that most had been boarded up. On others, front doors stood open, swinging back and forth in the hot breeze. Tattered curtains fluttered from broken windows.

Up ahead, two blackened mounds of wood showed the effects of devastating fires. McCoy stopped and studied them. The blazes had been so recent that the street was still peppered with ash, and the dank smell of destruction hung around them.

Plainfield must have been the unofficial Mormon Way, Spur thought as he moved on. If all the houses had once held Mormon families, they'd had hard times in Boise. At least Governor Evans had been honest about his feelings concerning them.

Spur finally found a freshly-kept, brightly painted two-story clapboard house. The Bancrofts? He knocked and the door soon opened.

A large-boned man peered out at him. "Yes?" His voice was wary.

"I'm looking for Jake Bancroft, but I don't know the address."

"You got him."

"Good. Mr. Bancroft, I'm with the U.S. Government, looking into problems in this town of yours."

Bancroft laughed. "Heck, Boise isn't my town!" He didn't open the door farther.

"Can I come in?"

"How do I know you're not one of those vigilantes?" Bancroft asked.

"I'm not. Besides, from what I hear, they work together. Six men." He gestured behind him. "I'm alone and I'm not wearing a kerchief mask. Okay?"

The man mulled it over and nodded. "Fair enough. Come on in."

Spur stepped into the house. It was a stark, brightly lit place with simple furnishings—hand made tables and chairs, two spinning wheels, a loom and a small shelf holding leather-bound books. The scent of cooking apples filled the air.

He heard laughter and feet shuffling in an adjoining room.

"Sorry about that rude welcome," Jake said, turning to him after closing the door. "But I have to be careful these days. Too many people in town I can't trust. Starting with Governor Evans."

"I understand," Spur said.

"Have a seat."

Spur did.

Jake paced. "I truly don't understand what these folks are afraid of! My family's not out to rape, loot or kill. All we want is a quiet, peaceful life."

"And spread the word about your faith. Right?"

"Sure, of course."

"These people aren't afraid of you, Bancroft. They're afraid of change. You represent new ideas, new ways of thinking. It threatens them and their own faith."

He lowered his head. "I know. But those—those—" He shook his head. "They think it gives them the right to burn down houses and force my people out of town!"

"That must not set well with you," McCoy probed. "All this anger and violence directed toward your people. Has anything happened to you or your family?"

Jake softened his voice. "Yes. Last week I was walking out of the general store. Someone slammed the butt of his pistol into my neck. When I turned around he was gone—just vanished." He rubbed the tender spot and winced. "I never told my family about it. Last thing I want is for them to worry about me."

"Have you received any threatening letters?"

The Mormon stared hard at him. "Matter of fact,

I have. Just yesterday. Candra found one shoved
under the door.''

''Can I see it?''

''I burned it up soon as I read it. It was written
in big letters, something about 'we don't like your
stink. Go back where you came from.' '' Bancroft
rubbed his palms together. ''First one we got, but
the other families—the Warners, the
Greenaways—they got letters. Two days later their
houses were torched. I don't mind saying I'm
nervous.''

The words were true, Spur realized. This wasn't
the kind of man who'd send notes to Governor
Evans. Bancroft was more than nervous. He was
scared, afraid for his life.

That ruled him out.

''Look, I don't know who you are, but if you can
do anything to calm these people down I'd—''

Spur grunted. ''Afraid there's not much I can
do. But I am looking into the vigilantes, trying to
find out who they are. They're behind all the
persecution. Right?''

Bancroft nodded so vigorously his lower lip
wobbled. ''Yes, sir! Those men are crafty. No one
knows who they are and they won't try to put a
stop to them.'' He shook his head. ''Boise sure is
different than Salt Lake.''

''You could always go back.''

Jake smiled. ''That's just what they want, isn't
it? No. We can't. It's our mission to bring the word
to these people. It doesn't matter if they want to
hear it or not. Some will, and that'll make all this
worthwhile.''

"Those are brave words, Bancroft."

As Spur rose from the chair he saw three women standing in the kitchen door, staring at him with wide eyes. They ranged in age from about 20 to 35, all unique ladies, simply dressed in non-provocative clothing.

"My wives," Bancroft said, his eyes shining. "Come on, girls. Get back to work!"

They frowned and disappeared.

"You must be some kind of man," Spur said, grinning.

Bancroft puffed out his chest. "They're a handful, alright. But we get along."

"Thanks for your help." McCoy walked out.

Halfway down Plainfield, Spur heard rapid footsteps behind him. He turned and saw a young woman racing toward him, her skirts flying in the air.

"Wait!" she said desperately.

As the woman neared him, he recognized her as the youngest of Jake Bancroft's wives. She panted and clutched her chest. "I have to talk to you."

"Fine, Mrs. Bancroft. Let's talk."

"Not here." She whipped her head around, sending her brown pony tails flying. "I snuck out the kitchen door. Jake doesn't know I'm gone. Let's go into town."

They went quickly. Spur tried to take her arm but the young woman brushed away his hand. Curious, he walked with her onto Goldrush. "Where now?"

She glanced both ways and shrugged. "Your hotel?"

"Mrs. Bancroft!" Spur said in surprise.

"The name's Candra," she said, her cheeks coloring. "And I'm only thinking about my safety. Let's go!"

Two minutes later, Spur closed the curtains and turned up the lamps. Candra Bancroft sat in the rickety chair that she'd thrust under the doorknob. In the soft light she looked older than her years— eyes low and dark, lips firmly set, shoulders slumped with defeat.

"What's the problem, Candra?" he asked, standing before her.

"My husband. And his other wives." She bit her lower lip. "I just can't stand it any more. Jake refuses to take us back to Salt Lake. He seems to think we'd all be better off dead or losing everything than face the church elders there, admitting defeat."

Spur nodded. "Your husband's faith is very strong. Unbreakable."

"I know. And so are his other wives." The word was harsh, strained. She looked up at him, raised the corners of her mouth and blinked. "But that's behind me now. I'm leaving town, going to Pocatella where I have friends. It's the only thing I can do, and I need your help."

"Sure. Can't you just divorce your husband?"

Candra rolled her eyes. "There's no time! We've got a few days at most before they run us out of town. If they burn the house and we're all asleep in it . . . ." The words trailed. She clutched her shoulders and stared at a spot on the wallpaper behind Spur's shoulder. "I can't wait for that to happen. Maureen and Lois—my husband's other wives—won't come with me. I tried to talk them into it but they're stubborn. So here I am."

"What can I do?"

"I checked yesterday when I bought eggs. The stage leaves for Pocatella in the morning at dawn. I just need a place to stay tonight."

"No problem. You can sleep here."

Her face melted with relief. "Thank you, Mr.— Why, I don't even know you're name!"

"McCoy. Spur McCoy."

"I hope I won't put you out," Candra said, swinging her leg.

"Not at all. It won't be the first time I've slept on the floor."

She smiled. "You—ah—you wouldn't have to do that." She looked directly into his eyes.

Spur smiled wonderingly at her.

"Mr. McCoy, I've been married for a year now. For the last six months I've slept alone. Sure, three other people were in bed with me, but I was *alone*. Do you understand what I'm saying?"

He smiled. "Yes."

She stood and walked to the window. Candra Bancroft ran her fingers up and down the green fringe that edged the curtains. "A woman has certain, well, needs. Her husband should fulfill them for her while he's fulfilling his."

"That's the way it's supposed to work." He looked at the back of her dress. She was a strange woman.

"But when a man has three wives, one of them can fall through the cracks of his needs."

He grunted affirmatively.

Candra unfastened her pony tails and let her lightly curled brown hair fall to her shoulders. She ran her hands through it until it shone in the yellow lamp light.

"I'm only human." She fumbled with something in front of her.

"Yes. You are that." He enjoyed the game she played with him.

"So it's only natural that when a handsome man walks into an unfulfilled woman's home, that she might . . . ."

"Perfectly natural."

She shifted her hips. "And when she's alone with him in his hotel room, shouldn't she . . . ."

"Uh-huh."

Candra turned around. Her cotton dress lay unbuttoned to the waist. She slipped it off her shoulders. Spur watched in fascination as it slid off her body with a hypnotic grace, slowly revealing her firm, rounded form. No undergarments veiled her beauty. When the dress touched the floor she was totally naked.

"Mr. McCoy, you don't know how long I've waited for a man like you!" She held out her arms. "Please. Now. Just do it! I need it so bad!"

The catch in her throat, her stunning nudity and the desperation in her eyes made him kick off his boots. His crotch pounded as he yanked off his socks and removed his shirt.

Candra silently watched him, looking into his eyes as he undressed. Then, bare and erect, he walked to her. Spur's penis stabbed her midsection before his hands fastened around her shoulders. She groaned at the erotic contact, at the closeness of him, and buried her face in his chest hair.

McCoy lifted the whimpering woman and laid her gently on the bed. Candra automatically spread her legs and thrust her hand between them, probing, flicking back and forth, pleasuring herself. "Please. Please!"

He didn't hesitate. Drunk on the young woman's musk, he entered her as gently as he could, pushing until their bodies were locked together at the waist. Candra moaned and tossed her head as he pumped.

"Faster. Faster!"

Grunting, he obeyed her animalistic command, gazing into the eyes of the woman who bounced below him. She rammed her hips up to his, meeting his driving thrusts with ever increasing urgency.

The old bed squeaked with their rhythm. Flesh slapped against flesh. Candra opened her lips, strangled out a cry and slapped a hand over her mouth. She shuddered with supernatural violence, twisting and thrashing under him as pleasure rocketed through her body.

Her contractions made his groin boil. Spur plunged faster into her, pistoning his hips. Candra rolled through a second and third climax until he lost control and joined her in a malestrom of erotic ecstasy.

The mattress came alive, bucking and buckling beneath them as their slick bodies shook together. A pure, sweet howl whistled through Spur's ears.

The moment infinitely stretched out, extending, lengthening with each powerful burst deep inside her.

Candra finally gasped and lay still below him, taking his last few pumps before he collapsed on top of the young woman. She clasped her hands around his wet back and puffed.

"I mean, it's only natural, isn't it?"

Spur mumbled something in her hair.

CHAPTER NINE

Spur did see Candra Bancroft safely onto the stagecoach the next morning. The young woman left everything behind in the dust that rose in the air behind the departing vehicle. As he watched it surge out of town, the horses fresh and eager to be out on the trail, Spur hoped she'd find her peace somewhere, sometime. And he was happy he'd given her some comfort during her last day in Boise.

Scratching an annoying itch on his chin, Spur straightened his hat and wandered down Goldrush. No reason to see the governor today, he decided, but he should let the service know he'd changed his plans. McCoy sent a telegraph to General Halleck informing him that the vigilantes were now his main targets.

He turned toward the hotel. Time for breakfast.

*   *   *

Just after sunset, five men rode into town, kicking their horses into full-out gallops. Women screamed and ran onto the boardwalk. Well fed boys who had been playing with pop-guns, aiming at tin can targets, shouted at each other in joy as they hid behind water barrels. Horses tied up at the hitching posts before the stately houses whinneyed in response to the neighs of their new equine friends.

Every man who heard them coming, who saw their careless, power-drunk entrance into Boise, wondered who they were behind their masks. And if they were the next to be killed.

They rode abreast, spanning Goldrush, forcing carriages and buggies to turn aside to let them through. As soon as they'd passed, the street returned to normal. People went back to their everyday lives, willfully crushing all memories of the vigilantes.

One dark clad figure watched in silence as the five men rode relentlessly down Goldrush. He hovered in a dark corner, moving the muzzle of a rifle in the street dust, waiting.

The five turned onto Plainfield and halted outside a house. They bunched together, whispering.

''You got the kerosene and rags?'' one asked.

''Yep.''

''You know what to do!''

All but their leader dismounted. Cloth was soaked with the deadly liquid. Suitable rocks were found, tested for proper weight and wrapped with

the rags. Ends were tied to ensure they wouldn't
fly off. In a minute, all was ready.

"No warning!" their leader said to them from
his mount as he was handed one of the deadly
packages. "Do it! Start the circle of fire. These
heathens'll burn in hell; we're just giving them a
head start!"

One vigilante ran around the house with a can
of kerosene, pouring a trail of the deadly liquid
on the sun dried plants and weeds. When he'd
surrounded the structure, he rejoined the others.

Three matches were lit and thrown onto the
ground. The kerosene quickly lit, rising up in a
curtain of flame that extended around the house.

More matches were lit and touched to the rag-
wrapped rocks until they burst into flames. The
men hurled them at the house. Three crashed
through windows. Two others landed on the
ground and were quickly quenched.

Soon, five more rocks broke the silence. Light
grew inside the house. The four men mounted up
and rode down Plainview as the unholy inferno
behind them exploded in a sea of brilliant
destruction.

As they passed another abandoned house, gunfire rang out. One of the vigilantes howled and
gripped his arm, nearly unseating himself.

"Damn! I'm shot!"

"Badly?" their leader called to him as they continued racing out of town.

"Don't think so but it hurts like shit!"

The man searched the area with his eyes.
"They're long gone by now. Ride on, men! We've

done our work!'' he yelled above the sounds of twenty hooves pounding into the dirt.

They left the last house behind them and rode over open countryside for two miles before slowing their horses and looking back.

A house on Plainfield lit up half the town.

''No more Mormons!'' the leader of the Citizens' Vigilante Committee yelled.

The men joked with each other as they pulled the kerchiefs from their faces. The wounded man clutched his leaking forearm and stuffed the kerchief in his back pocket.

They rested their horses and themselves before heading back into town from five different directions with five different stories.

Another victory for the vigilantes.

''Mr. McCoy! You are looking fit this morning,'' Vanessa Gilroy said as she approached him.

''Don't know how.'' He stared at her as she approached him. The widow had given up her black attire; she was wrapped in yellow crinoline.

''Bad night?''

''It was a strenous one. I got together a search party for the vigilantes. I actually had two men agree to help—they were fed up with them. We didn't find anything but tracks leading out of town that split up and led back into Boise.'' He snarled. ''And, as usual, no one had anything useful to say to me.''

''Somebody must know something,'' Vanessa said, retying the bow beneath her chin. ''But they're scared. There has to be four or five wives

wondering why their husbands came in so late last
night, but they'd never dare to connect that fact
with what happened to the Bancrofts." She shook
her head and squinted up at him. "Will you have
lunch with me?"

"Sure. I haven't eaten all morning."

"Then it's time. I know a wonderful restaurant
right down the street."

They walked there.

"Have you uncovered anything about the
vigilantes?" Spur asked.

"I don't know for sure. I'd hate to accuse the
wrong men."

"Hmmmm." She was stalling, Spur thought. But
why?

"I did hear that some folks around town think
that Sheriff MacElravie was one of them."

He looked at her in surprise. "Where'd you hear
that?"

"I don't know. Something someone said during
quilting yesterday. Course, we'll never know now
that he's dead."

"He did seem to be a little too happy to let them
run this town for him."

"And he never did a thing to find the men who
killed my husband." Vanessa shook off the
memories. "But let's not think about that now.
We're here."

She led him into the small, darkly lit restaurant.
They sat at a table in the corner. Appetizing smells
laced with garlic and tomatoes steamed from the
central rear door. Two couples sat digging into
plates of food and glasses of wine.

"Nice place," he said.

Linens covered the tables. The wall sconces dripped with cut crystal, and the silverware gleamed in the soft light.

"Reminds me of Philadelphia—I mean, what I think Philadelphia would be like. It's a little bit of civilization in this uncivilized place." She unfolded her napkin and placed it on her lap.

Spur followed suit. "You come here often?" he asked.

"Not since my husband—not for quite a while." She leaned closer to him. "I didn't bring you here for the food, Mr. McCoy."

"Then what?"

"In a few seconds, a man will walk out from the kitchen. I'll bet you a glass of wine he'll have a hurt arm."

He studied her. "I'm not the gambling type, Vanessa. What are you up to?"

Before she could answer a short, dark man emerged from the kitchen.

"Mrs. Gilroy!" he said expansively, smiling and holding his hands out as if to embrace her from across the room. "I am honored by your presence, as usual," he said in a thickly accented voice. The man's right shirtsleeve was pushed up, and a white bandage circled his forearm.

"Thank you; you're too kind." Her voice was sweet. "What happened to your arm, Sam?" Vanessa asked.

The restaurateur rubbed the white bandage and ruefully grinned. "A foolish accident, I am afraid. I chop onions, I chop myself." The short

Italian grinned and placed his hands on the table.
"Maybe I think about you when I do that? Not
think about work?"

Vanessa laughed. "Sam Delmonico, you're an
old tease. Bring us some steaks. Rare. And a bottle
of your finest red wine. Okay?"

"Anything. Anything for you, my dear!"

When he'd disappeared she grabbed Spur's
sleeve. "What did I tell you?"

"So he's a lousy cook. Or he isn't very careful."

Vanessa shook her head and moved her chair
beside his. "Didn't you hear the stories? Someone
fired a rifle last night as the vigilantes rode out of
town. Sam Delmonico didn't cut himself; he was
wounded after burning down the Bancroft place—
and them!"

"You can't know that!" Spur said. "It could be
a coincidence."

"Of course! That's why I wanted you to see for
yourself." She paused. "But I hadn't seen Sam for
weeks. There was no way I'd know he'd hurt
himself in the kitchen." Vanessa stared at him.

"But you knew he was shot?"

"Yes. Yes! When we were all crowding around
this morning, watching them pulling out the—the
bodies—this Mormon woman said she saw the
whole thing, the fire, the man getting shot. They
live right across the street, after all! And she said
the man was short. I just put two and two together.
Most of the fellas in this town are big mountains
of men."

He mulled it over. "You sure you didn't hire
someone to take a potshot at the vigilantes last

night?"

"How could I know they were going to attack the Bancrofts? Be reasonable, Spur!"

"That's hard to do in an unreasonable town."

"I know. I've lived here for long enough to know that only too well!"

They quieted as Sam brought out the wine and two glasses. He set them down and filled them. "Your dinners will soon be ready."

After he'd gone again, Vanessa looked at Spur and shrugged. "He's one of them."

"Great. Now all I have to do is prove it."

"And I'll do everything I can."

They sipped the wine. The front door burst open and Governor Martin Evans whisked into the room. Not pausing to look left or right he stormed into the kitchen, leaving two flapping doors in his wake.

Spur watched the doors swinging and turned to Vanessa. "I wonder what that's all about," Spur said, setting down his glass.

Vanessa licked her lips. "Sam and Martin are old friends. Sam's probably behind in his rent again."

"The governor owns this building?"

She nodded. "Half the town. And what he doesn't own, he has interest in. Governor Evans is so rich he can affort to throw around his money, and he does. He makes a lot of loans. You could almost say he's the unofficial banker of Boise. The First Bank of Evans."

"I see."

Vanessa lowered her voice. "Sam Delmonico

might have been too busy hanging innocent men
and killing Mormons to think about little things
like paying his rent. That'd be enough to set off
Martin Evans."

"Will you be happy if he's reelected?"

She looked into her glass. "Oh, I don't know.
But I don't have any choice, do I? At least he's a
known danger. This Judd Feingold—we don't
know what he's like, what he'll try to do to Idaho
Territory. At least he says he supports the
Mormons, which is a long way from wanting to
run them out of town." She shook her head. "I
haven't really thought about it."

"Yeah, you've had other things on your mind."

"I have at that."

Spur sipped the wine. No wonder Evans was
worried about these threats. He had a lot to lose
if he had to give up the title of governor.

Doors banged. Evans shot past them and walked
outside. He never saw the man and woman sitting
at the table, talking about him.

FEINGOLD FOR GOVERNOR, the sign in the
window said.

Spur knocked on the door and walked in. The
strong scent of tobacco smoke filled the air.

"Yes?" The thin man looked up from his desk,
pen in hand. His narrow eyes were heavily lidded;
his chin was blue with the kind of whiskers that
no razor could ever scrape off.

"You Feingold?" Spur asked.

"That's me. The next Governor of Idaho
Territory, if everything goes right." He smiled and

rested the pen against the inkwell. Dressed in his shirtsleeves and a black vest, the dark haired man straightened up in his chair. "What can I do for you?"

Spur closed the door behind him. "I'd like to talk about the election."

"Fine! Nothing I like better than that." He rubbed his hands together. "Do you live in Boise, or somewhere else in this great territory of ours?"

"No. Just passing through."

Feingold grinned. "Then I guess you're not here to kill me."

"How's that?" Spur asked, surprised.

"I said, I figure you didn't come here to blow my brains out." Judd Feingold ran a hand through his short, curly black hair and frowned. "Maybe I should explain."

"Maybe you should." Spur took a seat.

"I've been in the county courthouse all morning—I'm a lawyer, if you didn't know. When I got back here I found this." He handed a piece of paper to Spur.

"It's rather, er, vivid account of what'll happen to me if I don't drop out of the election and move somewhere else."

The note was familiar—too familiar. Same block lettering. Different words, but Spur thought it looked to be the work of the same man. "Have you received any other letters like this? Before today, I mean?"

Feingold squinted at him and rubbed his chin. "Look, I don't even know who you are."

"Spur McCoy, United States Secret Service, from Washington, D.C."

Judd Feingold nearly fell off his chair. "Whoa! I've heard about you boys. Never figured I'd meet one!"

"You have."

"What're you doing in Boise?" Feingold rested his boots on the marble desktop.

"Investigating."

"Investigating what, may I ask?"

"Different things."

Judd Feingold smiled. "Like the vigilantes, maybe?"

"Yes."

He slapped the desk. "Hot damn! About time we got some help around here, someone who's not afraid of those holier-than-thou types!" Feingold chuckled and stared at Spur, eyes wide, face shining.

"Is this the first letter you've received?"

"Yes sir, it is."

"You've heard about the threats against the governor's life?"

Judd grimaced. "Have I heard of them? No one within a hundred miles could have missed it. Evans is playing that up for everything he can, saying that ruthless, unsavory people are trying to force him out of office, and if he isn't reelected they'll take over the whole territory. If you'll pardon my expression, Mr. McCoy, that's a load of horse shit!"

"What makes you say that?"

"Facts. As a lawyer, I deal in facts. Nothing has happened to the sitting governor. Absolutely nothing. Sure, a few notes may have been dropped off at his house, but nothing else of substance."

"And now you've received one of those notes."

"Yes."

"You think the sender's just trying to rile you both up?"

"I don't know."

Spur ran his fingernails along the right seam of his pants leg. "Any idea who might have sent it?"

Feingold grinned. "Mr. McCoy, asking me if I think the opposition's trying to scare me out of the race is like asking a married woman if she's a virgin."

"Point taken."

"If it isn't just a scare tactic from Evans, I don't have the slightest idea. Perhaps someone's having some fun. Maybe it's the vigilantes . . . ."

"You talk about them in your speechifying?"

"No way!" Feingold thundered. He stood and walked to the window. "That's one ticket to oblivion I'm not going to stand in line for. I'll admit it—I'm afraid to even mention them. I'll talk about bringing in new business, the problem of water rights, taxes, fencing the land and all that, annexation—but not the vigilantes."

"And the Mormons?"

Judd spun toward him. "Where do you stand on them?"

McCoy shrugged. "As far as I'm concerned they're entitled to live their lives wherever they want. They have rights just like the rest of us."

"Sounds like my last speech. Thoughts, ideas like that are ripping this town apart. I say we should let them in. Evans thunders on and on about how they'll destroy our chances of ever achieving statehood."

"So this note could have been sent by someone who doesn't agree with you."

"Yeah. Like the vigilantes." He shrugged. "Now that the Bancrofts are gone, maybe the last family'll move out and there won't be any more problems." Judd shook his head. "If Evans wins and the Mormons move back in, I don't wanna have to watch what happens."

"I've heard a few of his speeches. Are you sure all that hatred against the Mormons isn't just campaign rhetoric?" Spur asked.

"Maybe he is feeding on what he assumes is the commonest reaction of them. Hell, I don't know." He looked at the letter. "But I won't give up now. The election's only three days away. If I leave, Evans'll have things sewed up."

"It takes guts to do that with the governor, the vigilantes, and half the town against you. That's pretty admirable of you."

Feingold slammed a fist into his left hand. "Or powerfully stupid. Sorry, I have to kick you out. There's a debate this afternoon."

After he left the man's office, Spur thought it over. Feingold obviously wasn't behind the letter that Evans had received. His gut feeling was that the man was innocent. A lawyer can talk a good story but McCoy sensed that he had been totally honest with him.

That led him back to the vigilantes. Suddenly, something occurred to him. He'd heard the stories that flew around the crowd watching bodies being pulled out of Bancroft's home. The latest incident had loosened up some of the populace, and whispers were passed from person to person.

Every eye-witness report of their entrance into town said that five men had ridden in that night.

Not six. Five.

Had one of them gotten cold feet? Had second thoughts? Maybe one man's conscience would not allow him to be party to killing the Bancroft family.

Or was Vanessa's comment that the sheriff was one of them true? If so, it made sense that only five vigilantes attacked the house. There were just five left.

He thought it over as he went to the Masonic Hall and waited outside for the candidates to arrive, keeping watch for a gang of kerchiefed riders.

CHAPTER TEN

"And so, fellow citizens of Boise, a vote for Evans is a vote for you!"

The packed building rattled with applause as the governor took a drink of water. Spur stood just below the speaker's platform, searching the crowd for signs of danger. He was there, he'd told himself, to protect both Evans and Feinhold.

The 200 men standing in the stuffy, hot hall quieted. The mass of humanity stretched out the door and onto the street that fronted the masonic hall.

"I'm a man of action, not empty words. Your vote will ensure that the Territory of Idaho is soon the State of Idaho, a place where we can raise our families and enjoy the riches of this great country of ours, unhindered by the seductive wiles of outsiders who'd infect us with their filthy ways!"

More applause.

Judd Feingold, sitting on the dais next to Evans, signed and shook his head.

"You don't like that, Feingold? Sorry, but they do."

Hot lead slammed into the wall behind the governor. As the explosion echoed throughout the room, the mob panicked, pushing and shoving, pressing onto each other in a mad attempt to leave. Spur bounded onto the dais between the candidates, weapon already drawn, sniffing the acrid scent of gunpowder.

"Ladies and gentlemen, please!" Evans shouted. "Calm yourselves!"

The group didn't hear his words. Spur stared down at the boiling morass of human flesh and shook his head. There'd be no way to discover who'd fired the shot.

In a few minutes it was over. McCoy stood with Evans and Feingold, looking at the boots, hats and jackets that had been dropped in haste on the floor.

"I can't believe it," Judd said.

"Didn't think I was in any danger, McCoy?" the governor asked sarcastically. "I'd say that bullet back there proves you wrong!"

Ignoring him, Spur turned to the man's opponent. "Feingold, things are getting too hot not to take threats seriously. You got any friends handy with firearms?"

He glanced quizzically at him. "Well, sure! I know a few men. Why?"

"Keep 'em with you. Wherever you go. And don't walk the streets without a pistol slapping against your thigh."

"McCoy, I can't—" Feindgold started.

"Even if you don't know how to use it, it might make some trigger-happy fool think twice. And Governor Evans, hire yourself some bodyguards." He stepped down from the dais and kicked a hat lying on the floor.

"Where the hell are you going?" Evans shouted.

"To find out who's really behind this shit!"

He walked outside. Four dozen people stood around, commiserating with each other, discussing the debate and that moment when a bullet had prematurely halted it.

But after he'd talked to 40 people he knew that no one—as usual—had seen anything.

It had all the signs of being the handiwork of the vigilantes.

"Care for more wine?"

"No, thank you. Just the check." Vanessa Gilroy opened her beaded purse.

"No, no!" Sam Delmonico said. "For you, it is on the house." He sat beside her at her table. "I—I miss you these months."

She saw the fire burning inside him. The repulsive little man took her hand. Vanessa fought off the urge to push him away. She forced herself to smile, and was astounded at the effect it had on him.

"Without you, my restaurant is dark and cold," the Italian said, his nostrils puffing. "Then you walk in and I see heaven in a green dress come down to bless me." He kissed her hand.

Widow Gilroy glanced around the room. "Isn't it about closing time?" she asked, lifting her right eyebrow.

He jumped. "I be ready in five minutes!"

As Sam Delmonico dashed off, Vanessa smiled and settled back in her chair. She was already prepared.

Ten minutes later she let Sam into her house, closed the door behind him and locked it. "Look, Sam, I won't play games. I need you. I want you!"

The Italian gasped. "That makes me so happy!" He reached for her.

The strong scent of garlic wafted over her. Vanessa took his hands. "Come to my bedroom!"

This is too easy, she thought as they climbed the stairs. Sam Delmonico was so nervous he tripped a half-dozen times before they reached the landing.

Once inside her bedroom, she closed the curtains. "Pull down your pants, Sam. I wanna see a real man!"

"Is this happening?" the immigrant said as he fumbled with his belt. Soon he unbuckled it, opened his fly and hauled down his pants and underwear.

Vanessa smirked at the tiny organ that stood there ready for her. Sam blushed under her intense gaze. It throbbed.

He ripped off the rest of his clothing.

"Onto the bed!" she said. "Now! Before I change my mind!"

"Yes—yes, Vanessa! I am dreaming this."

He took tiny steps to keep from tripping over his lowered clothing. Once there, he sat on its edge, saliva oozing from between his lips.

Vanessa quickly undressed to her chemise and

bloomers, then turned her back and went to her bureau. She extracted four lengths of black satin cloth she'd ripped into thin strips earlier that day and went to him.

"Woman of my dreams, you—you—what is this?" Sam asked in confusion.

"You know what they're for." She pushed him onto his back and hauled his skinny legs onto the mattress. Bending over him, she quickly tied his right wrist to the old iron headboard. "I will possess you, Sam Delmonico! You're mine. All mine!"

"Yes, yes," he whimpered.

Vanessa grabbed his left arm.

"Hurts!" he said. "My injury!"

"Sorry." She wrapped the satin around his wrist and tightened it. Vanessa laughed when the sudden pain went directly to his crotch.

She firmly secured his ankles to the bed's legs and stood over him, staring down at the helpless, exposed little man that she despised so much. "Do you want me?" she asked in a harsh voice.

"Yes! Please!"

Vanessa pressed her fingernails into the flesh above the knot of his left ankle and raked them upward along the hairy white flesh. Sam Delmonico shivered and pitched as she neared the point between his legs.

"You like that?"

"God, yes! Can't you see?"

Vanessa smiled and grabbed his testicles, closing her fingers around the heavy, warm sack and pulled.

"Not so hard!" he said, gasping in pain.

"Not so hard?" She yanked at the soft flesh pouch. "You killed my husband!"

Sam Delmonico howled with pain as the widowed woman's fingernails bit into his tender flesh. He struggled but the satin ropes held his wrists and ankles firmly to the bedposts. He was completely immobilized.

"Vanessa, this is not funny!" the immigrant said, bucking his hips, trying to throw off the hand that slowly tortured his crotch.

"It wasn't funny watching you and your friends string up my husband either, Sam!" she said. "At least it wasn't funny to me. But you must have enjoyed watching that innocent man die at your own hands!"

The gasping man's body reddened. "What—what do you talk of?"

"Don't try to hoodwink me, you Eye-talian murderer! I know all about it."

"You do not know what you are—"

"Sheriff MacElravie couldn't stop talking before he died." Vanessa released his testicles.

Sam Delmonico relaxed on the bed, panting, staring up at her in wide-eyed horror.

She put her face inches away from his. "Don't play dumb with me, Sam! Unless you want more of these!" She unfurled her fingers and held the sharp nails to his neck.

"No. No! I—I cannot stand that!"

"Then you better start talking." She sat on the bed beside him. "Now!"

The restaurant owner screwed up his face. "He

will kill me."

"Who? Who'll take your miserable little life? You mean your leader? Who is that, honey?" She touched his thigh. "Who's in charge of your gang?"

Sam twisted his face away from hers and stared at the ceiling. "Did you not hear my words? He will kill me if I talk to you!"

"Better him than me!" Vanessa said. "You have one minute to save yourself, Sam. One minute between me and oblivion."

Strange sounds choked from his throat. "Okay. Yes."

"Yes what?" she demanded.

"Yes. I am one of them. I was there when they killed your husband." He closed his eyes.

"There? Heck, you put the rope around his neck and cinched it up!"

"Yes."

"I know most of the other members, I've been watching your little raiding parties in town. Last night, in fact, when I heard you, I took my shotgun outside and waited for you to pass by. Once you'd killed the Bancrofts, Sam, I took a shot at you to see if my information was right." She smiled and touched the bandaged wound on his arm. "It was."

"That—that was you?" He glared up at Widow Gilroy.

She nodded. "I'm a better shot than you are, Sam. I thank my father for the day he taught me how to handle a rifle. All those afternoons of target practice. But enough of that." Vanessa pressed against the blood-stained cloth. ''Who leads you? Who's ultimately responsible for all these deaths?''

''Bitch!'' he yelled, spitting the word at her. ''I will tell you nothing. Nothing!''

''Have it your way, Sam. I gave you a chance. You just lost it.'' She yanked the pillow from under his head.

''Let me out now!'' the immigrant said.

Vanessa smiled down at him. ''I'll let you out. As soon as you're dead.'' She lowered the pillow.

''No. No!''

It molded to his face. The feathers trapped inside the pink cloth shifted as they pressed harder and harder against the man's nose and mouth. The Widow Gilroy sighed as Delmonico struggled, flailing his imprisoned arms so hard against their bonds that the iron bed banged against the wall.

''Darn it! Lie still and let me kill you,'' she said as she forced the pillow into his face. Muffled sounds from beneath it told her it wasn't working. She thought for a second, released it and squatted over his face. His gyrations hadn't yet freed his head so Vanessa sat fully on it, forcing the softly suffocating pillow into his mouth and plugging the man's nostrils.

''Bumpy ride!'' she said as the pillow shook beneath her.

His body vainly whipped from side to side. She raised her knees and forced her whole weight onto Sam Delmonico's face.

As the motions below her weakened, Vanessa Gilroy remembered her husband's face, the good times they'd had—when she'd surprised him with a glass of wildflowers just after they'd moved into their new home, the first suit she'd ever sewn for him, Michael coming to her with tender lust late at night after bolting out on some emergency call.

She thought of the babies that hadn't been born, the long days that would have stretched out into years with her husband, the plans they'd had to tour the capital cities of Europe when he had closed his dental practice.

Vanessa sniffed and realized that the pillow was still. She shook her head, slipped her legs to the side of the bed and stood on the floor. Gingerly, the widow lifted the pillow from Sam Delmonico's head.

The tortured expression on his face told her all that she needed to know. The terror and suffering he must have endured before he'd gasped his last breath didn't begin to pay back the horror she'd lived with these past few weeks, Vanessa thought, but it helped.

"You'll never kill another innocent man," she said, and went to her bureau.

Back at the bed with a knife, she bit its blade through the satin and laughed as his left arm flopped down, lifeless and slowly growing cold.

"I don't buy that, Evans!" Judd Feingold stabbed the air with his finger.

"Your spending habits are no concern of mine, Feingold," the governor joked.

"You paid someone to take a wild shot at you during the debate this afternoon!" He stabbed the air with his finger.

"Why?"

"I can say it in two words: sympathy vote."

The governor folded his hands and laid them on the oak desk. "Your imagination is matched only by your stupidity, Feingold."

The candidate advanced on him. "Yes. I've been so stupid, believing you'd run a clean campaign like the decent, honest man you say you are!"

Evans tapped his fingers on the desk. "Haven't you wised up by now? You should know how it is. There's no place in politics for an honest man."

Judd Feingold groaned. "That kind of thinking's what's wrong with this territory! It's men like you who're gonna run Idaho into the ground!"

"Give it up. Drop out now, Feingold. Get your ass outta town."

Silent, the man reached into his pocket and retrieved a folded piece of paper. "I got your note!" he yelled and threw it onto the desk."

"I don't send letters to assholes." Evans kept his hands folded and didn't even glance at the square of paper.

"Who'd you get to send it for you? Huh? One of your friends, the vigilantes?"

"I don't know what you're talking about and I don't care. Out!" Evans roared, rising to his feet.

Feingold smiled. "Tell your friend—the one who sent me the letter—that I won't back down now. I'll fight you all the way to the polls! I've got right on my side!"

"Aren't you forgetting something, Feingold?" Evans said. "Your support of those ungodly, perverted, heathen Mormons?" He said the word

like a curse. "They're against every principle the
United States of America was founded on. They
go against our laws and the will of God. And I'll
do everything in my power to keep men like you
from ever holding office!"

Judd Feingold shook his head. "You double-
talking bastard. You'd even kill me to win."

"Keep out of my way." Evans leaned across his
desk. "Just keep out of my way! I don't wanna
see your ugly face until after the election." He
curled his upper lip. "After I win, I just might
invite you to my celebration here at the mansion."

"If I ever do run into you again on the street I'll
stand upwind." Feingold walked to the door. "I
can't stand your smell!"

Evans smiled as his opponent walked out of the
room. He picked up the letter that lay on his desk,
unfolded it, read it and walked to the fireplace.

Might as well get a little blaze going, he thought,
and threw the paper onto the grate.

She fastened the last button and looked at herself
in the mirror. The dress suited her, Vanessa Gilroy
thought. She wasn't in mourning any more. She
was through with feeling sorry for herself.

As she glanced down at the reflection of her
shoes she saw the body lying behind her on the
floor. Not long until it was time to get rid of him.

But she couldn't put off the hardest part of her
task. The sturdy woman grabbed Sam's ankles and
pulled him out of her bedroom. Reaching the
stairs, she walked down them backwards,
carefully fitting her feet on each descending step,

watching as the dead man's head flopped up and down, banging into the wood. The effect was comical.

She hauled him to the front door and walked into the kitchen. Eyeing the barrel beside the pie-safe, Vanessa pumped spring water into the kettle and lit the stove. A good cup of tea would calm her down, she thought. As the water simmered over the yellow flames lapping up from the fire box, the widowed woman pushed the barrel into the entryway.

She'd never put a man inside a barrel before, but she set her mind to the task, stuffing the naked body inside the cask, rearranging stiffening arms and legs until she'd fully succeeded. That done, she hammered the lid onto the barrel with three nails until it was completely shut.

The whistle from the kitchen distracted her. She poured the water into a teapot and added a heaping spoonful of tea, replacing the top before the odor-laden steam could rise up to her nose.

Vanessa sat at the kitchen table and wrote a short note, detailing Sam Delmonico's crimes, stating that he'd been a member of the vigilantes and had been brought to justice—just like Sheriff MacElravie had been.

She copied the note, word-for-word, and stuffed the duplicate inside the barrel just in case the second one blew off. With another nail she fastened the first note to the lid and stood back, pleased at what she'd done.

After enjoying her cup of tea, Vanessa Gilroy rolled the heavy barrel out front and pulled her carriage beside it. Straining her muscles, the woman managed to finally heave it into the carriage. The vehicle creaked under the weight. She pulled the black scarf over her face and rode to the sheriff's office.

She halted the horse and looked around. The town was deserted. Besides, who'd notice if someone saw a barrel being dropped off a carriage? It could be a delivery or something.

The sheriff's office was dark. She pushed both feet against the barrel. It lurched forward and banged down onto the dirt. The dust softened the blow; the barrel landed intact.

Smiling, Vanessa drove back home, enjoying the cool evening air and the new freedom that surged through her.

It really was too bad though, she thought. He did cook a good steak.

CHAPTER ELEVEN

Spur McCoy yawned, rubbed the ache in his lower back and wondered why he couldn't get to sleep. It must be well past midnight, but something kept him awake.

Too many unanswered questions, he told himself, staring at the darkened ceiling. Too many bodies. Not enough suspects. And the election was just a few days away.

Hmmm. He rolled up to a sitting position and pushed his feet into his boots. Maybe a short walk would clear his head and let him get some rest.

He pulled on his coat and walked outside of the Goldrush Hotel. Everyone in town seemed to be asleep but him. He rambled down the boardwalks fronting the various businesses, wandering aimlessly, trying hard not to think about anything at all. Just breathe deep and smell the night, he told himself.

It worked for a while. He walked two blocks and was weary enough to return to bed. But he figured he might as well finish the third block before heading back.

He dragged himself down the street, his boots shuffling in the dirt, looking straight ahead. Something didn't seem right. Something was lying in the street.

McCoy peered through the darkness at the black lump as he approached it. It looked out of place, to say the least. Adrenaline coursed through his veins. He quickened his steps. What was it?

Spur sighed. Just a barrel, he thought, and kicked it. To his surprise, it didn't move. Both lids were firmly secured, he discovered while examining it. What in hell was inside?

He squatted and succeeded in rolling it a foot or so. It moved crazily as if a heavy object was inside. Strange, the Secret Service agent thought, as he sat on his heels and rested.

Then a lighter colored patch on the barrel's surface caught his eyes. Spur felt it. It was smooth, cold from the night air. And it moved.

It was too dark to tell, but Spur knew what it was. Must be a label of some kind. He tore the paper from its fastener. It easily came off. Rising, he stared at it.

The darker shadings that covered it seemed to indicate writing, but he couldn't be sure. Frustrated, Spur fumbled in his pockets and found one single match. He lit it on the bottom of his boot and held the flaring stick up toward the paper. The words roused him to full consciousness.

VIGILANTES BEWARE!

Sam Delmonico is no longer with you.
He's gone to his reward—in hell!!! I've
sent him there like I did his fellow
vigilante, Sheriff MacElravie. This judge
and jury found Delmonico guilty of
murder and executed him this night.

Don't try to find me . . .

The match flared up and flickered out, plunging
the note into darkness. Spur had seen enough.

Sheriff MacElravie a vigilante? And the Italian
restaurant owner, too? Who had found out? And
who was killing them?

He glanced at the darkened sheriff's office. They
wouldn't have a new sheriff until after the
election. Who could he talk to? Spur set his jaw.
He had no choice.

He ran toward Thistledown Avenue. The houses
and trees flew by him. It was a hard, fast run but
Spur was in shape. He was only slightly out of
breath as he opened the great iron gate and sped
up to the front door.

Lights shone in the downstairs windows.
Someone was up in the governor's mansion. He
banged the knocker three times and waited,
huffing.

"What in hell—Spur!"

He groaned. "Hello, Lacey."

"I knew you'd come back!" She pushed his chest
and stepped outside. "My father's here with

company, but we can go out to the garden again
and—''

''No. I'm sorry, Lacey. I have to see your
father.''

''Why?'' The young woman frowned. ''Don't
you like me anymore?''

''Of course I do. This is business. There's been
a murder and I've found the body.''

''A murder!'' She blew out her breath. ''I must
say, you do come up with the best excuses.'' She
backed inside the door. ''He's in the library.''

''Thanks, Lacey.'' He kissed her forehead and
went there.

''I don't know, John. I don't know if I want to
take the risk,'' Governor Evans said.

''Sorry to interrupt you!''

The two men, startled, turned and stared at Spur
as he walked into the library.

''No, no, Mr. McCoy,'' Evans said with an
obviously forced smile. ''What brings you here at
this hour?''

Spur glanced at the man who stood next to
Martin Evans. Thin, bearded and white-haired, he
was dressed in an expensive suit.

The governor laughed. ''John Shepherd, my
lawyer. You can trust him.''

''Alright. Since you're the highest elected public
official around here I thought you should know.
There's been another murder.''

The two men looked at each other.

''The vigilantes?'' Evans asked.

Spur shook his head. ''At least, I don't think so.''
He turned for the door. ''I can't wait to explain.

Bring a hammer and come with me!''

"A hammer? Okay, McCoy. Just let me grab my coat!''

He headed out to the entryway. Lacey stood there in a flowered blue robe, huddled against the chill air blowing through the still opened door. ''I figured you wouldn't be staying long so I didn't close it.''

"Thanks. See you soon!'' Spur yelled.

"Hold on, McCoy! What's all this about?''

"I don't know, governor. I found a barrel sitting in front of the sheriff's office. A note was attached to it. I figured you better be there when that barrel got opened.''

"Okay, that sounds fair. But how does murder fit into this?''

"We'll find out.''

Four minutes later they stood assembled around the ordinary wooden cask. Shepherd held a match to the note, and Evans read over his shoulder, his lips moving with each word.

"I don't believe it!'' Evans said. "It's not true! Sam Delmonico was a fine man. He wasn't the type to ride around at night burning down houses and hanging people! For God's sake, he was a family man!''

"His wife up and took the kids to Augusta,'' Shepherd pointed out. "That must've been two years ago, and she hasn't been back since. He's changed since then.''

Evans stared at his lawyer.

"You got that hammer?'' Spur asked.

"Sure.'' Evans handed it to him.

"We'll know for sure in a minute or two." Spur
rammed the tines under the lid and pried. The
nails resisted the pressure for a few seconds, then
loudly squeezed out from the wood. "Progress,"
he said, and grunted as he pulled the hammer
sharply toward him.

He repositioned it and yanked as hard as he
could. The lid was an inch from the barrel. In a
new position, Spur finally succeeded in popping
it off. He bent down. "Can't see a damn thing. Got
another match, Shepherd?"

"What? Ah, sure!" He handed one to Spur.

Evans and Shepherd crouched down behind
him. He struck the lucifer. Yellow light exploded
and danced from its tip, illuminating the contents
of the barrel.

Spur shook his head.

"I'll be damned!" the governor shouted. "It is
him!"

"That's Sam Delmonico alright, though I never
saw him like that."

The man's naked body lay crammed into the
barrel. His head lolled at an unnatural angle.
Sightless eyes stared up at the three men.

"You ever hear any talk about him riding with
the vigilantes?" Spur asked.

"No. Nothing. You, John?"

The bearded man shook his head. "Uh-uh. That
man was clean as a whistle."

"Someone sure thought he was one of them."

"Damn! This has to stop!" Evans said.

Spur stared at the dead man. "Seems like an anti-
vigilante group has sprung up."

The lawyer moved closer to the barrel. "But how'd he die? I don't see any rope burns on his neck, stab wounds or slashes."

Spur rose and stretched his calves. "Assuming there aren't any on the parts we can't see, I'd say there's only one way he could have been killed."

"Poison?" Governor Evans asked.

"Strangulation."

"I don't know who'd do something like that to old Sam. He was the best cook in town," Shepherd said, lighting a third match from the dying flame.

"What happens now, Evans?" Spur asked.

"What do you mean?"

"I mean, there's no sheriff. You're in charge. What do you want to do?"

He set his jaw. "Find the bastard who killed Sam. What the hell do you think?"

"Use your head, Evans!" Spur's voice was so sharp that the big man turned to him. "We can't leave a man's bare-ass body here in the street for the women to see in the morning. I know you have an undertaker in this town. With all the work he's had lately, I don't think he'd mind one more job. Go wake him up. Me and Shepherd'll bring the body."

"I'm not used to taking orders—"

"Just do it!"

Evans frowned, looked at the dead man again and threw up his hands. He walked away without a word.

"You know where the undertaker's place is?" Spur asked the lawyer.

"Huh? Sure, yeah."

"Something wrong, lawyer?"

"No. It's just—I don't know. It makes you wonder if anyone in this town's really safe."

"I know what you mean. Help me get him out of there. We've got work to do!"

Between the two of them they managed to extricate the cold, stiff body from the barrel. The lawyer gritted his teeth during the task, seeming to force himself through it. Spur was surprised at John Shepherd's obvious revulsion at touching the dead man.

"You're not running for sheriff, are you?" Spur asked.

"No!"

McCoy nodded. "Good!"

It was dawn by the time he left the undertaker. The sunlight seared his eyes. Moaning from lack of sleep, Spur rubbed his face, lowered the brim of his hat and walked down the boardwalk.

"McCoy! I just heard!"

The voice was familiar. He looked at the figure racing up to him.

"One of the vigilantes was killed and you found the body. Right?"

"That's about it, Feingold."

"Whoa, boy!" He hopped from foot to foot, practically dancing a jig. "Anything else?"

He forced himself to speak through his exhaustion. "Judging by your reaction, Judd, I'd say there's a lot more. The killer left a note with Delmonico's body. In it, he said that Sheriff MacElravie was a vigilante, too. Doesn't that news brighten your day?''

Judd reared back. "Don't misunderstand me, McCoy. I don't think murder's right, and I certainly don't approve of what happened to these men. But I'm glad they're gone. If those two were vigilantes that means there's only four of them left. Their ranks are dwindling, my friend.'' He looked up at the sky. "I just wonder who's doing it?'' He sucked his cheek.

"You and me both, Feingold. You and me both!''

Too weak, Vanessa thought as she sipped the tea. Was it too much water or too little tea? She sighed and put down her cup. She wouldn't worry about it. Nothing could worry her today.

She hadn't woken until ten that morning, but then it had been a long night. The widowed woman, still dressed in her underclothes, went to her bedroom and flung open the old walnut dresser. What should she wear today? Yellow? She smiled. Yes.

Yellow was a great color for an execution.

CHAPTER TWELVE

What the hell did she want with him?

John Shepherd clutched his books as he walked to Vanessa Gilroy's house. He'd been greatly surprised when she showed up at his office that afternoon, asking that he stop by just after supper to go over some of her late husband's papers.

Shepherd had readily agreed. He could always use some extra money—even from her—and it would get him out of Martin Evans's way for a while. That man was starting to get on his nerves, the lawyer thought. And she certainly wasn't too hard on the eyes—or other parts of his body.

He thought it was rather odd that she'd waited all this time. What was it, two weeks since her husband's death to settle things like that. But he figured she'd spent all her time mourning.

John Shepherd grimaced when he thought of the

lie he'd concocted for Governor Evans, saying he'd had to attend to a dying woman on the south side of town. She hadn't made out a will and he couldn't possibly get out of it. Evans didn't like sharing Shepherd with anyone else, but when he'd informed the governor that the woman would probably deed much of her estate to the city, and that she'd voted for him, the big man had given his permission.

A figure slowly approaching him made Shepherd readjust his shirt tails and straighten the position of his hat.

"Afternoon, Mr. Shepherd," Lacey Evans said.

"Good afternoon to you, Lacey." He turned and watched the young woman walk away, frowning. If only she wasn't the governor's daughter. And if only he wasn't on his payroll.

He put those thoughts out of his mind. That's dangerous territory, he told himself. Don't go exploring where you know you'll be in trouble.

He turned down Mapleview and quickened his steps. Dusk was deepening into evening; the last light faded from the western horizon, blotting out the church spire that had been outlined against it.

It was night.

He rapped on the door at 313 Mapleview and waited. Nothing. Was she hard of hearing? Frustrated, he knocked twice as hard and kicked the door for good measure. It slowly swung inward.

"Hello? Mrs. Gilroy!" he yelled.

Silence. The slice of the house's exterior he could see didn't contain the woman, so he pushed it fully open.

"Come on in, Mr. Shepherd!"

He turned and blanched at the unbelievable sight. "Widow Gilroy!"

"Thank you for coming. We have a lot of work to do together this evening," she said.

Confusion boiled in his mind. "But—but—"

"But what?"

Shepherd dug his fingers into the hard leather bindings of his legal books, pressing them to his stomach. "Mrs. Gilroy, you're naked!"

"I'm what?" She looked down at her body and smiled. "Why, so I am! I must have plumb forgot to put on any clothes!" She ran her hands through her perfectly curled red hair and approached the middle-aged man. "How silly of me!"

"I—I—" He stared at her. "What are you doing? Keep away from me!"

"Now, Mr. Shepherd, you aren't afraid I'll bite you, are you?" She grinned wickedly as she advanced toward him. "A big man like you?" She glanced at his crotch.

He pressed his back against the door, closing it. "Mrs. Gilroy! Your behaviour is scandalous!"

"What's wrong, John?" She placed her hands on her thighs and rubbed them up and down, miming kisses.

"Have you no shame?" he asked, confusion and sexual heat swirling in his mind. She was naked and beautiful, but he couldn't touch the woman. He couldn't bear the thought. It was too sickening after what had happened.

"No!" he shouted, shrinking from her. She was almost within arm's reach.

"No what?" She moved her head in a tiny circle,

staring at him from lowered eyelashes, moistening
her lips.

"Widow Gilroy, I'm a god-fearing, Christian
man! Stay away from me!"

"God-fearing? Hell, John! What's a little sin
between friends?" She throatily laughed.

"Stop. Please!" He panted.

Vanessa nodded and stepped back. "Okay, okay.
I just figured that we could—never mind. That's
not the reason I asked you here anyway." She
walked to the rolltop desk in the corner of her
parlor.

Shepherd relaxed. He'd almost allowed himself
to lose control. "What—what was it?"

"I need some legal advice. Mr. Shepherd, what
should I do? I found out the lawyer I'd engaged
to conduct my husband's business is crooked."

"What do you mean, crooked?" He looked down
at her round, pink buttocks as she bent over at the
desk.

"Unethical." Vanessa turned to face him. "He's
a thief. A criminal. A murderer!" She put her fists
on her hips and arched her back, lifting her
breasts.

John Shepherd smiled. His natural inclination
for legal work overcame his unease. "I was
wondering why you'd suddenly asked to see me.
Look, I'd be happy to counsel you, Widow Gilroy,
but do you think you could put something on?
That's rather, ah, distracting."

"Of course! How silly of me. I haven't been
thinking right for weeks now." She walked to a
chair which was draped with a pink robe.

"I guess that must be why you're dressed like
hat."

"You mean *not* dressed." She twirled her
obscenely exposed body like a girl showing off a
new dress, laughed and slipped on the robe. "Is
his alright?" she asked, tying it around her body.

He took one last look. "Ah no, Mrs. Gilroy.
Your—your chests are still out."

Vanessa looked down. "Oops!" She smiled and
pushed them under the cloth.

She was a strange woman. If she'd been any
other female in Boise he would have jumped her.
But not her. Not Widow Gilroy. Just his luck!

"Fine. I need your help in trying to figure out
what to do to this man. I have to find a way to
trick him into admitting everything he's done."

"I see." The thought of being instrumental in
bringing one of his colleagues to his knees
enthused him. "What can I do for you?"

"Well, start by putting down your books. On
that table there!" she brightly said.

He did so. "And now?"

"Turn around. Just turn around for a minute or
two. Let me work things out. I know I'll have to
surprise him from behind."

"Okay." As he stood there, facing the far wall,
Shepherd regretted his revulsion toward her. It
could have been fun. If only—

He felt her breath against his right ear.

"Pretend to be him. Pretend to be Gus Procter!"

"Sure!" So that was the name of her double-
dealing lawyer! Wait until I tell Evans, Shepherd
thought. He never did trust the big city lawyer.

A hand fastened around his stomach. A second plastered to his neck. Gentle pressure at both spots told him he wasn't supposed to move.

"Is this a good hold?" she asked, huffing.

"Yes. You'd have to do it tighter, though." His body felt warm and good against hers. Was she trying to trick him into pleasuring her?

"Like this?"

Her grip crushed him, digging into his belly. Vanessa Gilroy gripped his chin and yanked back his head.

"Hey!" he yelled.

"John Shepherd, shouldn't a lawyer who's killed an innocent man deserve the worst punishment?"

"Of course. Let me go, Vanessa!" Confusion washed through his mind.

"And shouldn't that man be punished without waiting for a trial?"

"Yes. Yes, of course!" The arm constricted his neck. This wasn't any fun at all. Pain stabbed into his body. "Vanessa, what're you doing to me?"

"What I should have done a long time ago, murderer!"

She was serious! John struggled against her, but the woman was surprisingly strong. His unused, underdeveloped muscles were weak.

"I don't know what you're—"

"Yes you do!"

Tight. Tighter. He couldn't move his arms. She crushed him, digging into his neck, throwing him off balance.

"Do you confess to your crimes, John Shepherd?" she hissed.

"What crimes?"

"Don't play strupid with me! You were there. You're one of them! You killed my husband!"

"I don't know what—" The agony spread through his body.

"You shouldn't have made me watch!" she screamed. "I recognized you and your horse the night you came with murdering thoughts in your mind!"

Her arm bit into his throat for a blinding second, then eased off. "Alright. I was there!" he gasped. "Let me go, Vanessa!"

"You killed him! You all killed him! And now you're going to get your reward!"

He gagged under the choking weight. John Shepherd lurched forward, desperately trying to extricate himself from the woman. But she held on, moving with him, squeezing his neck harder and harder until she cut off his air supply.

The ascetic lawyer gasped. The ceiling shimmered in his mist-filled eyes. He made one last effort to break free from her clutches as the pressure at his throat increased. His lungs seemed to explode. Sweet lethargy poured through him. The room dissolved as every muscle in his body went limp.

An odor penetrated the darkness of his brain. A harsh, poisonous odor that was somewhat noisy. A loud smell?

The thought was enough to rouse him. John Shepherd opened his eyes. The odor was strong, sickening, dangerous. He saw Vanessa Gilroy, fully dressed, splashing some liquid around the room.

Vanessa! Where was he?

He tried to sit up but couldn't—something was holding him down. "What—"

"Save your voice for the Almighty, John!" she said, walking to him. "You'll be talking to Him real soon!" The widow smiled as she worked.

Shepherd gyrated on the couch before realizing he was firmly tied to it.

Vanessa walked up to him, held the tin can over his body and tipped it, spilling its contents onto his body.

One drop landed in his eye, stinging it. The scent seemed familiar. Then he knew.

Kerosene.

"No, Vanessa! Don't do this!"

"I'm only following your advice," she said. "Taking the law into my own hands. Punishing a known murderer!" She threw down the can. "Besides, it was good enough for the Mormons!"

"I'll do anything—anything!" John pleaded.

This wasn't happening, he thought. This wasn't supposed to happen. He'd promised them!

"You've already done enough!"

The bound man lifted his arching head to look around the room. Everything was splattered and soaked with kerosene. He flopped back down when the pain in his throat threatened to make him black out again.

"No!"

She put a handled basket under her arm and tied her bonnet firmly onto her head. "Sorry, I have to be going now. I won't see you again"

''Please!'' The terror sickened him but he gave into it, firmly believing what was occurring. This wasn't a dream. This was cold, hard reality.

Vanessa Gilroy reached into the basket and took out a lucifer match. ''Goodbye, Mr. Shepherd.''

She struck the match and threw it onto his stomach. It flared up, igniting the liquid, turning his shirt front into an inferno.

The widow laughed, struck two more matches, threw them into the room and quickly walked out.

Adrenaline speeding his efforts, tortured pictures of that night when they'd hung Michael Gilroy whirling in his mind, John Shepherd arched his neck and tried to blow out the flames.

High. Higher. The curtain of fire spread along his shirt, burning through it, charring his chest hairs and scaring his skin.

The pain was too much. The screaming man closed his eyes as the blaze engulfed him.

CHAPTER THIRTEEN

I should go see her, Spur thought, picking his teeth after his supper. Maybe the good Widow Gilroy knew more than she was telling him.

As he walked out of the Goldrush Hotel, men with buckets ran past, yelling at each other. Young boys screamed as they raced after their fathers. Water?

Fire! Then he smelled the smoke, grabbed the fire bucket that hung beside the door outside the hotel and followed the contingent.

He saw the flames before turning down Mapleview. Orange-red light slashed the inky sky, boiling and billowing in its destructive fury. Ash fell to the street like dry snow. A shiny horse-drawn firewagon pulled up as he joined the bucket brigade.

It was Vanessa Gilroy's house.

The small quantities of water they hurled at the flames evaporated before they had the chance to do anything. The fire flared up. Flames shot out the lower windows of the old house, forcing the men back with blasts of heat.

Spur shook his head as he watched it burn, standing amidst gasping men and women whose faces glowed redly in the darkness.

It was hopeless, but he helped pass the buckets that were filled from the big metal tank that had been hauled there. Was she there? Was she safe, or already burned to a crisp?

"Anyone inside?" he asked the squat man in line beside him.

"Hell if I know. It just seemed to go up like tinder. No one could go in and check."

The fire fed on the dry wood. The men stood back as the top floor crashed in on itself and the flames rose higher into the black sky.

The house on Mapleview turned night into day. Bizarre, dancing shafts of light bathed the citizens of Boise as they watched the rushing flames bathe it, slowly eating away at the structure, reducing it to worthless rubble.

Spur set down his bucket, took off his hat and wiped the sweat that had formed on his forehead. Had this been the work of the vigilantes, too?

If so, why would they hurt Vanessa Gilroy?

Governor Evans strolled up and recognized Spur in the eerie light. "What in hell's going on here, McCoy?"

"I don't know. Maybe the citizen's committee again." He shook his head. "I just hope Vanessa wasn't inside.''

"That is her house! Or it was, anyway. But it couldn't have been them, McCoy. They haven't touched a woman in all their doings.''

"What about the Bancroft place?''

The governor frowned.

"They killed Jake Bancroft and two of his wives.''

Evans shrugged. "Not directly. Besides—''

Spur touched the man's shoulder. "Look, governor. I don't wanna hear any more of your reactionary rhetoric concerning the Mormons. Save it for your speeches.''

The husky man frowned at him.

"No. No!'' a woman screamed.

Vanessa Gilroy walked up beside Spur, her steps shaky, staring up at the blaze. She held a cloth-covered basket under one arm and clamped a hand over her mouth as she watched the carnage unfurl itself with increasing fury.

"Vanessa! Thank God you're alive. I didn't know if you were inside or what.'' Spur touched her shoulders.

"My house. Everything I own. It's just—just—'' Her hair glowed with the inferno's orange light.

"At least you're safe.''

She dropped the basket and took two faltering steps toward the blaze. The middle-aged woman shook her head, open mouthed.

The people standing around, drinking in the spectacle, slowly moved away from the woman, respecting her grief.

"Maybe you shouldn't watch.'' Spur took her

hands in his. "Don't you want to go somewhere else? Anywhere else but here. It won't help to look."

She violently turned to him. "No, Mr. McCoy. I have to watch!"

"Okay."

Her face shone in the red light. "I was just taking some food to a woman I know who's sick on the other side of town. I wasn't gone more than an hour."

Her voice was so weak and strained that Spur had to bend his ear to her mouth to hear her over the crackles and snaps issuing from the blazing building.

"I was just doing a good deed—and now look what those vigilantes have done! They've ruined me!"

Governor Evans walked up. "McCoy, I've been asking around and no one saw the vigilantes ride through here earlier this evening."

Spur gripped the woman's hands. "That's nothing new, is it, Evans? No one ever sees them. There's too much fear in this town, not enough guts!"

Vanessa Gilroy laid her head against Spur's chest. He gathered her in his arms and held the woman.

The fire seemed to die down momentarily. Then a tremendous explosion rocked the house, hurling the last remnants of window glass out all four sides. The building buckled and the lower walls crumpled into black splinters laced with darting red tongues.

"Salamanders," Vanessa said, still watching.

"What?"

"My husband used to say that salamanders played in the fireplace when we sat before it on cold winter nights. Little red lizards that bathed on the coals, enjoying the warmth, nourishing themselves on the fire."

She was going out of her mind. "Come on, Vanessa. Let's get you somewhere."

The woman pulled away from him. "No! I don't want to. I'll stay until the end!" Widow Gilroy walked closer to the blaze, clasping her hands before her.

A grizzled old timer walked up beside Spur.

"Nasty fire," he observed.

"That it is. You see who started it?"

"Mister, I live right across the street. I was home all night, and I didn't hear or see the vigilantes ride through here. I've always seen them before. Not tonight."

Spur grinned. "You've seen them?"

"Sure!" He rubbed his bald head. "I'm too old to get involved in the games all these other folks are playing. I've seen them two or three times. It's always been the six same horses, the same kerchiefs over the men's faces."

"Can you remember anything about their mounts? Something that might help a man find out who they are?"

The man smiled at Spur. "Why?" he asked sharply.

"It's time someone did something about the vigilantes. Don't you agree?"

"Hell, yes!" He stuck a finger into his right ear
and twisted it back and forth with so much force
that it seemed he was searching for something
buried inside it.

"Well?" Spur asked.

"Well what? Oh, them horses. One of their
beasts stands out. I've seen it clear two times. A
big horse, black as a moonless night. Its coat
shimmers. About 17 hands high, maybe." He
pulled out his finger and looked at it. "White blaze
on its forehead."

"Great. Have you ever seen this horse in town?
Tied up to a hitching post, or with an unmasked
man riding it? Any idea of who it belongs to?"

"I don't know. Don't get out of my house much.
I just sit in my rocker and watch what goes on
through the winders. The missus gets out more,
but she's got no sense about horses—or much of
anything else any more, the poor dear."

"You've been a great help, mister—"

"Steel. Johann Steel."

"Thanks, Mr. Steel."

"Yeah, well, a man's got to do something to keep
him from going crazy." He wandered off, the
excitement forgotten, back to his own home.

The blaze had nearly consumed its fuel. Jagged
timbers jutting erratically into the air framed heaps
of broken wood and charred furniture.

A paunchy man dressed in long johns with a coat
thrown over his shoulders shouted for attention.
"Okay, men! Let's put out the hot spots! Make sure
it don't spread nowhere else!"

The bucket brigade started again. The ten or so

men had things well in hand, so Spur turned back to Vanessa Gilroy. The woman stood silhouetted against the dying flames, surveying the destruction.

He went to her. "You have a place you can stay?"

"Yes," she said, her chin firm. "I'll stay with the Widow Parkin. Millie's lonely since her husband passed on and wants company. She said I could if I ever sold the house." Vanessa laughed. "Too late for that now."

"Look, Mrs. Gilroy, I'm sorry."

"Don't—don't say it. Please."

"Fine. You know where I am if you need me."

"I surely do. Goodbye, Mr. McCoy."

Spur nodded at the somber expression on her face. She walked away, leaving the basket she'd dropped lying in the dirt as a gust of wind covered it with fine, white ash.

"Shepherd! Shepherd!" Martin Evans walked through the crowd, searching for his lawyer.

Where the hell had that man gone, he wondered. First he says he has to take care of some old lady's will, and now he's disappeared.

Just like him to duck out in a time of crisis. The governor went to Shepherd's house; it was dark. A quick search inside turned up nothing.

His horse stood sleeping in the rickety shelter behind the lawyer's house. It hadn't been ridden lately.

Evans shrugged and returned to his mansion, enjoying the walk. As he stretched his legs he

remembered the burning house and Spur McCoy's
questions about the vigilantes.

Who the hell had done that to Vanessa Gilroy?

Millie Parkin had been more than kind, taking
Vanessa in without question. She'd counted on the
old woman and hadn't been disappointed.

Now as she pulled the lavender-scented sheet
up to her chin, trying to get comfortable in the
strange bed, Vanessa wondered if she'd done the
right thing.

Not the execution—John Shepherd had deserved
to die. That was obvious. But burning down her
own house? All those memories of her late
husband?

She shook her head on the goosedown pillow.
The past was just that—passed. And she still had
momentos—his knife, gold pocket watch and
billfold that she'd placed in the bank after his
murder. That, and the small diamond ring on her
finger, were enough.

Besides, the fire should stir up the citizens of
Boise into action against the vigilantes. She had
to work slower than she wanted in removing those
evils from this earth. Maybe the public outcry over
their latest crime would make them think twice
befor striking again, before they ended any more
innocent lives.

Then she could execute the others, one by one,
until none were left. The thought comforted her
and she turned on her side and tried to sleep.

Of course, there was still one man that she
hadn't identified. One man who always sat on his

horse when the others did the dirty work. The tall man who always rode a different horse and disguised his voice during every crime.

Their leader, Vanessa thought, biting her lower lip. Who was it? Would she ever find out? And if not, would she ever be able to blot out the memories of his raucous laughter as he forced her to watch her husband's murder?

Three men met in a valley outside Boise. Masked, they dismounted, secured their horses to a clump of saplings and squatted, talking in low voices.

"Where's Shepherd?" one asked.

"I don't know."

"Men, we can't afford to take any chances," the tallest said. "MacElravie and Delmonico are dead. People are starting to talk about this, and now someone's burned down Widow Gilroy's place and made it look like we did it. We're losing our grip on this town!"

"What the hell can we do about that?" a shorter man asked. "Hell, we don't know who's killing our own! It could be anyone at all!"

"Gentlemen. Gentlemen. Do I have to remind you of what'll happen to the rest of us if we don't discover the man who's decimating our ranks? You won't be doing any complaining with a knife buried in your back! So work on it. Spend every second trying to solve this little problem."

"And what'll you do?" the vigilante challenged their leader.

"Everything I can on my end. Now ride back into town!"

CHAPTER FOURTEEN

Goldrush Street was hot and dusty. A carriage rattled by, thickening the air with a brown haze that spurted up in its tracks.

McCoy was checking horses. A big black stallion with a white blaze on his forehead, the man had told him. If a vigilante had indeed ridden that horse it had to be in town. He couldn't know if the man was a reliable source of information. But then again, he didn't have anything else to go on.

So he searched the town, discreetly looking at every horse that walked or trotted by, or that stood drinking from the wooden troughs.

He saw dozens of them. Hipshot, whinneying beasts of every color and description were lined up before the businesses and homes of Boise, Idaho Territory. Bowed-backed nags barely able to keep on their feet; roans, sorrels and bays; the odd stallion or two looking for love; placid geldings simply waiting for the return of their owners and another long, hard ride through the countryside.

Some of the horses regarded him curiously as he passed, raising their heads, licking water from their mouths, flaring their huge nostrils. Brown eyes warily regarded the man.

After he'd traveled the length of Goldrush on both sides, Spur walked down the other streets. A few horses were tied up at the hitching post but no big black beasts with slashes of white on their heads.

Undaunted, he stopped by the two livery stables in town, posing as a potential customer, and checked out the merchandise. Nothing. The horse might as well not exist.

The man who lived on Mapleview could have been mistaken, or could have passed on false information. Or, Spur reasoned, the owner of this particular horse was being careful. Extremely careful.

Dusk deepened into the blackness of night.

Vanessa Gilroy straightened her bonnet and knocked at the back door of the huge brick building. It finally opened.

"Hello, Clem," she said sweetly as she walked into the bank.

"Hello yourself, Widow Gilroy. You're looking pretty this evening." The thickly-haired, short man sighed and locked the door. "Been a long day, it has. So you really came to get it? You're really going to do it?"

Vanessa patted the banker's shoulder. "Mr. Jackson, you don't have anything to worry about. I won't withdraw every cent my husband deposited in your bank. Just some of it—to help out with unexpected expenses. After all, I lost everything in that fire." She smoothed a mask of despair onto her face.

"You poor dear," Jackson said, shaking his head. "I understand. As long as you won't break the bank, I can help you out."

"Thank you!" She looked around the empty building and shivered. Only two lamps had been turned up in the vault. "It's cold in here. Do you think we could just do it?"

"Of course. Come this way."

"I won't feel safe until I'm back at Millie Parkin's place," she said, following the waddling middleaged man. "That's why I had you let me in the rear door after regular hours, don't you know. I don't trust the streets any more. Why, if someone saw me coming in here after hours they'd assume I was withdrawing a large amount of cash money. Heaven knows what would happen if one of the vigilantes found out about it!"

Clem Jackson turned to look at her, his big doe eyes softening in the thin light. "I don't think you have to worry about that, Vanessa. They don't rob folks. Leastwise, they haven't yet."

"Just their lives."

The banker grunted, held an oil lamp in his left hand, stooped over, cracked his fingers and twisted the dial on the face of the vault door. "I forgot and already locked the dang thing up."

"What's the matter, Clem? You in a hurry to leave work or something?"

"No, no. It's just that I could—"

"I know. I could use a drink myself!"

Jackson beamed. "Now that's being honest. Nothing I like more than an honest woman!"

She heard a click.

"Okay, you can come in now."

The banker swung open the door. She stepped up to the circular aperature and was amazed at the thickness of the walls.

The vault was the size of a small room, lined with metal shelves stuffed with numbered leather sacks. Each sack was simply tied shut—not locked.

"How'd you ever get such a big safe?" Vanessa asked.

"It's a vault, and they dragged it here during gold-rush times. Boise needed one this big because of all the money that flowed through her during those days." He looked around. "It's seen lots of riches in its day. More than you or I ever will." He walked inside, carrying the lamp with him.

Vanessa sniffed. "Where's my husband's deposit?"

"Oh, ah, right here."

Clem Jackson rummaged around for a second and turned to her, smiling. "Here it is. Deposit number 6-0-5."

"Thank you. Could—could you bring two chairs? This might take a few moments." She gripped the heavy bag.

"We could move outside—"

"No. No! I feel safer in here."

"Fine and dandy." Clem handed her the oil lamp. "Be right back."

Alone in the vault, Vanessa opened the bag and extracted $3,000. That was surely enough, she thought, as she stuffed the hundred dollar bills into her purse. For now. She retired the bag.

"Here we go." Clem pushed two chairs inside.

They sat facing each other. Vanessa pretended to open the bag for the first time and gaped at the amount of gold, silver and bills it contained. The thirty year-old woman glanced up at the banker. "This calls for a celebration of sorts. Doesn't it?"

He peered at her. "Celebration? What you getting at, Vanessa?"

She revealed the small bottle of whiskey she'd put in her purse before coming. "A drink or two?"

He licked his lower lip. "I never say no to a lady, Mrs. Gilroy."

The banker was practically salivating. Vanessa handed him the bottle. "You first!"

Clem straightened his back, removed the cork and took a healthy swallow. He closed his eyes as the numbing liquid slid down his throat and entered his stomach. "Ah! Fine stuff you brought there."

"Just the best money can buy," she said sweetly. "I figure if we're going to drink it might as well be good stuff."

He proffered the bottle to her, wiping a stray drop from his lower lip.

"No, you go again. I have work to do!"

Fifteen minutes later, Vanessa had three piles of bills on her knees. The bottle was nearly empty as Clem shakily set it on the vault floor.

"You—ah—heh, heh. You about done there, Vaneshy?" The man couldn't seem to keep his feet firmly on the floor. They kept slipping forward, threatening to spill him from the chair.

"Just about. I'm doing some figures in my head."

He was drunk, she thought. Almost time.

"Well, how about a drink?" She held the whiskey out to him.

He raised a coarse hand to his face. "Oh, no. Oh, no!"

Widow Gilroy stuffed all the money back into the bag.

"Something wrong, Clem?" she asked him.

"My God, it finally happened, just like my ma used to tell me when I was a squealing brat!" He patted his cheeks.

"Clem, what's the matter?"

The banker turned to her with sad eyes. "I done drunk so much my nose fell off!"

She deliciously laughed. "I told you—only the finest for you. That's why I didn't have any. Just a drop of that liquor makes me—well, you don't want to hear about it." She had cleared her lap and retied the string that kept the bag closed.

"It shore do the trick." He coughed and looked around the vault. "You know, sometimes I wish all thish was mine. It'd be sho easy to forget that it ain't, to clean it all out and go live somewhere else."

"Now Clem, you'd never do something like that." The widowed woman rose and replaced the bag on the second shelf. "Crimes have a way of coming back to haunt you."

"Ah heck, Vaneshy," Clem said, slapping his knee. "Not if you're careful! If no one knows you did it there's no danger."

"But if someone finds out?"

He fastened a red-eyed gaze at her. "Ah. Well, I guess it would be obvioush—me 'n the money disappearin' at the same time."

"Yes. Folks always know who did something like that. Bank robbery. Cattle rustling." She stood before him. "Murder."

"Well, yeah. Guess I'll leave it here." He looked up at her. "You about finished?"

"Yes, Clem." She picked up the bottle. "And so's this whiskey. You realize how much you drank?"

He screwed up his red face. "I'm sorry. Sometimes when I start I can't stop."

"That's alright, Clem." She released her fingers; the bottle crashed onto the metal floor.

Jackson looked around, startled, holding his ears as the sound echoed and reverberated in the small metal room.

"Oh! Look what I've gone and done!" Vanessa said.

"I don't mind, girlie. It'll clean."

The woman slipped behind him. "Here, let me help you out of that chair." She grabbed his shoulders. As the squat man rose, Vanessa Gilroy pushed him back so hard that he stumbled and toppled over.

"Hey! Take it easy! I'm not a well man!" he said

on his knees.

"I know why you've been drinking so much. It's your conscience. You can't live with yourself since you started riding with the vigilantes. Can you?"

Clem Jackson placed his palms against the floor and tried to rise from it. "Now hold on there, Vaneshy!"

"I know all about it."

"Stop talking nonsense," he said to the wall, unable to turn to face her.

"Nonsense? Why, Sheriff MacElravie, Sam Delmonico and John Shepherd all said you were one of their own before they died," she lied. "Besides, I recognized the horse you rode on your nightly raids. Not your brown gelding, but the one you keep out on your son's spread. The big black stallion with the white blaze on his forehead!"

He twisted over on the floor and landed on his buttocks. "You—you know what? What'd they tell you?"

She smiled. "Everything."

Vanessa Gilroy bent and picked up the remaining upper half of the bottle. "Everything except two small details. Who's the fifth man? And who led you into doing this, Clem, huh? Who told you to go out with him and kill my innocent husband in cold blood? Who was it?"

The banker dissolved into tears. "It—it sounded like a good idea at the time. I didn't wanna do it. But he—he—he talked me into it."

"Who? Who was it? Who's your leader?"

"No. I can't tell you." His shoulders slumped forward. "I can't tell you or anyone."

"Are you so sure about that, Clem?" Vanessa waved the deadly glass weapon in the air between them. "If you don't tell me right now I'll send you to the same place I sent George, Sam and John!"

The sobbing man gazed at her with bloodshot eyes. "You killed them?"

She laughed. "Of course. Haven't you been listening to me? I'll kill you, too, if you don't start talking. Now, Clem!"

He crawled back to the wall and leaned against it. "Vaneshy," he said, blubbering. "I just can't. Now you get outa my bank!"

"No. I've got work to do." She pretended to lunge at him.

Clem Jackson struggled to his feet and grabbed the woman's arm. "No! Don't do it!"

She wrenched free from his alcohol-soft fingers and stepped back. "Who else rides with you?"

"Alright. Alright!" He tore at his hair, standing on shaky feet. "Rex Cutshaw."

She laughed. "The saddle maker? I don't believe it. I don't believe that leather stitcher's the man in charge of the vigilantes!"

"He ain't. Cutshaw's his second. If you don't believe me, go ashk him! But I can't tell you anything elsh!"

"I'll ask him. Right after I take care of you!" Vanessa Gilroy advanced on the trembling, tear-stained man. "Don't worry about it, Clem. Maybe they have banks in hell!"

She slammed the broken glass onto his scalp with such force that it drove the man to the floor. Bright blood sprang from the wound as Clem

Jackson fell face-first. The sound of his impact—
flesh slapping against steel, the tinkling of coins
in his pocket—echoed in the vault.

Vanessa threw down the bottle. It smashed
beside his face. "Clem?" she called.

Nothing.

"Clem?" Louder this time.

Had that done it? Panting from her exertions,
Vanessa squatted next to the downed banker. She
smiled at the needles of glass that peppered his
right cheek, making it look for all the world like
a pincushion. She shook his shoulders but he
continued to lie still.

Vanessa touched his neck. The pulse was there,
but weakening. He was unconscious.

Good. She walked to the vault's door and looked
back inside one last time. He lay there surrounded
by spilled whiskey and broken glass—and two
chairs.

She breathed deeply and hauled them out,
replacing them behind the first two desks that
obviously needed them. No sense in taking any
chances, in having any questions asked.

Vanessa Gilroy pulled the door shut but didn't
spin the tumblers. It was Friday night. No one
should go into the bank until Monday morning.

By then Clem Jackson would be dead from loss
of blood or lack of air. As she straightened her
clothing and walked to the bank's rear door,
Vanessa remembered the first time he'd shown
her the huge vault and told her how it was air-
tight. Anyone who stayed in it for more than an
hour or so would die of asphyxiation, he'd said.

When his employees arrived on Monday morning, they'd find him and assume he'd gone into the vault to drink after work and swallowed down so much that he'd passed out and accidentally died.

Just what she wanted, Vanessa thought. She walked into the darkness outside the bank and calmly closed the door behind her. The last thing she needed was the remaining vigilantes to be too wary.

Especially a leather stitcher named Rex Cutshaw.

CHAPTER FIFTEEN

Spur spent a frustrating weekend. Between meetings with Governor Evans and Judd Feingold, he had questioned the people of Boise about the vigilantes but ran up against the same wall of silence that had hounded him since he'd arrived in town.

On Sunday afternoon, he'd provided security during the governor's final speech, held in the middle of town. It went smoothly. No problems.

And no further threatening letters were sent to either candidate. Judd Feingold apparently hadn't been scared off by the one he'd received, for he energetically waged his campaign of peace and co-existence, paying boys to plaster the whole town with posters and hiring white-haired women to spread the word, trying up until the last moment to change the voters' minds.

McCoy checked every horse in town, but the black stallion with a white blaze still eluded him. It wasn't in Boise, for he'd looked virtually everywhere—even poking his head into the small stables behind houses.

When he began questioning people about it he got even more discouraged. No one save for the man who lived across from Vanessa Gilroy's old place would admit to seeing it. Just the very mention of the beast made decent men and women uncomfortable.

Spur had napped Saturday night and walked the streets until about three A.M., on the alert for another vigilante raid. But all was quiet. He repeated the same schedule Sunday but once again, the power-hungry killers didn't disturb the town.

McCoy had figured things would heat up but they seemed to be simmering. What was going on?

On Monday morning, he sighed and glanced at his haggard face in the cracked mirror. Men who were named as vigilantes were dropping like cows in a waterless desert. If they didn't recruit more members soon they might as well disband entirely. Whoever was killing them was doing a bang-up job.

He shrugged at his reflection and unbuttoned his shirt, then used its tails to mop his forehead. This early in the morning, before nine o'clock, it was already hot in his hotel room. It was hot all over Boise.

It was election day.

Later that morning, Spur visited two saloons to

listen in on the local gossip. Clem Jackson, a banker, had been found dead in the vault. A broken bottle and a sticky stain on the floor seemed to indicate he'd gotten drunk, accidentally closed the door and suffocated to death.

Suffocated, Spur had thought, sitting in the saloon, listening to the young buck's words. Why did that seem so familiar?

And was this death accidental, or had this Jackson been killed? Was he mixed up with the vigilantes?

After leaving the saloon he spent the rest of the afternoon watching the polls. People were orderly, and it seemed every man in Boise lined up to make his mark on the town's political history. The governor's shills worked the line, urging the men to vote for Evans. Those that said that they had, received two dollars.

The shouted praises of the governor's record—and Judd Feingold's pained expression as he came to vote an hour before the polls closed—seemed to point out the inevitable.

Two hours later, a nervous young man stood up at the podium in the Masonic Hall. It was official—Martin Evans had been re-elected, but by a surprisingly narrow margin—269-231. Evans made a point of publicly shaking Feingold's hand and slapping him on the back, but his glee spilled out in his words and the quick movements of his squat body.

"McCoy," Evans said to him after the results were announced. "I'm having a victory celebration tonight at the mansion. Fifty or so of my closest

friends will be there. Why not stop by and have
a drink? Now that I'm out of danger and you're
out of a job."

"I'll try," he said, smiling at the man, "but I
might be busy."

Something about Evans rubbed him the wrong
way. It always had, but he couldn't determine
what it was.

"Then I'll be looking for you!"

Spur walked over to the losing candidate. "You
gave it your best, Feingold. I guess bigotry and
hatred ruled the day."

The thin man shook his head. "That's the way
it goes. Excuse me, I think there's a bottle of
whiskey somewhere with my name on it." The
man pushed through the crowd away from Spur.

McCoy blew out his breath and returned to his
hotel room. He should eat, but he wasn't hungry.
He could go to the mansion but he didn't feel like
celebrating. Thoughts about the vigilantes and
their killer boiled up in his brain. He worked out
so many possible explanations that he finally had
to put the subject out of his mind.

Spur answered the insistent knock on his door.
"Vanessa!" he said in surprise.

"I had to come see you." She pushed past him
and paced back and forth in his room. The woman
removed her bonnet. Red hair flashed back and
forth.

"How have you been since the fire?"

"As well as can be expected. Millie's been such
a dear, putting up with me these past few
days." The widowed woman touched her left

cheek. "I'm afraid I've been a terrible burden on her."

"I'm sure she enjoys your company. Well, it's election day. Did you hear who won?"

Vanessa halted at the window. "Evans?"

"Yeah."

"It doesn't matter to me. Nothing matters."

"What can I help you with?" Spur closed the door and went to her.

"You heard about Clem Jackson?"

"Was he the banker that they found dead in his vault this morning?"

She nodded. "Well, I have it from a reliable source that he didn't just drink too much and pass out. He was killed because he was one of the vigilantes."

It figured.

"Who told you this?" he asked, touching her shoulders.

"That doesn't matter. What does matter is the other piece of news I've received." She took a deep breath. "I need you to come with me on a visit to a man I think is one of the last two remaining vigilantes." Her gaze burned into him.

"Wait a minute. Slow down!" Spur said, shaking his head. "Who is this?"

She frowned at him. "Rex Cutshaw. You probably don't know him. He makes saddles here in town. Spur, if you don't go with me, I'll go alone!"

"And do what?" he asked her.

Vanessa bitterly laughed. "You can't imagine how it's been, knowing that some of the men who

killed my husband are alive and walking the
streets while Michael rots in the churchyard!'' She
broke from his grip and stepped back. ''If there's
anything I can do to bring them to justice I'll do
it—even if it means going there by myself.'' She
strode to the door.

''Now wait a minute, Vanessa!''

She paused, her hand at the knob.

Spur thought for a moment. ''Okay. I'll go with
you.''

''Fine!''

Five minutes later they were walking along a
tree-shaded street. The sun hadn't quite set, but
deep shadows cut into the ground.

''What are you planning on doing?'' Spur asked.
He figured it was best to be with her to ensure
that things didn't get out of hand.

''Among other things, find out if it's true. Most
important, I want the name of the other vigilante.
Their leader. If Rex Cutshaw is one of them, I'll
rely on you to force him to tell me—us.''

''Maybe you shouldn't be there.'' He tugged on
her arm to slow her quickening pace.

''Don't try to stop me, Spur!'' she said. ''I want
to know the truth! I want to hear him admit he's
one of them! Besides, you wouldn't even know
about him if I hadn't told you. You owe me this
one.''

He sighed. ''Okay. How far is this place?''

''Right up the street.''

Vanessa gripped her purse and hurried toward
it, with Spur struggling to catch up with the
determined woman.

They neared a small, ramshackle house on the outskirts of town. As they walked up to it and opened the rickety, paint-peeling fence, a man stepped out of the building.

"You Rex Cutshaw?" Spur asked.

"That's me." He nodded to Vanessa. "I'm just going to vote."

"Too late. The polls closed hours ago. Evans won."

The stocky man grinned. "Oh, well. Guess he didn't need my vote nohow."

"We have to talk." Spur walked toward the man and stood inches from him, waiting.

"Okay," Cutshaw said, his neck popping. "Come on inside the place."

"I thought you'd never ask, Mr. Cutshaw."

His house smelled of tobacco and old bacon. Spur watched Vanessa's nostrils flare at the unappetizing odor as they were seated in Cutshaw's parlor.

"Can I get you something to drink?" he asked, his face expressionless.

"A whiskey would suit me just fine!" Vanessa said. "And one for Mr. McCoy."

"Let me handle this," he whispered to the woman after Cutshaw walked out of the room.

"Fine. We'll do it your way." She crossed her ankles and primly placed her hands on her knees.

The saddlemaker returned with two small glasses filled with amber colored liquid. "Darn!" the man said, smiling to reveal two cracked front teeth. "I forgot all about your drink, Mrs. Gilroy. I'll be right back." He set down the glasses on a mall table and disappeared once again.

"I can't wait," Vanessa said. She walked over o the table.

"My, you're thirsty."

"Be quiet!" After a few seconds she returned o her rail-backed chair.

Rex walked past the table and handed the third lass to Spur, who took it and sipped the bitter iquid. "I see you've already started," he said, miling broadly as he went for his whiskey. The omplicated business over, he eased into a chair, nd took a swallow. "What can I do for you? Need special, customized, deluxe saddle or omething?"

"No," Vanessa said.

Spur cut her a look. "Mr. Cutshaw, I'm in wn inquiring about the dangerous situation ere."

The man looked into his glass. "Kinda bitter." Ie raised his eyebrows and downed its contents. What dangerous situation?"

"All the murders. The threatening letters that vere sent to Governor Evans a few days back. The riminal activities that have occurred here without o much as one citizen standing up to the men oing them."

Rex burped and licked his lips. "Why come to ne about all this? Mr. McCoy, is it? Mr. McCoy, know leather and I know horses inside and out. can make you a saddle that'll last you a lifetime. ut this talk about—about—"

Spur glanced at Vanessa, who smiled at him. Mr. Cutshaw? Are you feeling ill?"

The man set down his glass and yawned. "No. Guess I worked too hard today. Can't seem to hold up my darned eyelids."

"We'll be out of here soon, Rex," Vanessa said.

The middleaged man slumped in his chair. "Whoa! Boy, I am tired. Must be the whiskey . . ." He grabbed the curved wooden arms and held on for a second. His entire body went limp and slid to the floor.

"What in hell?" Spur asked, walking to him.

"Just something I put in his drink, Spur. Nothing to worry about!" Vanessa Gilroy smiled at him.

Spur grabbed the woman's arm. "Vanessa, I told you. I'm in charge here. I didn't tell you to slip a sleeping power in Cutshaw's drink!"

"It won't last long. I gave him enough to put him out, but only for a few minutes." She looked down at the unconscious man. "Rex always was a lazy sort."

"Vanessa, give me your solemn word that you won't interfere again. If you're right about this man he's a dangerous criminal, far too dangerous for you to be toying with him!"

"You're right. Doesn't he looking positively lethal right now, laying there passed out on the floor?" The red-haired woman laughed.

"You know what I mean," he said, irritated at the woman's boldness. He'd lost control and hadn't even been aware of it. "Just sit still and keep your mouth shut!"

The woman returned to her chair. "Yes, daddy." A wry smile played on her face.

Spur bent over Rex Cutshaw. "Wake up,

;odddamnit!'' he shouted. "I have some questions
needed answered!''

"He is drugged, after all. Give him fifteen
ninutes.''

"Okay, fine." He didn't turn back to her. "I need
ome rope,'' McCoy said, unbuckling the man's
unbelt. ''Might as well tie him up while he's
elpless.''

Vanessa clapped her hands together like a child.
'What a clever idea, Spur McCoy!''

"Did you think of it?''

"Why else would I have knocked him out?'' She
asped. "I'm not as dumb as you appear to think
am.''

"Let's not—'' Spur shook his head. "I'll be
ack.''

He went into the kitchen. Piles of dirty tin plates
nd stained coffee mugs spilled over from the table
nto the floor. Greasy rags and a half pound of
dorous green bacon sat on the stove, surrounded
vith flies. Spur breathed through his mouth as he
ummaged through the mess. No rope.

Frustrated and wary that Rex Cutshaw would
vake up while he wasn't there, Spur dashed out
he back door and saw a hank of hemp hanging
rom a hook by the door. He grabbed it and ran
ack into the parlor.

Vanessa looked up at him. "Don't worry. I
aven't killed him yet.'' She smiled brightly.

"Nice that you can keep your sense of humor
t a time like this,'' Spur said.

He rolled the man onto his stomach and quickly
ound his wrists, securing the knots tight enough

so that the coarse rope bit into his skin. That finished, he picked him up and dumped him into the chair.

"Would you have thought to do this?" he asked the woman as he tied the man's ankles to the chair legs.

"Don't underestimate me, Mr. McCoy!" She tapped her feet on the floor. "It's been just about long enough. Get some water and—"

He shot her a harsh, penetrating glance.

"I'm sorry." Vanessa's eyes were steely. "I'll do as you told me. I won't interfere."

Spur shook his head as he went to the kitchen. He found a salt-glazed jar filled with water and walked back into the parlor with it.

"Okay, Cutshaw, time to wake up!" He tilted the clay vessel over the man's face. A few drops spilled onto his cheek. When there was no sign of consciousness Spur upended it, sending a quart of water splashing down.

Cutshaw coughed, spluttering against the sudden rain, rapidly blinking. His shoulders surged back and forth in the chair.

"What—what—" he blubbered.

"Hello again, Cutshaw!" Spur said viciously.

"What—who tied up my hands?" He shook his head, flinging crystalline drops of water flying through the air. "What in hell's going on here?"

"This is a questioning, Mr. Cutshaw. You're going to answer my questions about your vigilante activities here in Boise. Now!"

"I don't know what the hell you're talking about," the man protested. He blew out liquidy breath. "You've got the wrong man, mister, and I'm damned mad about it!"

"I don't think so. And don't use that kind of talk in front of a lady!"

"Lady?" He looked around the room in confusion until he saw Vanessa. "Oh, yes, Mrs. Gilroy. You're still here."

"Rex—"

"Now then, Mr. Cutshaw," Spur said, cutting off the woman's words. "How long have you been riding with the vigilantes?"

"I already told you, you have the wrong man! Who in hell's been bad-talking my good name?"

McCoy glanced at Vanessa. "Someone in the know. Someone who knew the truth."

"Clem Jackson!" she blurted.

Rex stared at the widowed woman. "What?"

"Clem Jackson told a friend of mine who told me!"

"But old Jackson's dead."

"He wasn't last Friday afternoon when he pleasured Millie Parkin!" She gazed at him triumphantly. "Everyone knows a man can't keep a secret when he's—"

"That's enough, Vanessa!"

"—he's putting his thing—"

McCoy lunged at her. "Shut your mouth, woman!"

Vanessa stepped back and lowered her head.

"Cutshaw, I'm a federal law enforcement officer. I have the power to arrest and to kill if necessary. You don't want that to happen, do you?"

The saddlemaker struggled against his bonds. "Why? I didn't do anything! Let me out!"

Spur sighed and drew his Colt. "All Uncle Sam cares about is a body, a name to fit a crime. I guess yours is as good as any other man's."

"Now hold on!" Cutshaw drew in breath so rapidly that he hollowed his cheeks and whistled. "Maybe I do know something about all this."

"Uh huh."

He looked down at the floor. "Suppose I was one of them vigilantes. What'll happen to me?"

"That depends," Spur said, casually pushing the muzzle of his revolver to the man's throat.

Cutshaw inched back until his hair was plastering against the cushion. "On what?"

On how much help you are to me."

Cutshaw's wide eyes stared from Spur's hand, traveled up his arm and finally stopped at his face. "Okay. Alright! I'm tired of it anyway! It's gotten out of hand."

"What's gotten out of hand?"

"The—" He bit his lip.

"The killings? The murdering of innocent men and women? The fires? The rampages?" He bent toward the man. "The taste of blood gets sickening after a while, doesn't it? It isn't as much fun. You don't feel the rush!"

"Yes." Rex Cutshaw squeezed his eyes shut and gently shook his head. "I couldn't leave. They wouldn't let me stop, said I was in it as much as they were and if I didn't ride with them to burn down the Bancroft house they'd kill me." He opened his eyes. "Shoot me dead! There wasn't nothing I could do. I had to go. Don't you understand? I had to!''

Spur grimaced. ''You never should have started. Oh, the little lady has a question for you. Don't you, Vanessa?''

He heard the woman's boots clicking on the floor behind him. ''Yes. Who's your leader?'' she asked as she stood beside McCoy. ''Who tells you what to do? Who was it that forced you into killing those women?''

''It'll look good in court.'' Spur eased his Colt away from the man's neck and stepped back. ''Soften up the judge's heart. Make him lenient.''

''I don't know if I can tell you that.'' Cutshaw seemed incredibly interested in Widow Gilroy's boots. ''My life wouldn't be worth living.''

''Come on, now, Rex,'' the woman said. ''You don't want me to kill you, do you?''

Vanessa gripped a full sized .44 revolver in both hands. Her arms were strong and steady. This was a woman used to handling firearms.

''Damnit!'' McCoy yelled.

''Spur, back off. If you try to rush me I'll shoot him! I mean it! He killed my husband. It's only right that I make him pay his debt to me!''

The fury in her voice proved her point. ''Okay, okay Vanessa. We'll do it your way.''

''Now, Rex, who is it?'' Her voice was controlled, low. ''Who threatened you if you didn't keep riding with him. Hmmmm?''

Cutshaw whistled a little tune and looked at the ceiling, acting as if she didn't exist.

She lowered her aim toward his crotch.

Rex laughed. "Get off it, girlie! You ain't gonna use that thing."

"Maybe I won't kill you, but I'll be happy to ruin your future dealings with women!"

He looked at her aim and blanched. "You wouldn't!"

Vanessa smiled. "Are you willing to bet your thing on that?" She jabbed the barrel into his fat crotch, making the saddlemaker howl with pain.

"Trust me, she can do anything she puts her mind to." Spur stood back and watched the scene unfold.

Cutshaw pursed his lips. "Alright, alright, girlie! Just pull that weapon outta my crotch!"

"Not until you tell me who it is!"

Spur smiled as the man glanced at him. "Sorry. I can't control her. You're on your own."

"It's—it's—"

"Yes?" She forced the revolver harder against his genitals. "Yes, Rex?"

He sighed. "Hell, it's the most powerful man in town. The one who owns half the buildings, who built the Masonic Hall, who's got every politician wrapped around his little finger." Cutshaw took a breath and shook his head.

"You mean?" Vanessa asked.

Rex nodded. "Yes. It's him. Governor Evans."

CHAPTER SIXTEEN

"You just lost yourself a ball, Rex!"

"No, wait Vanessa!" Spur warily walked to her. "It all fits. What man in town would benefit most from the vigilantes? Who constantly needs to deal with enemies? And who's been screaming about the Mormons ever since I got here?"

Vanessa bit her lower lip, thought, and finally removed her revolver from Rex Cutshaw's groin. "Martin Evans. Governor Martin Evans! It has to be true!"

"It is!" The saddlemaker gritted his teeth. "The man's gone crazy. No one can control him!"

Vanessa turned to McCoy. "What do we do now?"

"Well, they must have elected a new sheriff today." Spur gently took the weapon from the woman's hand. "Maybe me and Mr. Cutshaw here should visit him."

"Yeah. Just get me away from that woman!" He shrank back in the chair and tried to force his knees together.

A half hour later, after delivering the man to a surprised greenhorn sheriff by the name of Tabor, Spur and Vanessa walked down Goldrush Street in the early evening air, arm in arm.

"Know why I brought you along?"

"Hmmm? Ah, no. Why did you?"

"I didn't trust myself. I thought I might kill him before he had the chance to tell me. Just like all the others."

He stopped. "What?"

"You know how it is, Spur. A woman's got to do what she thinks is best. When they made me watch my husband's murder I studied them. Memorized every detail I could—their horses, their clothes, their heights, even the kinds of kerchiefs they wore over their faces. I was right about George MacElravie, Sam Delmonico, John Shepherd and Clem Jackson, but I didn't have a clue who the other two were." She turned to him. "Clem was nice enough to tell me about Rex, though he wouldn't name Governor Evans."

Dark thoughts burned in his mind. "Vanessa, you didn't—"

"So I figured I only had one more chance to discover the truth. I brought you along for insurance."

He studied her face, but it was concealed by deep shadows. "Did you kill those men?"

"Of course!"

"All four of them?"

"Yes, Spur," she said impatiently. "Haven't you been listening to me? I had to bring them to justice. They destroyed my life. You understand, don't you? I had no choice—not with a dishonest sheriff!"

"I'm not sure. It's a big shock."

"Why Spur McCoy, you said yourself not an hour ago that I was capable of doing anything I put my mind to." She patted his arm. "Can we be going now? I can't wait to get back to Millie's and take a rest. These boots are killing me!"

Spur smiled at the comment and escorted her to the house. He'd worry about what to do with the woman later—after he visited the mansion.

Every lamp in the huge building must have been lit for the windows shined so brightly that a glow surrounded the mansion. As Spur walked up to the house the sounds of laughter and music issued from inside.

So Evans was celebrating. Why not? He'd won the election. He'd forced nearly every Mormon out of town. He was in complete control of everyone but the sheriff, McCoy thought. It was time to correct that.

The front door was wide open. Spur walked in. The hall was empty save for coat-covered chairs and that ancient domestic who'd given him a rude greeting the last time he'd seen her.

"Take your jacket?" the wrinkled woman asked.

"No, thanks."

She huffed. "Suit yourself. They're in the ballroom—down the hall to the right."

He nodded to her.

The noise grew louder as he moved along the panelled walkway, passing oil paintings of men who he assumed were the governor's antecedents. What would they think of him now?

The hall led into a huge, open-beamed room. Four musicians played something that seemed vaguely French on a small stage. Elegantly dressed men and women danced before it while others milled around the tables stocked with liquor and platters of food. Spur smiled in greeting to a few vaguely familiar faces and moved through the crowd.

Despite the opened windows the ballroom was hot, steaming with the sweat of the toadies gathered around their leader, eager to snatch a crumb from his overflowing plate. The men drank. The women laughed and flirted. But everyone seemed slightly uneasy, as if they expected the roof to cave in. Even the bright lamp light shimmering from the crystal chandeliers lining the walls couldn't sweep away the darkness within the people assembled there.

Evans wasn't in sight. He asked a few people if they had seen the Governor but they simply shrugged and moved away from him. McCoy walked past the rows of glasses and bottles of gin, whiskey and Scotch and out through the floor to ceiling double doors. He entered a garden. The same garden where he and Lacey had so much fun.

Where was Evans?

"Stop the music!" a voice boomed out.

Spur instantly returned to the ballroom. Martin Evans stood on the podium in front of disgruntled musicians who put down their instruments.

"Ladies and gentlemen, I propose a toast." The governor raised a glass. "To another four years of peace and prosperity for the people of Boise!"

Men yelled and stamped their feet. Liquor sloshed down throats. And above them all, looking down on his flock, Governor Evans drained his glass and threw it onto the floor.

The resulting crash cheered the celebrants. "Dance! Drink! Eat!" he said, gesturing in the air. "Tomorrow we go back to work!"

Another round of laughter. The two violinists, the cellist and the flautist started playing again, taking up where they'd left off. Spur sank back into a corner and waited.

Lacey breezed into the room dressed in a gown worthy of her name—an incredible concoction of lace and white silk that cast a veil of purity over her luscious body. Evans embraced his daughter, kissed her on the cheek and grabbed a glass out of a passing man's hand. He laughed and bolted down the contents.

Spur moved out of the line of sight. If Lacey saw him it could complicate things. He certainly couldn't touch the governor in front of fifty people—a veritible private army. No. He'd wait to make his move.

A mature woman, jewels dripping from her neck, asked Spur if he'd seen her blue and white brocaded purse. He smiled and shook his head.

"So what the hell good are you to me?" she said

in a heavy European accent.

He sighed and bided his time.

Fifteen minutes later, after two more visits from the drunken foreigner, he watched Evans slap two men on their shoulders and walk laterally across the ballroom, jokingly pushing aside the couples who whirled there.

Where was he going? Spur slowly moved toward him and quickened his pace as the governor disappeared into the garden. He hurried after the man.

Martin Evans stood facing a rose bush. Spur heard the soft trickle of liquid splashing onto its leaves.

"That isn't very elegant, Governor Evans. Pissing on flowers."

Surprised, Evans turned on him, recognized the face and turned away from him. "No. But I nearly flooded my pants in there, and that wouldn't be the best way to start a new term in office." He went about his business. "You, ah—decided to join my celebration after all?"

"No. I came here to talk to you about Rex Cutshaw. He's just confessed that he's a vigilante."

Evan's right hand shook up and down. "So?" he asked and faced Spur, buttoning up his black trousers.

"So he and you are the only vigilantes left. He said you led them. You planned the raids and ran them. Very efficiently, I might add."

Evans smiled and stepped toward him, searching his face in the dim light. "Thanks, McCoy. Coming from a man like you that's a real compliment. If that's all, I have to rejoin my guests."

"I've got some more news for you, Evans. I know who's been killing your friends—the sheriff, your lawyer, all of them."

The governor stopped before him. "Yeah? Well who is it?" His voice was harsh.

"Not me. Someone you'd never suspect." Spur worked out his words with care. "Someone who's damned mad at you, who's still walking the streets, waiting for the right time to send you into the next world."

Evans brushed a wet spot on his fly. "You trying to scare me, McCoy? Hell, my men can find anyone."

"Not this time. You don't have so many men left, do you, Governor? Four of the best of them are dead."

"Get to the point! What do you want? Money?" He laughed. "No."

Evans peered at him and frowned. "Get your butt off my property, McCoy! I don't take kindly to smart-mouthed double-talkers!"

"You're forgetting something, aren't you?"

"I'm trying to forget you."

"You're under arrest!"

"Shit. Boris, now!" he yelled.

Spur ducked a second before lead cleaved the air over his head. He rolled across the bare earth and slammed into the jasmine bush as screams and rustling feet echoed inside the ballroom. There, looking out through the tangled leaves, he drew his revolver and waited.

Evans had darted out of sight. The gunman who'd fired at him hadn't shown himself. Spur cursed. The man did indeed have protection who followed him everywhere he went. Even when he took a—

"There's no way out, McCoy!" Evans shouted. "You made a big mistake coming here and expecting me to let you drag me off to jail!"

Spur fired at the sound of the voice. One bullet.

"Good try, but not good enough!"

"Evans, the sheriff knows all about this," he lied. "If I'm not back there in ten minutes, he'll come looking for you!"

Gunfire exploded in the garden. The bush shook around him as bullets raced through it, dislodging a shower of white petalled flowers.

"Bullshit! Ralph Tabor's a friend of mine! Hell, I put that man into office!"

This wasn't getting him anywhere. Spur surveyed the land behind him. Three feet of dense yew trees fronted a brick wall.

McCoy used every trick he knew, silently moving through the dense tangle of trees, crouching, carefully pressing his feet one at a time to the ground. Then gunfire broke out over his head.

The explosions reverberated in the walled garden, zipping past him again and again until the silence consumed them. The smell of gunpowder burned his nose and the air was blue with it.

He looked out among the twisted trunks. The garden was about 30 feet square with plenty of shadows and bushes. Lots of hiding places.

"Father, what's going on?"

The voice electrified him. Spur turned to see Lacey standing in the doorway, lit up from behind ike an angel atop a Christmas tree.

"Father, is Spur McCoy out there?" Lacey yelled into the garden from the ballroom doors.

"Get back in the house!" Evans shouted. "Do you want to get yourself killed? The man's gone crazy! He's liable to plug you full of bullets!"

"No, daddy! You're out of your head!"

Spur finally got a firm position on the man. Evans must be behind the plaster garden bench that sat near the doors.

"Move!" the governor screamed.

"No!"

"Thomas, take her to her room and come right back!"

"Ah, yes sir!"

A man darted from the trees on the far side of the garden. Spur peeled off a shot. The lead slammed into the man's right hand.

Lacey screamed.

"Son of a bitch!" The gunman fired madly into the yew trees as he ran for the ballroom, grabbed the young woman and pulled her out of sight.

"You're endangering my daughter, McCoy!" Evans said, taking a shot.

It sailed harmlessly into the air. "No way. You've been doing it ever since you thought you were the law in Boise."

"I am the law!"

Now, Spur thought. The time was right. He hunched over and moved through the trees, gliding silently through the thin trunks on either side. Three seconds later he stood beside the bench.

"Don't move, Evans!"

The man stared up into Spur's barrel. McCoy

smashed his boot into the governor's right hand, sending his weapon flying away. "It's over."

"No. Damnit, no! I'm not gonna let a little man, a little, sniveling man like you take me down!" Evans said. He got to his feet. "No one tells me what to do!"

Spur backhanded the governor's chin. The stocky man reeled, cursing and rubbing the bruised skin.

"Bastard!" he spat.

"They say you see yourself in other men. I guess they were right. Let's go!"

CHAPTER SEVENTEEN

The next morning, Spur wired General Halleck the news and stopped by the sheriff's office. He jingled the big key ring as he walked in. Rex Cutshaw and Martin Evans glared up at him from their respective cells.

"If you don't have any food, I don't wanna see your ugly face," Cutshaw said.

"Sorry, fresh out of green bacon." His voice was bright.

Evans rose from his cot. "I'll see you hang for this, McCoy!"

"Save your breath. Did you hear, ex-governor? Judd Feingold's being sworn in this morning. They're putting together an emergency ceremony to make it all legal. Some of your friends won't be here to see it. They're packing up and leaving town. Just like Sheriff Tabor did last night."

"Damn you!"

Spur laughed. "But don't think I'd leave you here all day without someone to look after you."

The front door opened.

"That must be him now."

"McCoy? Where the hell are you?"

"Back here!"

A tall, clean-shaven man walked into the rear room. "That them?"

"Yup. Keep your eyes on those two. I don't trust either of them—especially the short, fat one." He pointed at Evans.

"Will do." The man smiled. "Sure was surprised to run into you on the street this morning."

"Same here, Forester."

"I wasn't planning on staying in town but you had to go and remind me."

"Right. Libertyville. Three years ago. I saved your ass, marshall!"

"A U.S. Marshal?" Cutshaw said. "Hear that, Evans? He's a marshall!"

Spur sighed. "I'll be back for them tomorrow morning to escort them. But I've still got some loose ends to tie up." He tossed the keys to the man.

Forester grabbed them and winced. "Sure. No problem. I didn't want to spend a week with my sister anyhow. My brains'd fall out if I had seven days of peace and quiet."

McCoy laughed as he walked out.

"You can't see her," Lacey Evans said as they lay panting in her bedroom.

"Why not? Are you jealous?"

"Of course!" She smiled. "But that's not the reason. Vanessa Gilroy stopped in here to say goodbye to me. She left town."

He sat upright. "When?"

"First thing this morning." Lacey arched her back and stretched. "She left on the eight o'clock stage. I guess she didn't like it here in Boise, and I don't blame her." Her voice was breathy; her face shone with the results of their morning exertions.

"That lets her off the hook."

"What?"

He laughed. "Nothing. Forget it." He kissed her white shoulder, marvelling at the young woman's beauty. "Are you sure you're okay, I mean with everything that's happened?"

She nodded. "I guess I never really trusted my father, but I had no idea that he was behind all that killing." She shivered and laid her head on his shoulder.

A familiar scent blossomed in his nose. "What's that perfume you're wearing?" He sniffed her hair. "It's been bugging me ever since I wrapped you in my arms. It isn't roses, is it?"

Lacey pushed him onto the mattress and flung her body on top of his. "No," she said, nibbling on his stubbly chin. "Jasmine."

by Dirk Fletcher

*The adult Western series that's got more
straight shootin' than a day at the O.K.
Corral and more wild lovin' than a night
in a frontier cathouse!*

#35: Wyoming Wildcat. Missing government surveyors,
long-legged hellcats, greedy ranchers, and trigger-happy
gunmen—they're all in a day's work for Spur McCoy. But
he'll beat down a hundred bushwhackers and still have the
strength to tame any wildcat who strays across his path!
__3192-2 $3.50 US/$4.50 CAN

#36: Mountain Madam. In Oregon's Wallowa Mountains,
murderous fanatics are executing anyone who stands in the
way of their fiendish conspiracy to reap a heavenly reward.
But with the help of a tantalizing godsend named Angelina,
McCoy will stop the infernal plot.
__3289-9 $3.50 US/$4.50 CAN

BUCKSKIN

By Kit Dalton

The hard-ridin', hard-lovin' Adult Western series that's got more action than a frontier cathouse on Saturday night!

Buckskin #35: Pistol Whipped. Rustlers are out to steal all the cattle in Oregon, and only Buckskin Lee Morgan can stop them. A six-shooter in one hand, a gorgeous gal in the other, he'll bushwhack and hog-tie the cow thieves—and mark all the lovely ladies with his burning brand.

_3439-5 $3.99 US/$4.99 CAN

Buckskin #36: Hogleg Hell. A demon-worshipping swindler is terrorizing Hangtown, California, and he has the lustiest lady in town under his spell. To save the tempting tart, Morgan will have to strike a deal with the devil's disciple— then blast him to hell.

_3476-X $3.99 US/$4.99 CAN

Buckskin #37: Colt .45 Revenge. Something is rotten in the state of Arizona, and Morgan has to put things right. Between hot lead and cool ladies, he'll have his hands full, his six-gun empty, and the Wild West exploding with action.

_3533-2 $3.99 US/$4.99 CAN

LEISURE BOOKS
ATTN: Order Department
276 5th Avenue, New York, NY 10001

Please add $1.50 for shipping and handling for the first book and $.35 for each book thereafter. PA., N.Y.S. and N.Y.C. residents, please add appropriate sales tax. No cash, stamps, or C.O.D.s. All orders shipped within 6 weeks via postal service book rate. Canadian orders require $2.00 extra postage and must be paid in U.S. dollars through a U.S. banking facility.

Name _____

Address _____

City _____ State _____ Zip _____

I have enclosed $_____in payment for the checked book(s).

Payment <u>must</u> accompany all orders.☐ Please send a free catalog.

KANSAN DOUBLE EDITIONS
By Robert E. Mills

A double blast of honchos and hussies—
two complete Westerns for one low price!

Trail of Desire. An able man with a gun or a fancy lady, the Kansan lives only for the day he can save the sultry Deanna from the snake-mean bushwhacker who kidnapped her.

And in the same low-priced volume...

Shootout at the Golden Slipper. Left for dead after trying to rescue his sweetheart from a low-down renegade, Davy Watson needs an Oriental angel of mercy's special care before he can head across the burning desert to kill an enemy who has made his life a living hell.

__3421-2   **$4.99**

The Cheyenne's Woman. When the vicious warrior Grey Thunder captures the lovely Deanna, the Kansan heads for a showdown that will be a fight to the finish for one man— or both.

And in the same action-packed volume...

The Kansan's Lady. It's Davy's last chance to save his sweetheart from ruthless sidewinders who want him dead. Either the Kansan evens the score—or he goes down in a final blaze of glory.

__3450-6   **$4.99**

LEISURE BOOKS
ATTN: Order Department
276 5th Avenue, New York, NY 10001

Please add $1.50 for shipping and handling for the first book and $.35 for each book thereafter. PA., N.Y.S. and N.Y.C. residents, please add appropriate sales tax. No cash, stamps, or C.O.D.s. All orders shipped within 6 weeks via postal service book rate. Canadian orders require $2.00 extra postage and must be paid in U.S. dollars through a U.S. banking facility.

Name _____

Address _____

City _____ State _____ Zip _____

I have enclosed $_____ in payment for the checked book(s).
Payment <u>must</u> accompany all orders.☐ Please send a free catalog.